Bluey's War

Herb Hamlet grew up in the Brisbane suburb of Wynnum and left school at fourteen to work in an iron foundry. At twenty-one he joined the army, serving with the Royal Australian Engineers for six years. During that time, he gained his matriculation by correspondence and upon his discharge, joined the Australian Public Service, rising to a management position.

Herb Hamlet now lives a quiet life with his wife, Lyn, on Queensland's Sunshine Coast. After accepting early retirement, he gained a degree in political science and international studies at the University of the Sunshine Coast. The writing bug then hit him and he has been busy ever since. *Bluey's War* is his second published work.

Bluey's War

HERB HAMLET

PENGUIN BOOKS

PENGUIN BOOKS

Published by the Penguin Group
Penguin Group (Australia)
250 Camberwell Road, Camberwell, Victoria 3124, Australia
(a division of Pearson Australia Group Pty Ltd)
Penguin Group (USA) Inc.
375 Hudson Street, New York, New York 10014, USA
Penguin Group (Canada)
90 Eglinton Avenue East, Suite 700, Toronto, Canada ON M4P 2Y3
(a division of Pearson Penguin Canada Inc.)
Penguin Books Ltd
80 Strand, London WC2R 0RL England
Penguin Ireland
25 St Stephen's Green, Dublin 2, Ireland
(a division of Penguin Books Ltd)
Penguin Books India Pvt Ltd
11 Community Centre, Panchsheel Park, New Delhi – 110 017, India
Penguin Group (NZ)
67 Apollo Drive, Rosedale, North Shore 0632, New Zealand
(a division of Pearson New Zealand Ltd)
Penguin Books (South Africa) (Pty) Ltd
24 Sturdee Avenue, Rosebank, Johannesburg 2196, South Africa

Penguin Books Ltd, Registered Offices: 80 Strand, London, WC2R 0RL, England

First published by Penguin Group (Australia), 2008
This edition published by Penguin Group (Australia), 2009

10 9 8 7 6 5 4 3 2 1

Cover & text design by David Altheim © Penguin Group (Australia)
Cover photograph of pasture at sunset: Jochen Schlenker/Getty Images;
girl: Todd Korol/Getty Images; man: Photolibrary
Typeset in 13/18 Adobe Garamond by Post Pre-press Group, Brisbane, Queensland
Printed and bound in Australia by McPherson's Printing Group, Maryborough, Victoria

National Library of Australia
Cataloguing-in-Publication data:

Hamlet, Herb.
Bluey's war / Herb Hamlet.
9780143009566 (pbk.)

A823.4

penguin.com.au

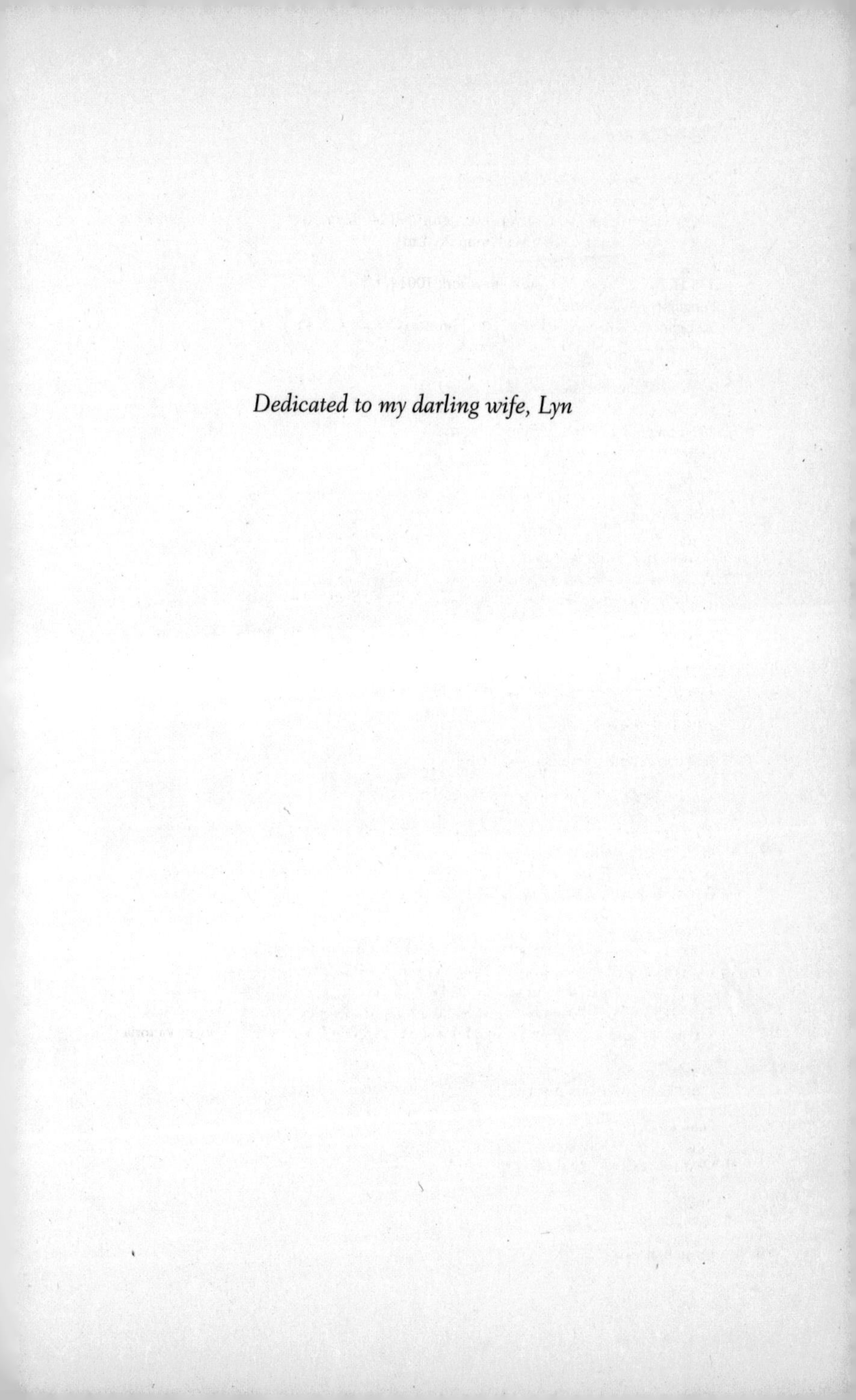

Dedicated to my darling wife, Lyn

Prologue

It took Bluey O'Donnell two lifts from Goondiwindi, followed by a long walk, but as dusk approached, he found himself at the front gate of Kilkenny. Intense heat still bore down from the setting sun that hung above the horizon like a ball of fire. The newspapers had been full of talk about the long drought decimating farms in southern outback Queensland, but Bluey was still unprepared for the devastation of his family's mixed wheat–sheep property. Dry, barren land extended for as far as the eye could see – everything a dusty yellow. He opened the gate and slowly made his way towards the bush homestead with its wide, bull-nosed verandah.

Home.

His father had built the weatherboard house with his own hands, and named it after the Irish county in which he'd been born and raised. Its metal roof now had a few rust patches, as did the large water tank that sat beside it. The front verandah was enclosed by a railing with uprights made of bush timber. Out the back there was an earth closet, a copper that his mother had used every Monday morning to wash the clothes, and a propped clothes line that now sagged after twenty years of washing. Bluey had many memories of his life in that house. His mother had made major events of holidays, birthdays, as well as his baptism and confirmation. His daughter had been born inside its walls.

Although he couldn't see them from the dirt road, he knew the chook yard and pig pens were behind the homestead. His father raised hens for eggs and roosters for the larder. Porkers also provided a change in the family's diet. And if things were bad, there were always rabbits. Mutton every night certainly did nothing to stimulate the palate. Just to the left of the homestead, which was fenced to keep the stock out, was the double garage. Beyond that, a windmill and corrugated-iron shed were silhouetted against the dimming skyline.

When Bluey was 150 yards from the homestead, a kelpie came running out barking aggressively. Once the animal caught the approaching man's scent, however, its ferocity turned to delight and it ran to Bluey, wagging its tail. 'Skipper! You're still alive, you old bugger!'

The dog jumped up and excitedly licked the sweat from his hands. Bluey patted the animal and rubbed its ears affectionately. The dog's welcome had momentarily distracted him from the task at hand, but as he turned towards the verandah, a knot formed in his stomach.

Can I do this?

He was tempted to run, but stood his ground. Heart pounding, he knocked softly on the front door and waited. When there was no response, he knocked again, this time a little louder. After several moments, which seemed like an eternity, he heard light footsteps approaching and the door opened slowly. He drew in a sharp breath, swallowed, and removed his hat.

Still beautiful . . .

Indeed, to Bluey's mind, Ellen had not changed one bit. He'd always admired her thick blonde hair, now cut short like a boy's, giving her a youthful appearance. He couldn't help but notice the trim figure that used to drive him wild in his youth. Her grey moleskin work trousers hugged her long slim legs and her blue checked shirt strained against her ample bosom. While Ellen's facial features were certainly striking, she could never be described as a conventional beauty. Yet there was something about her.

On seeing her estranged husband, Ellen stared at him, speechless, her emerald-green eyes flashing and her mind spinning. This was impossible to take in. Surprise quickly turned to anger. 'You!' she snapped.

'Hello, Ellen.' He paused, searching for the right words. 'H–how are you?' he stammered.

Her mouth opened then closed. This seemed such an inane question to Ellen that at first she could only stare at him. Then she found her voice.

'How am I?' she spat. 'You rotten mongrel! How the hell do you think I am? You leave me and the kids to run off with that . . . woman. I don't hear a word from you for fifteen months!' Rigid with rage, the tendons in Ellen's shoulders felt like steel strands. Temper had made her cheeks flame.

He searched her face, hoping to find some clue that the gentle woman he had married was still there, but he saw only hatred.

He let it wash over him. He knew he deserved this. Taking a deep breath he looked into her eyes and said softly, 'I want to come back.'

'Just like that, eh?' she answered stiffly. His gentleness was disarming.

He took a moment to answer. 'No.' He sighed. 'I don't expect you to take me back as your husband. I just want to come back here to live, to try to be a father to the kids, and to help you with Kilkenny.'

'It's a pity you didn't think about that when you shot through.'

Bluey winced and looked away.

'Look, can I come in?' he asked politely.

'I suppose I can't stop you.' She stepped to one side.

Bluey moved through the front door and into the openness of the homestead's interior. Everything was just as he remembered: clean, neat and tidy. Against the far wall of the kitchen, a kerosene refrigerator, his mother's pride and joy, still ticked away. In one corner the wood stove radiated its usual warmth. A kettle had just come to the boil. As Ellen moved over to give it her attention, Bluey eased into a dining chair at the bare timber table.

Ellen looked down at him. 'Where's Ruby?' Anger threatened to overwhelm her again. The hardship of the past year had been almost unbearable. She'd not only had to run a home, and take care of the children, but manage a property. And now here he was – the main cause of her suffering – sitting right in front of her. For an instant, her vision blurred and she heard nothing but the pounding of blood in her ears.

Bluey lifted his shoulders in a shrug. 'Don't know. Haven't seen her for nearly a year.'

'You left with her!' Ellen's voice was shrill in the silent house.

He sighed. 'Look. You know it wasn't a sex thing. It was just the grog. She was as bad as me.'

'That's what you say,' she scoffed.

'It's the truth. You more than anyone should know what booze does to a bloke's sex drive.'

Ellen made no reply as she took out a cup and saucer, but his answer seemed to have calmed her. 'You look like hell, Bluey. Are you still drinking?'

'No, I haven't had a drink in quite a while.'

'That's something, I suppose.' Although she'd waited years to hear these words, she felt suddenly drained. 'You want a cup of tea?'

'No thanks.' He waited while she poured herself a cup and sat opposite him. 'Even though Kilkenny's still legally mine, I won't stay if you want me to leave.'

Ellen was confused. This man – the source of all her hardship, offering himself as a solution.

'I don't know what to do,' she replied. 'The kids miss you. They wouldn't forgive me if I sent you away. But if you stay, you sleep in the shearers' quarters. Understand?'

'Fair enough.' He was relieved that she'd agreed to let him stay, but wondered if he would ever be able to win back her trust. He decided to steer the conversation to practical matters. 'The property seems to be in a bad way.'

'Like you care,' she said sarcastically.

He ignored her tone. 'I loved this place. My father built it up from nothing.'

'Pity you didn't take after him,' she retorted. 'Apart from being a wonderful man, he was also very responsible . . .' she trailed off.

'And I'm irresponsible?'

'You said it, not me.' She lifted the cup to her lips.

Bluey leaned forward. 'Look, Ellen, I think I know how you feel —'

'You bastard!' She cut him off. 'You have no idea how I bloody feel!' She slammed the cup down on the table and glared at him. Once again she'd lost control.

This is not like me!

She'd never been the type to resort to bad language. She breathed deeply, trying to calm herself, and looked at her husband coldly. 'Please listen to what I have to say, so you don't misunderstand my reasons for not sending you away. The truth is I desperately need you to help out on the property. We haven't been able to plant a crop and the drought has killed twenty per cent of the sheep. What's more, the bank wouldn't provide any financial assistance to see us through. "Couldn't loan money to a woman" the manager claimed. And anyway, I didn't own Kilkenny, did I? "Went against policy", he said – the arrogant sod.'

'I don't know how much help I'll be for a while,' he sounded a little sheepish. 'I've been a bit crook, but I'll do my best.'

'You'll do more than that,' she replied harshly. 'I had to let our help go – couldn't afford to pay them – so you'll start at daybreak and you won't finish until dark.'

'How in blazes have you managed?' he asked, incredulous.

'I don't know.' She shook her head slowly. 'But I couldn't have done it without David.' There was pride in her voice.

The guilt ripped through him. 'Poor kid.' He lowered his head, embarrassed. He'd never thought for a moment that his son would be bearing the load.

'You're the one who left.' The accusing tone was back.

He looked at her in despair. 'I'm sorry, Ellen.'

'It's too late to be sorry,' she answered simply.

'But surely you had some other help?'

'Len Humphries has given me some of his time,' she replied matter-of-factly. 'He comes out a bit.'

Her words were like a blow to the pit of his stomach. Bluey's mouth felt suddenly dry. He needed a moment to gather his thoughts. 'Does he stay over?'

'That's none of your business.'

Bluey pushed back his chair and walked over to the sink. He drew a glass of water and surveyed the depressing view before him. From the kitchen window, one could look out over the grain paddocks, where thick wheat crops once swayed in the gentle breeze. Now there was nothing to be seen but parched ground – sheer devastation. As Bluey took in the grim panorama, a strong westerly wind created whirlies around the homestead, filling the air with fine powdery dust.

'There goes the topsoil,' he observed, almost to himself.

'We've lost plenty already,' she responded quietly, joining him at the window. 'But it's not too bad, I suppose. If we could just get some rain, things would change quickly.'

Bluey noticed that Ellen's manner now seemed less aggressive. 'When will the kids be home?' he asked.

'They won't be home till late.' She continued gazing out the window. 'It's sports day so they'll miss the school truck. Brenda said she'd drop them off at the front gate.'

'I'll get out to the shearers' quarters and get settled then,' Bluey said in a low voice and retrieved his meagre belongings. Ellen watched him as he walked slowly along the path, the old kelpie following closely behind. She leaned heavily against the door frame, drained of all the emotion. A hot tear trickled down her right cheek and her eyes became emerald pools. 'Oh, Bluey, you stupid, stupid fool.' But there was no longer animosity in her voice, only sadness.

PART ONE

1933–1955

Chapter 1

Ellen Sommers moved to the regional centre of Goondiwindi in 1935 when she was just eleven years of age. She came with her mother, Joan, her father, Eric, and her older sister, Pam. With the onset of the Great Depression and the subsequent lack of work, the family had been forced to leave Brisbane's bayside suburb of Wynnum.

Ellen had loved living at Wynnum, 'the workers' suburb'. She particularly loved the beach, which was only a short stroll from the cramped, furnished workers' cottage her parents rented. The small weatherboard dwelling had a corrugated-iron roof and was lined on the inside with tongue-and-groove pine. It had two bedrooms, a kitchen, a combined living–dining area and a front and back porch. Attached to the rear was a rough bathroom-cum-laundry with a dirt floor. Ellen's mother had sewn hessian bags together to make a wagga rug for the floor. In the backyard stood a laundry copper, a woodheap and an outhouse. Council workers came once a week to empty the can of sewage.

Ellen shared her room and her bed with her sister. To escape the suffocating atmosphere inside the small house, Ellen spent every available moment at the beach. She especially enjoyed playing on the two piers that jutted some distance into Waterloo Bay. To enable swimming at high tide, enclosed bathing areas had been built at the end of each one. Both were fenced with wooden palings and wire netting to protect swimmers from the bay's sharks.

The old man who managed the tidal baths took an interest in Ellen as she tried to improve her swimming. He told her to kick as fast as possible, at the same time reaching out with her hands, moving them through the water with swift, fluid strokes, keeping her fingers together. She concentrated on this style as she trained. If she had the penny that gained her entrance, she continued to practise her swimming until she could complete twenty laps of the baths without stopping. On achieving this goal, she tried to swim the laps faster and faster each time. With such dedication, Ellen soon developed into a strong swimmer.

Unemployed relief workers were in the process of constructing a wading pool on the foreshore and Ellen took great interest in the progress of this work. To supplement the family's food supply, Ellen, together with her mother and sister, often fished or crabbed from the jetties.

Joan Sommers and her two daughters took long walks along the beachfront. On a clear day, Ellen loved to take in the view over the bay. There was always a breeze on even the hottest days. At high tide, the view over the water stretched out to St Helena and Green Islands, with Moreton and Stradbroke Islands much further out. Ellen yearned for the day she could be taken to St

Helena to explore the convict ruins and the old cemetery she had been told about so often. At low tide, however, the sea view was a very different one. One hundred and fifty yards of mud flats had to be crossed just to reach the shallow waters of the bay. Often, when the tide was at its lowest, men dug for the mud worms that made such excellent bait. The girls and their mother dug up large numbers of a thin variety that thrived in coarse sand near the high-tide mark. Life should have been idyllic. It was anything but.

Each night, when her drunken father finally arrived home from the hotel, Ellen often wished she was still on the beach, safe and relaxed in its peaceful surroundings. Instead, the young girl would be cowering in her room alongside her older sister, shaking and weeping, as their father showered his family with abuse. Eric Sommers' target was usually his unfortunate wife, but at various times, the door to the girls' bedroom was kicked open and his large form would appear in horrifying silhouette. She and her sister would then be subjected to a tirade of foul language, sometimes accompanied by physical abuse. The nuns at the convent often shook their heads knowingly and in sympathy when Ellen unconvincingly explained away the dark bruising that suddenly appeared on her arms and legs. When he was sober, Eric Sommers acted as if nothing had happened, and Joan and the girls were far too frightened to ever raise the subject. Ellen had seen the consequences when her mother answered back: a black eye, a split lip or bruised arms.

Sober again, Eric suffered a degree of remorse for his actions, but never sought to express his sorrow to his spouse or daughters. On one occasion, when he almost dislocated Ellen's elbow, he felt so bad the next morning that he took her to the local milk bar and bought her a chocolate sundae. His regret, however, did not stop him from becoming drunk and abusive again, and so the cycle continued.

Wynnum housed many of the workers who travelled to the large meatworks and bacon factories in the nearby industrial suburbs. Eric was a qualified and competent meat slicer, who'd worked for the Queensland Public Abattoir for five years. His rough-and-ready workmates were not to be messed with, nor was Eric for that matter. When the Depression finally forced the abattoir's closure, his drinking became even worse. Just the thought of her father coming home was enough to make Ellen's stomach churn, and nervous tension became her everyday companion. As a consequence of the stress, she developed a severe rash on her scalp – the doctor called it psoriasis – which needed ongoing medical attention. The constant itch and Ellen's scratching only made the condition worse. When Joan found she could no longer afford professional treatment, she allowed Ellen to swim more often, hoping that the salt water might help the problem in some way.

In the first few years of her schooling, Ellen attended the local parish school, Guardian Angels, set on top of a hill boasting panoramic views over Waterloo Bay. The church and presbytery stood in the grounds, and Mount Carmel Convent on the opposite side of the street.

Being part of a traditional Catholic family, it was only natural that the girls be educated by the church. The school often overlooked the girls' tuition fees in return for Joan undertaking domestic duties at the convent. The convent had a chapel, a dining area and kitchen, reception rooms, and cells for the nuns – a big job for any domestic. It even had its own bathing boxes on the beachfront, where the nuns would swim in summer. They could be seen on hot afternoons splashing and swimming in the enclosure at the end of a short jetty. In their black bathing caps and black neck-to-knee bathing costumes, they looked, to Ellen, like dolphins frolicking.

Although the nuns were strict, school was like a sanctuary for Ellen. In the first two years, the prep years, she used a slate and slate pencil to write down her letters and numbers. Like the other children, she often sharpened her slate pencil on the school wall, and had to bring a dampened cloth to school to wipe her slate clean. As the children went about their tasks, the only sound in the classroom was the shrieking of the slate pencils. Any naughtiness was met with a strap across the buttocks, girls as well as boys. She was pleased when she progressed to paper and pencil in grade 1, where the children sat on long forms at desks that had holes for inkwells.

The playground during recess was a popular place to practise skipping, using a long rope with a girl at each end to turn it. Her best friend at school was a tiny lass with a thin face and curly blonde hair named Beverly Walker, whose father was the railway stationmaster at Wynnum.

Each Sunday the Sommers family attended Mass. Here, Ellen would see the Sisters of Mercy nuns who taught her. They were so different, she thought. Sister Theresa was kind and gentle while Sister Madonna had a voice like a sergeant major and handed out the strap at the drop of a hat.

Ellen just loved the pomp and ceremony – the priest decked out in his colourful vestments. One of her earliest memories of going to Mass was gazing at the Stations of the Cross at Easter and wondering at the significance of each one. She'd been so nervous making her first communion. Gazing up at Father O'Reilly with due reverence, she'd opened her mouth to receive the sacred host – the body of Christ. The moment brought a shiver of excitement and awe. Yet, even after her confirmation, the need to confess her sins still puzzled her. Why should she have to confess her sins to a priest when God already knew everything she'd done wrong? It didn't seem logical and it was embarrassing having to divulge your thoughts to a shadowy figure on the other side of a lattice screen. However, she always felt better after saying the allocated number of Hail Marys and Our Fathers to make up for her minor transgressions.

Joan Sommers was at her wits' end. Her unemployed husband's continual drinking meant there was little money left for the household, and she was struggling just to put food on the table. Relief came in the form of a letter from Eric's brother, Mick, who lived and worked in Goondiwindi. In the letter, Mick explained that a vacancy for a slicer had come up at the local meatworks where he worked, and that he'd personally approached the manager on his brother's behalf. Eric had extensive experience, so the manager had little hesitation in offering the position to him. There was also one of the firm's workers' cottages available, which cost company employees only a nominal rent. All Eric had to do was make his own way to Goondiwindi. He could see no alternative to his family's uncertain future, so two days later the decision was set in concrete.

For the journey, the Sommers family dressed in their best clothes – Eric in his navy-blue single-breasted suit, and hat; Joan in a plain grey, waisted dress with a matching beret. The two girls wore light-green cotton dresses their mother had made on a friend's treadle sewing machine. They then packed their possessions and caught the local train to Brisbane where they boarded the *South Western Mail* for the long journey to the border town of Goondiwindi. This was a particularly exciting event for Ellen, for she had never travelled any further than Brisbane.

Ellen was both happy and apprehensive, alternating between excitement and anxiety. She'd always lived in the city suburb by the bay, and here she was heading towards a town in the country, far, far away from her beloved beach. She had never met her uncle, either, and knew very little about him.

What if he's like Dad?

After the steam train had passed through Ipswich, it headed due west into the Lockyer Valley, an area renowned for its small crop-farms. She stared out the window and all she could see was open spaces – ploughed fields with row upon row of vegetables and other crops. The family made good progress until they reached the Great Dividing Range, where the train almost came to a standstill it was travelling so slowly. At the top of the range they stopped at the large Darling Downs provincial centre of Toowoomba to take on more passengers. For the next stage of the journey, the train turned south, chugging its way along the flat, open countryside at full steam, through Allora, then on to Warwick. With all the stops along the way, the journey took up most of the day.

Approaching Goondiwindi, Ellen was surprised at the uniform flatness of the surrounding countryside: not a hill to be seen. It was late in the afternoon when the train pulled in to the town's railway station. Uncle Mick and his family were waiting on the platform to meet them.

Ellen liked Michael Sommers immediately. He had an open, friendly face, sandy hair and eyebrows, and a ruddy, sunburnt complexion. He was dressed in a dark brown suit and wore a wide-brimmed hat. Ellen's Aunty Pat was a tiny slip of a woman who'd barely reach seven stone wringing wet. Her small-featured face and bright, inquisitive eyes were almost possum-like, and lit up every time she smiled. In keeping with current fashion, she wore a lemon floral dress that hung well below her knees. Her outfit was complemented by a black hat, set at a jaunty angle, with a yellow flower. The two boys, the eldest of the siblings, were tall, strapping lads for their ages with full, open faces and snowy hair. They were dressed in their Sunday best in matching blue shirts, navy-blue serge shorts, shoes and socks. The two girls were quite plain, but they were dainty, and their mousy-coloured hair was thick and well cared for. They were dressed in floral frocks and sandals.

'So I finally get to meet my little nieces,' Uncle Mick said with a twinkle in his eye. 'Well, Ellen, what do you think of moving to the bush?'

'I don't know yet, Uncle. I'll miss the sea, I think.'

'We have a river here, you know. It's called the Macintyre and it's pretty big. In good seasons it flows strongly. You can swim and fish in that if you like,' Uncle Mick suggested. 'And you've got a lot of cousins here to play with.' He indicated his brood with a wave of his hand. 'This is Kevin.' He placed his hand on the shoulder of the largest lad. 'He's the oldest – thirteen. The next one is Rodney, he's twelve.'

'He's only eleven, Mick.' Aunty Pat clicked her tongue in mock disapproval.

'Righto, love,' he continued, undeterred. 'This is Sheila, she's nearly ten. Birthday next week, she told me.' He grinned. 'And the youngest here is Mary. She's eight.'

The cousins' responses were less than friendly towards Pam and Ellen. Thinking they were out of sight of their father, the two older boys screwed up their faces, while the two girls poked out their tongues. Uncle Mick was onto them in a flash, clipping the boys behind the ear and tapping the girls on the backside. The girls screamed.

'Shut up that blubbering or you'll get another one,' Uncle Mick warned. There was immediate silence. 'Righto, folks. Let's grab your luggage and get you settled,' he said cheerfully. 'On the way, I'll show you around a bit so you know where you're going.'

Uncle Mick instructed the porter to take the luggage out to his old flat-topped Dodge, which was parked just outside the entrance to the station. Uncle Mick and Aunty Pat piled into the front with their two girls, while the two boys and Eric's family climbed into the tray.

Michael drove through the business centre until he reached the narrow bridge over the Macintyre. He parked beside the road.

'There you are, Ellen,' he said, when everyone had alighted, 'that's the river. Lots of fish in there. Over the other side,' he pointed, 'is New South Wales.'

Ellen thought it was a pretty scene, not quite like the bay views she was used to, but lovely just the same. On the clear, windless day, not even a ripple disturbed the waters. Majestic white river gums were mirrored in its surface, and native shrubbery hugged the bank at the water's edge. Wild duck and water fowl foraged in the shallows.

Uncle Mick continued. 'Before the bridge was built, a ferry at this spot was the major border crossing for the area. It was also the customs collection point until Federation in 1901.' He pointed to a building from the town's past. 'That's the old Customs House. Lots of shenanigans used to go on to get out of paying state customs duties, I can tell you.' Mick was proud that he knew a little about Goondiwindi's past. 'Right, let's get back on board.'

Backtracking through Goondiwindi's deserted streets they reached the workers' village, where identical houses lined both sides of the road. Mick pulled up in front of a low-set cottage with a corrugated iron roof and a paling fence. Mick led the way through the front door.

'No key?' Joan queried.

'No need for 'em, love. People are pretty trustworthy here, and they look out for each other.'

The front door opened wide, creaking in protest, to reveal a hall which ran down the centre of the four-room rental that was to be Ellen's new home. The two bedrooms at the front each had a battered double bed, wardrobe and chest of drawers.

The slightly larger of the two rooms also boasted a dressing table with a hat drawer and a fly-specked swing mirror. The sash windows had torn roller blinds hanging haphazardly from their fixtures. The living room featured a threadbare lounge and a small sideboard with leadlight doors. In the kitchen stood a plain timber table and chairs, an ice chest, a wood stove and an old dresser. A kerosene tin that had been cut in half with the exposed edges folded over was the only sink. From the back door, just off the small porch, a tank sat on a wooden platform while on the other side was a lean-to bathroom–laundry. The house was similar to the one they'd rented at Wynnum, the one big difference being the brick fireplace in the living room. Uncle Mick had warned them that freezing temperatures were common in winter.

Joan felt her heart sink a little at the starkness of the cottage, but her mind was soon filled with thoughts of how bright new curtains and wagga rugs on the floor would make the place more homely.

For Ellen, the fact that she would again be sharing a bed with her sister was no great surprise. In working-class families, such practices were considered the norm. Leaving the bayside had made her feel a little unsettled, but she knew her father had had no choice but to move to Goondiwindi.

Despite Eric's new job and his family's brighter economic circumstances, nothing much changed in their domestic life. Most Saturday nights were just as they had been in Wynnum – a nightmare. Ellen's father would come home from the pub drunk and abusive; Joan and the girls would often be left with bruises. The next morning the family would attended nine a.m. Mass at St Mary's with Uncle Mick and his family as if nothing had happened. Deep down, Eric was always filled with remorse, but could never admit his feelings to anyone, except to the priest during confession. The whole scenario had become a sort of ritual in which the participants felt trapped. After the service, the adults would gather in the parish hall for tea and scones with the other parishioners, while the children played outside. On just about every occasion, Ellen and Pam became targets for their male cousins, who pelted them with twigs and nuts that had fallen from the trees in the church grounds. The boys teased their cousins mercilessly.

The two families would then assemble at Uncle Mick's for a roast-beef lunch. He had his own home, a three-bedroom affair that seemed like a mansion to Ellen. After clearing the table and helping with the washing up, and if the weather was warm enough, the children changed into play clothes and usually made their way down to the river for a swim.

Being the eldest, Kevin was always placed in charge. Yet this responsibility did not stop him from trying to belittle his two cousins. 'Hey Rod,' he once said to his brother, 'we don't have to worry about Ellen. She's as skinny as a stick. She'll float.' The two boys would laugh, bringing the colour to Ellen's cheeks.

'What about Pammy?' Rodney would reply. 'She's a bit podgy. She'll probably sink to the bottom.'

Being much younger, Ellen's two female cousins only giggled

or stood silently by their brothers. Then they would all run down the bank, pushing and shoving each other while stripping down to their underclothes and diving in. A rope had been suspended from the bough of a large red gum growing at the river's edge. The two boys swung on the rope, dive-bombing all the girls with a whoop. Pam and Ellen would then be ducked. The two sisters began to hate the sight of their large, rough male cousins.

On one particularly hot Sunday, when the river was swollen and flowing swiftly, Kevin said, 'You'd better not go in, Mary, it's too fast.' Despite his teasing, Kevin took his responsibility as watchdog over the younger children very seriously. 'There's to be no skylarking or dive-bombing today,' he continued firmly.

After a short swim, they towelled themselves down and pulled dry clothes over their still-damp undergarments. Without further thought, Kevin led the others to the track that would take them through the riverside scrubland to the road leading back to their house. Unbeknown to him, Mary had hurried to the edge of the stream to throw in the stones she'd collected while waiting for them to finish their swim. The bank was wet and slippery, and as she hurled the first small pebble, she slipped and fell into the fast-moving water.

Ellen, who was bringing up the rear, heard Mary's squeal of fright. She turned and sprinted the short distance back. Mary had already been swept downstream and was bobbing up and down, arms flailing, screaming with terror. Ellen didn't hesitate. She was ahead of the two boys and dived in, swimming strongly after her cousin. Kevin dived in behind her. The others ran along the water's edge, following them. Ellen quickly gained on Mary who had run out of breath and could barely stay afloat. Just as Ellen reached her, Mary slipped from sight beneath the dark, murky waters. Ellen made a desperate grab for her, just managing to take hold of her collar, and dragged the young girl's head above the surface. Mary, in a desperate state of panic, began clawing and clutching at Ellen, who felt herself being dragged under. She had to yell at Mary to be still or they would both drown. Fortunately for them both, the youngster reacted to her pleas. Ellen placed an arm under Mary's armpit and began sidestroking towards the water's edge, assisted now by Kevin who had finally caught up. Ellen had saved her cousin's life.

Back on dry land again, Mary began to cry uncontrollably with the shock of it all, her sister stroking her hair gently. Kevin knelt by Mary, panting, almost in tears. 'Thank you, Ellen,' he began in a shaky voice. 'If it wasn't for you, Mary might have . . . she might have . . .' He trailed off.

Kevin helped his sister back to the house. When Mick heard what had happened, he wrapped his big arms around Ellen in a warm embrace. 'You wonderful girl,' he said, his voice breaking with emotion. Even her own father said he was proud of her, a moment she would never forget, as he rarely praised anyone.

From that moment on, Ellen's two male cousins placed her on a pedestal. 'Me and Rod'll never tease you again,' Kevin told her later. She could do no wrong in their eyes.

Even though the Sommers family regularly attended Mass, there was no assistance program to enable the girls to be educated at the same convent school in Goondiwindi that their four cousins attended, so Ellen and Pam had to attend the local state school. For the first few weeks, Ellen found it very difficult. It was so different. There was no uniform and hardly anyone wore shoes. While Pam was quickly accepted by her classmates, Ellen was immediately ostracised. On her first day, the teacher enquired about her previous education and Ellen told him she'd attended a convent school in Wynnum. In the background, she heard a mumble begin in the classroom. Then she heard a low voice behind her. 'She's a Mick!'

In the schoolyard, the teasing really began in earnest. Some of the girls pulled her hair, while the boys pushed and pulled her around calling her 'tyke', 'Mick' and 'pope-lover'. Still, she was determined not to cry.

Can't give them that satisfaction!

After a week of constant harassment, Ellen had had enough. When a much larger student named Helen Humphries pulled her hair, Ellen pushed her over, tearing her new blue-linen dress and grazing her knees. Ellen almost smiled as the other girl's loud wail reverberated in the hot, dry air. A few of Helen's schoolmates quickly gathered and began scolding Ellen, attracting the attention of a large boy from the other class. He wore dark-blue shorts and a white shirt and was one of the few boys wearing shoes.

'That's my twin sister you hurt,' he accused.

'She was hurting me,' Ellen answered firmly. 'I didn't start it.'

'You're that Mick sheila,' the boy said nastily.

'So what!'

'It's time you learned a lesson. Nobody hurts my sister!'

Ellen swallowed. 'She was a lot bigger than me.'

You're a lot bigger than me . . .

'I don't care!' And with that, Len Humphries twisted Ellen's arm behind her back until she cried out in pain. In between sobs, she tried to threaten him. 'I'll tell my cousin, Kevin. He'll belt you up if you don't stop.'

Len applied more pressure. 'He's not here, is he? Him and his brother go to that Mick school over the road.'

Just as Ellen again squealed in pain, she heard a strong male voice. 'That'd be like you, Humphries, you big bully. Pick on a girl.'

Len Humphries released Ellen and turned to face his accuser. Ellen held her sore arm, her attention drawn to the boy who had come to her aid. He was a head shorter than the larger boy, and was even a little shorter than Ellen. She took in his curly ginger hair and the spray of freckles covering his nose and cheeks. He was dressed in grey shorts and a red open-necked shirt. Like most of the other children, his feet were bare. She knew only that he was in the other class; she had not paid much attention to him before. Now she noted his bright-blue eyes and nice-looking face.

He's almost pretty.

The redhead looked contemptuously at Humphries, who sneered back. 'This has got nothing to do with you, O'Donnell. I'm just looking after my sister. This Mick pope-lover hurt her.'

O'Donnell took a pace forward. 'Your sister's big enough and ugly enough to look after herself, Humphries. She doesn't need you.'

'I'll do you over for that you little twerp,' he growled.

As Len Humphries moved in, he raised his fists. O'Donnell did likewise. They came together under the shade of a large jacaranda tree in a flurry of punches. When the first exchange ended, both boys were breathing heavily. O'Donnell had landed three or four heavy blows to the bully's protruding stomach, and avoided most of the heavy punches directed at his face.

He's so quick, thought Ellen.

In the fast and furious scrap that followed, it was plain to see that although blood gushed from O'Donnell's nose and his lip had split open, he was more than a match for Humphries, who was now beetroot-red in the face and was having great difficulty catching his breath. Finally a teacher intervened, grabbing both bloodied eleven-year-olds by the scruffs of their necks. He then proceeded to give the pair a severe tongue-lashing as well as a detention for their 'brutish' behaviour. After the two boys were dismissed, Len Humphries went to console his still blubbering sister, while the small lad started to walk across the schoolyard, using his handkerchief to wipe the blood from his nose and lips. Ellen approached him. 'Thank you for helping me,' she said shyly.

'That's okay.' He shrugged. 'I hate that rotten, fat turd anyway. He's always throwing his weight around.'

'But weren't you afraid?' she replied admiringly. 'He's so much bigger than you.'

'I suppose he is.' He felt embarrassed by her attention and his cheeks began to turn pink. 'But my dad taught me to fight a little and he told me to always go for the guts first.'

'I heard him call you O'Donnell. What's your first name?'

'Bluey.'

'Your hair, of course.' She smiled. 'But what's your real name?'

'Just call me Bluey,' he answered, a little stiffly.

'Okay.'

'What's yours?'

'Ellen.'

He exhaled slowly, finally daring to look into her eyes. 'They giving you a hard time about being Catholic?'

'Yes.'

'My dad's Catholic, you know.' He again looked away. 'But he doesn't go to church no more. My mum's Church of England and I am too. Don't know why everyone makes such a fuss about what religion a person is. After all, it depends on what sort of person you are, doesn't it?'

'I suppose so,' she answered lightly.

'Okay. See ya.'

Ellen watched him walk briskly away.

He seems to do everything quickly.

After that, Ellen looked for him almost every day at school, and the more she saw of him, the more she liked him. Sometimes their eyes would meet across the schoolyard, but he would always look away shyly.

Although ostracised in the beginning, Ellen was soon able to make friends with a few of the girls. She discovered that not everyone was like Helen Humphries. Margaret Smith became a good friend. She was the smartest student in the class and a lot of the other girls were jealous of her, particularly Helen Humphries. Margaret's father owned one of Goondiwindi's grocery shops. However, it was Brenda Wilson who became her very best friend. She was a stout girl with long, straight blonde hair that her mother plaited each day. She had a warm, generous nature and a great sense of humour. The pair soon became inseparable.

Chapter 2

Bluey O'Donnell thought Ellen Sommers was the prettiest girl he'd ever laid eyes on, and tried to work up the courage to speak to her, but a suitable occasion never seemed to present itself. At odd times he acknowledged her with a nod, but there was rarely any conversation.

Over the next three years, Bluey proved himself to be extremely popular with his classmates, except of course Len Humphries and his friends. He was also very athletic. In fact, by grade seven, apart from three Aboriginal boys who could run like the wind, Bluey was the fastest runner at the school. Much to Humphries' disgust, he was also captain of the school cricket and rugby league teams.

At fourteen, Bluey left school to help his father on the farm, and Ellen sought employment in town. In a country centre like Goondiwindi, the Depression was still biting and jobs were difficult to get. After canvassing all the businesses in town, she found that only the Chinaman, Jimmy Wan, offered her work. He owned a mixed business – groceries, fruit and vegetables. Two days a week, Ellen started at seven a.m. and finished at five p.m., filling orders for outlying properties. Jimmy had great difficulty pronouncing her name, eventually settling on 'Missy'. Most of the money she earned for her two days' work, she paid her mother in board. On the days she didn't work, she helped her mother at home, washing, ironing and learning to cook. One of the orders she filled at Jimmy's was for the O'Donnell property. As she carefully packed the produce, she often daydreamed about Bluey. In her mind he was her hero, even though he was half a head shorter!

The outbreak of World War II, which quickly brought to an end the nation's chronic unemployment problems, coincided with Ellen's fifteenth year. Australia's workforce was mobilised as it had never been before. Because Ellen's father was in a protected occupation, he made no attempt to sign up for military service. Many others rushed to enlist, accepting that Australia should make every effort to assist Great Britain in its time of need. They believed vehemently that Germany and its allies had to be stopped, just as they had been in the Great War.

Ellen's cousin, Kevin, was one of the first in Goondiwindi to enlist, leaving his job at the dairy to join thousands of other young Australians in the armed forces. He looked so proud at the farewell party Uncle Mick and Aunty Pat threw for him. Aunty Pat insisted that Kevin wear his uniform, although he protested. Ellen thought he looked so dashing in his summer khaki outfit, the shirt with its distinctly Australian badges and army emblems. He'd completed his basic training and had been posted to an infantry battalion.

'You take good care of yourself, Kev.' She felt her voice waver.

'Thanks, Ellen. This blue shouldn't last for too long. I'll be home before you know it.'

'Where are you heading?'

'Back to my battalion. From there, I don't know. The army doesn't tell you these things. We'll be in Australia for a bit longer, I think. Then, who knows?' He lifted his shoulders in a shrug.

'Well, good luck, Kev.' Ellen kissed him on both cheeks. She felt proud of her cousin, and did not dwell on any uncertainties.

The highlight of the week for both Ellen and Bluey was Saturday afternoon when they attended the local picture theatre for the matinee session. Goondiwindi had two theatres: the unroofed Empire, which ran night programs; and the Civic, a high-roofed building with an imposing facade, which was filled with row after row of removable seats. The program usually included two full-length movies, trailers of upcoming attractions, the news, a serial and a comic – all good value for sixpence. Not that the two youngsters ever sat together. Bluey would sit with his mate, Sean Murphy, on one side of the darkened theatre while Ellen usually sat with her sister in the centre. That arrangement quickly changed when seventeen-year-old Pam found herself a boyfriend. Since leaving school, she'd been working as a sales assistant at the town's drapery which, along with the other retail businesses, closed its doors at noon on Saturdays. Ellen usually waited for her sister on the footpath outside the drapery, and then they strolled to the pictures together.

Although Pam was a little more solid in build, they looked so much alike that passers-by could have been forgiven for thinking they were twins. Both girls were tall, although Ellen was just a shade taller, and both had shoulder-length honey-blonde hair, high cheekbones and emerald eyes. The sisters themselves were quite unaware of how attractive they were, despite turning many a man's head as he passed them by.

Even though she paid a large percentage of her wages on board, Pam still had enough left over to buy a few new items of clothing for outings. Ellen, however, only had the one good dress that she wore to church. For the pictures, she usually wore Pam's cast-offs, which had been altered to fit.

Once inside the theatre, Pam sent Ellen away to sit by herself. She didn't want her little sister beside her while she sat with her new boyfriend. On the first few occasions she was left on her own, Ellen thought Bluey was going to approach her, but he turned away just as he reached the end of her row.

The new seating arrangements had not gone unnoticed by Helen Humphries, who brought them to the attention of her brother, Len. Helen was surprised at the look on his face. A little half-smile played at the corner of his mouth and his eyes narrowed. He was like the cat that had swallowed the canary. Len had actually become infatuated with Ellen. He'd covertly watched her at every school sports day, hardly able to take his eyes off the long, trim legs that disappeared beneath her sports skirt. She had developed into a real stunner. Having now left school, he'd made sure his visits to Jimmy Wan's grocery coincided with the days she worked there. Watching her pack the boxes, he had slyly ogled her, allowing his eyes to run over her body, then feeling his blood run hot through his veins.

On this particular Saturday, Len made his way towards her in the picture theatre with a friendly smile on his face. He had developed into a reasonably trim young man, and was feeling very smart and confident in his new cream cotton slacks and dark green blazer. 'Hello, Ellen,' he said, his eyes wandering to her breasts, which curved against the soft fabric of her faded, v-necked lemon blouse.

Ellen noticed his lascivious gaze and to her it seemed more objectionable than if he had touched her. 'Hello,' she whispered back, her cheeks turning pink.

He gazed steadily at her until she looked away. His eyes strayed down to her slender calves. Her straight, light-brown skirt had slipped up almost to her knees. 'You're by yourself.' It was a statement rather than a question. He watched the pink spread over her face again, her embarrassment creating a pleasant conflict between longing and expectation within him.

'My sister's over there,' she indicated with a nod to where Pam sat with her latest beau.

'Want to sit with me?'

'No thanks.' Ellen had never forgotten his appalling behaviour in the playground. Although it was more than five years ago, and Len had scrubbed up well as a young man, she knew that the bully lurked just beneath the surface.

'What?' Humphries seemed genuinely shocked that he had been turned down.

Ellen shook her head, a noticeable frown creasing her brow as she looked up at him. 'No, I don't want to sit with you.'

He looked at her, annoyed. 'Why?'

'Because you were mean to me.'

'That was a long time ago.' He gave a short dismissive laugh. 'Things are different now.'

'The answer's still no.'

'That's what you think,' he said angrily and sat heavily in the seat beside her. Ellen did not know what to do. She could barely breathe she felt so self-conscious and embarrassed. At that moment the lights dimmed. Len moved closer and attempted to put his arm around her shoulder. This brought about an instant response from Ellen, who pushed his arm to one side and jumped to her feet. As she struggled to pass him, he grabbed her by the arm.

'Where do you think you're going?' he hissed.

'I'm going to find another seat,' she said defiantly, her green eyes blazing.

'Oh, no you're not,' he said between gritted teeth. 'You're sitting with me.'

'I'm not!' Ellen tried to pull away, but Humphries only tightened his grip.

Ellen felt a hot tear roll down her cheek. 'You're hurting me,' she whimpered.

'What's going on?' said a gruff voice.

Ellen turned and saw Bluey standing in the aisle at the end of the row. 'He's trying to make me sit with him,' she said and the tears began in earnest.

'Piss off, O'Donnell,' Humphries exploded. He was in no mood for interference, especially after the embarrassment of Ellen's rejection. To rub salt into the wound, the person he hated most in the world was glaring at him. Humphries was now considerably taller than Bluey, but the smaller teenager was not fazed.

'Leave her alone,' he said in a low voice. 'She doesn't like your ugly mug.'

'I'll give you ugly, you little prick!' Humphries stood up. 'I'm a lot bigger than you, so don't mess with me.'

Bluey's lips curled contemptuously. 'You know what they say, the bigger they are, the harder they fall.'

'That's it, O'Donnell. Now you're for it.'

Bluey raised his fists and waited for Humphries.

The ensuing fight, which took place towards the front of the old theatre, had the younger patrons rushing to catch a glimpse of the action. Nearly all of Goondiwindi's youth were aware of the animosity between Bluey O'Donnell and Len Humphries. Most of the cheering was for gutsy Bluey. During the altercation, the pair rolled over the seats and onto the timber floor. Again, Humphries had the upper hand at the beginning of the fight, but like the previous occasion, when the boys were just eleven, Bluey outlasted the larger lad who finally capitulated. Humphries stormed from the theatre humiliated, his clothing ruined. Bluey's mates stood around patting him on the back. Surprisingly, during the fracas, there was no interference from theatre management, perhaps because it was over so quickly.

Breathless, Bluey made his way back to Ellen and sat down beside her. She used her white handkerchief to wipe the blood from his nose and lips. A few drops had fallen onto the collar of his blue, open-necked shirt.

'Don't do that,' he objected shyly, 'you'll mark your hanky.'

'It doesn't matter.' She looked at him adoringly.

'Is it all right if I sit here, Ellen?' he asked, his voice barely a whisper.

Her eyes shone brightly. 'Yes, of course.'

The young pair settled down to watch the program, though neither of them was able to concentrate on the show. An unfamiliar warm feeling flowed through Ellen. Eventually, Bluey squirmed in his seat.

'Is everything all right?' she asked.

'Ellen, I want to ask you something.'

In the darkness, she was looking at him, her eyes sparkling. 'Yes?'

'I never said anything to you, but I always thought you were a bonza sort.' His voice was barely a whisper, but she heard every word. 'And I like you a lot as well.'

Ellen felt a wave of happiness wash over her. 'That's nice, Bluey. I like you too,' she whispered back.

'There's more.' He paused, taking a deep breath. 'I want to ask you something else.' The darkness of the theatre and the drone of the film's dialogue had provided cover for Bluey, and he found he had the nerve to say the words he'd been turning over in his mind for so long.

'Yes?'

'Will you be my girl?'

'Oh, yes!' she said, unable to disguise the joy in her voice. She would have loved to bury her head in his shoulder and allow him to caress her, but she resisted the temptation. Instead, she had to be content with him cementing the new relationship with a brief peck to her cheek.

From that day on, the two of them were inseparable – well, as far as possible given their responsibilities at home and at work. They could hardly wait for the end of each week, for every Saturday they dressed in their best outfits and went to the pictures together.

At home, Sally O'Donnell noticed the change in her son. 'You seem happy,' Sally commented to him one morning as he sat down to breakfast.

'I'm okay, Mum,' he replied evasively.

'I just wondered, seeing there was blood on the blue shirt you wore to the pictures last Saturday afternoon and you had cuts on your lips when you got home. It's not like you to be fighting.'

'It was nothing. Len Humphries was trying to force a girl I know to sit with him.'

'A girl?' Sally turned away to hide a smile.

'Yeah.' Bluey said self-consciously.

'Why were you the one to rescue her?' she asked, feigning innocence.

'She's nice,' he said matter-of-factly. 'He was being rough with her.'

'I see. Is she pretty?'

'Why are you asking all these questions?'

'I'm just interested, son.'

'Yes. She's pretty,' he said tersely.

'You're sweet on her, aren't you?' she teased.

'That's it, Mum,' he snapped. 'Enough!'

Bluey stormed out of the house, leaving his mother giggling to herself. That night at the dinner table, the teasing continued. 'Dave, have you heard? Our Bluey has a girlfriend.' She smiled broadly at her husband, and gave him a wink.

Bluey ignored his mother's comment, and continued eating his steak and vegetables. Dave took in the mischievous look on his wife's face and returned the wink. 'Begosh and begorrrah, what's this little Colleen's name?'

The exaggerated Irish brogue annoyed Bluey, who thought his father bunged on the accent at times. 'I don't want to talk about it.'

'Is she a good sort, son?' Dave choked down a laugh.

Bluey put down the knife and fork, feeling as spiky as the prickly pear growing in the paddocks. He looked from one parent to the other. 'I know you two think this is funny, but I don't. If you both want to know, her name is Ellen Sommers and yes, she's very pretty.'

Sally knew when enough was enough. She reached over and patted his hand. 'Sorry, son, but what great news.'

Ellen's mother got to hear about her youngest daughter having a boyfriend from her neighbour, who'd seen them at the pictures. 'Jean tells me you have a boyfriend,' she commented one day when Ellen returned from work.

Ellen's cheeks flushed. 'Yes, Mum.' She looked down. 'His name is Bluey O'Donnell.'

'Jean says he comes from a good family. Is he a nice boy?'

'Yes, very.'

'That's comforting to know, Ellen.' Conscious of Ellen's good looks, Joan struggled to express her concern. 'We've had our little talk, you know, about life and all that.' She paused. 'Don't be doing anything silly, will you, pet?'

Ellen shook her head. 'Don't worry, Mum, I won't.'

'And don't let your father find out about this Bluey or he'll have a fit.'

Ellen already had a fair idea of that, and didn't really need the warning.

After a few weeks, and in the darkness of the old picture theatre, Bluey and Ellen experienced the delight of their first real kiss. What started out as brief pecks soon developed into long, passionate embraces which often left them gasping for breath. They felt bewildered and shaken by the strength of these new sensations and feelings. Some months later, after their first kiss in the dimly lit theatre, the relationship had progressed to the stage where Bluey placed a tentative hand on her breast. At first Ellen was appalled, but could not help the little shiver of excitement and desire. She drew away from the embrace, embarrassed and uncertain about what to do next. She feigned feelings of indignation. 'Bluey, what are you doing?'

'Sorry, El. I didn't mean to upset you.'

'I know some of the girls let boys do that,' she sounded offended, 'but I'm not like that.'

'Okay,' he agreed, dejected.

After Ellen's negative response, Bluey was reluctant to carry things any further. A few more weeks into the courtship, however, she had no objection when his hand accidentally touched her breast. Emboldened, he gradually progressed to actually fondling her. Ellen positively swooned when he began exposing her breasts in the darkness of the theatre, kissing her nipples, which hardened at his touch. It seemed a natural progression, then, when Bluey placed his hand on her thigh, eventually easing his fingers inside the leg of her pants. The experience brought both youngsters to new levels of sexual excitement.

The demands of Kilkenny usually required Bluey's presence there on Sundays, but not always. On rare occasions, Bluey and Ellen were able to meet up in town on that day. They would spend the afternoon strolling hand in hand along the river, talking. One Sunday, as they embraced on the Macintyre River's grassy bank, Ellen finally placed her hand on his hardened penis. Bluey groaned with pleasure before feelings of guilt forced Ellen to draw away. 'I shouldn't do this. It's sinful.' She sat up, looking around in distress, straightening her blouse. With her Catholic upbringing, she couldn't reconcile her excitement and guilt – wanting to, and not wanting to.

'Don't listen to all that malarky the priests and nuns tell you,' Bluey replied scornfully.

'But I shouldn't do it,' she said sorrowfully, brushing her golden hair back with one hand. In keeping with current fashion, she wore it shoulder length.

In the hushed silence that followed, he said, 'We could go one better, you know.'

'What?' Her eyes opened wide. 'Have sex?'

'Yeah.' He knew his tone was beseeching, but he didn't care.

Her pounding heart seemed to stop. 'No, I couldn't. I just couldn't. What if I got pregnant?'

'I could get a frenchie.'

'I don't know, Bluey.' She looked at him, her eyes troubled. 'I do want you, but I'm scared.'

'I'm nervous as well,' he admitted. 'It would be the first time for me, too.' He took a deep breath and tenderly brushed the hair from her eyes. 'I don't want to force you into anything. But I know I love you.'

'Oh, Bluey,' she beamed. 'You've never said that before.'

'I don't like talking about these things,' he mumbled.

'I love you, too.' She leaned over and kissed him lightly on the lips. Her heart soared.

He took her hand and held it. 'With this bloody war, I might have to join the army soon.'

'But you're only sixteen!' Ellen felt a sudden hollowness in her stomach.

'When I'm seventeen they'll take me if my parents approve.'

'But not overseas,' she added, remembering discussions around the dinner table at home. She felt relieved that they had been given a reprieve.

'Yes, you're right. Not until I'm nineteen.'

She swallowed. 'Oh, Bluey, I never really thought about you having to go into the services. What do your parents think?'

'Dunno. Haven't talked to them about it yet.' A small smile played across his face. 'My dad hates the English and calls this their war. Says we shouldn't be involved.'

'What do you think?'

'I don't agree with him.' His tone was serious. 'I mean, if our country decides to go to war, then we're all in it together. But I wouldn't say this to him.'

'What will I do without you, sweetheart?'

He looked at her coyly. She'd never called him that before. For a long moment, Ellen was quiet and thoughtful. 'Bluey, you get the protection and next time we'll do it.'

'What? Sex, you mean?'

'Yes.' She sounded determined.

And they did. On the banks of the muddy Macintyre River one week later, Ellen and Bluey lost their virginity. As Ellen lay in his arms a few moments later, she wondered if this brief activity was what everyone got so excited about. Finally, she couldn't resist making a comment. 'It didn't take long, did it?'

'No.' He was feeling a little despondent. 'I just couldn't hold it in.'

As the weeks passed, their lovemaking slowly improved, much to their delight and mutual ecstasy.

Chapter 3

Ellen stood out of sight of the newsagent, browsing through a *Women's Weekly* in the town's only newsagency. Like most other girls of the same age, she often hid from counter staff to peruse the various magazines she could not afford to buy. She jumped with fright when she heard a pleasant female voice behind her.

'You're Ellen Sommers, aren't you?'

Ellen turned towards the speaker, a petite woman in her late thirties who was pretty in a girlish sort of way.

She's lovely.

Although she had never met this woman before, she seemed somehow familiar, with her bright blue eyes and thick, wavy, shoulder-length auburn hair. She wore a simple skirt and blouse and carried a beaded handbag.

'Yes.' Ellen admitted shyly.

'I thought so. I'm Sally O'Donnell, Bluey's mother,' she said sweetly, holding out a hand.

Ellen took the woman's hand, acutely embarrassed. 'P–pleased to meet you, Mrs O'Donnell.'

'I'm so glad to meet you at last,' Sally said warmly. 'Bluey's always talking about you. "Ellen says this" or "Ellen says that" is all I hear at times,' she said with a small laugh. 'Come down to the milk bar with me, and I'll buy you a malted milk.'

'I couldn't possibly —' Ellen began, but that was as far as she was allowed to proceed. The older woman simply linked arms with Ellen and steered her out of the newsagency.

The milk bar was a favourite meeting place for the town's youth. Still relatively unused to the new attraction, youngsters could choose one of the stools lining the counter, or if there was a big group, one of the six booths, in which to sip their drinks and talk. Sally and Ellen chose the high stools.

'What flavour, Ellen?'

'Chocolate, please.'

'Make that two chocolate malted milks,' she said to the waitress.

'How did you know me, Mrs O'Donnell?' Ellen asked.

'Bluey keeps a photo of you on his bedside table. You know, the one he took of you by the river.'

Ellen remembered that day. It was the first time they'd made love. The memory caused her colour to return.

'You look a little red, my dear. Is everything all right?'

'Y–yes, of course.'

Sally liked Ellen immediately. She was impressed by her neat appearance as well as her courteous and pleasant manner. Even though there was a significant age difference, there was an immediate rapport between the two women. As they drank their malted milks, Ellen slowly felt more comfortable in the older woman's company. Sally enquired about Ellen's past, her job at Jimmy Wan's, her sporting interests, her family and finally Bluey. Ellen, on the other hand, was anxious to hear about Kilkenny. She told Sally that she had never ever visited a farm, even though she had now been living in Goondiwindi for seven years. Sally immediately invited the girl to the property. 'You must come out home for tea on Friday night. I'll pick you up in front of the Council Chambers at four p.m.,' she said enthusiastically. 'You can stay over. Then Bluey's father can drop you both at the pictures on Saturday. He goes to town every Saturday, anyway.'

'I don't know if I'd be allowed,' Ellen replied, crestfallen. 'I'll have to ask Mum.'

Ellen was uncertain about the invitation. Her father had no knowledge of Bluey, and she dreaded his reaction should he discover that she had a boyfriend. Ellen remembered her sister's comment, 'He's not very big, is he?'

'You know the old saying,' Ellen had responded indignantly, 'good things come in small packages.'

'But he's not even as tall as you. Don't you feel embarrassed walking with him?'

'Girls develop sooner than boys,' Ellen said defensively.

'My Mark is the same age as me and he's taller than I am.'

'Yeah. And he's also got a face full of pimples!' Ellen retorted.

'What about Bluey?' Pam was now the indignant one. 'He reminds me of Ginger Meggs!'

'He does not.'

'Yes, he does. In fact, from now on, I'm going to call him

Meggsy!' She strode from the room and Ellen could still hear her laughing as she walked down the hallway.

Sally's words brought her back to the present. 'Your parents don't know about Bluey, do they, love?' She had been quick to analyse the situation.

'Mum does.' Ellen sighed. 'But if my father even suspected I had a boyfriend, he would accuse me of all sorts of things, especially when he has too much to drink.' Ellen was surprised to feel her eyes brim with tears. She'd never told anyone about her father before, but somehow she felt she could trust Sally.

Sally left her stool to take Ellen into her arms. 'You poor darling.' There was a lump in her throat. 'Looks like we have something in common, love. My dad was a drinker, too.'

Ellen wiped her eyes, relieved to be able to share her awful secret with someone who understood. From that moment on, all awkwardness dissolved and the two women chatted like old friends until Ellen had to race home to her chores.

Later, when Ellen approached her mother about the invitation, she was surprised that her mother agreed.

'How are you getting out there?'

'Mrs O'Donnell is picking me up in town.'

'What about getting back?'

'Mr O'Donnell will drop me in and I can walk home.'

'It'll be a nice change for you.'

'I'm really excited, Mum. Bluey said he would take me horseback riding.'

For a moment, Joan's face clouded. 'You be careful if you do, my girl.'

'Yes, Mum, I will.'

Joan decided she would tell her husband that Ellen was sleeping overnight at a girlfriend's house.

Friday finally arrived. Ellen packed a change of clothing and toiletry items in a small, worn suitcase which she carried into town. Right on time, the O'Donnell utility pulled to a halt in front of her. Sally quickly jumped from behind the wheel and greeted Ellen warmly before darting off to the grocery store. Bluey got out and stood smiling, at a loss for words. Having his girlfriend stay over was a completely new experience for him. 'You look nice,' he said simply.

Ellen looked down at the old frock she was wearing. Its only redeeming feature was that it hugged her figure. 'Thanks, Bluey,' she replied shyly.

He took her suitcase and placed it in the rear of the ute. Ellen looked around nervously. Although her father usually started work at six-thirty a.m. and there was little chance he would see her with Bluey and her suitcase, she couldn't help feeling apprehensive.

'Can I hop in?' she asked.

'Sure,' he said, opening the passenger door. Unfortunately, at that exact moment one of Eric Sommers' drinking mates pedalled by. Ellen didn't see him, but he certainly saw Ellen, and made a note to tell Eric.

Sally returned a moment later and they were soon on their way. Ellen felt as though she was going on a little adventure. As the ute bumped its way along the unsealed corrugated road, she looked out the window and took in the green open countryside, paddock after paddock, most of them dotted with merino sheep.

Only a very few properties grew wheat. Sally named a couple of the farms as they passed. It was interesting for Ellen to see where some of the boxes she packed at Jimmy Wan's store ended up.

'There's the river.' Sally pointed. It was easy to identify the river's snaking course over the cleared paddocks by the trees and thick foliage growing along its banks.

'The properties on our left all run right down to the water,' Sally informed her.

Bluey didn't have much to say. Although he was excited to have Ellen visiting, he felt uncomfortable talking to his girlfriend in front of his mother.

Driving through Kilkenny's front gate, Ellen shook her head in wonder, for the scene before her was even more beautiful than she'd imagined. The pretty farmhouse had a long verandah, and a neat garden with plenty of shade trees.

'What a lovely place!' Ellen exclaimed. 'And how do you find the time to tend the garden?'

'Bluey does the vegetable garden,' Sally said proudly. 'He's got a rare talent. We'll be sampling some of his fresh beans, peas and cabbage tonight.'

Ellen smiled and looked at Bluey, 'You never mentioned this before.'

'Oh, it's nothing – just another job that I do,' he replied modestly.

As the three walked from the garage to the house, Sally placed her arm around Ellen's waist. It would be lovely to have a young girl visit, she thought to herself. In the past, it had only been Bluey's friend, Sean Murphy, who'd been over.

Ellen immediately felt at ease in the peaceful environment

of the O'Donnell home. As Sally showed her around, she realised it was much more spacious than the workers' cottage in Goondiwindi. There were cheerful homemade cushions and throws in the sitting room, and in the sleep-out where Ellen would be staying, a bowl of roses adorned the bedside table and a gorgeous quilt covered the bed.

A bed to myself at last!

At dusk, Dave O'Donnell could be heard singing as he made his way towards the homestead. When Ellen looked up from peeling the vegetables, she noticed the extra sparkle in Sally's blue eyes as her husband entered the kitchen.

Sally went to kiss him before turning back to Ellen. 'We have a young visitor, Dave. Ellen Sommers, Bluey's friend.'

He smiled warmly at Ellen before winking at his wife. 'An' a lovely picture she is, eh, Sal?'

Ellen felt her colour rise.

'Don't you be teasing her now, Dave,' Sally scolded before turning again to Ellen. 'Don't take any notice of him, love.'

'Don't you mind me, young Ellen. Welcome to our home.'

'Thank you, Mr O'Donnell,' she replied shyly.

Through all this conversation Bluey had remained quiet. Finally he looked towards his father. 'Is it all right if I take Ellen riding in the morning, Dad?'

'Sure t'ing, lad.' Dave patted him on the shoulder. 'After you've done your chores, mind.'

'Okay.'

'Have you ever ridden a horse, young Ellen?' Dave enquired.

'No.'

'Ah!' His face lit up, 'There's nothin' like bein' on a horse for the first time.' He turned to his son. 'Blue, you'd better saddle up old Dolly for Ellen here.' He smiled reassuringly. 'She's a sweet old t'ing. She'll look after you.'

'Thank you,' Ellen said, clearly delighted.

'Just take it easy,' he added, 'and you'll be right.' He turned back to Bluey. 'And you can take Bert, son.'

'Aw gee, Dad,' Bluey complained. 'I thought I'd take Bullet out for a run.'

For the first time Dave's tone was serious. 'You keep off that bloody chestnut, you hear? He tried to kick me yesterday. He's dangerous.'

'All right, Dad.' Bluey nodded.

Ellen thoroughly enjoyed the meal of roast lamb and vegetables which was followed by homemade apple tart and fresh cream. The atmosphere around the dining table in the O'Donnell's house was in stark contrast to that of the Sommers'. On the rare occasions Eric ate with his family, no one dared talk during the meal, and there was always tension in the air. It was like walking on egg shells. Eating with the O'Donnells was a much more carefree affair – they chatted and laughed incessantly. Bluey's parents enquired about both youngsters' days, and Dave brought his family up to date with his current planting activities while Sally made light of some of her daily chores. Ellen sat back, basking in the warmth and congeniality.

Waving aside Sally's protests, Ellen insisted on doing the washing up. Dave chipped in. 'All right, if young Ellen's going to do the dishes, Bluey can still clear the table and dry up as usual.

Sal, you come with me to the lounge room and we'll listen to the radio.'

As she lay in the quiet of the homestead's sleep-out that Friday night listening to the light rain on the metal roof, Ellen could not remember a time she'd ever felt so at peace. The room was long and narrow, with casement windows along its entire length. It contained a single bed, bedside table and a set of drawers with a mirror attached to the wall above it. Dismissing the rain, Bluey's mother had opened two of the windows slightly to let in a bit of fresh air. 'Too stuffy in here with all the windows closed,' she observed. 'A little bit of water on the floor won't do any harm.'

Ellen sighed contentedly. At least for one night, there would be no lying awake anxiously waiting for the hotel to close, and her father's drunken arrival at home and the abuse that would follow. She couldn't help but feel a little envious of the harmonious, loving family environment in which Bluey had been raised. She was pleased for him, but also considered him to be extremely fortunate. In the peaceful atmosphere of the country homestead, Ellen Sommers slept more soundly than she could ever remember.

It was still dark when she felt Bluey's hand on her shoulder. 'Come on, Ellen. We've got to do the animals.'

Ellen yawned. 'What's the time?'

'Quarter to five.'

'That early?'

'It's all right for you townies who can sleep in.' He grinned down at her. 'We're the ones who have to get up early.'

'Go outside so I can get dressed,' she ordered.

'What about a kiss?' he asked mischievously.

'No!' she chided. 'I told you there'd be no mucking about in your parents' house.'

'Okay.' He sounded a little disappointed, then changed the subject. 'What do you think of my mum and dad?'

'They're wonderful,' she said admiringly. 'I like them a lot.'

'Yeah, they are pretty good I suppose.'

'All right, now out you go so I can get up.'

Ellen dressed herself in a pair of navy-blue slacks and a long-sleeved flannelette blouse she had borrowed from Pam. With a cold westerly wind now blowing, she was grateful for the jacket Sally had loaned her the night before. Bluey wore his favourite brown jodhpurs, a red and grey checked shirt and fawn jacket.

Pink tinged the eastern horizon as they walked the short distance from the house to the barn. When Bluey told her to watch out for snakes she screamed and jumped to one side, then admonished him because he laughed at her. As Ellen entered the building, she noticed that four horses were penned along one side, each having access to an outside yard. The rest of the barn was used for feed storage – lucerne hay, oats and molasses. The barn walls were made of rough-cut, hand-dressed timber which had weathered to a silvery grey. The building itself was constructed around three thick tree trunks embedded in the ground. Thick boughs had been bolted to the tops of the trunks as cross members. These supported the roof trusses and the outside walls. In the far left-hand corner was the milking pen, which was currently occupied by what Ellen considered to be a black and white monster.

'Are you going to have a go at milking her?' Bluey asked.

'What? That big thing?' Ellen looked back at him, horrified.

'Old Betsy's not that big, and she's pretty gentle, too.'

With that the Friesian cow turned towards Ellen and began lowing, a sound that in the confines of the small barn was like a foghorn. Ellen jumped with fright and Bluey chuckled.

'Look, I'll show you what to do,' he offered. Placing a spotlessly clean stainless-steel milk bucket under the cow's udder, he positioned himself on a small stool. Ellen watched him rub a creamy substance into his hands. He then reached for one of the cow's teats, taking the bulging nipple in his right hand. He squeezed firmly as he moved the grip down. A stream of warm milk squirted into the bucket. He repeated the process several times before selecting another teat.

'Right, your turn.' He rose to his feet. 'When you get the hang of it, you can use two hands.'

Ellen looked uncertainly into the face of the cow. 'All right. I'll give it a go.' Nervously she moved closer to the giant Friesian.

'Don't let her see you're scared or she'll play up,' he warned.

'All right.'

Just as she arranged herself on the small stool, the cow thought it timely to empty her bowels. As the dung fell steaming onto the barn's dirt floor, she screwed her nose up in disgust. 'I think I'm going to be sick.'

'Don't be a sook. It's not that bad.' He grinned. 'Come on, let's see you milk her. Here's some cream.'

As she rubbed the cream into her hands, she eyed the large udder uncertainly.

'Take that one.' Bluey pointed to a large teat.

Ellen took hold and attempted to imitate Bluey's action, but not one drop of milk made its way into the bucket.

'Do it again, El, but grip it harder. You won't hurt her.'

Ellen followed his instructions and took a firmer hold. Squeezing the teat downwards, a small stream of milk spurted into the bucket. When she repeated the process, the stream of milk became stronger.

'There. What did I tell you? Not that hard, is it?'

At that moment the cow stepped back, nearly knocking over the bucket with its front hoof. Warm milk sprinkled onto Ellen's sandshoes. She repositioned the bucket and selected another teat. Half an hour later, her arduous task was completed, and the cow had been released into a back paddock. Together she and Bluey fed and watered the pigs and the poultry.

When they returned to the house, Sally served up large portions of bacon and eggs followed by toast and golden syrup. As she poured milk for them, she asked. 'Where are you taking Ellen on the ride, Blue?'

'I thought I'd take her along the river to the cave.'

'That's a nice ride.'

Back in the barn after breakfast, Bluey pointed out Ellen's mount, a light-grey mare of about thirteen hands. While Bluey fitted the bridle and began saddling her, Ellen stroked the animal's neck. The old mare just loved the attention and snickered with satisfaction, nuzzling Ellen's upper arm.

'She's lovely, Bluey.'

'Yeah, I suppose so. She's getting on a bit.'

'How old is she?'

'About twenty-four, I think.'

As Ellen stood stroking the mare's neck, her attention was drawn towards a beautiful, reddish-coloured horse in the next stall. When the flashy chestnut looked back at Ellen, she could see white round its eyes, but had no idea that this was an indication of its instability. Because of its showy appearance, she was attracted to the gelding and moved closer to try to pat it. The chestnut snorted loudly, thrust its head over the door and took hold of Ellen's shoulder, biting down hard. She let out a terrified scream that shattered the early morning quiet and echoed in the barn. Fortunately for her, as she pulled away, its thick teeth were only able to latch onto the thick woollen material of her jacket. Yet she was still dragged towards the door of the horse's enclosure. The next thing she heard was the crack of a stock whip and the snorting animal immediately released her and ran out into the yard.

Strong hands pulled her to safety. 'Ellen! Ellen! Are you all right?' Bluey's hands trembled as he held her close, his face contorted with anxiety.

Ellen had never seen him like this. Still in shock, she nodded. 'Y–yes. I don't think I'm hurt.'

'Let me have a look at your shoulder.'

Ellen unbuttoned the jacket and slid her blouse sideways to expose bare skin. 'Doesn't look too bad. There'll be a bruise,' he said after examining the area. 'The mongrel of a thing!' he exclaimed angrily.

'Oh, Bluey!' She licked her lips. 'I was so scared.'

He exhaled slowly, and gazed into her eyes. 'I don't know what I'd have done if anything had happened to you, El.' He again took her in his arms, holding her for a long moment. After they had settled down he said, 'We'd better go and tell Mum what happened. She'll probably want to put ointment or something on that bruise. I hope that mad chestnut hasn't put you off riding,' he added anxiously.

'Oh, no. I still want to go,' Ellen assured him.

Ellen and Bluey set out on their adventure, full of anticipation. It was one of those magical autumn days where a night wind has swept away the rain clouds, leaving a clear, crisp, sunny morning. When a slight westerly wind drifted across their path, Ellen was grateful for the thick woollen jacket and brown leather gloves Sally insisted she wear. She shivered, not only from the autumn chill, but also with nervous excitement.

Following Bluey's instructions to the letter, it didn't take long for her to adapt to riding. Bluey even remarked that she was a natural. A gentle nudge with her heel or a slight tug to the rein, as he instructed, and the old grey mare responded accordingly. The bay horse Bluey rode was two hands taller than Ellen's and it, too, appeared to be a gentle animal. Ellen only became a little concerned when Bluey's bay broke into a trot or canter. Not to be outdone, her competitive mount would do exactly the same. The trot caused her to bounce up and down in the saddle, and it took a while to adjust to the proper rhythm. The first time the old grey actually broke into a canter, Ellen was afraid she would fall off altogether. But thanks to Bluey's coaching, she soon found the required rhythm and began to enjoy herself.

After they made their way through two grain paddocks, currently lying fallow, Bluey dismounted to open one of the gates to the river paddock. In the distance, the sunshine glinted off the Macintyre. Mobs of healthy sheep sheltered from the sun under large gums that dotted the lush paddock.

Ten minutes later, the two were riding along the banks of the Macintyre where majestic red gums and weeping willows crowded the water's edge. 'All this land,' Bluey waved his hand expansively, 'was where the Goomeroi people used to live. Dad says the river provided a lot of food for their diet – things like crayfish, mussels and fish. There are still a few middens along the bank. I'll show 'em to you later.'

'What are middens?'

'It's where they used to prepare their food. They left behind a lot of shells and other stuff.'

'Oh.' Ellen was impressed.

Bluey was on a roll. 'Dad says they used their spears to catch the fish from wooden canoes that they carved from tree trunks.' As they rode on, Bluey identified the scar trees for her.

From her schooling, Ellen knew that the river flowed west, changing its name to the Barwon before linking with other streams and finally flowing into the Darling River. This long waterway joined up with the Murray River at Wentworth, a town on the border of New South Wales and Victoria. The water she was looking at now would eventually flow into the sea on the South Australian coastline, a thousand or so miles to the south-west.

Bluey interrupted her thoughts. 'You like fishing, don't you, El?'

'Yes. I used to do a lot when we lived at Wynnum.'

'Good fishing here, you know. Black bream, freshwater jewfish, yellow belly and Murray cod.'

'Murray cod are the big ones, aren't they?'

'Too right,' he said enthusiastically. 'I'll take you fishing for one the next time you come out. See if you can't catch a big one.' He grinned. 'We never have.'

Stopping at the stream to rest the horses, the abundant birdlife on the waterway caught her attention: brolga, jabiru and spoonbill fed in the shallows while a lonely duck paddled idly by. They again mounted, slowly following the water downstream. A short time later, they came upon an area of scrubland.

'That's where we're going,' he pointed along a narrow track through thicker bushes.

Bluey steered his horse onto the trail and Ellen followed. Fifty yards or so later, Bluey came to a stop and began to dismount. Ellen looked around, puzzled. 'I see a rocky outcrop, but I don't see any cave.' She dismounted.

'It's hidden from view. I'll show you. It's bonza.' Tethering the horses to a tree, he took a bicycle torch from his saddlebag and led Ellen along a narrow pathway between the rocky walls. A moment later, she saw the opening. 'Come inside,' he beckoned her, 'I want to show you something.' He took her hand, leading her a little further into the muted darkness of the cave. 'You see that?' He shone the torch onto faded paintings of kangaroos, emus and other Australian fauna. 'Abos did these thousands and thousands of years ago.'

Ellen's eyes opened wide in wonder and she moved closer to inspect. She stood in awe, overcome by a feeling of reverence.

'Not many people have seen these,' Bluey said proudly.

'Oh, Bluey, this is wonderful.' Her skin tingled.

'Yeah,' he admitted, 'I always get a funny feeling when I come here.'

'Who knows about it?'

'No other white people apart from us, and that's the way Dad wants to keep it.'

Bluey placed his arm around Ellen's shoulder. She turned her face to his, and they kissed gently.

'Do you want to do it here, El?'

She detected a note of expectancy in the casual request. 'No,' she said, aghast. 'I just couldn't, Bluey. This is a special place. It would almost be like doing it in church.'

'All right.' He tried not to sound disappointed. 'Let's go home and get ready for the pictures.'

When they returned to the homestead, Ellen noticed something different. Beside the open corrals was a large mound of freshly turned earth. Dave stood sweating beside the heap, shovel in hand.

'Have a good ride, kids?' he asked.

'Oh, yes, Mr O'Donnell.' Ellen glowed. 'It was wonderful.'

'I showed her the cave, Dad.'

'What did you think?' Dave asked.

'I thought it was very special,' she said quietly.

Bluey's eyes turned to the mound beside them. 'Bullet?'

'Aye, son,' Dave answered seriously. 'It's Bullet.'

Ellen looked at the mound, shocked. She couldn't believe that Bluey's father had actually killed such a beautiful and valuable animal. Certainly its behaviour had frightened her, but she didn't expect it to be put down.

'I thought you were going to sell him,' Bluey said.

'Couldn't sell a dangerous horse like that,' he answered gruffly. 'Not after what he did to young Ellen here. He might have killed someone.'

For the first time, Ellen realised that life on the property had a harsher side. Sometimes difficult and costly decisions had to be made. It could be a hard life.

Chapter 4

Ellen walked home from the pictures feeling dreamy and relaxed. Even though it was getting late in the afternoon, the sun still hovered above the horizon. It had been a perfect day, one she would never forget.

What wonderful people they are.

Singing to herself as she entered the front gate of her home, she put her suitcase in her bedroom and rushed to the kitchen to tell her mother all about her time at Kilkenny.

'Mum! I've had the most amazing —' was all she could utter before she felt a heavy blow to the left side of her face. Dazed, her head spinning, she heard her mother's terrified scream.

'Been waiting for you, harlot.' The slur in his voice told Ellen her father was drunk.

'Don't, Eric,' Joan pleaded, moving towards her daughter. 'Please leave her alone.'

Eric shoved her aside. He grabbed at Ellen again and she stumbled sideways against the sideboard, smashing a small mirror. Her mother again tried to intervene. Ellen heard the sickening sound of another blow, followed by her mother's cry of pain. Her father then lunged after Ellen, striking the right side of her face. She collapsed, fighting against the swirling darkness that threatened to envelope her. Out of the corner of her eye she saw a small red pool forming on the waxed surface. It was only then she realised that blood was streaming from her nose and from the other injuries to her face. Turning her head, she could just make out the outline of her drunken father standing over her.

His eyes narrowed. 'Slut!' he yelled at the top of his voice. Alcohol had fuelled a mindless rage. 'You were seen going off with some boy,' he shouted.

Ellen staggered to her feet. 'I didn't do anything wrong, Dad.'

The next blow was so hard that she was knocked to the floor again. For a few moments, she lost consciousness. When she came to, she knew she had to get away and that her father was capable of killing her. With great effort, she scrambled to her feet, and swayed towards the hallway. She needed to reach the front door and get out. Her father anticipated the move, viciously wrenching her arm.

'Where do you think you're goin'?'

As Eric brought his hand back and forth across her face in sharp slaps, Ellen could feel the blackness closing in. Suddenly her father bellowed in pain and released her. Blinking to clear away the fog, she saw him slump to the floor. Behind him, her mother stood holding a heavy cast-iron frying pan.

Joan Sommers wept as she took her daughter in her arms. 'Oh, look at your pretty face, sweetheart. This has gone too far. He'll be out cold for a bit, so you'd better go while you can. Stay with a friend overnight. I'll tell you when it's safe to come home again.'

Ellen's mouth was suddenly dry. 'What about you?'

'I'll be fine. I doubt he'll even remember what happened,' Joan answered. 'He'll have a headache, but he'll get over it.'

Ellen again embraced her mother, before retrieving her suitcase which was still packed from her visit with the O'Donnells. Her legs felt like jelly as she walked away from her home. She could hear her father ranting and cursing again, but he made no attempt to go after her.

He'll take it out on Mum.

Ellen felt a terrible guilt at leaving her mother, but knew that Joan only wanted her to be safe.

With her suitcase in hand and her head swimming, Ellen attempted to retrace her steps to the spot where Bluey always waited for his father after the pictures. An elderly woman, on her way home from the town centre with a string-bag full of parcels, stopped to offer assistance, but Ellen couldn't hear her – she was oblivious to everything. Her mind could focus only on finding Bluey. In a daze, she tottered from one side of the footpath to the other, not noticing the stream of blood that slowly soaked the front of her white blouse. She finally saw Bluey, as though in a mirage, in the distance. She tried to call out his name, but lost her footing and collapsed. Lying on the grass she looked heavenwards at the late-afternoon sky with its wispy clouds. And then Bluey was above her, his face white with shock.

'Ellen! Ellen! What happened, sweetheart? What the bloody hell happened to you?' He was weeping.

'What the —' Dave O'Donnell was by his son's side. 'Jesus, Mary and Joseph, she's been beaten! Come on, Blue, snap out of it. Help me get her into the ute. We have to get her to a doctor.'

Ellen felt herself being lifted onto a soft blanket in the rear of the utility.

'You get in the back with her, Blue.'

Sweet blackness soon enveloped her. When she woke, she heard an unfamiliar male voice. 'She's sustained a depressed fracture of the right cheekbone, Mr O'Donnell. A man's fist most likely.' The voice sounded angry.

'Has she suffered any permanent damage, Doc?' Dave asked, concerned.

'Once the swelling and the bruises are gone, she'll be fine,' the doctor assured him.

'Who'd do such a dreadful t'ing to this lovely girl?'

'I don't know, but it possibly happened at home.'

'What makes you think that?'

'It's not right for me to say, but between you and me, her mother has been treated for similar injuries.'

'The father?' Dave raised an eyebrow.

'Most likely.'

'The bloody coward.'

When Ellen awoke the following morning, she tried to open her eyes, but could only let in tiny slits of light. Her cry of anguish was answered by Sally O'Donnell.

'Don't worry, love. You're with us out at Kilkenny. You can't see properly at the moment because your face is too swollen.'

Tears trickled down Ellen's cheeks, but she made no sound. 'Don't cry, sweetheart,' Sally implored her. 'You'll be fine. You wait and see.'

'Has Bluey seen me like this?' she asked shakily.

'He'd be no son of mine if it made a difference,' Sally answered firmly. 'Bluey's just worried about you, that's all. You rest again and then I'll get you something nice to eat.'

'I don't feel like anything, Mrs O'Donnell.' She turned her head away.

'That'll be enough of that, my girl.' Sally used her no-nonsense tone. 'You'll need to eat to keep up your strength, and eat you will, you hear?'

'Thank you, Mrs O'Donnell,' Ellen replied meekly, laying her head back on the pillow.

When she woke again, Bluey was waiting patiently by her bed. 'How do you feel?'

'I've got a headache and I can't see much,' she said wanly, 'but apart from that, I'm okay I suppose.'

'That's good.'

'I must look a mess.'

'Oh, it won't be long before you're back to being the best-looking sort in Goondiwindi.'

'You really think that about me?'

'Too right,' he said with a smile, before becoming serious. 'Who did this to you, El?'

'I can't say.' She stared down at her hands.

'It was your bloody father, wasn't it?'

'Oh, Bluey, please leave it alone. Please,' she implored him.

He held her hand, his eyes searching her battered face. 'I wanted Dad to report it to the cops, but he said they don't do anything about domestics. He says they don't want to get involved.'

'Please don't go near my father, Bluey,' she pleaded. 'He's a very big man and he can be very mean.'

'Don't worry about me, El,' he replied. 'I can handle myself.'

'Please, Bluey. You've no idea what he's like.'

Bluey gritted his teeth and said nothing, but his eyes flashed, and his pupils were pinpoints of fury. As he'd desperately run towards Ellen on that terrible afternoon, he had never felt so frightened or helpless. He'd barely been able to catch his breath as he'd taken in the damage to her lovely face. As he looked at her now, fears about her future continued to plague him.

But will she be safe when she goes back home? It might happen again. I have to protect her.

He confided these fears to his mother as she entered the kitchen after bathing Ellen's face. 'Mum, what'll happen when she goes home?'

'I don't know, love,' she answered uncertainly. 'But things probably won't change for her when she does finally go home.'

'I can't let her go back.'

'There's nothing you can do,' she said calmly.

'I can't let this happen to her again, Mum.' His face crumpled and tears streamed down his cheeks. 'I love her.'

Sally wrapped her arms around her son. 'Oh, Blue! You're too young to know if you love someone —'

Bluey cut her off. 'I'm not! I'm not!' he almost shouted, pulling away from her embrace. 'I know how I feel.'

Ellen remained in bed for the rest of the day while Sally fussed over her as if she were her own daughter. She brought her meals on a tray and in the afternoon read *Treasure Island* to her. That night, Ellen took the two tablets that had been prescribed by the doctor and again slept soundly. The following day, however, she decided she could not spend any more time in bed with the O'Donnell family waiting on her. It didn't seem fair when she was feeling so much stronger. She got up and tiptoed to the bathroom, closing the door quietly. When she caught sight of her reflection in the mirror, she cried out in shock. Not only was her entire face swollen, it was also dark with bruises. A deep cut marked the left side of her nose, and her normally soft, full lips were puffy and split. Ellen's sparkling emerald eyes were hidden behind swollen lids. Her legs buckled and she sat on the edge of the claw-foot bath and began to cry, gut-wrenching sobs convulsing her body.

After a few moments Sally entered and sat down beside her. She placed a protective arm around Ellen and held her. 'Don't be upset, love,' she cooed. 'You'll be back to your old self in no time.'

'But what will I do?' she asked dejectedly. 'What about when I go home again?'

'Why don't you stay with us for a while?'

'What? Here?' Ellen was astounded.

'Yes.' Sally replied evenly. 'I mentioned it to Bluey's father and he thinks it's a good idea. Bluey does too.'

'That's very generous of you, Mrs O'Donnell,' Ellen was

embarrassed by the generosity of this offer, 'but I couldn't impose on you and Mr O'Donnell. And what about my mother?'

Sally paused. 'I've spoken to your mother. She's okay about you staying with us for a while. And don't worry, you wouldn't be any burden to us, love.' Sally's voice was reassuring. 'In fact, it'll be a pleasure to have some female company around the place.'

'But I'm just Bluey's friend. It's not like I'm a relative. And what about my job?'

'You are Bluey's special friend and you've become my special friend as well,' Sally answered emphatically. 'And I'll phone Jimmy Wan and explain everything. When you're well enough, you can help out here at Kilkenny.'

'But my mother will be so worried.'

'We'll get a note out to her to explain everything and we'll get your sister to pack your clothes. If things ever improve, you can always go home. Your mum and sister can come out to Kilkenny to visit, can't they, and you can meet them in town? So there, that's the end of it.'

'Oh, Mrs O'Donnell, I don't know how to thank you.'

'Seeing you safe and happy is thanks enough.'

On the following Saturday, when Bluey and Dave left for Goondiwindi to pick up a load of feed from the produce store, Bluey seemed withdrawn. He had hardly spoken a word to anyone that morning, not even Ellen, which was unlike him. When Ellen had heard Sally warn him to stay away from the Railway Hotel, a new fear took root. This was the place where Ellen's father drank with his meatworker mates, and she knew Bluey wouldn't be put off by her father's size. His determination and youthful pride would see to that. But she was also certain that Bluey would be no match for the man who'd beaten her.

He could be hurt badly.

As she waved them off, she turned to Sally. 'I hope Bluey doesn't do anything silly,' she said anxiously. 'You've no idea what my father's like.'

'Unfortunately, love, I think I do.'

'Oh, yes. Of course you do.'

In spite of the same fears growing in her own mind, Sally tried to play down Ellen's concern. 'Well, Bluey has to go to town some time, doesn't he?'

But Ellen could not so easily dismiss her anxious feelings. The memory of her father's brutality was still too fresh.

Chapter 5

Goondiwindi's Railway Hotel was no place for the meek and mild. Almost everyone knew the pub to be a hangout for rough and ready meatworkers, a place where a fist fight could break out at the drop of a hat. Bluey stood outside the hotel, marshalling his courage. He'd told his father he would stay in the truck while Dave went inside to do the paperwork at the produce store, and that he'd be there to help with the loading. But he'd been unable to resist the urge to run to the pub to see if Eric was there.

Brushing away the fear, he pushed his way through the hotel's doors. The first thing to hit him was the smell – an acrid mix of stale beer, cigarette smoke and body odour. A blue cloud hung in the air above the twenty or so men who stood around the U-shaped bar, talking and drinking. They looked a rough mob. Most of the men were dressed in work clothes, many wearing hats. A few of the braver ones wore shorts and navy blue singlets on the unusually warm autumn day.

Bluey looked uncertainly from one end of the bar to the other, took a deep breath, and called out loudly. 'Is that coward Eric Sommers here?'

The thickset man who turned to glare at the youngster was well over six feet tall. Bluey could see some resemblance to Ellen in the man's rough face that carried a full day's stubble. He immediately removed his hat and placed it on the bar. 'I'm Eric Sommers and you must be looking for a bloody hiding, you little bastard.'

'Anyone who would belt up his daughter is a coward.' Bluey's voice rang out defiantly.

Eric's drinking mates turned from the bar, anticipating a good scrap. The large man's face turned purple with rage. 'You must be the little shit she's involved with,' he snarled. 'Right, ya little prick. Let's have ya.'

Bluey stood his ground, watching a thick vein throb in the big man's temple. Every instinct told him to flee, but he could not bring himself to run from the man who had done such a terrible thing to Ellen. He raised his fists.

One of Eric's mates called out scornfully, 'Don't hurt the little bugger too much, Eric.'

Momentarily distracted by the speaker, Bluey was quickly felled by a large fist that appeared from out of nowhere. Face down in the sawdust he tasted the blood that began to gush from his mouth. The next thing he knew he was being pulled to his feet by his hair. He tried to raise his fists to protect his face, but he was too weak and disoriented.

'Now this is what you get for messin' about with my daughter, you rotten little shit,' he said, drawing back his fist.

'You t'row dat punch an' I'll kill ya. If you don't, I'll restrict it to a hiding.'

Eric released Bluey, who slumped to the floor, and swung around to face Dave O'Donnell. Eric quickly sized him up. He was several inches shorter and had a wiry build, at least three or four stone lighter. A confident sneer twisted the bigger man's lips. 'You must be this little shrimp's old man.' He pointed down at Bluey, who was struggling to raise himself from the sawdust.

'Yes, that's my son you just king-hit,' Dave snarled.

'He had it comin'.' Sommers took a step forward. 'Been shaggin' my daughter.'

'You've got a foul mind.' Dave was trying to keep a cool head. 'I saw what you did to young Ellen. Pity your mates didn't,' he added, waving his hand in disgust in the general direction of the bar. 'It was the act of a coward, but it was your own family's business. Now that you've laid hands on my son, the situation changes.'

Sommers roared with laughter. 'You! What can a short arse like you do? I'll give you what I just gave your boy here.'

A cheer went up from his meatworker friends. 'Yeah, give the little prick heaps, Eric,' one called out.

'Not in here you don't. Get out the back,' the publican shouted.

There was a sudden, noisy exodus as the clamorous drinkers made their way through the double back door to a large concrete area at the rear. Just outside, a number of empty wooden beer kegs lined the hotel's wall. Bluey stumbled after his father. Out in the open, Dave removed his hat and shirt and laid them over an empty keg. He turned to face Sommers who'd already positioned himself in the centre of the concrete arena. The eager onlookers formed a ring around the two combatants, who moved towards each other with raised fists.

Eric Sommers sneered. 'No Marquess of Queensberry rules here, you Irish twit. Anything goes.'

'Suits me, Pommy scum.'

Five minutes later, Dave was straddling the huge man, raining blows on him mercilessly. One of Sommers' meatworker friends could see Eric was at an end and called out, 'He's had enough!' But Bluey's father couldn't stop.

Another man moved closer. 'Dave,' he said quietly, 'I think it's time to stop. You might kill him.'

Dave lowered his fist, took hold of Eric's shirt front and pulled his bloodied face towards him. 'Now you listen, big man. If I ever hear of you beating up women again, I'll find you and finish the job. Do I make meself clear?'

There was no response.

'Do I make meself clear?' he yelled.

The reply was barely a mumble. 'Yeah.'

Dave released Eric, who slumped to the ground. As he walked away, two men went to Eric's aid.

The hands on the kitchen clock had hardly seemed to move as Ellen waited for Bluey and Dave's return. All that morning, she'd agonised over what might be happening in town. When she finally heard the old Fargo utility pull up, she rushed to the front verandah. Bluey got out and it was clear that her worst fears had been realised. The side of his youthful face was bruised and swollen.

Sally joined her. 'You couldn't leave it alone, could you, son?' she said bitterly.

'I couldn't let him get away with it.'

'Oh, Bluey, look at you!' Ellen said, a tear running down her battered cheek.

'We make a good pair, don't we, El?' Bluey said sheepishly.

'And what's your excuse, David?' Sally looked accusingly at the few small marks on her husband's face.

'David now, is it, Sal?' he said a little stiffly. 'Eric Sommers hit our son. That's enough.'

'Did he hurt you, Mr O'Donnell?' Ellen asked.

'No. Dad gave him a proper hiding,' Bluey interjected proudly.

Ellen shook her head, amazed. 'But how?'

As Bluey attempted to provide a full account, he was stopped by his father. 'Never mind.'

Sally was relieved that Ellen would be spared the detail. 'Okay, then. Let's get you both cleaned up.'

Eric Sommers continued to drink heavily. After work each day he'd join his mates at the Railway Hotel for three or four hours of drinking, then weave his way home on foot at around seven p.m. Back home he'd demand his evening meal, sit in surly silence to eat it, and with luck, would head for bed to sleep off the booze. If he was in one of his dark moods, which were becoming more frequent, it would be Joan and Pam who would bear the brunt of his aggression.

Their precarious situation finally came to a head one Saturday when, just by chance, Uncle Mick called around after Eric had assaulted his wife. He stood at the front door staring in disbelief at his sister-in-law's battered face.

'What in blazes happened to you?' he demanded, his disgust at his own brother's behaviour momentarily overriding his concern for his sister-in-law.

She held her hand up to cover her bruised and swollen left eye. 'I . . . bumped it on a cupboard door when I bent over.'

'Pig's arse you did,' he replied angrily. 'Where's Eric?'

'Please, Mick,' she pleaded. 'You'll only make things worse.'

'Like hell I will. Now where is the gutless bastard?'

'He's not here —' Joan began, and then realised that Mick could hear the sharp crack of an axe splitting wood.

With his sister-in-law's protests ringing in his ears, Michael Sommers stormed through the house, out the door and into the backyard. In his haste to reach his brother, he nearly tripped over the prop holding up the washing line. Eric's face lit up when he saw his older brother approaching, but his smile soon faded when he caught sight of Mick's thunderous expression. Joan and Pam wrapped their arms around each other, watching proceedings from the relative safety of the back porch.

'G'day, Mick.' Eric looked uncertain.

'I thought you might have learned your lesson after what Dave O'Donnell gave you,' Mick almost spat the words.

'You heard about that?' Eric replied, putting down his axe.

''Course I did,' Mick exploded. 'Everyone in town knows about it and what brought it on.'

'Oh.' Eric paused, then his expression turned to anger. 'I could have taken that little prick. He just got lucky.'

'Bullshit! Listen, you stupid bloody idiot. Dave O'Donnell was the welterweight boxing champion of all Ireland before he emigrated to Australia.'

'He wouldn't be able to take you, Mick.' Eric tried to curry favour.

'I wouldn't come up against him anyway. He's a good bloke.' Michael Sommers' eyes narrowed. 'Anyway, that's not the point. When I heard what caused the fight, I didn't want to believe it. Ellen saved my Mary's life . . .' He trailed off.

'Mind your own bloody business. It's got nothing to do with you.'

'Now that I've seen Joan's bruises, I know what you're capable of, you gutless wonder.' Mick eyed his brother critically. 'I often wondered why Joan missed Mass some Sunday mornings. Now I know. They should give you the Victoria Cross for bravery.'

'She opened her mouth at the wrong time. Don't tell me you never hit your missus?' Eric replied with a knowing leer, recoiling slightly at the look of utter contempt and condemnation on his brother's face.

The idea of such an unspeakable act was too much for Mick and he struck his brother hard on the side of his face. Eric fell to the ground, bright spots dancing in front his eyes. He felt as if he'd been hit by a pile driver. The next thing the groggy man saw was his brother kneeling over him. *How could this be happening again?*

Mick took him by the scruff of the neck, pulling him to a sitting position, then leaned closer and whispered so Joan and Pam couldn't hear. 'Now, listen very closely, Eric, because this is your only warning. I know our father used to knock us around, but that's no reason for you to take after that old mongrel. You know, I always thought you were a weak prick, but you're my younger brother, so I always felt a bit obligated to you. But that's over now, you bastard. If you ever take your drunkenness out on your wife or kids again, I swear to God I'll thrash you to within an inch of your life. Do I make myself clear?'

Eric tried to speak, but no sound emerged.

'Do you bloody well understand?' Michael Sommers yelled, shaking his brother by the scruff of his neck.

'Y–yes, Mick,' he stammered. 'I understand. I . . . I didn't mean it, you know.'

'Tell it to Joan,' he muttered before yanking his brother to his feet. 'You have a lovely family, you fool. If you keep this up, you'll bloody well lose them.'

'I told you. I didn't mean it.'

'But you *did* it, didn't you? You should lay off the grog, and stop knocking about with those lazy troublemakers from work. I got you this job.' His bushy eyebrows came together. 'If you don't buck up and do the right thing, I'll tell the boss he should give you the sack.'

Eric watched, humiliated, as his older brother turned and strode back to the house.

Inside, Mick said his goodbyes to Joan and Pam. No one mentioned the altercation in the yard, and instead turned to polite conversation. 'Have you heard from Kevin?' Joan asked.

'We get a letter every month or so.'

'Where is he now?' Pam enquired.

'Still in North Africa fighting Rommel's lot.'

Joan placed a hand on his arm. 'We pray for him every night, Mick.'

'Thank you, Joan.' He kissed them both before leaving.

Eric quietly made his way to the house where he remained in the bedroom until called for dinner. He'd thought long and hard about his behaviour and his relationship with his wife and children. What if Joan left? His life would be nothing without her. And if he lost his job too . . . He had already driven away one daughter. He still couldn't believe he'd done those terrible things to her. He'd gone to confession, but it couldn't take away the stain of guilt. The words of the priest echoed in his head.

'The Lord emphasised a loving relationship in marriage. I have told you this on many occasions, Eric. If you continue to sin in this manner, you will never attain the purity and holiness necessary to enter heaven. You risk languishing in purgatory.'

Eric knew he would never have done such a thing if he'd been sober, but he also knew he could never give up the drink. Now he'd even alienated his brother.

Sitting at the head of the dining table that evening, he could not bring himself to look at his wife or daughter, despite the fact he now had a black eye that matched his wife's. Nobody said a word. After the meal, he took a deep breath and began the longest speech of his life. 'I feel pretty bad about all this. Ashamed as well. I've always blamed the grog. Like it wasn't me who was doing these things. There's also the rotten thing I done to Ellen.' He faltered.

Joan's eyes filled with tears. She wanted to reach out and put her hand on her husband's arm, but was concerned it might disturb the moment. This was the most he'd opened up since long before they were married.

Eric continued. 'I'll be honest, Joan, I don't know if I can give up the grog. I'm scared to try. Been drinking too long. But from now on, I'll make sure you won't be affected by it.'

To his family's amazement, Eric Sommers kept his word. Sure, there were times he came home worse for wear after a few drinks, but instead of hurling abuse at his wife and daughter he went straight to bed. On the occasions he had a blinder, he had the good sense to sleep it off at a mate's place. He knew better than to go home, where even the slightest provocation might send him into a rage, and he would be tempted to lash out. He knew if that happened, he'd have his older brother to contend with and there was also the threat to his job hanging over his head.

The women could not believe the change in their lives. No longer did they live in fear when they heard him coming. His new job paid well, so with Eric's regular wage and Joan's capable management, for the first time the family was able to save a bit of money. The one thing missing was Ellen. Joan longed for her voice and the sound of her laugh. With Eric's turnaround in behaviour, she'd hoped for a reconciliation between father and daughter, but knew Ellen would take a lot of convincing to come home.

Chapter 6

With a million Australian men and women in the armed services, few families were spared the worry about friends or loved ones fighting overseas. As the months passed, the realities of life changed greatly. All available resources were needed to support the troops, who had to be fed, clothed and armed, and this led to constant shortages of food and other essentials like clothing and petrol. Ration coupons had to be handed over along with money to buy essential items like butter and tea, and restrictions were placed on horse racing, alcohol sales and gambling. Women were recruited in their thousands to fill the vacancies in factories and workshops.

Like most other communities in Australia, the people of Goondiwindi were doing their best to assist. Local air-raid wardens were appointed to ensure blackout regulations were observed. Schoolchildren were drilled in evacuation procedures. The Salvation Army, the local Red Cross and other community support groups assisted the families of men in the services. Clothing and scrap-metal drives were organised to help with the war effort.

Because of the shortfall in labour, Dave was grateful to have Bluey and Ellen helping out on the property. Even seasonal workers were hard to find, and much of the work was now undertaken by women. Ellen milked the cow each morning, fed the pigs and poultry and collected the eggs. She also assisted Sally with domestic chores and helped Bluey with the vegetable garden. Bluey took responsibility for the flock, giving Dave time to attend to the wheat crop.

After he turned seventeen, Bluey was anxious to enlist. Many of his mates from school were already in the services.

'I hate the thought of you going away,' Ellen said when he mentioned it.

'Everyone has to do their bit, El.'

'What about Kilkenny? Your dad needs you.'

'I know, I know. But my country needs me too.'

Ellen dreaded the thought of him going away, and could barely bring herself to think of the danger should he be sent overseas.

He could be hurt or even . . .

At the dinner table one night Bluey broached the subject with his father. 'I feel so guilty, Dad, with all the other blokes joining up.'

Dave had been waiting for this. 'Believe me, I know how you feel, son. But I need you here for a bit longer.'

'We all do.' Sally had felt her chest tighten.

Every Monday, Ellen went to town with Dave to meet up with her sister and mother at a local cafe. Sometimes her Aunty Pat and one or both of her daughters joined them. With rationing beginning to bite, Sally always gave Ellen some eggs and fresh vegetables to take with her, which Joan gratefully accepted. Sipping their tea, they chatted and laughed as they brought each other up to date with their respective lives.

'Dad's much improved. You could come home if you like,' Joan offered on one visit. She missed Ellen, and felt embarrassed that her youngest daughter was living apart from the family.

'I'd love to come back home, Mum,' Ellen put her hand on her mother's forearm. Joan's words had tugged at her heart. 'It's just that Mr O'Donnell is short-handed at the moment and I'm helping out. It's my way of doing my part for the war.'

Joan sighed. She knew Ellen was happy and being well cared for. What was more important, she was safe. Life with Eric had improved greatly, but it was still uncertain.

Pam steered the conversation in a more cheerful direction. 'You'll never guess, Ellen. I've met someone!' Pam went on to explain that her new beau's family had only been living in the town for a couple of years and that Ellen didn't know him.

Ellen was excited for her sister. 'What's he like?'

'He's a bit taller than you and he's got a nice build,' she replied dreamily. 'And he's so handsome.'

'He sounds nice.'

'Oh, he is. He's so thoughtful and attentive. I've never met anyone like him.'

'Watch out,' Ellen joked, 'he might be the one.'

'I hope so.' Pam sighed.

While Ellen stayed in regular contact with her mother and

sister, she'd had no contact with her father since the day of the beating. She'd never even laid eyes on him. That situation changed with the news of Kevin Sommers' death at Tobruk, an event that shattered the whole Sommers clan. Everyone in the land knew the Australian 9th Division had been engaged in an ongoing conflict with Rommel's forces at the Libyan port. The siege had gone on for many months, and the Australian soldiers had become known as the Rats of Tobruk, probably because they'd dug tunnel networks to supplement their trenches and gathered equipment each time the enemy was routed.

Pam had phoned Ellen at Kilkenny to tell her. 'Aunty Pat won't come out of her room and Uncle Mick is devastated, as is everyone else,' Pam sobbed.

'I can't believe it.' Ellen wiped tears from her own cheeks. His sincere promise to her after the incident by the river flashed through her mind.

Me and Rod'll never tease you again.

She hung up and ran to her room, crying. Bluey followed her, but was at a loss as to how to comfort her. He sat on the edge of the bed, stroking her back. Finally, Ellen looked up.

'He seemed so happy to be going off to do his bit. He was so brave.'

'Yes, he was.' Bluey was surprised to feel a twinge of jealousy at Ellen's deep respect and admiration for her cousin. While he could not have explained it in so many words, Bluey wanted Ellen to feel the same way about him. Indeed, the young man's death did not deter Bluey at all, and only seemed to strengthen his determination to enlist.

The following week a requiem Mass was held at St Mary's Catholic Church to honour the life of Kevin Sommers. Ellen sat with Pam, a few pews behind her mother and her father, who kept glancing back at her. After the service, she gave her condolences to Uncle Mick, Aunty Pat and the other members of the family, hugging them all, Pam and her mother included. Just as she was leaving, Eric Sommers walked awkwardly towards his estranged daughter. There were tears in his eyes.

'You look well, pet.'

The softness in his tone caught her by surprise. 'Dad, I —' She faltered. The hurt was still there.

'I'm so sorry, love,' he said sincerely. 'That was a terrible thing I done to you.'

Ellen nodded, waiting for her father to continue.

'I spoke to the priest about it,' he said. 'And he showed me how wrong it was. You see, I grew up in a family where that thing went on all the time, sort of normal, if you get what I mean.' He looked her in the eye. 'I know that's no excuse, but that's how it was.'

Ellen recognised the genuine remorse in her father's face. He was close to tears. 'I'm glad to see you, Dad,' she said gently.

'You don't know how much I hoped you'd say that.' He swallowed the lump in his throat as she walked into his outstretched arms. They held each other for a long moment. 'Why don't you come home? We miss you.'

'Oh, Dad, I would, but I'm needed on the property.'

'This bloody war.'

A couple of months before Bluey's eighteenth birthday, the Japanese entered the war. They'd been fighting the Chinese since 1936, but entered the global conflict with their sneak attack on the American Fleet at Pearl Harbor on 6 December 1941. Australia was now virtually isolated from the rest of the world and appeared to be in an extremely vulnerable position. Her protector, Great Britain, was in no position to come to her aid. The old country was barely holding on itself under Hitler's constant barrage.

Like most young men his age, and even though he knew it would leave his father short-handed, Bluey was determined to do his bit. He had been feeling increasingly frustrated as he helped his father on the property, watching as most of his friends from school enlisted. Australia was under threat and he longed to join up. And then Darwin was bombed, and he knew he couldn't wait any longer. He approached his father. 'I know you need me, Dad, but I've got to join up.'

'I t'ought it wouldn't be long, son,' he said with a heavy sigh. 'It's not every day a man gives his son permission to go off to war. You do what you have to. We'll survive.'

'Thanks for understanding.'

At the dinner table that night, the discussion turned to Bluey's enlisting. 'But you're so young!' Sally blurted out.

'Most of the blokes are my age or a bit older, Mum.'

Ellen would have liked to agree with Sally and express her own fears, but she held her tongue, aware that Bluey already felt enough pressure. Later as she and Bluey stood on the front verandah, she told him quietly, 'I can't believe you're going away.'

'It won't be for long. Just for some training.'

'But what about later? They'll surely send you overseas.' She almost choked on the words.

He took her into his arms and kissed her gently. 'We'll cross that bridge when we come to it.'

As soon as Bluey heard that the recruiting team had set up in Goondiwindi's School of Arts building, he made his way there. Perusing Bluey's application, the middle-aged sergeant either didn't realise that Bluey had made himself a full year older than he actually was, or didn't think it a grave concern. Recruiting targets were difficult enough to fill without worrying about mundane things like a mistake in a prospective recruit's year of birth.

Ellen's cousin Rodney was also keen to enlist, but his father had thrown a spanner in the works. Uncle Mick had opened his own butcher shop with a small slaughterhouse at its rear. He had taken Rodney on as an apprentice butcher – a protected occupation. 'No father should have to lose two sons in any bloody war,' he had stated bitterly, defending his actions.

To Ellen's despair, the day finally arrived when Bluey had to travel to Brisbane for basic training. She went with Sally and Dave to see him off.

The station was abuzz with townspeople who had come out in force to say their farewells. The ladies were a colourful sight with their floral dresses, picture hats and gloves. They wanted to look their best and leave their loved ones with a lasting impression. Mothers, wives and girlfriends put on brave faces with bright smiles and forced cheerfulness as they said their goodbyes. Some could not keep up the pretence, and dabbed at their eyes with their handkerchiefs. Fathers and other male relatives dragged heavily on cigarettes to calm their nerves. The new recruits themselves, in their best casual clothes, had an air of suppressed excitement. They had little idea of what lay ahead, but they expected adventure.

'I'm proud of you, me boy.' Dave shook hands with his son. 'It's not just the bloody English's war now.'

'You take care of yourself.' Sally hugged him.

'It's only basic training, Mum.' He shrugged self-consciously. 'It's not like I'm going off to the front line or anything.'

'You're going away, though. That's enough.'

Bluey turned to Ellen. 'Take care of yourself, darlin'. I'll miss you.'

'Oh, Bluey! I don't know what I'll do without you.' Ellen threw her arms around his neck and hugged him close. She summoned a smile when all she wanted to do was lean against him and cry.

The sound of the steam train's whistle was the signal for the two young lovers to break their embrace. A guard ordered the travellers on board. The picture of Bluey leaning out of the window, waving as the train pulled away, would stay with Ellen for the rest of her life.

Chapter 7

A burly infantry sergeant was waiting for the recruits at Brisbane's Roma Street station when the train arrived late that afternoon. 'Right, you lot,' he began in a thunderous voice. 'Get your luggage from the baggage car and be on the truck outside in five minutes.'

A small lad from Warwick made the first mistake. 'What if we can't get our baggage out in time, Sergeant?' he asked meekly.

'Well, that'll be a pity for you, son,' the sergeant began sweetly, before screaming, 'If you sheilas are not outside in five minutes, you all fucking walk. Do I make myself clear?'

Bluey jumped a foot in the air and the young men looked at each other. This was the first indication of what was to come.

For a country lad like Bluey who had never been away from home, the army was a totally new experience. He was allocated to No. 13 platoon along with thirty-five other recruits under the supervision of one sergeant, three corporals, and a second lieutenant who all seemed hell-bent on making the recruits' lives a misery.

On arrival in camp at Wacol on the city's outskirts, they lined up at the quartermaster's store. Here they were all issued with one khaki felt hat, one hat badge, one groundsheet, one tooth brush, one set of anklets, webbing, one jacket, two pairs of khaki shorts, two pairs of khaki trousers, three shirts, one blanket, two pairs of boots, a knife, fork and spoon, a sewing kit to repair socks and clothing (otherwise known as a housewife), a clasp knife, one safety razor and blades, three singlets, identity discs, three pairs of socks, two towels, a hairbrush and a helmet. They were informed that the uniforms had to be pressed with creases down the legs, and the boots spit-polished to the satisfaction of the company sergeant major. The first morning was taken up with medicals and dental inspections.

The first time he dressed in his summer uniform and slouch hat was a special moment for Bluey. He felt his chest swell with pride.

What will Ellen think about me in this? I can't wait to show her.

Bluey had anticipated they would be tested both mentally and physically – after all, they were being prepared to fight against a battle-hardened enemy and they were untested and inexperienced. He knew he just had to grin and bear the pain. For many of his mates in the platoon, however, it was a living nightmare, with every task having to be completed at the double. When the platoon pulled to a halt outside the huts, a corporal would yell at the top of his voice, 'Right, you lot. Two minutes to get changed into PT gear and be outside again.' He'd look at his wrist watch. 'Failure will result in two extra duties. Dismiss.' Anyone too slow on the uptake was liable to be run down in the stampede.

Nicknaming was an important part of mateship, and the men usually picked an obvious physical characteristic to create one. The tallest in the platoon was known as 'Stalky', the shortest 'Shorty'. Surnames were also a starting point, and anyone with the surname Rogers became known as 'Buck', and anyone called Robson or Robertson was simply 'Robbo' and so on. Bluey was used to this, and it made him feel at home.

Much of their time was devoted to fitness and weapons training, supplemented by long periods of drill on the hot, dusty parade ground where flies crawled over the young recruits' faces, even into their ears. Anyone who dared to brush the flies away was immediately admonished by the drill instructor. 'Stand still, you men. You may not be aware, so I'll tell you only once. Those flies are my pets. Any man who attempts to strike at them will be sorry.'

During their short breaks they stood around talking in small groups, most of them smoking cigarettes. Like his father, Bluey had never taken it up, and because he didn't like the smell, he always stood upwind of his mates.

Can't be good for you.

At mealtimes in the large open mess hall, Bluey usually sat at a bare timber table with Buck Rogers, Jimmy Fielding and a large bloke he'd befriended named Digger Belford. After wolfing down the food, which Bluey always considered ordinary compared to his mother's tasty meals, they would sip their teas, light up smokes and share small insights into each others lives.

Buck came from Maryborough, north of Brisbane and was stout, with mousy coloured hair. Wiry Jimmy was from Charleville and had worked as a drover. He had a ruddy complexion and creases around his eyes from squinting into the sun. Digger was from Coolangatta on the south coast. Twenty years old, he stood six foot three in his stockinged feet and weighed fifteen stone. He had the brightest smile and sunniest disposition Bluey had ever encountered. There was an easy-going quality about him that Bluey instinctively liked. He was a good-natured fellow and difficult to rile, but once the big man became upset, those around him needed to stand clear.

'How'd you get the name, Digger?' Bluey once asked during a break in training.

'From when I was little,' he replied dragging on his cigarette. 'I always wanted to join the army and my second name's Digby. So I got called Digger.'

As basic training progressed, long route marches became an everyday part of their lives, and soon the recruits could strip and clean a .303, an Owen submachine gun or a Bren gun in the dark. Buck Rogers was particularly adept at these tasks and the NCOs saw him as infantry material.

At a subsequent range shoot, Bluey was ranked among the platoon's top three marksmen. His father had taught him to handle the family's .22 rifle from an early age. As they gathered up the valuable, expended brass shells, placing them in hessian bags, the platoon sergeant clapped him on the back. 'Well done, O'Donnell. You'll make a fine infantryman.'

'Actually, I want to join the engineers, Sergeant.'

'The Gingerbeers! Why would you want to join that lot?'

'Because they do all the things I'm interested in, Sergeant.'

When they moved on to grenade training, however, everyone was a novice. After initial instruction at the grenade firing range, every man had to install a primer into the device, arming it. They then took turns hurling it from a trench. On a command from the NCO, the recruit removed the pin, nervously holding the live grenade in his hand. On another command, he threw the explosive device and crouched down on his heels. The resultant detonation was almost deafening.

After four weeks, it was announced that a boxing tournament would be held at the camp. The other recruits in his platoon had watched the professional way that Bluey had attacked the punching bag in the temporary gym, and were keen for him to compete. The NCOs also provided encouragement because company pride was on the line.

Each fight would be held over three rounds, with Bluey in the light welterweight division. He was confident in the skills he had learned from his father, but he was still a little nervous when the actual day of the tournament arrived. He had never taken part in a formal boxing contest before. His dark-haired, swarthy opponent smiled with self-assurance as he looked over his much younger and less experienced adversary.

The fight began with Bluey's opponent trying to deliver a number of jabs to the head which he easily avoided. Bluey was able to land three heavy rips to the swarthy man's midriff. He heard him grunt as the wind left his lungs. In the next exchange, the dark-haired man attempted to hold on, pinning Bluey's arms, so he couldn't raise his fists. To Bluey's surprise, his opponent began to manhandle him towards a neutral corner, and tried to hit him below the belt. Bluey had been warned of such tactics by his father and knew how to avoid them. Lunging to one side, he was able to weave out of harm's way. The more experienced fighter attempted to dart after him, but Bluey landed some stinging body blows and a series of jolting lefts and rights to the man's face, and he fell to the canvas gasping for breath. To the cheers of C Company, Recruit O'Donnell was chaired out of the building.

One of the NCOs supervising the platoon, Corporal Sanders, had a particularly vicious streak and took a set against Digger, perhaps because he didn't respond to orders as quickly as the others. Whatever the reason, Digger often bore the brunt of his ire. Amongst the men, there was a simmering discontent towards Sanders, but they took everything the aggressive corporal dished out without complaint.

One particular day, during a locker inspection, the situation reached boiling point. Corporal Sanders inspected the interior of Digger's closet and removed a photograph of an attractive teenage girl dressed in a bathing suit. He let his hands slide caressingly over the snapshot in a way that seemed obscene, his leering eyes never leaving the photo. 'Who's this, Recruit Belford?'

'My sister, Corporal,' Digger answered.

The corporal licked his lips. 'Not bad, not bad,' he said slyly. 'I'd sure like to give her one.' He then went on to describe in offensive detail what he would do.

Digger lunged at the corporal, grabbing him by the shirt front and pinning him to the bed. Ignoring Sanders' yells of protest, he pummelled him in the face and body, anywhere he could. He was eventually restrained by Bluey and several other recruits, who knew he would be in serious trouble.

It took every ounce of their strength, but finally the men were able to drag their outraged friend from the corporal.

'Calm down, Dig,' Bluey implored. 'Calm down, cobber.' He held onto one of Digger's arms while Buck Rogers held the other.

Sanders struggled to his feet and glared at his attacker. Humiliated at losing face in front of his subordinates, he was now in a full-blown rage.

'You're on a charge, Belford,' he screamed. 'You'll go to jail for this, you bastard.'

Bluey came to his friend's defence. 'I saw what happened, Corporal.' His tone was even. 'It was you who brought this on.'

'You wanna be on a charge too, O'Donnell?' he threatened, dabbing at his bloodied chin.

'Do what you like,' Bluey shrugged, 'but you baited him with those disgusting remarks about his sister.'

'That doesn't matter,' Sanders said defiantly. 'He hit me, and for that he'll go to jail.'

Every time the NCO spoke, Digger attempted to break free to get at him.

'Settle down, cobber.' Bluey tried to placate his friend. He turned back to the injured NCO and his eyes narrowed. 'I want to give evidence when the charge is heard.'

'That'd be a stupid thing for you to do, Recruit O'Donnell,' he replied scornfully. 'It could backfire on you.'

'Is that a threat, Corporal?' Bluey asked tightly.

'Treat it as you like.'

'I'll still give evidence.'

'Suit yourself,' snapped the corporal. 'Now you lot bring that bludger along to company headquarters.'

The first thing Bluey saw as he entered the company commander's office was Digger flanked by two armed guards. He looked crestfallen, resigned to whatever punishment awaited him. Corporal Sanders stood to one side of the OC's desk, the company sergeant major by his side. It was difficult to judge the age of the greying, moustached major who sat behind the small oak desk, but there was no doubting his authority. Recognising Bluey, the officer raised his eyebrows and a glint of appreciation appeared in his deep-set eyes. 'You fought in the boxing tournament?'

'Yes, sir!' Bluey stood to attention and saluted.

'Good fight too, lad. C Company's proud of you.' Major Sinclair extinguished a cigarette in the ashtray in front of him. 'Did you know the chap you knocked out was a rising welterweight in Sydney?'

'No, sir.' Bluey's eyes opened in genuine surprise.

'Who taught you to box?' the major continued.

'My father.'

He looked at Bluey in disbelief. 'You mean to say you've had no formal instruction?'

'No, sir.'

'Remarkable,' he said slowly. 'Bloody remarkable.'

Pleasantries over, the major coughed, and fitted his peak hat to his head. 'Very well, let's get to it,' he said in a businesslike manner and handed the charge sheet to the company sergeant major.

The CSM read the charge, which was immediately followed by Corporal Sanders' evidence. Naturally, the corporal neglected to mention his provocative remarks about Digger's sister. Blood still trickled from Sanders' nose and lips.

'You wish to give evidence, Recruit O'Donnell?' The major raised his eyebrows.

'Yes, sir,' he replied smartly.

Bluey noted the corporal's threatening look, but was undeterred. In a firm, clear voice he provided an outline of the provocation that had caused Digger to snap. When Bluey had completed his evidence, Major Sinclair glared at the junior NCO. 'Is it true you made such despicable comments about Recruit Belford's sister, Corporal?'

'It was just in fun, sir. I —'

'That's enough!' interrupted the OC. 'Recruits are here for basic training to prepare them for war, not to have their families insulted. Is that clear, Corporal?'

'Yes, sir.' Sanders answered meekly.

The OC turned towards the sergeant major. 'CSM, Corporal Sanders is to remain here after this issue is resolved.'

'Yes, sir,' the warrant officer answered crisply.

The major then directed his attention to Digger, who had remained quiet during this phase of the proceedings. 'Despite being severely provoked, Recruit Belford,' he looked sideways at Corporal Sanders, 'you did strike an NCO, and I must inform you that the punishment for that is severe. Under normal circumstances, such an offence would land a soldier in military prison for some months. In your particular case, however, the provocation was such that a detention of two weeks will suffice.'

'Yes, sir.'

After the hearing, Corporal Sanders was given a formal dressing down by the company commander, and allocated six extra guard duties. The other NCOs assigned to No. 13 platoon made the remainder of Bluey's recruit training a misery. He was given extra picket and guard duties, and if there was a staff shortage in the kitchen, the NCOs always selected Bluey to help. Yet he took everything they could dish out. He had done the right thing and felt proud for standing up for his new friend.

After his time in the Provost Detention Centre, Digger returned to camp, where he approached Bluey. 'Thanks for helpin' me, Blue.' He held out his large hand.

'That's okay, cobber.' Bluey took his friend's hand in a strong grip. 'What was it like in there?'

'Bloody awful, mate. Those bloody screws are a pack of bastards. Thanks to you, I only got two weeks.'

'You shouldn't have got any time in there. That prick, Sanders, deserved what you gave him.'

Digger was quiet for a moment. 'Look, I've been thinkin'. I don't wanna go into the infantry with the rest of the blokes.' He threw his kit bag on his bunk. 'I wanna get into the engineers with you.'

'Hope you do, Dig.'

Before joining up, Bluey had read about the Royal Australian Engineers and planned to do everything in his power to join them. When the time arrived for corps allocation interviews, he pushed long and hard for his first choice. He told the interviewing officers everything he knew about the corps and that he possessed a mechanical aptitude. He'd often helped his father strip down the tractor's engine when new piston rings were required and had a great deal of practical knowledge about construction. Digger had worked in a local garage so was also considered engineer material.

As luck would have it, the two recruits were successful and were delighted to learn that they would be posted to the School of Military Engineering just outside Liverpool in New South Wales for corps training. On their last night in camp, they got a chance to even up things with Corporal Sanders by placing a dead rat in his bed roll. Both giggled like schoolchildren when they heard a loud wail followed by a list of expletives coming from the NCO's hut. Sanders' eyes were daggers the next morning at their final roll call.

'It was you two bastards that done it!' He pointed at Bluey and Digger in front of the assembled recruits.

'Did what, Corporal?' Bluey asked deadpan.

'Put that bloody dead rat in my bed!' With that the entire platoon burst into uncontrollable laughter. 'Shut up!' Sanders screamed, his eyes darting wildly. 'Shut up, I said.' But the laughing continued. Even the sergeant grinned.

At long last, basic training was over.

Chapter 8

Ellen was determined to learn to help Dave O'Donnell with the merino flock while Bluey was away. He and Sally had taken her in and treated her like a daughter, and this was her chance to repay them in some small way. Instead of looking for a job in town, she'd made a decision to help out on the property. This was the least she could do for the people she had come to care for so deeply.

Dave was a good teacher – patient and methodical – and Ellen was a fast learner. Out in the field he taught the ex-city girl how to mend fences, how to drive a tractor and how to assist with crop spraying and fertilising. He taught her how to drive the ute and she soon got her licence at the local police station. He explained that rain was needed before planting wheat, and that follow-up rainfall was needed to ensure a bumper crop. He told her that at any one time, Kilkenny's wheat paddock took up about a thousand acres of the property's total area, with the remaining six thousand acres allocated to the merino flock. She learned that there were three, thousand-acre paddocks for growing wheat, but that only one was planted each season, the other two lying fallow and used as pasture. After harvesting, sheep grazed on the wheat stubble – a vital source of nutrients.

'There's not many of us growing wheat here yet and I'm proud to say we were one of the first. The land is perfect for the crop, and in the future, I'm sure some of the paddocks will be so large that it will take a tractor over two hours to complete just one circuit of sowing.'

'When do you plant, Mr O'Donnell?' Ellen asked.

'Usually around April, lass, if we get rain. Then harvest in October. It's a busy time when the harvesting contractor is here, I can tell you. The crop has to be bagged and then loaded on trucks to be taken to the railway goods yard in town.'

After dinner most nights, Ellen sat with Dave and Sally to listen to the radio. They listened to the war news on the ABC and enjoyed shows hosted by the ever-popular Jack Davey, shows such as *Rise and Shine* and *Star Parade.* Ellen rarely missed an episode of *Dad and Dave*, her favourite. If there was nothing to listen to, Dave took the opportunity to teach Ellen a little more about the farm, especially the tasks associated with raising two thousand prime merino sheep. She learned about the shearing season, and about the need for crutching twice a year.

'There are three steps,' Dave informed her. 'Crutching, wigging and ringing. You crutch around the tail and then you wig them – you take a couple of inches from around their eyes so they can see where they're going. Ringing is when you remove four inches or so of wool from around a wether's penis to prevent urine from staining the wool and attracting blowflies. You see, lass, in a wet season, the sheep's belly is rarely ever dry. During this period, you get a lot of blowfly strike.'

'Blowfly strike?'

He went on to explain. 'One of the most important things is to prevent the animal from being infested by blowflies. Blood poisoning can occur after three or four days in a bad outbreak. This condition can kill the infested sheep, which to us, is a serious loss. When you're out in the paddocks, lass, it's important to keep your eyes peeled for any sheep that are lying on the ground. If they do not move as you approach, then they probably need your help.'

'What do I do?' she asked uncertainly.

'You don't get squeamish, young Ellen, do you?'

'I don't know,' she answered honestly.

'All right. I'll be tellin' you.' Dave smiled.

'You see, lass, when dung fouls the wool near the animal's behind, it attracts flies, which lay eggs in it. And they soon hatch into maggots. That contaminated wool needs to be removed with shears and the area around the backside sprayed. If it's not done, then the animal will remain down and will probably die.' His tone was serious. 'You should always check a sheep that's down. Sometimes they just need some help getting up.'

'I see.'

'Don't worry,' he assured her. 'I'll show you how to do it, and I'll put a pair of shears and some spray in your saddlebags.'

'You were talking about a wether,' she reminded him. 'What's that?'

'That's a male sheep that's been deknackered.'

Ellen looked at him blankly. Although she had been on the farm for over a year, she had mainly worked around the homestead.

Dave realised that she had no idea what this meant. 'Well, you see young Ellen, we can't have all the male lambs growing into rams, or there would be chaos at breeding time, wouldn't there?' He gave a short laugh. 'There are only about two per cent of rams to ewes. To put it simply, lass, we have to remove the male lamb's breeding equipment.'

'Oh, but —' Ellen looked worried.

'Don't you be frettin'. You don't have to do it. When the time comes I'll employ someone to help me. But you can help with the dipping.' He went on to explain. 'You see, lice and itch mite can drive the poor sods mad, so we put the flock through a dip twice a year to stop the pests from breeding.'

Sally looked up from her mending. 'And another thing you have to watch out for is crows.'

'Crows?' Ellen replied.

'Oh, yes. The rotters pick the eyes out of sick newborn lambs when they've been deserted by the ewe. Then the lambs have to be put down.'

'How dreadful,' Ellen shuddered.

'I leave poison baits for them around the property,' Dave added. 'Keeps the numbers down.'

'How do you avoid poisoning the sheep and your dogs?'

Dave laughed. 'Well, Lass, I usually leave the baits above ground, out of reach of four-footed creatures.'

Dave was only too happy to continue talking about the farm,

his pride and joy. Ellen learned more in one night about sheep than she had learned in her entire life.

The next day Ellen rode out to the paddocks where Dave gave her on-the-job training. At first Ellen thought she would be sick when she caught the foul smell of the maggot-infested area around a downed ewe's anus. As the day progressed, however, she became accustomed to the smell, and was soon removing her shears from the saddlebag and carrying out the unsavoury task unsupervised. Dave had also stressed the importance of getting the infected animal to its feet, once the clipping had been completed. He explained that the animals need to be on the move to feed and drink, otherwise they die. After her first week, Ellen did not give any of these tasks a second thought – they were just part of the job.

Over the next few days, Ellen helped Dave and two rouse-abouts, Ben and Mac, with the dipping. The concrete dip was about ten yards long by a yard or so wide, and had a slope at one end. It was filled with a murky, milky, foaming substance. Aided by the dogs, which ran over the sheep's backs, it was Mac's task to keep the animals moving into the shute which led to the dip. As each creature plunged into the trough, it was Ellen's job to push them completely under as they passed. She had a leather saddle about eighteen inches wide with a long handle at one end. By simply placing the saddle on the sheep's back and pushing down hard on the handle, it wasn't difficult to dunk the animal. Dave had explained that the sheep had to be totally immersed, otherwise the parasites would make for the dry head area and survive.

Despite her work on the farm, Ellen always made time to see her mother and sister. She had her own money now – Dave had insisted that she accept payment for her work, brushing aside her protestations – and she enjoyed being able to buy lunch for Joan and Pam. One day after lunch, she bumped into Brenda Wilson.

'Haven't seen you for ages.' Brenda hugged her.

'You look fantastic,' Ellen replied.

As a child, Brenda could never have been described as pretty, but she had blossomed in adolescence. Her honey-blonde hair was drawn back into a ponytail, and her now-trim figure was enhanced by her gingham dress.

'Let's have malted milk and a yak.' Brenda took her by the arm.

'I just had a sandwich and a cup of tea with Mum and Pam.' She rubbed her stomach. 'But okay, why not.'

They sat themselves on stools in the milk bar, with their drinks in front of them. 'You still living with the O'Donnells?' Brenda asked.

'Yes.'

'I heard Bluey enlisted.'

'He's away at basic training at the moment. He gets a short leave after that.'

'You must still love him.'

'More than ever,' Ellen replied warmly. 'What about you? Who's the lucky man in your life these days?'

'Michael Murphy,' Brenda replied, her voice tremulous with excitement. 'He's a bit older than me, but he's so nice.'

'I know the Murphys. Their property's not far from Kilkenny. He didn't go to school here, did he?'

'No. He was a boarder at Downlands College in Toowoomba.'

'Oh, I see.'

'He's joining up and he wants us to get engaged!' She was grateful to have a friend to share her news.

'Going to school at Downlands, he must be Catholic, like me.'

'Yes, he is. But I don't care. I love him.'

'If you want to marry him, you'll probably have to convert. You know that, don't you?'

'Yes. I've thought about nothing else lately.' Worry lines creased her forehead. 'Mum and Dad won't like it. But I've been thinking. I mean, it's the same God and it's what sort of person you are that counts, isn't it?'

'Of course it is,' Ellen replied.

Good luck!

Despite her youth and energy, after a full day's work in the paddocks, Ellen was completely drained. She bathed and changed, and was always ravenous as she sat at the dinner table. Sleep came almost as soon as her head hit the pillow. Bluey wrote to her only twice a week – his training schedule allowed him little time for personal matters. Ellen waited impatiently for his letters, reading each one over and over, savouring every word.

Bluey didn't talk much about army life, but he did tell her about the corporals who made their lives a misery and he complained about the nine-mile route marches. She was surprised at how easily he seemed to be able to write things that he found difficult to say face-to-face. He told her how much he loved and missed her. In one letter, he expressed some concern about his father.

I'm glad Dad's got you to help him, El. Otherwise he'd be working himself into the ground. Please keep an eye on him.

Bluey's comment got Ellen thinking. Dave O'Donnell was up before daybreak and didn't return to the house until after the sun had set, and he did this seven days a week. One Saturday morning when the two women were alone enjoying a cup of tea, Ellen broached the subject. 'Mr O'Donnell works so very hard, doesn't he. Does it worry you?'

Sally was silent for a moment, a faraway look in her eyes. She gave herself a little shake and smiled. 'Oh, no,' she replied simply. 'He just loves this place.'

'If it's not a rude question, how long has he been here?'

'No, love, it's not a rude question. He was only twenty or so when he came from Ireland. He'd been involved in some anti-English activities in the old country and was wanted by the authorities.' Sally saw the frown on Ellen's face. 'No, it wasn't anything like that. He didn't set bombs or hurt anyone. But he did allow his name to be put to some Irish nationalism propaganda, and under the emergency laws in place at the time, he became a wanted man.'

'I see.'

'The IRA and the like also wanted Dave for their cause because he was a sort of working-class hero. He was a champion boxer over there and the people loved him. He had to leave Ireland just when he was about to make some real money out of the sport. He didn't care, though, because once he set foot in Australia, he fell in love with the country and its people. But he hates the English with a passion. Still blames them for letting so many Irish people die in the potato famine.'

Ellen leaned forward in her chair. 'How'd he come to live here in Goondiwindi?'

'I'm getting to that,' Sally looked thoughtful. 'Dave had an uncle who had struck it rich on the Victorian goldfields. Instead of drinking and gambling his fortune away like a lot of the other miners, Dave's Uncle Patrick bought seven thousand acres of freehold land. But mind you, Ellen, the land wasn't anything like it is now. It was covered with scrub and trees, and of course there was no house or outbuildings. Dave's uncle kept the property as an investment, but never visited. He just let the land sit idle. He had no family of his own, so when he died, he left the property to Dave.'

'So Mr O'Donnell had to start from scratch when he came here?'

'Yes, we both did.'

'You knew him then?' Ellen said, surprised.

'Yes, we were already married then. You see, when Dave first came to Australia, he answered an advertisement for a job on a wool and wheat property just outside of Dubbo. He had no experience, but the owner, Mr Holdsworth, liked him so much that he took him on. Dave started as a rouseabout and ended up a leading hand on the property.'

'Where did you meet, if you don't mind me asking?'

'I lived in Dubbo at the time. My father worked on the Dubbo Council's road gang. Ours was not a happy household, Ellen, as I've told you before. But believe it or not, I met Dave at a dance.' She smiled warmly. 'I noticed him as soon as he entered, and when our eyes met across the room, I just knew he felt the same. We danced together all night. Then he took me home.'

'Did he —' Ellen stopped, embarrassed.

'Kiss me?' Sally smiled. 'No. Not on that occasion.' She chuckled. 'The silly goose just stuck his hand out and said what a good time he'd had. But he did ask me to a CWA concert the Saturday after, and when he took me home *that* night he kissed me.'

Ellen sighed. She loved hearing such romantic stories. 'When did you get married?'

'Not long after that, love. Things came to a head at home and I had to get away. I came home one night to find all my belongings strewn on the grass outside my bedroom window. My father had done it. When I tried to go inside, he wouldn't allow it. He was drunk and tried to hit me.'

'So did you leave then?'

'I stayed with a girlfriend for a week. Dave tried his best to talk my father around, but Dad took a drunken swing at him. Dave told me he loved me and asked me to marry him. I accepted, but since I was under the legal age, we had to get permission from a magistrate.'

'Did you get married in a church?'

'The priest wouldn't marry us unless I became a Catholic,' Sally replied stiffly.

'I see.'

'Dave went to a lot of trouble explaining the circumstances to the Church. In fact, he even wrote to the bishop. But the old fart of a priest wouldn't reverse his decision. So we got married in my church and Dave hasn't set foot in a Catholic church since, although I'm sure he still considers himself to be a true Catholic.'

'Did you come up here then?'

'News that his uncle had died came just after we were married. Dave's employer had put us up in a little shack and I worked in the homestead as a domestic. I'd never done that sort of work before, but the boss's wife was a good woman and gave me lots of encouragement. Six months later, we found out about the inheritance. It was actually the boss who suggested that Dave work the land instead of selling it. That's why we came.'

'It must have been hard,' said Ellen.

'Yes, it was, love, very hard. We lived in an old tent at first. Dave had to use a fair bit of the money to get the grain paddocks cleared and fenced. That was his first priority. Then we built the agricultural shed and lived in that for a while. After our first crop went in, we bought some top-grade merino stock from his previous employer who also threw in a truckload of five-year-old wethers for meat. The two of them had built up a good relationship and the boss was keen for Dave to succeed. And that's how we started. When I found out I was pregnant, Dave built the homestead.'

'Bluey?'

'No,' Sally replied sadly. 'Anne. We had her for two years. She died of meningitis.' Her voice caught.

'Oh, Mrs O'Donnell, I'm so sorry. I had no idea.'

'Of course you didn't, love.' Sally patted Ellen's hand reassuringly, and took a deep breath. The pain was never far from the surface.

As the weeks without Bluey slipped by, Dave and Sally came to think of Ellen as their own child, and an unspoken bond was established between them. For Sally, Ellen also provided much-needed female company, the two chatting whenever the demands of the property permitted. On one such occasion, Ellen finally asked Sally a question that she had been longing to ask. 'Mrs O'Donnell, I've always wondered about Bluey's real name. I've asked him over and over, but he won't tell me.'

'No, he's not happy about the name his father chose. But it was Dave's father's name, so there was no talking him out of it.'

'What is it?' Ellen asked expectantly.

Sally smiled. 'Bluey won't be happy with me telling you, but here goes. Our Bluey's real full name is Kinsella Liam O'Donnell.'

'Kinsella?'

'Yep.'

'Kinsella from Kilkenny!' Ellen's eyes danced with mischief. 'I think I'll stick to Bluey.'

'It would be a good idea, I think.' They both laughed.

Chapter 9

As the old steam train chugged up the range, Bluey's heart began to thump with anticipation. He had a bad case of the fidgets and couldn't sit without his feet tapping or his fingers drumming. He had three days' leave and couldn't wait to see Ellen. If only he didn't have to waste their precious time together with travelling. The impatience he felt became almost too much to bear. He stood and began pacing up and down the corridor with several other uniformed servicemen. It was plain to see they were all anxious to get home.

At last the steam locomotive pulled into Goondiwindi's old station and there she was – beautiful as ever. She was dressed in her Sunday best – a cream tailored straight skirt that outlined her trim figure, a white cotton blouse and a tan half coat. Her blonde locks caught the afternoon sunlight. When she saw him, her face lit up and her lips broke over a devastating smile. With kitbag in hand, he jumped from the carriage and ran to her, taking her in his arms, holding her as though he'd never let her go.

'Oh, El, I couldn't wait to see you,' he whispered in her ear, taking in the scent of her perfume.

'Me too,' she replied softly.

Sally raised an eyebrow. 'Does a loving mother get any of that, son?' Bluey smiled, enveloping her in a fierce hug, before shaking hands with his father.

'Looks dashing in the uniform, doesn't he, Dave?' Sally commented proudly.

'That he does, Sal. That he does.'

Back at Kilkenny Bluey and Ellen couldn't wait to be alone. He quickly changed into civilian dress and informed his parents that he was taking Ellen for a long ride to inspect the paddocks. When they reached the banks of the Macintyre, she spread the blanket and they lay down side by side looking up at the cloudless blue sky.

'A penny for them, Bluey?'

He turned to face her. 'I was just thinking I feel at peace when I'm here with you,' he murmured.

'Me too,' she turned to him.

As their lips met, she circled her arms around his neck. Soon they were lost in the passion of the moment.

Under the shade of a weeping willow, she lay contentedly in his arms. 'That was wonderful,' she murmured.

'Mmm . . .'

During the two days that followed, they spent as much time as possible together. Bluey helped his father with a few heavier chores, but at every opportunity, he and Ellen made love, though never within the confines of the homestead. It was the most wonderful few days of their lives. But it was also an anxious time, because neither knew what the future held.

At Bluey's last meal in the homestead, before leaving to catch the train, Dave thought it time to make enquiries about his son's future in the army. 'Where to from here, son?' he asked hesitantly, not sure if he would be allowed to talk about such things.

'I have to go to Sydney for engineer corps training. I'm going to learn about explosives, mine warfare, bridge building and water supply.'

Ellen and Sally exchanged fearful glances. 'Sounds a bit dangerous,' Ellen said quietly.

'It's better than the infantry.' Bluey noted Ellen's worried tone. 'Don't worry, most of the time the engineers only have a supporting role.'

As the train steamed out of Goondiwindi's station, the ache in Ellen's heart was so fierce, she didn't think she could bear it. But it was more than that. She felt a kind of eerie foreboding, and even though it was a warm day, she shivered and goose pimples broke out on her arms.

'You all right, love?' Sally asked as they made their way back to the ute. 'You look as though someone walked across your grave.'

'I'll be fine,' Ellen replied, but still the feeling would not leave.

That evening, Bluey caught an overnight passenger train to Sydney with Digger. Although he was excited about beginning his corps training, he felt empty. Would he ever get used to missing Ellen? He felt her absence like a hole in the pit of his stomach.

Digger was also quiet and reflective on the trip, smoking a lot, and not talking much at all. He did tell Bluey that he'd enjoyed himself at home. It had been great to see his parents and his sister. The waves at Greenmount Beach were up and he'd spent most of his time bodysurfing.

By army standards, the School of Military Engineering turned out to be quite a small centre. Situated on the banks of the Georges River, just outside of Liverpool on Sydney's outskirts, the school had a U-shaped barracks surrounding a small parade ground. A mess area and ablution block adjoined the barracks, and the three large sheds near the river housed the equipment and stores needed for training budding field engineers.

Bluey's troop was supervised by three corporals, who carried out the majority of the instruction. The three junior NCOs were in turn supervised by a Sergeant Copeland and a Second Lieutenant Andrews.

'We're not a spit-and-polish outfit like the artillery or the infantry,' Sergeant Copeland explained to the trainees on arrival. 'The engineers are the workers of the army, but they're also first in and last out of battle, so a lot of their work can be extremely dangerous. It is therefore critical that instructions are carried out to the letter. A mistake here can cost you your life.'

The first phase of field-engineer training involved bridge building – a process overseen by two experienced warrant officers, who provided in-depth instruction on the building of both temporary and permanent structures. Speed was an important factor. Indeed, the ability to swiftly cross a river or a stream could mean the difference between an operation's success or failure. Men and machines had to be moved as fast as was humanly possible.

Bridge building was followed by amphibious-transport training. During this phase, barges were constructed, with vehicles of every sort ferried down or across the Georges River day and night. The trainees then became conversant with all types of knots and lashings, before going on to receive instruction in water supply and purification. It was the engineers' responsibility to supply the army with its drinking water. Mine warfare and explosives, including booby traps, were the last topics covered. It was a nervous time for the trainees, most of whom had no experience with explosives. When it came time for Bluey to disarm a live mine for the first time, he did not think he would stop shaking. Because his life depended on his skill, he forced himself to remain calm while the dangerous task was completed. By the end of the course, he could almost perform such a job blindfolded.

The day Bluey was urgently summoned to Second Lieutenant Andrews' office, he wondered what he had done.

'Ah, Sapper O'Donnell.' The young officer looked up as Bluey came to attention in front of the desk and saluted.

'Reporting as ordered, sir.'

'Right, let me see.' The officer reached for a file marked 'confidential'. 'This information is not to be discussed outside this room. Clear?'

'Yes, sir!'

'There's a task force leaving in three days for an undisclosed overseas destination. It requires engineer support, and the OC has requested graduates from your course. He has left it up to me to choose ten men to accompany the task force. I'm happy to say, Sapper, that you are one of the ten who have been chosen.'

'Thank you, sir,' Bluey answered, his stomach turning a cartwheel.

'I'm afraid, Sapper O'Donnell, that there won't be time for the usual pre-embarkation leave. It can be added to your leave credits and taken further down the line.' He paused. 'I see you're from Queensland.' He looked up from the file.

'Yes, sir. Goondiwindi.'

'Unfortunately you won't be able to say goodbye to your loved ones.'

Bluey's heart sank. 'I see,' his said, his tone leaden.

'Is there a problem?' the officer asked.

'Just a little disappointed, sir. But I'm fully prepared to go.'

'Good man.' Second Lieutenant Andrews grinned. 'You'll have to undergo a further medical, accompanied by the necessary immunisation shots. I'll also arrange with the quartermaster for you to be fully kitted out for the tropics.'

'Yes, sir.'

'Good luck, Sapper.'

Back in the barracks, Bluey was pleased to discover that his mate, Digger Belford, had also been chosen as one of the ten. It was a great comfort to know his friend would be there beside him.

The next day, waiting in line at the quartermaster's store, Digger asked, 'Where do you think we're going, Blue?' Digger dropped his cigarette butt and ground it with the toe of his boot.

'Wouldn't have a clue, cobber.' He lifted his shoulders in a shrug. 'Doesn't really matter, as long as we're fighting Japs.'

'Yeah, that's right, mate. It's time the little yellow bastards were stopped.'

In the afternoon, Bluey reported to the Royal Aid Post for his pre-embarkation medical and shots. 'Bloody hell!' he yelled loudly when they gave him the cholera shot. 'Watch what you're doing!'

The army doctor just grinned. 'You'll get over it, soldier.'

The remainder of the time at the School of Military Engineering was taken up with briefings by the task force's liaison officer. There were no surprises for the ten young men in the group: if they were required to attack a beach, they would be called upon to blow up barriers impeding their progress, even those in the sea. They also knew they had to clear mines and carry out various demolition duties as well as ensure an adequate supply of drinking water. The role described was nothing more than what they had been trained for.

Chapter 10

Standing on the wharf, with a clear view across the harbour to Sydney's Circular Quay, Bluey wondered what Ellen and his parents would think when they received his letter.

Q72431
Sapper K. O'Donnell
School of Military Engineering
C/- Military Post Office
Liverpool NSW

18 July 1942

Darling Ellen, Dear Mum & Dad

By the time you get this letter, I will be on my way overseas to fight the Japs. I know I'm not supposed to go till I'm nineteen, but what's the difference? I didn't join the army just to swan about Australia. I joined to fight the Japs and that's what I'm going to do. I don't know where we're going. Some of the fellas say it will be New Guinea. Others say it will be Burma. Who knows? I'm sorry this is so sudden and I hope you won't be too upset. I'm in a hell of a hurry. The ship is leaving shortly. I wanted to post this letter before we leave. I'll write when I can.

All my love, Ellen, and love to Mum and Dad

Bluey

Bluey looked up at the old ship on which he would sail, the SS *Wilhelmina.* It was the largest and oldest of the three ships that had been selected for the job of transporting the task force overseas. Named after the Queen of the Netherlands, the former cargo ship was manned by a Dutch maritime crew. Since Holland was now occupied by the Germans, the Americans had seconded the *Wilhelmina* as a troop carrier, its crew reporting to Uncle Sam.

A number of the waiting soldiers laughed and joked while others stood in stony silence. Most were drawing deeply on cigarettes, some chain-smoking. Behind the barriers separating the onlookers from the soldiers, locals called out encouraging words to the young diggers. Those soldiers with loved ones in the crowd waved and blew kisses. Bluey felt a wistfulness that there was no one there to bid him farewell.

Like the hundreds of other recruits gathered around them on the wharf, Bluey and Digger had been issued with a coloured ribbon designating the order in which each group was to embark.

Line after line of men slowly made their way on board while the others watched. At long last, they heard the word 'yellow', which was a signal for their section to proceed to the gangplank. Stepping onto the *Wilhelmina*'s deck behind Digger, Bluey looked towards the stern where a constant stream of army equipment was being loaded into the vessel's holds.

His group had been allocated to G deck, which he quickly discovered was situated below the waterline. Entering the claustrophobic confines of the sleeping quarters, the first thing he noticed was the false ceiling that had been installed in what had previously been a large open storage area. As a result of the remodelling, many more soldiers could be accommodated. On attempting to rise to his full height of five feet eight inches, Bluey struck his head on the metal ceiling above. Digger, who was much taller, remarked that too long in there and he'd develop a permanent stoop.

Two hours later, Bluey and Digger struggled onto the main deck to watch the spectacle as the old ship made its way out of Sydney Harbour towards The Heads. Bluey felt a wave of disappointment, realising he had missed an opportunity to explore Australia's largest city. But at least he had seen Sydney's main attraction, its world-famous harbour, a magnificent sight on the brilliant sunny day. Bluey looked back towards the city centre, and the Harbour Bridge gleamed at him in the mid-morning sunlight.

The *Wilhelmina* was soon through The Heads and out into the open ocean. Within an hour, land could not be sighted in any direction. Some of the soldiers claimed that Japanese submarines operated in waters off the Australian coast and that the troop carrier would be a target. The three ships transporting the task force were accompanied by a Royal Australian Navy destroyer, which was constantly on the move around the small convoy. During the early stages of the voyage, when the sleek grey vessel slipped by the *Wilhelmina* at speed, soldiers waved at the sailors, who waved back. After a few hours, the novelty had worn off, and the navy vessel went about its important business without any further response from the soldiers.

Bluey did not have to wait long to discover how the soldiers would fill in their long day on board. The largest part of every day would be spent in slow queues waiting for meals, which were served on the rear deck. From the serving point, the queue snaked in a crowded S shape. Bluey thought it would have been easier for the queue to line the circumference of the main deck, but this would have taken the waiting soldiers directly past the quarters of the Dutch maritime officers, who the Australian infantry officers did not wish to offend. The remainder of the time was taken up with physical exercises, under the control of an infantry sergeant, as well as the maintenance of their rifles and equipment.

On the first night at sea, when Bluey laid out his bedroll on the floor of the allocated sleeping quarters, he knew he would never be able to sleep in its claustrophobic confines. He was used to wide open spaces and found it difficult even to breathe. After tossing and turning for an hour or so, he turned to Digger. 'You awake, Dig?' he whispered.

'Yeah. Can't sleep here. Feels like the walls are caving in on me.'

'Me too. Let's go.'

Carrying their bedding and leaving their rifles and equipment behind, they made their way up the series of stairways until they reached the main deck, where they joined scores of others with the same idea. With the low throb of engines resounding in the still, sub-tropical night, the old vessel sliced through the dark ocean. Bluey and Digger laid their bedding out on the deck under the stars and were asleep almost as soon as their heads touched their mattress.

The following morning, a strong south-easterly had whipped up a broad ocean swell, forcing the ship to dig deeply into the blue Pacific as it surged northwards. Whitecaps foamed as far as the eye could see. The accompanying destroyer's deck was flushed with tons of salt water each time it ploughed through a swell. The constant rolling caused many of the men to come down with acute seasickness, which at least reduced the number of soldiers waiting in the long meal queues. Bluey felt sorry for the many who lined the rails, bringing up their insides. Although he was a country boy who had never been on a ship in his entire life, or even seen the ocean, he was grateful to have what appeared to be a natural immunity to the condition. Sea legs, he was told.

After five days at sea, the soldiers still had no idea about their final destination. For security reasons and in accordance with common practice, the commanding officer said the goal would remain top secret until just prior to their arrival. Only then would they be informed. Not knowing, however, did not prevent the Australian soldiers from speculating. New Guinea appeared to be the main choice, while others suggested India, Burma, Singapore or Malaya.

The following day, noting a change in the sun's position, many soldiers concluded that at sometime during the night the *Wilhelmina* had changed course and was now heading due west. Four days later, as he waited in line for lunch, Bluey was not sure, but he thought he spotted the outline of land on the horizon.

He turned to his friend excitedly. 'You see that, Dig?' He pointed towards the north.

'Yeah, mate.' The big man squinted. 'It looks like land.'

'Probably an island of some sort,' Bluey suggested.

'Yeah.'

That same night, as Bluey lay on the *Wilhelmina*'s main deck, he woke with a start. Something wasn't right. For a long moment, he could not explain what it was. Then it dawned on him – he could hear the sea lapping against the side of the ship. The *Wilhelmina*'s engines were silent.

Bluey shook his mate. 'The ship's not moving, Dig.'

'Be buggered,' the big man growled. 'What's that mean?'

He shook his head. 'I don't know.'

The pair joined other soldiers who lined the rail looking at the outline of the two other ships as they moved further away in the moonlight.

After half an hour's anxious wait, there was an announcement over the ship's loud speaker from the commanding officer. 'The *Wilhelmina* has some engine problems. The captain has been forced to stop altogether or risk permanent damage.' The OC paused to let the words sink in, and a buzz of conversation began amongst the soldiers. The senior officer continued. 'Please remain where you are for the moment. The ship's engineer and his assistants are working to rectify the problem. The other ships have had to move on and the destroyer has had to accompany them. I'm reliably informed the problem should be fixed in a few hours. Please don't light matches or smoke for the time being.'

'Bloody hell!' Bluey exploded. 'We're sitting ducks for a Jap sub. Especially in this moonlight.'

'Shit!' Fear had dried the saliva from Digger's mouth.

Some more soldiers had joined the men on the main deck, though most were still confined in the bowels of the ship. They stood around in small groups talking quietly. Not one returned to his bed. Apprehension and fear would not permit it.

Bluey looked at his watch. 'Only half a bloody hour,' he snapped. 'Shit, it seems like we've been stopped for ten hours.'

'What's the time, Blue?' Digger tried to sound calm, but his voice was strained.

'Half past one.' Bluey pointed towards the sky. 'Look at that bloody moon. Where's the clouds when you need them?'

The Japanese torpedo struck the forward section of the *Wilhelmina* at 3.30 a.m., the explosion throwing all the waiting soldiers on to the ship's metal deck. Bluey heard screams of pain and trepidation, and in that single moment knew what war was all about. Pandemonium broke out, a small number of officers and senior NCO's barking orders in an attempt to maintain some control. The majority of soldiers on the main deck responded to their directions. A few others, overcome by fear and panic, ran amok. Wild-eyed, they ran one way then the other, looking for some means of escape, ignoring all commands and directions from their superiors.

Two minutes later another torpedo struck *Wilhelmina*'s amidships and almost immediately, the old vessel began listing to its port side. Just as the crew attempted to release two of the lifeboats, a third torpedo hit, and a tremendous explosion shook the vessel from bow to stern, throwing all the soldiers and crew onto the deck. A few more desperate men struggled from below decks, some badly burned, but the submarine attack had been so swift, and the damage so extensive, that most of the men could not escape. The Australian soldiers still below were either already dead or were trapped in a sinking tomb.

An infantry corporal approached Bluey and Digger. 'Poor bastards.' He was breathing heavily. 'Japs must have hit the explosives store. We'll have to jump for it.'

Bluey turned to Digger, his eyes wide open with apprehension. 'Can you swim, Dig?'

'Yeah, like a fish, mate. How about you?'

'Not too well, I'm afraid,' was the shaky reply.

'Don't worry, Blue. I'll look after you,' he said removing his boots and shirt. Bluey did the same.

'Keep your sapper's knife, Dig. You may need it.'

Suddenly the crippled ship listed alarmingly, and they knew they could waste no more time. Looking over the safety rail on the port side of the main deck, Bluey did not relish the thought of leaping into the debris-littered surface of the tropical waters, but they had no choice. He was about to throw a leg over the railing when he saw the flames. The sea around the sinking vessel had become a watery inferno. He stared at the moonlit scene before him, horrified, and began to shiver uncontrollably.

Digger took him roughly by the shoulder and shook him. 'Get a hold of yourself! All we have to do is dive into the water and swim under the surface until we get clear of the flames. You understand?'

'B-but I told you,' his lips quivered. 'I don't swim well.'

'Grab a hold of my belt and I'll help you.'

'Okay, Dig,' he said, entrusting his best friend with his life.

Bluey and Digger climbed over the rail and, on the count of three, jumped towards the fiery surface. By the time Bluey registered the searing heat of the flames, he was under water. Digger grabbed Bluey's hand, tucked it in his belt and began a powerful breastroke. Bluey hung on for dear life, breaststroking with his free hand and kicking with all his strength. At one stage, he opened his eyes and looked up at the boiling light above. He knew he could not hold his breath much longer.

I'm done for. Goodbye, Ellen.

Digger felt Bluey's hand start to slip from his belt, and seized his mate's wrist. The salt water entered Bluey's lungs just as they broke the surface, gasping, their chests heaving. Digger supported his mate's head as he began coughing to clear the water from his lungs. Eventually the coughing and gagging eased.

'You right now, Blue?' Digger gasped anxiously, trying to catch his own breath.

'Yeah,' he choked.

'Just tread water for a while. You'll be fine.'

They turned towards the *Wilhelmina* just in time to witness her final death throes. In the brightness created by the fire, they watched in awe as the ship's stern rose out of the water before beginning its final journey to the bottom of the sea. In a last act of defiance, the ship's remaining boiler exploded, leaving an eerie silence, interrupted only by intermittent cries for help.

Bluey's heart was pounding. 'I – don't – know – how – long I can keep this up, Dig.'

Why did I do this? Why did I have to be a hero?

'Look, mate, you gotta try not to panic. Just hold onto me.'

'I'll try.'

'I'll find something we can both hold on to.'

In the darkness, Bluey and Digger listened to other panic-stricken cries around them. In a desperate effort to keep their own heads above water, the two friends whispered words of encouragement to each other. After what seemed like an eternity, they found a crate, but it would not support their weight.

'How long do you think we've been in the water?' said Digger.

'Don't know, Dig.' He looked at the pink-tinged sky in the east. 'Shouldn't be long before the sun's up.'

As the minutes crawled by, the glow on the horizon gradually brightened until a misty dawn light dimly illuminated the surrounding seascape.

'Look, Blue.' Digger indicated with a nod of his head. 'There's something floating in the water. Let's take a look.'

They swam over and discovered it was a large chunk of timber lining, just big enough to accommodate the pair of them. After a number of unsuccessful attempts, they finally clawed their way on to its surface. Their combined weight, however, forced the small, unstable platform to sink just below the water's surface. After the hours spent treading water they were just thankful to be able to lie still and catch their breaths. Even though Digger had been helping him stay afloat, Bluey didn't know how much longer he could have kept going.

Bluey and Digger surveyed the flotsam and debris that littered the sea around them. They counted twenty-nine other heads bobbing in the tropical waters, noting that each man had managed to support himself in the water. The three men nearest them had dragged themselves onto a T-shaped piece of timber. It appeared to be part of the derrick used for cargo lifting.

'Land over there, I think.' Bluey pointed northwards to a low, dark outline on the horizon. A few of the other men waved in acknowledgment. 'Let's start paddling this thing with our hands, Dig.'

'Okay.'

Working together, the group of Australian survivors began paddling. They had no idea how far away the land was, and considering their precarious position, morale was high. Then the sharks arrived. There was only a brief warning. One man screamed in terror as he was dragged below the surface, where his body quickly became the target of a feeding frenzy. His comrades watched helplessly, the attack area boiling with activity. Bluey and Digger could do nothing but look on in horror. Pandemonium broke out among the survivors. Men tried desperately to climb onto the various objects they clung to. In the process, weaker comrades were pushed further back into the water. Other men helped their mates as they attempted to scramble onto floating debris that could not possibly support them. One by one the hapless victims fell back into the sea and into the vicious jaws that awaited them. Agonised screams filled the air, and the once clear blue sea was now stained with blood. Eventually, only Bluey, Digger and six others remained. Lying on his stomach, Bluey couldn't stop shaking. It was too much for his young mind to absorb. Digger was pale with shock, but in control. Bluey knew that he had to get a hold of himself or panic would take over. If they were to survive, they had to reach land and make their way from there. He swallowed down the bile in his throat and looked out across the calm waters. The three men on the huge timber post were still safe. Another pair had gathered together an assortment of floating debris and had dragged themselves on top. The infantry corporal they'd met on board was holding onto a floating box. With his legs in the water, he knew he was vulnerable.

'Help me, please!' he shouted.

Digger was the first to respond. 'Hang on, mate. We'll come over and get you.' He and Bluey began paddling. 'Just keep as still as you can!'

It was slow going, but they gradually inched closer. And then, just when they were a few yards away, the corporal panicked and began kicking and paddling in a flurry of limbs to try to reach his two rescuers.

'No!' Digger yelled, then watched, frozen in horror, as a tiger shark dragged the screaming corporal below the surface. Other fins sliced through the water to join the frenzied attack.

The two men stared at the swirling red water in shock.

'We're floating targets, Dig.'

Bluey didn't have long to wait for the truth of his observation to be verified. The man-eating pack turned its attention to the remaining survivors. As the sun rose higher in the sky, their unstable platform became the centre of a large group of circling sharks. The three small groups called out encouraging words to each other.

'We've got to keep paddling,' Bluey tried to encourage his friend.

'Shit mate, I'm scared to put my hand in the water.' Digger looked around helplessly.

'Yeah, but we've got to move away from here,' Bluey said. 'Just make sure you keep your hands close to the edge.'

'Okay,' Digger muttered.

The other men followed their lead. And so continued the long and onerous task of paddling towards the long strip of land. Digger suggested, hopefully, that a current might be helping them because the land seemed much closer than it had before. But because their platform was partly submerged, the other five seemed to be making much better progress, the gap between them widening to the stage where the two other groups were almost out of earshot. Bluey yelled at the top of his voice. 'Good luck. See you on dry land!'

'Same to you,' a fading voice called back.

As the long hot tropical day dragged on, the sharks did not give up their circling, sometimes even lunging at the floating timber in an attempt to dislodge their human prey. But there was one factor in their favour on that fateful day. There was little wind, and the sea's surface remained smooth and glassy. A choppy sea would have increased the risk of capsizing.

As dusk approached, they found themselves closing in on a long sandy shoreline edged with palms and dense tropical foliage, a small mountain range some distance inland. They could hear the sound of surf. 'Hear that, Blue?' Digger sounded hopeful.

'Yeah, mate,' Bluey said quietly. 'This float'll tip over in that. Then we're done for.'

'Maybe not, Blue. Back home, the sharks usually keep outside the break.'

The pair increased their paddling rate and the noise of pounding waves became louder. They knew that at some stage soon, a swell would pick them up and make it impossible for them to control the float. They did not have long to wait. Moments later, they felt the small platform being lifted high in the air.

'Hang on tight, even if it tips over,' were Digger's last words before the large roller broke. Predictably, the platform did capsize, but they both managed to hold on as the float was propelled to shore. Salt water poured through their nostrils, their arms ached, and their fingers were swollen from hours at sea, but still they hung on. Then, just when Bluey thought he could not hold on for another second, his feet touched the sea floor. They struggled out of the water and collapsed on the sand. Too tired to speak, they crawled up the beach and, spreadeagled on the sand, they gave way to complete and utter exhaustion.

Chapter 11

For Ellen, the past ten days had felt like a lifetime. There was still no word from Bluey, only the rushed letter he'd sent on the day he boarded his ship. She told herself that this was normal, that it might take much longer for him to even reach his destination, but she could not stop herself from worrying about him. She tried to follow Dave's advice and prayed for Bluey every night.

Blessed Father, please keep him safe. Bring him home to his family.

One morning, when Ellen rose early to milk the cow, she suffered a bout of nausea, her stomach turning over. She rushed to the bathroom to be sick, but it did not relieve her queasiness. She carried out the rest of her morning duties with the same feeling of nausea. When Ellen sat down to breakfast, Sally turned from the stove.

'Bacon and eggs, love?' she asked cheerfully.

Just the thought of bacon was enough to send Ellen running to the bathroom again. Sally followed, knocking lightly on the door. 'Is everything all right, love?'

Ellen washed her face and composed herself before opening

the door. 'I've been feeling a bit off the last few mornings. I've probably got stomach flu.'

Tiny furrows creased Sally's brow. 'Do you think you should go to the doctor?'

'No. I'm sure I'll be fine.'

The same symptoms continued to plague Ellen every morning for the following week, until Sally finally asked, 'No better, Ellen?'

'No, Mrs O'Donnell.' There was a lump in her throat. 'I don't know what's wrong with me.'

'Look, love, tell me to mind my own business, but I must ask.' She shifted uncomfortably on her chair. 'Have you missed a period?'

'Yes,' Ellen admitted. 'But that's nothing new for me. I'm not that regular anyway.'

'Have you considered that you might be pregnant?'

'Pregnant?' She looked around in despair. 'Oh, my God.' She couldn't meet Sally's eyes, guiltily turning away, her mouth dry. 'What will you think of me if I am?'

'No different, I expect.' Sally saw the look of abject misery on Ellen's face. She reached across and took hold of her hand and said gently, 'Look Ellen, we didn't come down in the last shower. Blind freddie could see how much you and Bluey love each other. And he was going away. You wouldn't be the first ones to give in to temptation under such circumstances. Anyway, you might not even be pregnant. We'll phone and make an appointment with the doctor.'

Ellen's pregnancy was confirmed one week later, when Sally drove her into Goondiwindi to obtain the results of her test. The

GP informed her that the baby was due some seven months later. At first she was delighted, but then the reality of her situation dawned on her.

Why is this happening to me? It's the worst possible time.

Her cheeks grew hot with shame. How could she face her family, or the townspeople? She tried to get her thoughts in order as Sally drove her home in the ute.

'I don't know what to do, Mrs O'Donnell. Bluey doesn't know about it and he mightn't be back for a long time.' Her voice broke on a sob.

Sally pulled the vehicle over to the side of the road. 'First of all, Ellen, since you're going to be the mother of my grandchild, I think it's time you called me Sally. Now, with regard to you being pregnant, there's no need to do anything. You'll stay with us as you have been. And when Bluey comes home on leave, whenever that is, you'll be married.'

'What will everyone think?' she was crying openly now.

'Let them think what they like.'

'My dad will think he was right about me.' She lowered her head.

'"Judge not, lest you be judged" is a saying all good Catholics should be familiar with.' Sally reached out for her hand and squeezed it. 'Don't you be worrying.'

When Dave heard the news, the Irishman didn't say a word. He just rose from the table, placed his arms around Ellen and held her. Then he kissed her on the forehead. 'A little tyke around the place will do us all good.'

Goondiwindi's postmaster, Fred Kearney, sat at his desk looking down at the two official telegrams on the desk before him. God, he hated the sight of them.

Some poor bastards have been killed or are missing in action.

A less diligent postmaster might have allowed the wires to go out with the mail delivery, but Fred had always been conscientious about such matters, and what was more, he had a son serving in New Guinea. He understood how terrible they would feel receiving news in such an impersonal way, and knew of religious groups who'd volunteered to deliver such news and provide support to families. He reached for his notebook to obtain the phone numbers of Father Donovan and Captain Garvey of the Salvation Army.

Ellen was first to hear a vehicle coming up the driveway. 'Someone's here,' she called to Sally and Dave. A black Plymouth was pulling to a halt as they reached the front verandah. When Sally recognised their visitor, one hand reached for her heart and the other covered her mouth. The sharp stab of fear almost brought her to her knees. They all knew Father Donovan delivered bad news about loved ones who were serving overseas.

In a sad voice, he said, 'I wish I wasn't delivering this.' He handed the wire to Dave and waited.

Ellen felt her knees buckling and could hardly breathe.

With fingers trembling, Dave ripped open the telegram and read it aloud, his voice faltering. 'Sorry to inform, troop ship torpedoed. Q72431 Spr O'Donnell missing.'

Ellen was in a daze. Nothing seemed real. She could hear Sally repeating over and over. 'No, no, it can't be. I won't believe it. It can't be.'

Tears streamed from Dave's eyes.

'Don't give up hope yet,' Father Donovan implored them. 'Miracles happen. We must all pray for one.'

Dave put his arm around his wife. 'Thank you, Father, for coming all this way to tell us. Would you like to come in?' Dave asked.

'No, my son. You need time to come to terms with this news. Is there anything I can do?'

'Just pray for him,' Dave replied.

'We'll pray for Bluey at every Mass.'

As he drove out the gates, the enormity of the news hit Ellen like a sledgehammer. Overcoming the trembling in her legs, she ran to the sanctuary of her room.

Oh, Bluey, darling, please don't leave me.

The pain that tore through her left her gasping for breath. Deep wrenching sobs racked her body.

Blessed Father, I love him so much. Please keep him safe.

Dave and his wife sat numbly at the dining table. All of a sudden, Sally came alive. With blazing eyes, she looked into the tear-stained face of her husband. 'I don't believe he's dead, Dave,' she said defiantly. 'I'd know if he was.'

'It's best not to get your hopes up too much, Sal.'

'I tell you, Dave, I'd know. Just as I knew our dear little Anne wouldn't survive the meningitis. It's the same feeling. It might sound strange, but I know in my heart it's true. He's alive.'

On the Saturday following the news about Bluey, a friend dropped Joan Sommers and Pam at the O'Donnell's front gate. When Ellen saw her mum and sister walking towards the homestead, she ran out to meet them. The three embraced in the warmth of the early morning sun.

'I heard about Bluey,' Joan said sadly. 'We wanted to come straight out, pet, but we couldn't get here.'

Ellen put on a brave face. 'We just can't believe it, Mum,' she said, wringing her hands.

'I'm so sorry, sis,' Pam said soothingly. 'How're his parents coping?'

'Sally's sure he's alive, but Mr O'Donnell doesn't say much.' Her green eyes dissolved into liquid pools as the three reached the verandah where Sally was waiting.

'I'm so sorry, Sally,' Joan patted her shoulder awkwardly.

'Me too, Mrs O'Donnell,' Pam added, not knowing what else to say.

'Thank you. But he's all right you know.' Bluey's mother quickly changed the subject. 'Come on inside and I'll put the kettle on.'

Once the women were settled with a hot cup of tea and a piece of sultana cake, Ellen turned to her sister. 'Are you still going to Brisbane?'

'Yes. Barry says they urgently want women to work in the factories down there. You know, for the war effort. And I'll be in Brisbane when his ship docks —' She paused, unsure whether she should share her news. Ellen noticed her coy look.

'Is there something else?' Ellen knew her sister too well.

'Oh, El! Barry's asked me to marry him.'

'That's wonderful.' Ellen said flatly and kissed her sister on the cheek.

'He says he has a lovely engagement ring waiting for me. He's due in Brisbane the day after tomorrow. I'm catching the train in the morning. I just came out to say goodbye, Ellen. I'll miss you,' she said, her voice quavering. 'I know it's wrong to be going on about Barry with Bluey gone and all —'

Ellen shushed her. 'Don't be silly. Of course I'm happy for you.'

'He's a very nice fella. Nice family too.' Joan nodded approvingly.

'How's Aunty Pat now, Mum?' Ellen asked.

'Now that the girls have left home, she's a bit lonely. Did you know that Mary's working as a jilleroo on a sheep station near Cunnamulla?'

Ellen nodded.

'Well, Sheila has taken off to Brisbane to work at one of the factories down there.'

'I'll go and visit Aunty next time I go into town.' Ellen paused. 'How's Dad?'

'Much better, pet,' her mother assured her. 'You're welcome to come home any time you like, you know.'

'I know, Mum. But I'm needed here, especially now that Bluey's – away.' She paused. 'And there's something else.'

Joan and Pam looked at Ellen expectantly.

'Mum, Pam, I don't mean to hurt you, but I have to tell you that I'm pregnant.' Ellen saw the shocked looks on their faces. 'I didn't mean to blurt it out like that. I'm sorry.'

Her mother placed her empty cup and saucer on the table and sighed deeply. She looked into the fresh, young face of her daughter.

She's so young.

'I'm the one who's sorry, pet. It'll be very hard for you without Bluey around.'

'We'll help her until Bluey comes back,' Sally piped up.

'Yes, I'm sure you will, Sally,' Joan said gratefully. 'You and Dave have been very good to our Ellen.'

'This'll be hard for you, sis,' Pam said finally. 'You know what some people are like.'

'I don't care what other people think,' Ellen said tightly.

Her mother nodded. 'Good for you, pet, good for you.'

An hour later, Ellen waved goodbye to her mother and sister. Sally O'Donnell had kindly offered to drive them back to town.

When will I see Pam again? I hope she'll be all right.

She couldn't help feeling a little envious of her sister – she was getting married.

I wish it was me!

Chapter 12

Bluey woke to the sound of breaking waves. He sat up and looked up and down the beach. At any other time it would have been an idyllic setting, a paradise with a sandy foreshore, clear tropical waters, rolling surf and lush undergrowth. He shook his partner. 'Wake up, Dig.'

Digger groaned as he sat up. 'Shit, I'm sore. I can hardly move me arms.'

'Mine too.' Bluey stretched his shoulders, which ached in protest. His mouth felt dry and sticky, and his head ached.

'You feeling dizzy, Dig?'

'Yeah, mate. I can hardly swallow.'

'We never had anything to drink yesterday. We need to find water.'

Despite being accustomed to long days in the sun, both men were badly sunburnt. Bluey, the fairer of the two, could feel his lips burning from erupting blisters. He stood and took hold of Digger's hand, pulling him to his feet.

'Christ, Blue. I never thought we'd make it through those

bloody sharks. Those poor blokes . . .' Digger's big shoulders started to heave.

Bluey looked at his friend. Despite his bravery and strength, Digger was a soft-hearted, generous person. 'Dig, why we and the others were spared, we'll never know. The important thing now is to stay alive. Okay, mate?'

Digger took a deep breath. 'Okay.'

Moving to the cover of the thick bush that edged the sand, they searched the beach for some sign of civilisation, but there was nothing. In the tropical forest behind them they could hear the loud chatter of monkeys and the screeching cries of birds that Bluey thought sounded a bit like cockatoos.

'Where do you think we are?' Digger asked.

Bluey shrugged. 'Let's see. After we left Sydney we were heading north. Then a few days later we turned west. Someone said that was probably Torres Strait, you know, between Cape York and New Guinea. I reckon this has to be an island in the East Indies somewhere.'

'Which one, do you reckon?'

'Wouldn't have a clue, mate. But from what we saw yesterday, it looks like a real big one.'

Digger again looked at the long coastline that disappeared in both directions.

'The Japs probably control all these islands,' Bluey warned him. 'We'll have to be bloody careful.'

'We got no damn weapons, no damn food and no damn clothing, except for the shorts we got on.'

'But we're alive!' Bluey gripped Digger firmly by the arm. 'And all those other poor sods are dead.'

The big man lowered his head, looking a little sheepish. 'You're right. But what'll we do?'

'Water shouldn't be a problem. This is the tropics. There's bound to be plenty of streams with fresh water. And I noticed some coconut palms up that way.' He pointed in an easterly direction. 'Then there's the local people. They might help us. What do you reckon, Dig?'

His friend brightened. 'Yeah, mate.'

'So let's go.'

'Ah, which way?'

Bluey crossed his arms and looked thoughtful. 'How about east? At least we'll be heading back towards Australia.'

Bare-chested and barefoot, Bluey and Digger were an incongruous sight on the pristine beach. They trudged along the sandy shoreline, keeping as close as they could to the tropical foliage that provided some form of cover. On one occasion, a loud roar erupted in the undergrowth.

Digger jumped. 'What the hell was that?'

'I don't know,' Bluey replied nervously.

They guessed they had covered three-quarters of a mile when they came across a grove of coconut palms.

'I don't reckon I could climb up there.' Digger looked at the coconuts clustered at the head of the palms.

'Don't have to, cobber.' Bluey pointed at a couple that had fallen on the sand. They only had to find some way of reaching the white flesh inside the hard fibrous shell. Carrying the nuts in their arms, they continued their trek. The early tropical sun burned into their already sun-reddened bodies and blistered faces. Both men glistened with perspiration. After another hour they reached a wide, shallow creek of fresh water running into the sea.

'What'd I tell you, Dig?' he said cheerfully. 'Drinkable water.'

The pair moved upstream for some distance before taking their fill of the clear cool water.

Bluey used his hands as a scoop. 'My oath that's good.'

'Better not drink too much at once, Blue. We might get a guts ache and spew it all up.'

'Right, Dig.' Bluey began looking around. 'Now if we can just find a couple of sharp rocks, we'll be able to smash our way into these bloody coconuts and get some tucker.'

Digger found two large flat rocks in the stream, and Bluey discovered a particularly sharp stone protruding from the bank. Bluey placed the larger flat rock on the ground and held the sharp stone on the coconut's surface. 'Right, you use one of those big rocks to hit this sharp one while I hold it. But be careful.' He kneeled down. 'Don't hit me.'

'Okay, Blue.'

It took some time and plenty of sweat, but the hard copra covering was finally removed, leaving the coconut's inner shell. Using the claw fitting on their versatile sappers' knives they broke through the inner shell, drinking the sweet milk before feasting on the white flesh.

Bluey was first on his feet. 'Let's go.' For a reason he couldn't explain, even to himself, he was anxious that they keep moving, even though he had no idea of their present whereabouts or what lay in the direction they were headed.

When the torrid tropical sun reached its highest point, they found themselves on a small rocky point, jutting a hundred yards or so into the sea. On the other side, the sandy coastline seemed to go on forever. At last, exhaustion and the unrelenting humidity forced them to seek refuge in a small shaded clearing within the thick undergrowth bordering the beach. Here they lay down to rest and were soon asleep.

Bluey was awoken by the sound of an engine. He turned over onto his stomach and peered through the branches out to sea. He drew in a sharp breath – a Japanese patrol boat was motoring around the rocky point, about a hundred yards or so beyond the breaking surf.

Bloody hell! A bit sooner and they would have caught us out in the open.

He placed his hand over Digger's mouth before whispering, 'Japs. Don't move.'

The big man's eyes opened wide in alarm, but he remained still. 'Do you think they seen us?' he whispered.

'Don't think so. They're not changing direction or coming back. Different story if we'd been on that bloody point, though.'

Digger rolled over onto his stomach to join his friend. 'Do you reckon they patrol this beach a lot?'

'Don't know, Dig. They were probably looking for the *Wilhelmina*'s survivors.'

'Yeah, I suppose so.'

'We'll wait till they piss off and then be on our way.'

An hour or so later, they were again on the beach. After the Japanese sighting, their trek continued with renewed care. Every few minutes, Bluey checked the ocean horizon in every direction. It was almost dusk when they came upon a wide river blocking their path.

'Bloody mouth's probably full of sharks or bloody crocs,' Bluey said tersely.

'How'll we get across?'

'We won't. We'll follow the river inland. There's bound to be a village along it somewhere.'

The steamy tropical night descended upon them as they made a meal of the remaining coconut flesh before settling down to rest. In the darkness, they were besieged by clouds of mosquitoes that continually attacked their unprotected skin. The incessant buzzing made it difficult to give way to the sleep their tired bodies desperately craved.

In the light of a new dawn, they continued inland and were confronted with a network of swamps. They looked at the task ahead and despaired.

'A bloody mossies' breeding ground, if ever I saw one.'

'Probably full of snakes, too,' Digger added.

As they began to negotiate the waist-deep lagoons, the unprotected soles of their feet were cut and grazed on sharp tree roots and knife-like reeds. To add to their misery, swarms of mosquitoes continued their relentless onslaught as the pair struggled on, trudging through the stagnant waters. Digger looked up at the monkeys that were watching their slow progress. 'I know the small ones are monkeys, but what are those big red ones?'

'Could be orang-utans. Thought they were from Borneo, though.'

'Maybe that's where we are,' Digger offered thoughtfully.

They fought their way through the lagoons for several hours, until finally Bluey saw an end to their torture. 'Look. Dry land.' He pointed. They forced their way through a tangled mass of undergrowth into a small clearing where Digger called for a rest. 'Didn't think I could go on much longer,' he grunted breathlessly.

Lying in the shade of a leafy shrub, they dozed in the peaceful tropical arbour.

Bluey awoke with a start. A strange sound had brought him out of his slumber, but he did not recognise the noise. He quietly shook his sleeping companion.

'What's up?' Digger stretched.

'Something woke me,' he whispered.

'What was it?'

'Dunno. Shh!'

A moment later, they heard a crackling movement in the undergrowth on the opposite side of the small clearing. This was soon followed by a low growl.

Digger jumped to his feet with fright. 'Shit!'

They both heard another growl. The animal, whatever it was, had moved closer.

Bluey pointed to a strong sapling that lay at the edge of the clearing. 'Grab that heavy branch,' he ordered. 'I'll get another one.'

Standing with their backs to the thick shrub, they faced the clearing. On the opposite side, the shrubbery began to rustle and then all of a sudden a tiger entered the clearing. It stood still for several moments, head high, sniffing the air. Its yellow eyes came to rest on the petrified, gaping men standing before it. As tigers go, this was not a large specimen, Bluey thought to himself. He had seen full-grown ones at the circus and knew that they were the largest cats of all, even bigger than lions.

This is probably a young one.

But Bluey was also well aware that regardless of its age, the animal was potentially dangerous and certainly more than a match for the weakened humans standing before it. He came to a decision. If he and Digger were to survive, they would have to use some form of bluff.

'I'm shittin' meself, Blue,' Digger whispered.

'Me too, mate.'

The animal didn't move a muscle. Unfazed, it stared at them.

Bluey thought it time to break the stalemate. 'When I count to three, lift the branch and slam it on the ground and scream as loud as you can.' He paused. 'Righto. One – two – *three*.'

They lifted the boughs high above their heads. For the first time since entering the clearing, the tiger appeared uncertain. They brought them crashing down, all the while screaming at the tops of their voices. The frightened animal bounded into the undergrowth.

'Shit, Blue.'

'That was close.'

'Do you think it would've attacked us?' Digger's stomach was still churning.

'If there was only one of us it would have.' Bluey took a deep breath to stop his heart from pounding. 'Anyway, maybe it wasn't that hungry. It might have made a kill recently.'

'I thought tigers were in Africa.' Digger sounded bewildered. 'Where the hell are we?'

'Well, I remember from school that some of the islands in the East Indies have tigers, so we could be on one of those.'

'Do you think it'll come back?' Digger's eyes darted around the edge of the clearing.

'I dunno. But maybe we should sleep in a tree tonight just in case.'

'Yeah. Good idea.'

That night, they might have been too frightened to sleep on the ground, but they were just as afraid of falling out of the tree. To overcome the problem, they used vines to tie themselves into the fork. To protect themselves against the persistent mosquitoes, they also covered their exposed skin with a thick layer of mud. Despite such ingenuity, only utter exhaustion allowed them to fall into a fitful sleep.

The next morning they continued following the muddy river inland, noting that it was gradually beginning to narrow. Fighting their way through the undergrowth, they were bemused to discover themselves at the edge of another wide swamp. Once again, the deep lagoon had to be traversed at a painstakingly slow rate. By the time they reached the other side, their feet were red raw and bleeding. By midafternoon, they could smell smoke and soon found themselves crouching behind some undergrowth, gazing out at a small village in a clearing by the river.

The village was made up of thirty or so bamboo huts on stilts. The roofs were thatched with interwoven banana leaves and grass. In the centre of the small community was a much larger building with a metal roof. Canoes and other small water craft were tied to poles embedded in the muddy riverbank. At the far end of the village, two small elephants stood inside a corral constructed of tree branches. They moved their heads from side to side, swinging their trunks in a repetitive rhythm. Bluey crept closer. 'Look out for Japs,' he whispered.

Bluey was in two minds. He knew that they would eventually have to approach the villagers. Yet he wanted to remain in their present position, undetected in the cover of the thick undergrowth, and keep watch for as long as possible. Even when a clutch of children walked in their direction, he did not attempt to make contact. One small boy finally spotted them, and shot off like an arrow towards the central building. He was quickly followed by the other children. Fate had intervened to deny him a choice.

'Should we run?' Digger asked nervously.

'We need help, big fella. Food and rest. We'll have to take a chance on them.'

A babble of loud voices burst from the central building. Moments later, half a dozen village men emerged, walking slowly towards Bluey and Digger's hiding place. The men were quite small, and were dressed in loose fitting, dark coloured pants and shirts. All wore small caps with no brim. Their leader called to Bluey and Digger in an unfamiliar language. He was a small man with a dark, lined face and penetrating brown eyes. He could have been aged anywhere between forty-five and sixty-five – and had three of his front teeth missing.

'Here goes, Dig.' Bluey broke his silence. 'We're Australians.' He called out loudly. 'Anyone speak English?'

The leader stepped forward. 'I speak little English. Dutch masters teach.'

The two filthy Aussies limped from their hideout, both on the point of collapse. As the village men circled the foreigners, they looked expectantly at the wiry man who had spoken. What he lacked in height, he made up for in confidence as he addressed the two intruders. 'What you want?' he asked.

Bluey hesitated, feeling vulnerable under the village leader's stare. 'Food and shelter.'

The man continued to scrutinise the faces of his visitors. Finally, he raised his eyebrows and smiled. 'Allah say man must help other in need.'

'Who's Allah?' Digger whispered.

'That's their god,' Bluey answered.

'Allah only God. You unbeliever!' The village headman corrected them shrilly. They were in no position to argue.

'We're Australians.' Bluey's tone was courteous. 'We were on a troop ship that was torpedoed near here. But we don't know where we are.'

'You on Sumatra. This, Aceh, north of Natal.' The leader beckoned to the two Australians. 'Come. I have salve for feet. You be hungry.'

As the small group entered the circle of huts, Bluey noticed the women in the background who were watching their every movement. All the adults had their hair and faces covered, and were dressed in loose-fitting clothing that covered every part of their bodies. A number were gathered around a communal cooking plate and oven in the centre of the compound. They stared suspiciously as the white strangers passed. Bluey and Digger were led through the entrance of the main structure into a large room with two long tables surrounded by a number of chairs. All were fashioned from rough timber. The room appeared to be some sort of community meeting place. On each side, a head-high bamboo wall screened off two smaller door-less enclosures. The leader led them into one of these.

'This village building.' The leader indicated with a wave of his hand. 'Mosque behind wall. Infidel not enter mosque.' His voice was stern.

'Of course not,' Bluey assured him.

'You sleep here.' The headman then pointed out the window towards the river. 'First, you wash.'

On their way to the river, the two Australians were followed by many of the village children. They watched as the White strangers stood in water up to their waists and tried to remove the thick layer of mud caked on to their hair and skin. The youngsters laughed and giggled when a small branch floated into Bluey and he yelled in fright and ran from the water shaking.

'What's the matter, Blue?' Digger looked jumpy, ready to dash from the water as well.

'Sorry, cobber.' He was still breathing heavily. 'When the branch touched me, I thought it was a bloody crocodile.'

Their army issue shorts were still dripping when they re-entered the communal building. The headman sat waiting at one of the rough timber tables.

'Here.' The village leader handed a small jar of salve to Bluey then led them into one of the smaller rooms to show them the two straw mattresses on the floor. Two sets of light-coloured baggy pants, shirts and black vests were laid out on the bedding. There were also two pairs of rough sandals to protect their injured feet.

'Thank you.' Bluey bowed slightly to the headman.

'Yeah. Thanks,' added Digger.

'You change now.' The headman left them.

Once Bluey and Digger had applied the soothing ointment and changed, they at last experienced some degree of bodily comfort, although every muscle still ached and their skin stung from the sunburn and abrasions.

'Come. You eat.' The headman was again at the door, beckoning them.

'Thank you, sir,' Bluey answered appreciatively. 'We haven't had much to eat lately. Er . . . I don't know your name.'

'I sorry.' He bowed. 'Indula Mohammed, village imam.'

'Imam? What's that?' Bluey asked courteously.

'Imam, prayer leader.'

'Pleased to meet you.' Bluey held out his hand which was reluctantly taken in a loose grip. 'I'm Bluey O'Donnell and this is my mate, Jimmy Belford.' For the first time since the sinking of the *Wilhelmina*, Bluey felt a surge of hope. They may yet survive.

They followed the imam outside into the light provided by cooking fires. A male villager handed the visitors a tin plate with some type of roasted meat and boiled rice on it. Bluey caught the attention of the headman who quickly nodded at the food. He lifted a small joint of meat to his own mouth.

Ravenous, they followed his lead. The juicy meat tasted like roast pork. 'Pig?' Bluey enquired.

'No. Monkey,' the headman answered matter-of-factly, then laughed at the look of revulsion that appeared on the faces of his two guests. 'You Europeans not like?'

'We're Australian,' Bluey corrected.

'Hmm,' he shrugged dismissively.

'We saw lots of monkeys in the jungle.' Digger bit into his meat.

'Yes. Have monkey and orang-utan.'

'You have elephants, too. Where do they come from?' Bluey asked.

'Sumatra. Also rhinoceros here.'

'Well, stone the crows. I never knew that.' Bluey changed the subject. 'Are there many Japanese around here?' he asked casually.

'No, not see them,' Indula replied, looking Bluey squarely in the eye.

'We saw a patrol boat from the beach the day before yesterday.'

'That long walk from here.'

'Can we stay here with you until we figure out what to do?' Bluey asked.

The imam's smile seemed false. 'Allah say we give help to man in need, even unbeliever.'

'Thank you, Indula.'

'What you do?' he asked disinterestedly.

'Try to get back to Australia.'

'You not succeed,' the headman replied in the same deadpan manner.

'All we can do is try.' Bluey sat up straight. 'I mean if we can get to the southern point of Sumatra, we might be able to get a boat to take us across the strait to Java. Then we could island hop until we got to Timor. From there, it's not that far to Darwin.'

'Darwin?' Indula looked puzzled.

'A town on Australia's northern coastline.'

The village leader solemnly shook his head. 'No. You not be successful. Too difficult.'

'We have no choice.' He turned to his friend. 'We're not giving up, are we, Dig?'

'Not on ya life, Blue.' Digger clapped him on the shoulder.

'Dig?' The headman enquired, baffled. 'Like garden?'

'It's a special name for him,' Bluey said.

'Oh!'

Once they had eaten, the Imam led the pair back into the communal building and the two straw mattresses awaiting them.

'How do you stand the mosquitoes, Indula?' Bluey slapped at the insect drawing blood from his arm.

'Ah. Allah give us potion from leaves in jungle. Also, mosquito nets. Allah help you to sleep, my friends.' He turned and left.

'Not a bad bloke, eh, Blue?' Digger commented.

'I don't know, mate.' Bluey stroked his chin. 'Something about him doesn't ring true.'

After their previous nights in the jungle, the straw mattresses felt almost luxurious. Bluey's mind returned to the events of the past three days.

All those poor sods on the ship and those poor bastards taken by sharks. Must stop thinking about that. I'm lucky. I have to be.

His thoughts turned to Ellen and his mother and father. He hadn't even made it to the theatre of war, and was now lost in the middle of nowhere on a Japanese-controlled island. What would they think?

She'll hear about the ship. She'll probably think I'm dead. Oh, El. Somehow, I'll find my way back to you.

Chapter 13

At first light, Bluey and Digger were violently awoken by a group of village men. As the two Australians struggled in vain, the headman stood at the open doorway, busily barking out instructions. The villagers bound their wrists and forced them onto their stomachs. It took five of them to hold Digger still. In the background Bluey could hear the throb of an approaching engine.

'What the hell are you doing?' Bluey snarled.

The guests were dragged to their feet.

Indula Mohammed smiled sweetly before answering. 'We rid of you, European unbeliever.'

'We're bloody Australians!' Bluey snapped.

'You say before,' the small man replied smugly. 'That what we tell Japanese friend on radio.'

Bluey was in a fury. 'You traitorous bastard!' he screamed.

The headman drew his hand back and slapped Bluey hard across the face. Digger struggled violently and was only restrained with the help of an extra two men.

'Keep foul European word to self, Australian,' the headman said curtly.

'All that talk about Allah, you bloody hypocrite. Do you think Allah would be pleased with you using his name so falsely?' He looked at the imam with disgust.

For a few seconds, the headman looked taken aback. The accusation had caught him off guard. Then the smugness returned. 'Allah forgive. I do this for my people. You, infidels. Like Dutch colonial master,' he said accusingly. 'You want we follow your ways.'

'The Japs will just take their place,' Bluey shot back.

The headman smiled triumphantly. 'Japan free Asia from European and American colonial master.'

'Like they did with the Chinese and Koreans?' Bluey spat. 'The Japs just murdered them and made them slaves.'

'We not fight like stupid Chinese and Korean people!' Indula Mohammed was becoming agitated. 'We cooperate and we be free.' Then he added thoughtfully. 'Even if you right, it better to have Asian colonial master than European one.'

Before Bluey could respond, a Japanese junior officer and four soldiers strode into the building. Indula Mohammed and the officer began conversing in a language neither Bluey nor Digger understood.

Bluey could not believe what was happening. He had never been exposed to such treachery.

The Japanese officer approached Bluey and Digger. 'You spy. You be shot.'

'Bullshit. We're Australian soldiers,' Bluey answered defiantly.

The officer's reaction to this insubordination was immediate.

He began slapping Bluey hard across the face, snapping his head from side to side. But when he saw that the young Australian's eyes were still blazing with indignation, the officer called to his men who quickly set upon Bluey and Digger with rifle butts. Cowering on the floor, Bluey quickly learned the first rule that applied to a Japanese prisoner.

'Prisoner not talk! Must respect Japanese soldier at all time,' the officer screamed.

Struggling to their feet, the men tried to breathe through the pain. Bluey then made his second mistake – he looked hard into the eyes of the officer. The Japanese man issued further orders to his soldiers, who repeated their punishment.

'Second rule,' the junior officer shrieked. 'Not look at Japanese soldier face.' He pointed to the floor. 'Prisoner must look down.' Apart from a moan of pain from Bluey, the pair remained silent. The officer rattled off a succession of commands to the four soldiers accompanying him. Prodded with rifle butts, Bluey and Digger were forced out of the communal building and into the village compound. The locals egged the Japanese soldiers on as they manhandled the two prisoners down a pathway leading to the patrol boat moored by the river. Indula Mohammed followed closely behind.

At the foot of the gangplank, the headman again bowed to the Japanese officer, before turning to Bluey and Digger. 'Keep clothing Australian. Allah go with you.'

Bluey mouthed the words, 'Get fucked,' then he and Digger were roughly driven on board and pushed to a sitting position on the open, metal rear deck. The villagers untied the mooring rope and threw it to a waiting sailor. The patrol boat then slowly edged away from the bank, the Japanese skipper slowly bringing the craft around until it faced downstream. Staying within the boundaries of the stream's narrow channel, he began to manoeuvre the craft back towards the river's mouth. Unlike the Australians' long arduous journey following the waterway inland, their return trip took just over an hour. Once the craft entered the open sea, it increased speed, heading in a south-easterly direction. As mid-day approached, the Japanese soldiers were all handed a plate of food which they consumed with gusto in front of their prisoners. During the meal, the guards tormented and heckled their two captives, all the while laughing. Despite the provocation, Bluey and Digger sat in silence.

Bluey started to feel depressed. To think he had survived the horrendous events surrounding the sinking of his ship, only to find himself a Japanese prisoner-of-war. He had not even fired a shot in anger. The bitter irony of the situation almost made him weep.

He knew there was no point in trying to dive over the side of the speeding craft. Where could they go? Anyway, their hands were tied behind their backs. He would have to bide his time before attempting any form of flight.

Some time later, the patrol boat passed a small group of islands. Peering though the rails he could just see the outline of a coastal town. As the craft moved in closer, he noticed two more Japanese patrol boats tied up to a run-down wharf. After disembarking, the pair were pushed along the pier and into a small dilapidated building that smelled strongly of rotting fish. They were then marched through a series of narrow alleyways by the waterside, enduring a tirade of abuse from the townsfolk. Although Bluey could not understand a single word, there was no misunderstanding the intense hatred. He wondered if the abuse was due to the colour of his skin or his nationality.

Maybe they think we're Dutch?

To please the crowd, at intervals, the Japanese escort pushed the Australians with their rifle butts. This action brought immediate applause from onlookers. Eventually they arrived at a sandstone colonial building with a rising sun flag fluttering from its portal. Inside, they were taken to a large windowless room containing only a table, four chairs and a solitary ceiling fan ineffectual against the intense humidity and heat.

On entering, no one attempted to sit. Bluey thought he would faint. His clothing was wringing wet with perspiration. He and Digger were in acute pain from the large bruises and welts covering their bodies, their breaths coming in short gasps.

At last, after what seemed an interminable wait, the group were joined by three Japanese officers and a senior NCO, who carried two bamboo canes. The officers sat themselves at the table. The Japanese escort sprang to attention and saluted. Bluey judged the senior officer to be a colonel, but he had no idea about the rank of the other two. The colonel sat at the head of the table examining the contents of a folder. From time to time he glared at the Australians. Finally, he spoke. 'You spy!'

Bluey and Digger knew better than to look at the man or to answer him. 'You talk,' he ordered crisply.

'We're Australian soldiers,' Bluey said. 'We were on a ship that was sunk.'

'Yes, by heroic Japanese submarine,' the officer beamed proudly.

The Australian pair remained silent.

'Where your convoy headed?' The Japanese man's eyes narrowed.

'We do not know. We weren't told,' Bluey replied.

'You lie!' the colonel accused.

'No. It's the truth.'

The officer barked a command and the escort began beating the prisoners with the bamboo canes. Bluey fell to the floor. Digger lasted a little longer before he too collapsed from the brutal onslaught. Bluey closed his eyes.

I can't survive this.

'You answer now!' the officer ordered sharply.

Bluey groaned with pain as he rose to his feet. 'If I knew, I'd tell you. It's army policy not to tell soldiers where they're going.' He could barely talk through his bloodied lips.

The officer examined his bruised captives. 'What unit?' he commanded.

As politely as possible, and mindful not to look the Japanese officer in the face, he replied, 'O'Donnell K, Sapper Q72431.'

'What is your unit?' the senior officer shouted.

Bluey repeated his name, rank and serial number, all that the Geneva Convention required.

Enraged, the colonel ordered another severe beating, draining the two of any further resolve. They went on to tell the officer everything they knew, which, thankfully, was virtually nothing. At the end of the interrogation, the colonel addressed the two prisoners. 'This town, Padang. You go to camp now. You work good, you survive.'

The small compound was about two acres in size and entirely enclosed by two ten-foot-high perimeter fences, three yards apart. Each fence was topped with barbed-wire strands, and a guard tower stood at each corner of the outer fence. After passing the sentry at the main gate, Bluey and Digger were led to a low, rough timber building to the right with a dormitory adjoining its rear. The flagpole at the front suggested that the dormitory housed the Japanese soldiers who guarded the prisoners.

Inside the main building, Bluey and Digger stood before a short, slightly built man impeccably dressed in a grey uniform with a white-collared shirt.

'I Major Harada,' the man began softly. 'I only one here speak *good* English.' Bluey and Digger remained quiet. 'You Australian?' He looked at them expectantly. 'Speak!'

'Yes, sir.' Bluey almost choked on the words.

'I commandant of all camp here.' He paused. 'You prisoner.' His voice hardened. 'You follow all rules or be punished. First rule, not talk to Japanese soldier unless he talk first. Second rule, prisoner bow to Japanese soldier and to Japanese flag at all time. Third rule, you work hard for Japanese cause. If you obey all rules and work hard, Japanese give you food. If not, no food and you be punished.' He slammed the palm of his hand down on the table. 'Last rule, prisoner who try to escape will be shot. You understand? Speak!'

'Yes, sir,' the Australians answered in unison.

'What you do before army?' Major Harada lowered his voice, pointing to Digger.

Keeping his head bowed, Digger replied. 'I worked in a fish market.'

The major looked disappointed. 'You clear jungle here. You understand?'

'Yes, sir.'

'You. What you do?' He jabbed a finger at Bluey.

'I worked on our family's farm,' he answered.

The major smiled. 'What you grow?' he asked.

'Wheat.'

'Rice?' It was almost a plea.

'No, sir.'

'You grow much rice and other food here,' the officer commanded sternly. 'For Japanese soldier. You understand?'

'Yes, sir.'

'You know horses?'

Bluey looked up, surprised. He quickly lowered his head. 'Yes, sir. We had horses on the property; four of them.'

'Very good, Australian, very good.' He sounded pleased. 'You also look after my horse. He important to me.'

The major retrieved the sappers' knives from the table where they had been placed by the escorting guards. He opened the small, folded blade and frowned for a moment, tapping the knife on the desk. 'You keep. May need,' he said.

He then barked out further instructions in Japanese to a hulking sergeant who had just entered. The man approached the table, his long swagger stick under his arm, and saluted smartly.

The officer returned the courtesy. 'This Sergeant Kyoshi. He in charge of all prisoner. He speak some English.'

The man who was to be their keeper was unlike any Japanese soldier the two Australians had so far encountered. In the main, the Japanese soldiers were short and wiry. Sergeant Kyoshi was well over six feet in height with a broad, solid frame. The senior NCO glared at the Australians, pointing his swagger stick towards the door. 'Go!' he commanded sternly.

The sergeant again saluted his CO and followed his new captives outside into the sweltering compound. It was getting dark, and as they walked towards the three low huts at the far end of the camp, they were joined by two armed soldiers. At this point, Kyoshi began poking the Australians in the back with his swagger stick.

When they reached the dilapidated huts, the sergeant stamped a foot on the ground. 'Six a.m. parade, here, then work, all day. You,' he pointed to Bluey, 'you work in garden there.' He pointed to a cleared area behind the Japanese soldiers' quarters in the distance. 'You grow food, but not eat. I look many time. Make sure you not take.' He raised his lip in a sneer. 'I give prisoner food only if prisoner work. Understand?'

'Yes.'

'You use prisoner and Japanese soldier waste on garden to help grow. You clean out daily. Understand?'

'Yes.'

The sergeant pointed to Digger. 'You go now.' Bluey also turned away, but the sergeant's command brought him to a halt. 'You stay!'

Digger walked slowly to the first hut and waited inside.

Kyoshi turned to Bluey and leered. 'I not see man with red hair.' He pointed to the unkempt crop of copper curls that adorned Bluey's head. 'I like.' He gave a twisted smile. 'You be nice, yes?' He reached out to touch the curls.

Bluey could not stop himself in time. 'No!' he shouted, pushing the sergeant's hand away in disgust. The senior NCO's response was swift and brutal. He beat Bluey about the body and arms with his stick until the young prisoner fell groaning to the ground. Hearing the commotion, Digger raced from his hut, but was stopped by the guards.

'Not touch Japanese soldier!' Kyoshi growled at Bluey through clenched teeth as he departed with his men.

Digger rushed over to help Bluey to his feet. 'Crikey, mate. What'd you say to get him mad like that?'

'He's a bloody faggot. He wanted to touch my hair.'

'He's also a sadist and an extremely dangerous man,' added a voice with a cultured English accent.

The two Australians turned to see a tallish blond and bearded man with clear blue eyes. The only item that covered any part of his emaciated body was a dirty loin cloth wound around his hips and between his legs. 'Welcome to hell, chaps,' he said, extending his right hand.

Bluey put on a brave face and took the outstretched hand in a firm grip. 'G'day.'

'Roger Adams is the name.' He pronounced each word precisely. 'You're Australians?'

'Yep,' smiled Digger, introducing himself and Bluey.

'Three other Aussies were brought in yesterday. They're in the next hut,' Roger offered.

'Must be others from the ship, Dig!' Bluey remarked to his friend before turning back to Roger. 'Take us to them, will you, mate?'

The three Australian infantrymen were outside their hut talking when Bluey and Digger approached.

'You made it!' Bluey cried excitedly, introducing himself and Digger. He felt awash with relief to see other Australians.

One was tall and thickset with slightly receding dark hair. The second was short and thin, with snowy blond hair and a large nose. The third man had brown, wavy hair and an oddly studious air. The tall one pointed to himself before moving on to the others. 'I'm Scrounger Morgan, the little fellow's Skeetah Davies and the normal-looking bloke is John Fitzpatrick, or the Professor, as we like to call him.' They all shook hands.

'Good ta meetcha.' Skeetah had a high-pitched voice.

'Pleased to meet you.' John Fitzpatrick spoke evenly and precisely.

'How'd you get the name, Scrounger?' Digger asked.

'Because the big boofhead can lay his hands on just about anything,' Skeetah jumped in.

'That will be a handy attribute here,' observed Roger.

'What the fuck's an attra-beaut?' Scrounger turned to Fitzpatrick.

'I suppose you would call it a positive quality or a skill.'

'Oh.'

'What about Skeetah?' Bluey asked.

'I thought you'd know that one.' Scrounger had a girlish giggle.

'Mosquito. Get it? Little prick used to be a jockey before he put on too much weight.'

They later learned that John Fitzpatrick had been a trainee teacher before enlisting – hence the nickname 'the Professor'.

Were you the three blokes hanging onto the ship's derrick?'

'Yeah, that's right,' Skeetah answered.

'What happened to the other two?' Digger asked.

The men looked away, or at their feet.

'You tell 'em, Professor,' Scrounger said.

Fitzpatrick sighed. 'We all made it to shore safely but when the patrol boat spotted us, the other two tried to run off. They were mowed down and killed by the Japs.'

'Little yellow ratbags haven't got much of a sense of humour, have they?' Scrounger rubbed the heavy welt on his cheek. 'We told them we didn't know anything, but they still belted the shit out of us.'

'Where are you from, Scrounger?' Bluey asked.

'I go anywhere there's work, mate,' he replied. 'Steelworks at Newcastle, coalmines in the Hunter Valley, picking fruit. Too many jobs to remember. Grew up in Orange, though. My mum still lives there.'

'What about you?' Digger looked at Skeetah.

'I come from Yarra Glen in Victoria. I was an apprentice jockey to a horse trainer down there for a while. Then I moved out to the bush, breaking horses and doing a bit of stock work.'

Before Bluey could ask, John Fitzpatrick beat him to the punch. 'I come from Bankstown in Sydney.'

'He's also engaged to a good-looking sort named Jenny. We saw a picture of her.' Skeetah whistled appreciatively before changing the subject. 'Where'd you blokes get that clobber?'

Bluey started to reply, but Roger interrupted. 'Come on you two, their hut is full up. We'd better get back to ours and get you settled. I'm sure we have a couple of vacancies.' He smiled without humour.

'Okay, you blokes, see you tomorrow.' Bluey waved.

Inside the hut, gaunt, tired, bearded faces turned to examine the new arrivals. At first Bluey thought the men were too tired or too ill to offer a greeting. Looking around the interior of the hut, he counted ten sets of bedding lining each side. Outside the back door, they could see the burning embers of a cooking fire.

What a shit hole!

'Sorry, my friends. We've already eaten.' The Englishman's tone was apologetic. 'I'm afraid you'll have to wait until tomorrow night.' A middle-aged man rose from his mattress and addressed Roger in a foreign language. The Englishman answered him in the same tongue. He noticed the puzzled expression on Bluey's face. 'Sorry, old chap.' He forced a small chuckle. 'With all the excitement, I forgot to mention one important fact. The majority of the people incarcerated here are Dutch. They've been interned by the Japs.'

'So, what are you doing here?' Bluey asked.

'I worked for the Dutch East India Company in Batavia. They were offering terrific pay for a Brit who could speak Dutch. Unfortunately, I was in the wrong place at the wrong time when the war broke out.'

'How'd you get to this shit hole?' asked Bluey.

'When the Japs came, I was interned and brought here with a large group of Javanese men who had been forcibly mobilised.'

'Don't the East Indians object to their people being used like this?' Digger asked.

'The Japs have indoctrinated, trained and armed many young East Indians, and have given nationalist leaders like Sukarno a political voice. On the other hand, the poor have missed out completely. You see, the overriding concern of the Japs is the extraction of resources like oil, copper and other minerals. On Java, food and other vital necessities have been confiscated and this has caused widespread misery and starvation.'

'What is everyone doing here?' Bluey enquired.

'There are two major projects in Sumatra: the construction of an airstrip and a rail line.'

'A railway?' Digger looked surprised.

'We might think it's hell here, but we consider ourselves fortunate we weren't chosen for the Pekanbaru railway project. One of the Dutch chaps says it's a nightmare of suffering and that the poor sods working on it are dropping like flies.'

'Are there any other English people here?' Digger asked.

'Yes. There are three soldiers here who were part of a British strike force. It was attempting to start an underground movement with the locals.'

'What happened to the others?' Bluey asked.

'All dead, I'm afraid.'

'How long have you been here?'

'Most of us have been here around nine months. Some less. A handful of the local Dutchmen hid out in the jungle for a while, but were eventually captured.'

'What's it like here?' Digger asked.

'Bloody awful, old chap. One meal a day. Usually rice with a small quantity of fish, which is usually off. Gives you a pain in the tummy, if you know what I mean. We supplement the food, if you can call it that, with anything we can lay our hands on.' He looked hard into both Australians' faces. 'Right from the start, I must emphasise that it's extremely important to keep your eyes open at all times for any sort of food, and hide it from the Japs. That type of vigilance has kept us alive. But only just. Disease is the main killer. We lost two chaps only a few days ago – malaria. The blighters won't give us any medicine, although one of our own chaps knows how to gather the substance the locals use to combat malaria. Speaking of the locals, don't expect any help there.'

'We've already found that out,' Digger said bitterly.

'So what's the news from the outside world?' Roger changed the subject.

'Can't tell you much,' Bluey replied. 'Hitler still has Europe and Great Britain has withstood his onslaught from the air.'

'Good show.'

'But Singapore has fallen.'

'Blast! They said it was impregnable.'

'Don't know much else, sorry.'

'How did you pair get here?' Roger asked.

They recounted their story to the Englishman, Digger taking over when Bluey became emotional.

When they were finished, Roger shook his head in wonder.

'You chaps are extremely lucky to be alive. And because you didn't surrender, but were captured, the Japs shouldn't treat you as harshly as those three English fellows in the bottom hut.' He turned towards two spare straw mattresses at the far end of the room. 'You chaps can take those. They belonged to the poor sods who died.'

Digger looked at Roger in alarm and screwed up his nose. 'We might catch what they had.'

His concern was met with a wry smile from the Englishman. 'Chances are, old thing, you'll eventually catch it anyway. Right,' his tone became more businesslike, 'you'd better get some rest now. You'll need it.'

As he lay on the foul-smelling mattress, Bluey's body was one giant ache from the beatings. Though he yearned for sleep, pain and anxiety kept him awake. He lay there, castigating himself for his naivety. When he enlisted, he thought he would be considered a hero by everyone, someone to be admired. But all he had become was a prisoner of the enemy.

Chapter 14

It seemed to Bluey that he had only just closed his eyes when he was awoken by a shrill whistle.

'Quickly! Outside!' Roger urged them.

Bluey followed Digger and the other prisoners out into the tropical drizzle. He watched as the men from the three other huts shuffled towards his group in three straggly lines. Bluey guessed there were around sixty men in all. Sergeant Kyoshi stood in front of the motley group, shouting at his six subordinates, who began counting the inmates.

'I watch.' The sergeant narrowed his eyes. 'You work hard for Japanese army. All men must work harder or no food.' He pointed to Bluey. 'You come me, now.'

Bluey approached the sergeant, keeping his eyes riveted to the ground. 'You follow,' Kyoshi ordered and strode towards the rear of the Japanese soldiers' quarters. Bluey saw that someone had unsuccessfully tried to establish a garden of sorts in a cleared area. The beds, however, were now unkempt and overgrown with tropical weeds. Twenty yards or so further to the right of the barracks was a small shed and stable, and a corral with a fine bay gelding. As they approached, the friendly animal snickered a greeting. Bluey would have liked to stroke its neck, but resisted the urge.

'Major's horse,' the sergeant said stiffly. 'You see to. Horse food in here.' He opened the door to the timber shed. Inside was a jumble of gardening tools as well as a saddle, some chaff and half a box of oats. Out in the open again, Kyoshi continued his instructions. 'Use tools in garden.' He waved his hand towards the open area. 'Need food for Japanese soldier. People bring plants soon. Outside,' he pointed to the fence, 'you make rice paddy by creek. Come.'

Sergeant Kyoshi began walking towards what Bluey assumed to be the Japanese soldiers' privy. Unlike the prisoners' latrine, which was open to the weather, this enclosure had timber walls and a metal roof. Inside, two seats had been constructed over shallow trenches that currently held a foul mixture of excreta and urine. Sergeant Kyoshi hit the timber supports with the swagger stick, and a cloud of blowflies rose from the maggot-infested contents. Three rats also made a quick exit. Bluey, overwhelmed by the vile stench, screwed up his nose and made a face. Sergeant Kyoshi's retaliation was quick. He grabbed Bluey by the throat and thrust him against the wall, leaning over him so that his face was only inches away. 'Not insult honourable Japanese soldier! You take all waste and use for plants.'

The sergeant's grip tightened and Bluey felt himself becoming faint, his breath rasping and laboured. When the large man finally released his vice-like hold, Bluey refused to let the sadistic sergeant see him cower.

Kyoshi leaned closer. 'I want you for jungle,' he said, leering. 'But major want you for stupid horse,' he spat in disgust. 'You be mine one day. I wait. Time come. You work now. Major ride horse soon.'

The sergeant strode out of the latrine, and Bluey wondered how he could cope with the man's animosity. Meanwhile, he had other more important duties to consider. When he entered the horse's enclosure, the bay immediately came up to nuzzle him. He gave the animal a good brush down and fed it a mix of chaff and oats. He filled the horse's small drinking trough from the forty-four gallon drum that collected fresh water from the barracks roof. Stroking the animal's neck, the irony of the situation was not lost on him.

Bloody thing eats better than anyone here.

Yet the horse had a kind eye and seemed to appreciate affection. The smell of the animal reminded him of home. How he wished he was back there!

While the horse munched on its feed, Bluey removed a crude mattock and hoe from the shed. The drizzle had eased, and in the early morning heat, he made his way to the cleared area and began digging up the earth, meticulously turning it over and over. His body was already drenched with sweat. He stopped, scooped up a handful of the earth, still damp from the morning shower, and examined its worth.

Poor quality. Not like the dark loam back home. Won't grow much in this.

The previous gardener appeared to have had little or no understanding of what was required. The few plants that remained were disease infested, or wilted in the heat. The earth had not even been dug deep enough for the roots to take hold.

He noticed the horse at the fence, so he returned to the stable to saddle the animal, pleased to have a rest from the backbreaking digging. Just as he tightened the girth strap, the Japanese commandant, wearing riding apparel, approached. Bluey bowed as the man passed by.

'Horse look good, Australian,' he said approvingly.

Bluey remained silent, well aware of the rules.

'Talk,' ordered the major.

'Yes, sir. He's a fine animal.'

'Local chief give to me.' He stroked the horse's neck. 'Was owned by Dutch planter.'

The officer mounted the animal and rode off towards the main gate. Bluey resumed work on the garden plot with a new intensity. He marked out an area about fifty yards by thirty yards before setting to it with the mattock and hoe. Hunger, and the increasing heat, began to sap his strength, but Bluey worked on regardless.

The major returned the horse an hour later and Bluey washed and groomed the animal, which showed its appreciation by nuzzling him.

At various times during the morning, Japanese soldiers came by to inspect the Australian prisoner's progress. One soldier stood out from the rest of the sour-faced troops. He was short and overweight, with black hair clipped close to his scalp, and a rounded, chubby face. He approached Bluey, smiled, then removed his hat and wiped the sweat from his head with a cloth. Bluey bowed, and the small man began to chatter away to him in Japanese. He didn't understand a single word the man uttered, and what was more, the Japanese soldier knew he didn't. But that didn't stop him from talking. Finally, the little man shrugged, grinned sheepishly and walked away.

That one doesn't seem too bad.

Careful not to be seen, Bluey took a long drink from the horse's water supply. Around midday, the humidity was so intense he thought he might pass out due to lack of nourishment. Perspiration dripped from every pore and his wet clothing clung to him as he worked on. By midafternoon, he had turned over half the plot. By late in the afternoon, he'd completed three-quarters. Increasingly, the heat, combined with lack of food, began to take its toll. He hadn't eaten for thirty-six hours.

As dusk fell, Bluey heard the low voices of the other prisoners returning from their work in the jungle. He walked to the horse's enclosure to prepare its evening feed. As he stood stoking its neck, the affectionate animal nuzzled him on the arm.

'He like you.'

Bluey turned and bowed to the major.

'You speak.'

'I like him too, sir.' Bluey replied truthfully, eyeing the ground in front of the officer's feet.

'How many horse you have at home?' It was a friendly enquiry.

'Four, sir.'

'No room for horse at my home in Tokyo.' He sighed. 'But I still ride in park.'

The officer pointed towards the prisoners' huts. 'You go now and eat.'

Bluey bowed. 'Yes, sir.' He could not disguise his relief. He was midway across the compound when he heard a harsh voice behind him. 'Not go! You work more!'

Kyoshi had seemingly appeared from out of nowhere. Bluey almost took the risk of repeating the major's words, but instinct warned him of the likely consequences and he remained silent. Kyoshi, in turn, was silenced by another commanding voice.

'Prisoner go now, Sergeant.' The major appeared from beside the barracks. 'He work tomorrow.'

The sergeant responded in Japanese, and saluted smartly, then turned to Bluey and whispered nastily, 'You lucky, now. But I wait.'

Inside his hut, malnourished, exhausted men languished on their rough, straw mattresses. Three of the Dutchmen lay shaking from the dreaded malaria. The more able-bodied inmates attended cooking fires at the rear of the hut, and others prepared the meagre evening meal. Again, Bluey was struck by the gravity of his situation. This was to be his lot for God knew how long. He approached Digger and Roger Adams by the fire. They were joined by Scrounger, Skeetah and John who carried their meals on metal plates.

'How'd it go, Dig?' Bluey asked.

'Bloody awful, mate. Chopping down trees and digging out stumps. I'm knackered.'

'The bush is thick as buggery, and the bloody tools they give us are all blunt or broken. Hopeless little billygoats,' Scrounger said with disgust. 'What about you, Blue? What'd you do?'

'Worked my guts out all day digging a garden plot,' he grunted. 'The best part was looking after the major's horse.'

'Wouldn't mind that job, myself,' Skeetah observed with a faraway look in his eye. 'Always been good with horses.'

'Bloody thing eats better than us,' Bluey commented. 'Old Bluto and the guards kept their eyes on me though.'

Roger looked blankly at Bluey, who attempted to explain. 'Have you ever seen a Popeye comic at the pictures?'

Roger nodded.

'You know the big prick who's always the baddie? Bluto?' He grinned. 'That bastard sergeant looks just like him, except for the eyes.'

Raucous laughter filled the night air. 'Yes. Now that you mention it, he does.' Roger turned back to the two Australians, all traces of humour vanished. 'There's nothing funny about him, though. He's a murderer.'

'Murderer?' John repeated. 'That's a bit strong isn't it?'

'I'm sure of it,' the Englishman replied. 'You see, I arrived here with a group of Dutchmen that included a young, blond-headed fellow with a flawless complexion – you know, like a girl's.' He took a deep breath. 'From the moment the sergeant set eyes on the boy, he couldn't keep away from him. You've already discovered that he likes the boys, haven't you, Bluey? Well, this confirms it. One day, when we were in the forest, the rotten blighter took the lad away from the work detail. We never saw them for the remainder of the day. When the sergeant returned, he was alone. He told the major that the youngster had escaped. We all think the bugger had his way with him before doing him in.'

'Jesus!' Digger chimed in

Bluey felt a chill run through him. 'Didn't the major do anything?'

'Not a blasted thing. The truth is the major's as weak as water. He may be officially in charge of the camp, but make no bones about it, the sergeant runs the place.' He eyeballed Bluey. 'So watch out, my friend, because the stinker has taken a fancy to you.'

'He won't be able to do that to Blue,' Digger piped up. 'He can go.'

'Go?' A puzzled Roger had never heard the term.

'Fight, mate,' Digger explained. 'Bluey can really stand up for himself.'

'Won't make any difference. This blighter's so much bigger and stronger, especially with his three meals a day. The rotter's also well into jujitsu. I've seen him working out many times with the other Japanese soldiers, who are all scared to death of him, by the way. I'm sure some of them wouldn't be as bad if he wasn't around. With our appalling diet, Bluey, your strength will soon deteriorate.'

Bluey looked at the boiled rice with its few flakes of fish. When the cooking pan was removed from the stove, the three joined the others inside the hut where the scanty provisions were shared. Each hut was responsible for its own rations.

Lying awake on his mattress, Bluey thought about Ellen: the way she smiled, the sound of her voice and the smell of the cologne she always wore. He knew it wasn't an expensive brand, but on her it seemed especially sensuous. Pictures of Kilkenny filled his thoughts; his father working out in the paddocks, his mother preparing the evening meal and he and Ellen riding along the river to the cave.

Oh, El, why did I do it?

His spirits once more hit rock bottom. If he was to survive, he knew he must find more food. But there was one huge problem. The Japanese soldiers would continually monitor his work and would know if he removed anything from the garden. Stealing from the Japanese was therefore not an option. He lay back thinking about it, wondering what he could possibly do to increase their food supply.

After attending to the horse, Bluey's first task the following morning was to dig a series of narrow, deep trenches in the loose tropical soil. He took as long as he dared to do this, but then the job he had been dreading could not be put off any longer. In the tool shed, he found a four-gallon drum with a wire handle, some wire and several smaller cans. Using stiff strands of wire and one of the smaller cans, he fashioned a scoop that would enable him to carry out the revolting task ahead. Once prepared, he walked to the Japanese soldiers' latrine where he was forced to wait outside until one of the guards left. Inside, the stench from the latrine pit turned his stomach. As he began scooping the revolting contents into the four-gallon drum, the noxious smell increased and Bluey began to gag, and then vomited. His stomach empty, he toiled on, occasionally dry-retching.

Once the drum was filled, he carried the container and its

objectionable contents to the garden, where the human fertiliser was deposited along the furrows he'd dug earlier. He then covered the waste with a layer of soil. Time and time again he returned to the latrine until the trench was empty.

Thank God.

As he worked on, Bluey's skin and clothing were covered in a black mass of flies and other insects attracted by the smell. The malodorous stench, however, had one positive outcome. When the Japanese soldiers approached the newly ploughed area to check on his progress, the smell forced them to choose an alternative pathway.

Suits me.

The small, chubby soldier was not put off. On his rounds, he would approach Bluey and pinch his nose and grin before continuing on his way. Bluey nicknamed him 'Little Mudguts'.

That afternoon, two villagers arrived with a handcart filled with plants for the Japanese soldiers' new garden. They stood some distance back with Sergeant Kyoshi and watched Bluey remove them. There were pawpaw seedlings, banana suckers, sweet potato, yams, as well as what looked like cabbage seedlings.

'We know what here,' Kyoshi shouted. 'Villager count all. You be punish if all plant not grow.'

To Bluey's relief they had failed to notice the pawpaw seeds that had fallen amongst the seedlings. Two tiny banana suckers were also caught in the burlap bag at the bottom of the cart. As Kyoshi and the villagers walked away, Bluey made his move, hiding the seeds and the two suckers under his loose-fitting clothes. He then planted everything the villagers had brought.

Accompanied by Little Mudguts, Bluey next carried the four-gallon can to the small stream running beside the camp. He filled the container to its brim before making his way back to water the seedlings, which were already wilting despite it being late afternoon. He again returned to the stream, but before refilling the drum, he indicated to the small Japanese guard with hand actions that he needed to relieve himself. Little Mudguts laughed and pointed to thick foliage growing beside the stream.

Bluey scrambled through the thick undergrowth until he found a small clearing. Out of sight, he hurriedly dug a small trench with his bare hands and planted the pawpaw seeds and banana suckers.

They'll have to make do with rain.

On his return to the stream, Bluey found Mudguts had removed his boots and was happily paddling around in the cool running water. The little man's delight was short-lived. He jumped with fright, almost falling over, when Kyoshi let fly with a tirade of abuse from just inside the perimeter fence.

Bluey trekked to the stream repeatedly until he was satisfied that the new garden had been adequately watered. If it had been the wet season, he thought to himself, there would have been no need for him to carry water, as torrents of rain fell almost every day during this period.

That evening Digger asked Bluey about his day.

'Been doin' things I don't want to talk about.' His face contorted in disgust. 'Anyhow, I'm too bloody stuffed.'

'Come next door.' Digger beckoned. 'We got a little surprise for you.'

His curiosity overcoming his fatigue, Bluey followed his friend to the next hut where a group of prisoners were gathered around the cooking fire. The odour of cooking meat brought saliva to his mouth. 'What's that smell?'

'Scrounger killed a snake. A big bugger, you know, like a python. Hid it in the jungle till it was time to come back. Wrapped it around the belly of that skinny Dutch bloke over there while the Japs weren't looking,' he said pointing to a thin Dutchman in a loose shirt.

'Good one, Scrounger!' Bluey patted the big man on the back.

'Thanks.'

'Roast bloody snake.' Skeetah shuddered.

'Beats starving,' John offered quietly.

The meat was evenly divided between the inhabitants of the three huts. Although unsettled by the fact that he was eating a snake, Bluey knew the protein would do him good. It had an oily quality, and tasted a bit like chicken, though with a stronger, gamey flavour.

Not that bad.

'I'll catch a monkey next time.' Scrounger wiped a hand across his mouth and giggled.

'Now you see why we call him Scrounger,' Skeetah smiled.

Bluey had an idea. 'What about the rats?' They were almost in plague proportions, and ran all over the men at night, biting them while they were asleep. 'We could try them for tucker.'

'We've tried to catch them,' Roger shrugged. 'But we haven't been successful.'

'Leave it to me,' Scrounger offered. 'I'll make a few traps. I've done it before.'

Bluey smiled with some satisfaction when he heard the tropical downpour that night.

That'll help our little garden.

The next day, Sergeant Kyoshi instructed Bluey on the basic principles of rice growing.

'Prisoner dig pond beside stream.' Kyoshi's voice had a sharp edge to it. Bluey could tell he was in a foul mood, and that he was on the verge of erupting. Just a simple question on procedure brought about a violent response from the Japanese man, who raised his stick in a threatening manner. 'No talk!'

Under the watchful supervision of a guard, Bluey used crude digging implements to fashion what was to eventually become a large square pond beside the swiftly flowing waters. It took him three days of digging to excavate the paddy, which he then lined with topsoil.

His next task was to clean out the prisoners' latrines and use the contents as fertiliser for the future rice paddy. As he undertook the appalling assignment, he could not control the retching and vomiting that kept his shoulders continually heaving. On the fourth day, he dug a shallow trench to the edge of the waterway. As soon as he connected the trench with the stream, water started flowing along the shallow ditch, flooding the dug-out area and creating a wide pond beside the creek.

He was grateful when it was again Little Mudguts' turn to supervise his work. In recognition of Bluey's efforts, the guard nodded his head in approval as he inspected the pool. The morning after, villagers brought rice shoots which Bluey planted in the newly established pond.

During the following days and weeks, Bluey kept to a strict routine. First thing every morning he would attend to the horse, a task he enjoyed immensely because it was a reminder of home. There was something comforting about caring for an animal. For the rest of the morning he worked in the garden, pulling up the endless procession of tropical weeds that threatened to overrun his hard work. If there was no rain, the garden also had to be watered by hand. Insects were a major problem, one he overcame by covering the plants with mosquito netting his captors provided for the purpose. The Japanese failed to provide similar protection to the prisoners, who were at the mercy of the unrelenting hordes of mosquitoes that swarmed into their huts every evening. In the afternoons he spent most of his time in the rice paddy. Twice weekly, he would remove the foul-smelling contents from the soldiers' and prisoners' latrines and mix it with grass and leaves to create compost for future use.

The first time Bluey noticed birds feeding on maggots in the compost heap, it made him shudder. But as time passed, he noticed the birds becoming fatter and fatter. One day he shared his observation with Roger.

'Good God man! You're not suggesting we eat maggots?'

'We could cook them with sambal,' Bluey suggested. 'You should see those birds. They're so fat.'

'But maggots?'

'Desperate times call for desperate measures, mate.'

Roger screwed up his nose and thought for a few moments. 'Why not?'

From that time on when he emptied the latrines, Bluey

separated the maggots and washed them. The legless larvae were fried over the open fire, a sambal sauce added to them to make them more palatable. The chillies for the sambal grew wild in the jungle and were often collected by the Dutchmen. The maggot meal was fed to the sick who visibly improved because of the extra protein.

Some nights Bluey was too exhausted to think about anything but sleep. This was a relief. Most nights he lay awake thinking about Ellen and home.

I miss them so much. Please, God, let them know I am alive.

Chapter 15

Ellen was almost grateful for the endless hard work that living on a farm demanded, as sometimes several hours would pass where she didn't think about Bluey. But every night as she lay down to sleep, the worry and grief would return to haunt her.

Where is he? Has he been injured? Did he drown? Is he alive?

In the first few months of her pregnancy, Ellen continued to carry out the chores that had become her responsibility. Sally had taken over feeding the pigs and poultry and collecting the eggs, but Ellen still rose early each morning to milk the house cow, and spent much of the day helping Dave out in the paddocks.

Six months into her pregnancy, Dave and Sally approached her one evening as she sat in an armchair listening to the radio.

'Me an' Sally have been talkin', young Ellen,' Dave said with a serious expression. 'First of all, I must tell you that you've been doin' a great job out there in the paddocks, lass. Good as any paid hand I've ever employed. But from now on, we t'ink you should stop doin' that heavy work. An' we also t'ink you should keep off the horses, too. We don't want you to have a fall or anythin' like that.' He looked at Sally for backup, who smiled encouragingly. 'From now on, you take over from Sal in the house and she'll help me out in the paddocks. Is that okay with you?'

Ellen could see that Bluey's parents were not going to brook any argument. 'Very well. If that's what you want.'

Later that evening Ellen gave a startled cry.

'What's up, love?' Sally asked, concerned.

'The baby kicked me!' Ellen's mouth made a small 'o'.

Sally smiled and joined Ellen on the sofa.

'Put your hand here.' Ellen placed Sally's hand on the right side of her perfectly rounded stomach.

Sally felt a little ripple of movement. 'I feel it! Come and feel this, Dave. Quick!'

He looked embarrassed. 'Ellen doesn't want me doin' that, Sal.'

'Come on, Mr O'Donnell,' Ellen urged him happily. 'It's really lovely!'

Hesitantly, he placed his hand on her tummy. When he felt the tiny movements, Dave's eyes filled with tears.

Sally took her husband in her arms. 'He's alive, Dave. I know it. And that's his baby alive and well too.'

'I'm sorry, girls.' Dave wiped his eyes with a handkerchief. 'I was a bit cut-up when I felt the little bub move.'

'I get emotional too, Mr O'Donnell.'

'For the last time, young Ellen,' he scolded her in fun. 'Why can't you call me Dave? You call Sal Sally, don't you?'

'I'll try, Mr O'Don— er, Dave,' she answered self-consciously.

'That's better.'

During the long pregnancy, Ellen remained at the farm for most of the time, only venturing into town on the occasions she had appointments with the doctor. She used these opportunities to have lunch with her mother who sometimes brought a pair of booties, a bonnet or matinee jacket she'd knitted for the baby. Ellen appreciated her mother's efforts, and wondered how long she'd been saving the baby wool – with the war, wool was in short supply.

As the time for confinement drew near, Dr Elliot booked her into the maternity ward of Goondiwindi's public hospital. 'The maternity wing is quite new and very nice.' He put her file on the desk. 'Only one month to go, Ellen. You're in great shape.'

'Out of shape, you mean,' she replied despondently. 'I feel so enormous.'

'No you're not,' he chuckled. 'I've seen much larger.'

'I feel like I'm the size of a house.' She forced a smile.

'It's probably Sally feeding you all that extra milk.'

'You can say that again.' She rolled her eyes.

A week before the baby was due, Ellen was sweeping the floor when she noticed black clouds threatening the washing she had hung out earlier that morning. She immediately put down the broom.

The sweeping can wait.

Feeling the first spots of rain, she made her way into the backyard as quickly as she could. Just as she reached for the last sheet, she felt warm fluid slowly trickle down her inner thighs.

My waters have broken!

She stumbled back to the rear verandah to ring the bell Dave had installed for her. Sally and Dave had programmed their activities so that one of them would always be in earshot of the homestead. The instructions were made abundantly clear to Ellen. She was to ring the bell at the first sign of going into labour. Within five minutes, Ellen could see them through the back window as they galloped towards the rear of the house.

'Where's the bag?' Dave was puffing as he entered the back door.

'In my room. It's packed. But there's no rush if you want to clean up first.'

The prospective grandparents had a quick wash, changed their clothing, and the old Fargo was on its way to Goondiwindi. On arrival at casualty, Ellen was transferred to the maternity ward. When she was finally settled, a doctor entered the room and checked Ellen's contractions. 'It'll be some time, yet.' He returned periodically over the following few hours to check on her.

As the contractions came and went, Sally comforted her through the pain. Dave sat patiently in the waiting room, reflecting on the births of his own children. Nothing much had changed – men were still not allowed in the labour ward.

Finally, the contractions seemed to be coming all at once. It was time. Bluey's mother looked into Ellen's lovely face, now contorted in pain. An assertive nursing sister politely ushered Sally towards the door while the young doctor attended to Ellen. 'I'll call you when the baby's here,' she assured Sally.

'But I've seen it all before, Sister,' Sally replied, desperately wanting to witness the birth.

'Sorry, hospital policy,' she said, with a firm hand on Sally's back as she propelled her through the door.

After a few more contractions, and much encouragement by the doctor and nurse to bear down, the little baby's head appeared, followed by the body and legs.

'A healthy boy,' the doctor confirmed, as he cut the umbilical cord. He handed the crying baby to the sister, who wrapped the infant and placed him in his mother's arms. Enraptured, Ellen gazed at her baby's dear little face, his eyes still tightly closed. She felt a surge of love wash over her, swelling her heart to burst. Tears welled up in her eyes.

If only Bluey was here. Oh, my darling! Please be alive. Please come home to me and our son.

'You can come in now,' the sister beckoned to Sally and Dave, as she and the doctor left the room. Slowly, Sally approached Ellen and the little bundle she now lovingly held in her arms. Ellen looked up at Sally, smiling through her tears of joy. 'He's got red hair, just like his father.'

After the long months of denial, grief finally overcame Sally O'Donnell. She flopped into a visitors' chair beside the bed and poured out her heart. 'He won't ever see him,' she sobbed bitterly, laying her head on the bed. 'He won't ever see him.' Dave stroked his wife's back.

'Don't give up, please, Sally. I'm not going to.'

Sally sat up and wiped her eyes. She looked at this young woman and her little son and felt terrible for spoiling her special day. 'I'm sorry, love. Can I hold him?'

Ellen held out the infant. 'He's got your hair, too, you know.'

She looked down at the scrunched-up little face. 'Yes, young man,' she cooed. 'I bet they'll call you Bluey too.'

'What are you going to call him, Ellen?' Dave looked at his newborn grandson with pride.

Ellen caught his eye and held it, and with a tremulous smile, answered, 'David Liam O'Donnell. What else?'

For the remainder of the day, Bluey was never far from her thoughts.

Will our son ever see his father?

She brushed the negative thoughts away and focused on the joy he would feel when he met his beautiful son.

Dave and Sally returned the following night to find Ellen had been moved into a bright, airy maternity ward which she shared with four other nursing mothers. That morning she'd had two other visitors. Her mother Joan was the first to enter, kissing her daughter as she reached the bed. Joan was followed by her husband Eric who Ellen had not seen since Kevin's funeral.

'Dad!'

'Hello, Ellen. It's lovely to see you,' he said warmly.

'I'm glad to see you, Dad.'

Eric could see she meant it. Tears materialised in her eyes, and she brushed them away with a sleeve of her nightie.

'Any word about Bluey?' he asked.

'No. There's no more news.' She looked suddenly pale. 'Missing is all they tell us.'

'I'm sorry.' He took her hand and gently squeezed it. 'He's a gutsy young bugger. He'll survive.'

'I've been praying for that.'

'And so have I,' her father responded softly.

Joan changed the subject. 'I wrote and told Pam. She can't wait to see the baby.' Joan looked around the room expectantly. 'Nor can I. Where is he, pet?'

'In the nursery.' Ellen's face lit up. 'You can see him when you leave. He's beautiful.'

'A grandson! A male in the Sommers family at last,' Eric said and chuckled. Ellen couldn't recall the last time she'd heard her father laugh. Things were good, now. She knew she didn't have to worry about her mother any more. They would be okay.

When her parents finally said their goodbyes, Ellen lay back and thought about the great change that had taken place in her father. He now spoke softly and his eyes seemed to light up every time he looked at her. The transformation was so remarkable, it seemed like a miracle.

The next evening, after Dave and Sally had visited in the afternoon, her mother came to see her alone.

'Dad has changed so much, Mum.'

'Yes, he has.' Joan looked away.

'Is anything wrong?'

'Sorry, pet, I didn't really want to say anything at this time, but you have a right to know.'

'Tell me,' Ellen said quietly.

'Dad has a lump in his stomach.' Joan's voice cracked. 'The silly bugger won't do anything about it. There's blood every time he goes to the toilet and I know he brings up blood as well.'

'Has he seen a doctor?' Ellen felt her mouth go dry.

'He won't.'

'Oh, Mum,' she said helplessly. 'It sounds so serious.'

Joan played with her wedding ring for a moment as memories came flooding back. 'You know, Ellen, he was very handsome when I first met him, and he was nice, too. I loved him so much. I still do. It's hard to explain. He's a good provider, and he always worked hard – worked as hard as he drank.'

'I was always so scared of him . . .'

'Yes, I know, pet.' Joan sighed. 'But he's changed so much now. Since he became ill he can't drink. He goes to Mass three or four times a week. And he talks to the priest a lot as well. He was tickled pink that you forgave him and you should have seen the look on his face when he set eyes on young David.'

'I'm really glad.' Ellen hugged her mother.

'So am I,' said Joan. 'And I want you to know what a great relief it is for me to know that you and the baby are well cared for.'

Six days after the baby's birth, Ellen was discharged from hospital. On entering the familiar surroundings of the homestead, Ellen turned to Sally. 'It's good to be home,' she whispered, careful not to wake the sleeping infant in her arms.

'It's good to have you back,' Sally patted the younger woman's arm.

Ellen carried the baby to the sleep-out that had been converted into a nursery, and placed him in a bassinet.

'There you are, little one,' she cooed. 'Have a good sleep. Dear God,' she whispered, 'please let his father get to see him.'

Chapter 16

Weeks turned into months, and the Japanese soldiers' garden blossomed under Bluey's care. Due to his attention and knowledge, the bay gelding's coat also gleamed. The commandant nodded with satisfaction each morning as he approached the newly groomed and saddled animal.

At first, the night jungle noises had unnerved Bluey – the screeching of a monkey or the roar of a tiger – but he'd soon become used to these. Then one night he came out of his sleep with a start. A high-pitched human scream had awoken him. Growling sounds and other cries followed. Then there was silence.

'Did you hear that?' Digger whispered beside him.

'Yeah. I think some poor bastard copped it.'

In the morning, there was no six a.m. whistle for morning assembly. Looking out the hut door, they could see Kyoshi and other soldiers outside the perimeter fence. There was much arm waving and discussion. Later, as they were marched to the airstrip site, the soldiers' eyes darted in every direction, and their rifles were held at the ready. During the day, Roger was able to glean what had transpired the previous night. Only one Japanese guard had been assigned to patrol the perimeter fence. He had been attacked and eaten by a tiger. Soldiers would now conduct night patrols in pairs.

Finding more food was a constant problem for the prisoners, but fortunately, Scrounger was living up to his reputation. His rat traps had proved most effective. The rodents had white flesh, even whiter than rabbit pieces, and just a small amount of the meat added to their meal left the prisoners feeling a bit fuller. Scrounger also often returned to the camp with some item of food hidden on his person, or on someone else's. To the amazement of the other prisoners, he was somehow able to charm the Japanese soldiers who, with the exception of Sergeant Kyoshi, gave him the latitude they denied the others. He only had to indicate that he needed to relieve himself and the guards waved him towards the jungle. It was on these occasions that he set his traps. Using thick twine he'd found in the back of a Japanese truck, he laid a loop on the ground and tied the remaining twine to a bent sapling, secured by a trip wire. The unsuspecting animal, stepping into the loop, set off the trip wire, releasing the sapling and the noose tightened around its leg. On his next visit he would use a burlap bag to hide his quarry. Before leaving the work site, he'd retrieve the bag and hide it anywhere he could, usually under their work tools. The guards, becoming increasingly lax as time wore on, never carried out any inspection – they knew the prisoners were unlikely to try and escape, and anyway, in their weakened state they wouldn't get far. As a consequence of Scrounger's ingenuity, once or sometimes twice a week, an item of Sumatran fauna appeared on the menu to supplement the prisoners' meagre diet – monkeys, large lizards and native rodents. On one occasion, he even trapped a small tapir.

The prisoners' secret garden also thrived in the clearing, but unfortunately, Bluey was unable to provide any protection against the insects that infested the plot. When the time finally arrived for harvesting the results of his work, he pondered how he could possibly get the produce into camp without being detected. For most of the time he was followed around by Little Mudguts, and although the small man was good natured, Bluey knew he would not turn a blind eye to food smuggling. If Bluey was caught, Little Mudguts would certainly be punished too. Stroking his ginger beard, Bluey arrived at the only possible solution. He would have to get the food into the compound by sneaking out at night – a dangerous undertaking. As soon as he noticed the first signs of ripening in the hidden garden, Bluey knew the pawpaws and bananas would have to be gathered quickly or they would rot or be spoiled by birds and insects. Fortunately, the harvest coincided with a low point in the lunar cycle. He waited until the moon was a narrow crescent, and for two nights he monitored the guards' nightly patrol of the perimeter fence. He judged the interval between rounds to be just enough time to collect the fruit and carry it back to the safety of the huts.

Although it was pitch black when he slipped outside the hut with Roger and Skeetah, Bluey still felt anxious. Digger and Scrounger had stayed behind because they were too big. On hands and knees, the trio covered the thirty or so yards to the side fence of the compound. By the time they reached the fence, they were dripping with perspiration. The sound of their short, careful gasps seemed intolerably loud. Leaving Roger behind the inside perimeter, Bluey and Skeetah dug their way under the first, and then the second barbed-wire fences, using sharpened saplings that Scrounger had specially fashioned for the purpose. Once safely on the outside, Bluey whispered, 'Follow me, cobber,' and began walking towards the stream. Although he'd taken this trail countless times, Bluey became a little disoriented in the darkness.

Everything's so different at night.

Eventually, he and Skeetah were across the stream and through the thick jungle undergrowth that provided cover for the prisoners' small garden. Once in the clearing, Bluey used his sapper's knife to hurriedly cut the ripening pawpaws. He carefully placed the treasure in a burlap bag and handed it to Skeetah. Just as he cut a huge bunch of ripening bananas, a loud roar froze him to the spot.

'Let's get out of here,' Bluey whispered.

'I'm with you, mate,' whispered a terrified Skeetah. Struggling under the weight of their load, they made their way back across the stream, around the rice paddies and back to the fence where Roger waited nervously. With his breath coming in short gasps from the exertion, Bluey whispered through the furrow, 'Quick! We have to make the passage bigger for the bananas.'

Just as Skeetah and Roger set about it, they heard the sound of voices interspersed with laughter. The guards were still some distance away and didn't seem to have noticed anything. As quietly as possible, the men worked at a furious pace to enlarge the narrow openings. Once the trio and their loot were safely under both fences, they lay motionless, barely daring to breathe in the darkness. The two Japanese guards were still talking and laughing as they strolled by, their faces illuminated by the kerosene lanterns they carried. The guards were oblivious to the three prisoners lying a mere six feet from them. Once it was safe, the small trenches to the outside were carefully refilled and camouflaged. 'Bloody Japs! Blind, deaf and stupid,' Skeetah whispered as they struggled with the load.

Roger shook his head but didn't make a comment.

Stupid they are not, my friend.

Back inside Bluey's hut, the provisions were shared equally between the three huts. With five large pawpaws, there was just sufficient for a small slice each. The large bunch of bananas was not quite ripe enough for eating, so it was temporarily stashed. Three nights later, the bananas were ripe and each man was allocated one and a half. Bluey was amazed at how just that small quantity of fruit improved the prisoners' morale.

I'd forgotten what it's like to enjoy eating.

Most days, Bluey was able to hide a handful of the horse's oats in his clothing, adding it to one of their cooking pots when he returned. Sometimes, hungry and tired, he was tempted not to share the oats, but his conscience would not allow it. Even though it was a small amount, he knew it would help.

If Scrounger can share everything he finds, I can too.

When left unguarded, Bluey would also strip a leaf or two from the cabbage-like plants, quickly stuffing them in his mouth.

In spite of his best efforts, his body weight, and that of all the prisoners, continued to fall at an alarming rate. This also meant that their resistance to disease was very low.

Tired and malnourished men had no defence against the malaria that ravaged the camp. To counter the more adverse effects of the illness, Roger was able to use a local remedy with some positive results. One of the guards actually gave Scrounger some quinine, which he then gave to Skeetah when he fell victim to the dreaded fever. This generous gesture brought home to Bluey just how dependent they all were on each other. You did what you could for your mate, and he did what he could for you.

Two men in the end hut, one an English soldier, died from malaria as did another in Scrounger's hut. Dysentery was a constant companion, with almost every one of the inmates affected at one time or another. The poor quality of the drinking water and the unhygienic food preparation only made things worse. Bluey watch helplessly as his friend Digger slowly began to waste away. Like the others, he became gaunt, his cheeks sunken and his eyes hollow. His once solid frame was almost skeletal. A dark beard made him appear older. Bluey wondered about his own appearance, and was thankful they had no mirrors.

Most of the inmates also suffered from tropical sores, the decaying flesh emitting a terrible odour. There was no disinfectant to stop the spread of the germ. A recent Dutch arrival came up with a cure. He told Roger he had learned of a native remedy. Maggots were placed on the wound which was then bound with a cloth. The infected area was consumed by the larvae, leaving a clean sore. With nothing to lose, the treatment was tried. To their delight, the affected areas healed nicely. They marvelled that such a vilified form of life could play such a positive role in their health.

When it came time for each Japanese crop to be harvested, Bluey was ordered from the garden or paddy field. The Japanese soldiers preferred to carry out the work themselves to ensure that none of the produce was pilfered. Once that section of the garden was bare, Bluey was instructed to plant a new crop, with seedlings again provided by local villagers. After a bunch of bananas had been harvested, he removed the useless trunk to make way for the new sucker growing beside it. He then chopped the trunk up for mulch. Pawpaw trees produced bumper crops. He was provided with more pawpaw seeds to increase the number of trees. Thus the cycle continued, one month following another, with no end in sight.

When Bluey was struck down with a mild dose of malaria, he was still required to carry out his duties in the garden. At nights, Digger watched over him, wiping the sweat from his face and upper body with a cloth dipped in cool water. 'You'll get better, Blue,' his friend encouraged him.

'Tell me about Coolangatta,' Bluey asked through chattering teeth.

It was a subject close to Digger's heart. 'It's a beaut place, mate. Clean beach, good surf and nice people.'

'Do you live near the beach?'

'Not that far. Our house is on a hill. It's got a good view of the sea and the river.'

'Sounds nice.'

'Yeah.' Digger sighed.

When Digger was struck down with beri-beri, they didn't know what was wrong with him at first. He felt so weak he could barely rise from his bed. He suffered from nausea and severe cramps in his legs. His toes felt numb and he experienced a burning sensation in his feet.

'What's wrong with him?' a worried Bluey asked Roger after work.

'I'm not sure. I'll speak to one of the Dutch chaps who's lived out here for most of his life.' Roger was back in a few minutes. 'I'm afraid it's not good news. Hank thinks Digger has beri-beri.'

Bluey had heard of the condition, but knew little about it. 'What can we do?'

'Hank says beri-beri is caused by a lack of thiamine, an essential vitamin. Lack of it creates muscle weakness causing extreme fatigue. It is also life threatening.'

'Shit! What can we do?'

'He needs fruit, vegetables and meat.'

'That'd be bloody right! Everything we don't have.'

The next day when there were no guards around, Bluey took a risk and dug up a sweet potato which he hid in his clothing. That night he crept out of the camp to the secret garden where he knew a pawpaw was beginning to ripen. Digger was fed a portion of the sweet potato, the pawpaw, and was allocated a larger portion of the cooked rats. What was left would be fed to him over the next few days.

Bluey tended to him during the long nights, keeping him

company with stories of home. He told him about Kilkenny – the flock, shearing season, the horses and the wheat. A shaky voice responded, 'Never been on a horse.'

'Nothing to it, big fella.' Bluey wiped his friend's brow and the sweat from his dark beard. He spoke of his parents and about Ellen.

'I bet she's lovely,' Digger croaked.

'Yeah, she sure is.' He lifted a mug of water to his comrade's lips. 'What about you, Dig? You got a sheila?'

Taking a couple of swallows, Digger laid his head back. 'Nah, not really. Used to take a girl to the pictures, but it didn't work out. There's a girl two doors down I'd like to ask out, but I haven't had the guts yet.'

'Make sure you do when you get home, you silly bugger,' Bluey castigated him good-naturedly.

The Japanese soldiers allocated prisoners' rations by the number who worked each day. As there were always a few men who were too sick to work, this meant a cut in rations for everyone. Without Scrounger's traps and Bluey's secret garden there's no doubt many men would have starved to death. To the Japanese, illness, no matter how serious, was no excuse for not working. During the long hot tropical nights, Bluey would shiver feverishly in the darkness. Roger obtained some of the chalk-like substance the locals used for malaria and mixed it with water.

'Where do they get it?' Bluey asked from his mattress after he'd taken a drink of the potion.

'From the bark of a certain tree in the jungle,' the Englishman answered.

'Can you get more?' he asked anxiously.

'Yes. I know the species,' Roger reassured him.

The local medication, however, could not prevent the deaths of three more prisoners from malaria. Another two passed away from beri-beri. Five crude crosses marked their graves, joining other crosses in a rough area of ground just outside the perimeter fence. Initially, the deaths reduced the overall number of inmates in the camp, but only for a short time. Another ten internees arrived to take their place, among them a Dutch father and son. Roger Adams was particularly concerned for the seventeen-year-old youth, who soon gained the perverted attention of the Japanese sergeant. 'Look at the way that bastard looks at him,' the Englishman whispered to Bluey at morning assembly.

Two days later, while the working party cleared the undergrowth, Kyoshi suddenly beckoned the youngster to follow him into the jungle. Terrified, the teenager walked away from the group. Late that afternoon the prisoners returned to the camp to find the sergeant waiting for them – alone. Without a word being said, the boy's father knew at once what had happened. With a howl of anguish, the Dutchman threw himself at the sergeant. He was no match for his brutish Japanese keeper. Kyoshi's face seemed to shine with delight as he chopped again and again at the man's throat, before kicking his unconscious form on the ground. Roger, Digger and the other prisoners stood mute in horror. Kyoshi had beaten the poor man to death in front of the full company of soldiers and prisoners. Roger shuddered as he related the events to Bluey that night. Digger was strangely quiet.

'Watch your back, Bluey. If he gets the chance, old chap . . .' the Englishman's voice trailed off.

'I'm okay while I'm in the garden,' Bluey replied.

John Fitzpatrick, ill with malaria, muttered, 'I hope he gets his just deserts one day.' Malaria had ravaged his body and Scrounger and Skeetah had been trying to lift his spirits for days.

The morale of the inmates was at a low ebb. It wasn't only the lack of food, the constant illness and the back-breaking work, it was that the men could see no end to their hardship. No one knew what was happening in the outside world. Were the Japs still winning or had they been turned around? What about the Americans? The inmates felt hopeless, without a future. It was this sense of despair that became too much for John Fitzpatrick. Scrounger had called Roger to their hut to take a look at their ailing comrade. Bluey and Digger accompanied him.

Roger kneeled beside the professor. 'He's almost wasted away, poor chap. Dysentery on top of malaria – too much.'

That night, John died in his sleep, the first Australian to pass away. 'Poor bastard.' Skeetah was trying to come to terms with his friend's death. 'A good bloke. So bloody young.' This death, more than any other, shook Bluey and Digger to the core. It was hard not to reflect on their own fate – who would be next?

The months dragged on until one day, Bluey realised they'd been in camp for fifteen months. Roger did his best to boost their morale. The unflappable Englishman even arranged singing sessions at night and fashioned a set of crude playing cards from some cardboard. Unfortunately, most of the inmates were too exhausted or too apathetic to participate.

Each morning Bluey would bow to the major as he arrived for his daily ride. There was little conversation between the pair. One morning, however, the major turned to Bluey. 'Long time ago, Red Cross in Japan enquire about Australian prisoner.' He paused for a moment. 'I tell Red Cross I hold five and give name. This help your family, yes?'

'Thank you, sir.' Bluey kept his eyes on the ground. But once the major had ridden off, he smiled, his hopes soaring.

They'll know where I am! They'll know I'm alive!

Chapter 17

Little David was three months old when the news about Bluey finally came through. Ellen had just called Dave and Sally to the dinner table and was the first to spot the lights of the black coupé as it entered Kilkenny's front gate. With telegram in hand, Father Donovan ran from the vehicle to the front verandah where the family waited expectantly, their hearts fluttering. 'I pray it's good news,' he said breathlessly.

Dave ripped the wire open and began to read aloud. '"Red Cross advises Q72431 Spr O'Donnell held as Japanese Prisoner-of-War. Will advise if further information is received." He's alive!' he cried excitedly. 'He's alive!'

The news was almost too much to absorb. Ellen felt her heart begin a tap dance and her knees buckle. As she collapsed to the floor, she could hear Sally screeching with joy. Kneeling on the floor, arms across her chest, trying to catch her breath, trying to take in the wonderful, stupendous news, Ellen watched Sally and Dave hug each other and dance around in the porch light. Father Donovan was delighted and stood beaming at them all. It was far more gratifying being the bearer of good news. Helping Ellen to her feet, and giving her a hug for good measure, he said, 'We must all continue to pray for Bluey's safe return to our midst.'

'Yes, Father,' she beamed.

'Thank you!' Sally yelled after him as he walked to the car, before swinging back to the other pair, her eyes shining. 'I knew it! I just knew it!' She hooted with delight once more.

They made their way back to the dining table and the evening meal which was getting cold, but no one even noticed. Ellen hardly knew what to say. In her entire life she had never experienced such feelings of relief. 'I've prayed every day and often said the rosary for him.'

'I wish I'd known, young Ellen.' Dave seemed surprised. 'I would've said it with you. I haven't said it in such a long time.'

'Well, you two Micks had better teach it to me.' Sally looked from one to the other, chuckling. 'It seems to have worked doesn't it?'

Their laughter was broken by the sound of the baby who was due for his seven p.m. feed.

'Bring him out, Ellen, and let his grandfather nurse him,' Sally said with tearful happiness. 'Then we'll all celebrate.'

In her prayers that night, Ellen gave thanks before making one final request.

Dear Lord, please bring him safely back to us. Amen.

To be a single mother in a country town in 1943 was not a pleasant experience. Despite the liberalisation that had occurred with the war, there were still those who adopted a puritanical stance where unmarried mothers were concerned. Such people thought of single mothers as loose women to be scorned. Unfortunately, a number of those critics lived in the provincial town of Goondiwindi. Every fortnight, when she and Sally took baby David into town to visit the sisters from the Maternal and Child Welfare, she was keenly aware of the stares and whispers.

'Old biddies.' Sally glared back at the women, for it was only the women who were judging harshly. 'Don't take any notice of them.'

'I don't really,' Ellen answered quietly. 'But I can't help feeling a little embarrassed.'

'They rely on that, the old bags.' She spoke loudly so that the titterers could hear, and grinned when she heard the gasps of shock.

On her visits to town, Ellen occasionally encountered old schoolmates including Brenda, and Margaret Smith. Once, she also came face to face with a former classmate who could never be described as a friend – Helen Humphries. Helen now held an office position in her family's retail agricultural machinery agency and service centre. At first, Ellen thought the girl would walk right past. In fact, she hoped she would. But her hopes were soon dashed. The other girl's eyes widened in surprise when she recognised Ellen.

'Ellen. It's been a long time.' Helen scrutinised her. 'How are you?'

'I'm fine,' she replied politely, pleased that she'd regained her trim figure. She was dressed in her favourite outfit, a straight, dark-blue skirt and figure-hugging white shirt with short puff sleeves, an outfit that always drew admiring glances.

'And this is O'Donnell's kid, is it?' Helen looked down at the six-month-old infant with disdain.

'Yes, this is little David,' she answered proudly, ignoring Helen's look.

'Have you heard from him?'

'No. We've only just found out that he's a prisoner-of-war.'

'Pity he left you in such a predicament.' Her tone was slightly critical.

Ellen felt her colour rising. 'How was he to know? He was missing before I found out I was even pregnant!'

'Sorry. I didn't mean to upset you.' Helen said insincerely.

'You didn't.' Ellen replied, still miffed. 'Why isn't your brother in the services?'

Helen's complexion darkened. 'His is a protected occupation,' she answered indignantly. 'I thought you knew that. He tried to enlist, but they wouldn't take him.'

'Oh. I didn't know,' Ellen felt a twinge of guilt.

'Look, if you're in town again,' Helen said pleasantly, 'let me know and we'll have lunch together.'

Ellen didn't know what to say. The girl's change of heart was unexpected. 'That would be nice,' she lied. 'Well, I'd better get little David home. '

'Bye, Ellen. Take care of yourself.' On her return to work, Helen Humphries related details of her conversation with Ellen to her brother, Len. For the rest of the afternoon, Humphries sat at his desk, struggling to concentrate on work-related matters. His thoughts, however, were constantly drawn back to Ellen Sommers.

A great sort like that. What a bloody waste.

He was fully aware that a faithful person like Ellen would never consider him, not while her man was in a prisoner-of-war camp. He would have to bide his time and wait. It was a good thing, he thought smugly, that she believed he had tried to enlist. Like his sister, she had fallen for that bullshit, hook, line and sinker.

Len Humphries had been a spoiled, pampered child. His father had hoped for many more children, but had been blessed with only two, so he lavished his only son with attention. Even his sister, Helen, who should have at least experienced some degree of jealousy, ran after him from an early age, catering to his every whim. It was little wonder, then, that Len grew up with an unrealistic perception of himself.

His father, Eden, owned the town's largest retail agricultural equipment business, and had built it up from virtually nothing. As a prominent businessman, he maintained a high profile in Goondiwindi's social set. Unlike the majority of Goondiwindi's mainly working-class residents, the Humphries family lived in a plush two-storey brick house near the centre of town.

Len couldn't help feeling cheated when the only woman he'd ever really fancied ended up with someone else, that someone else being Bluey O'Donnell, his old foe from childhood. He was not used to losing out to anyone. To Len, Ellen Sommers was the perfect woman – beautiful, intelligent and with plenty of personality. In fact, when he really thought about it, there wasn't a single thing about her that he didn't like. He finally realised, with a shock, that as much as he could love anyone, he loved her. The fact she belonged to O'Donnell only intensified the attraction he felt. She was the forbidden fruit.

Many local girls considered Len Humphries to be a good catch. He was tall, well built and pleasant looking, and always dressed in the most modern outfits – in fact he was the first man in town to own a striped Windsor double-breasted suit with its fashionable sloping lapels. But there was one other important factor that made him attractive to certain women. He would at some time in the future inherit a thriving business worth an enormous sum of money. Len had courted a few of the local girls, one or two of them quite lovely, but there was never anything serious in the relationship, much to their disappointment. At one stage, he'd even had a girlfriend in Warwick – he'd met her at a dance there. She was the niece of the mayor, and for a while he seemed smitten, but the relationship soon fizzled out. No girl could match the immense attraction he felt for Ellen Sommers.

At odd times he'd seen Ellen from a distance in town, but she was always with someone, and it was too tricky to approach her. Now that O'Donnell was in a Japanese prisoner-of-war camp, he knew things had changed.

Chances are the little shit won't survive. Then I'll make my move.

Ellen hadn't said anything to the O'Donnells, but her parents were insisting that baby David be baptised as soon as possible, and raised the subject every time she and the baby visited. Most recently, they'd asked her at Pam and Barry's wedding, which had been held at St Mary's Catholic Church two weeks previously. Ellen had been the only bridesmaid.

When the baby was eight months of age, Ellen decided it was time to broach the subject.

'I think we should have him baptised,' she told Sally and Dave one evening.

'Hmm', Sally said quietly. 'I wondered when this would come up. He'll be baptised a Catholic?'

'Do you have any objection?' Ellen raised her eyebrows.

'Not really,' Sally replied. 'Apart from the fact that his father's not involved in the decision.'

'I can't wait any longer,' Ellen pleaded. She couldn't tell Sally that the real reason was her own mother's anxiety. Like all good Catholic grandmothers, Joan believed that if a child died before being baptised, it could not enter heaven.

Dave looked at Sally. 'There'd be no harm in baptising the little fella.'

'No, I suppose not,' Sally sighed, not wanting to cause a rift. 'And another Catholic in the family isn't going to make that much difference, is it?' She grinned mischievously. 'Excuse my ignorance, but does it matter that his parents aren't married?'

Dave interrupted. 'Oh, the priest will shake his head, tut, tut and carry on a bit. And Ellen'll have to go to confession and be reconciled back to the church, but when it all boils down, he'll baptise young David.'

'Right then,' Sally said. 'Who will you ask to be his godparents?'

'I'll ask my sister to be godmother, but the godfather should come from your side of the family. Who do you want?'

'We don't have anyone around here,' she said despondently.

'What about his grandfather?' Ellen smiled and kissed Dave on the cheek. 'Couldn't be a better choice.'

When she went to see Father Donovan, Ellen provided him with a full and candid explanation of how she became a single parent. He knew that Bluey was a prisoner-of-war, having hand-delivered the telegrams to the family, and was very understanding. She confessed her sins and was accordingly reconciled.

'Is the father Catholic?' the priest asked.

'No, Father,' she admitted. 'He's Church of England.'

'Hmm,' he looked back at her thoughtfully. 'That's a bit of a problem.'

'With the baptism?' she asked, bewildered.

'No. Later, child. When he gets home and you're married.' He checked his notes. 'Now, let me see. Are the godparents Catholic?'

'Yes.'

'No problem there.' He rose from his seat. 'Bring the little fellow to seven a.m. Mass next Sunday and we'll baptise him then. No doubt your mother and father will be there? As poorly as he is, I don't think Eric will miss his grandson's baptism.'

'Yes, I'm sure they'll be there,' she answered, her thoughts once again turning to her father, who had become a shadow of his former self. It was pitiful to watch him now. At Pam's wedding his pallor had been a sickly grey and he rarely left his chair. Eric's condition had reached a stage where he was in chronic pain, which restricted his capacity to move around. The agony could not, would not, deter him from holding his beloved grandson. When Ellen and baby visited the workers' cottage, he would sit in his favourite chair, intently watching David crawl around the floor. After taking more of the pain-killers the doctor had prescribed, the torment would finally subside to a bearable level. He would then call on Ellen to hand the infant to him.

'He's very heavy, Dad.' The little baby was very lively, and she was anxious he didn't cause her father more pain.

'I don't care, Ellen,' he assured her. 'I just want to hold him for a while.'

For the baptism, she thought her young son would look particularly adorable in the little white brocade outfit Sally had made for the occasion.

But what shall I wear?

The bridesmaid's dress she'd worn at Pam's wedding had been borrowed from her sister's friend.

'Why don't you buy yourself a new outfit?' Sally suggested. 'We'll pool some of our ration coupons and get something for you.'

For once, Ellen didn't argue. It had been years since she'd bought a new dress. 'Oh, thank you, Sal.'

Excitedly going though the outfits on display at the local drapery, she felt like a schoolgirl on her first date. She finally decided on a dark-grey, light-woollen dress with long sleeves and padded shoulders. To go with the dress, Sally and Dave bought her a black leather bag and matching kid gloves. These were luxurious accessories that she would never have considered buying for herself. She was overcome by their generosity.

On the following Sunday morning, both sets of grandparents

beamed with pride in front of the town's Catholic congregation. As the priest splashed holy water on the baby's forehead, young David O'Donnell let out a full cry of defiance over what was taking place against his will. Ellen looked very smart in her new outfit – Sally had used bobby pins to set Ellen's hair. Uncle Mick and Aunty Pat were also there to celebrate the occasion. After the service, and on the pathway just outside the double doorway leading into the church, Eric Sommers came face to face with Dave O'Donnell. They hadn't spoken a word to each other since their altercation a few years earlier. So much water had flowed under the bridge since then. Bluey's father looked into the ashen face of the tall, emaciated Englishman and extended his hand.

'I pray for Bluey every day, Dave.' Eric took the outstretched hand in a firm grip.

'Thank you, Eric. We appreciate that.'

One week after the christening, Ellen's father's suffering came to an end. Pam travelled from Brisbane for the funeral and stayed with her mother while Uncle Mick took charge of the arrangements. After such a long and painful illness, it was more a relief to everyone when he passed away. The tears had already been shed.

Because Pam was living on her own in the city, Ellen's mother made a surprise decision to return to Brisbane to live with her. The meatworks management had been supportive during Eric's illness, but now they required the cottage the Sommers family had lived in for all those years. With the war, accommodation was at a premium in the country centre as it was everywhere. Joan would live with her eldest daughter, who was a shift worker in an arms factory down there. As Barry was at sea for an indefinite period, she knew she could be a help to Pam, and although she would miss Ellen and her treasured grandson, she felt her other daughter needed her more.

'Pam and I will write every week,' Joan called from the window of the train.

Ellen's eyes filled with tears as the steam engine and carriages pulled away from the platform. Her mother had been the rock in their family and now she was going. Ellen would miss her.

With her mother now in Brisbane, Ellen took to visiting Aunty Pat more frequently than she had in the past. On her visits to town, she usually popped in to the butcher shop to buy some beef from Uncle Mick and Rodney. If the two men weren't busy, they'd chat for a few minutes and always seemed pleased to see her. Ellen had a close bond with Aunty Pat, and the older woman adored seeing young David. Since Kevin's death, her aunt had never been the same. Her once lively, twinkling eyes seemed dull and full of pain. The loss of her eldest son had dealt her a mortal blow. Lately, however, a noticeable change had come over her. On Ellen's last visit, as she lifted a cup of tea to her lips, Aunty Pat said in a quiet voice, 'Kevin is with our Lord, Ellen. I know that.'

'Yes, of course he is, Aunty,' she replied.

'He visits me, you know.' A faraway expression filled her eyes. 'When I wake up at night, I see his shadow at the bottom of my bed. I know it's him. Mick says I'm just imagining it, but I know it's him.' Her face lit up. 'I can feel his love.' She paused for a moment. 'You believe me, don't you?'

Seeing the paradisiacal glow suffusing her Aunt's face, Ellen could not help but believe her. 'Yes, Aunty. I do.'

It was almost the end of October and not one sheep had been shorn at Kilkenny. Because of the labour shortage, the family were permitted to assist with shearing the flock, something unheard of in Australia's industrial past. Under the wartime manpower legislation, the Australian Workers Union, which covered shearers, was in no position to argue.

Ellen had often watched experienced shearers – they seemed to remove a fleece with consummate ease. Now she had to learn to master the difficult and back-breaking task herself. Dave showed her how to hold the clippers when cutting or combing.

'Dump the animal in as small a space as possible,' he instructed, 'control her, reach for the shears, pull the starter cord and you're away, lass. I'll show you.'

He quickly removed a large ewe from the pen and demonstrated, removing the fleece in one piece.

It looks so simple.

He selected another ewe and held her. 'Remember, open up the belly first.'

Dave held the animal while Ellen attempted to remove the fleece. It fell into several pieces.

'Sorry,' she said, crestfallen.

''Tis all right, Ellen. Just remember. Keep her small and under control. Don't worry. You'll learn.'

Dave went on to tell her about the role of the rouseabout or 'picker-upper', whose task it was to spread the fleece out on a table for the wool-classer to inspect and grade. He grinned when he mentioned that the wool-classer earned more than the shearers, who were paid on the number of sheep they had shorn. He told her that after grading, the classer placed each fleece in its respective bin. The wool was then ready to be pressed into bales, a task normally carried out by hand.

'Kilkenny produces fine-grade wool, Ellen. Our yarn count is on a par with anyone's in the game.'

'Yarn count?'

'Ah, let me see.' Dave paused, trying to think how to put it into layman's language. 'The yarn or spinning count describes the number of hanks of yarn that can be spun from a pound of wool. The more hanks that can be spun, the finer the wool.'

Not really much the wiser, Ellen muttered, 'I see.'

She was surprised to learn that shearers were the responsibility of the shearing contractor, not the property owner. The contractor also supplied the cook. Dave said that just before the start of shearing season, many property owners frequented the stock and station agents in an attempt to pre-empt the likely price they might receive for their wool. At the same time, the buyers sought to obtain the cheapest bales.

After Sally took her turn at shearing practice, Dave was confident enough to let them work. The two women tentatively took their places alongside the older shearers, who grinned knowingly at each other. Ellen entered the pen and reached down to take hold of a ewe under its front legs. Standing upright, she backed through the swinging door and dragged the sheep to her stand.

She held the squirming animal firmly between her knees and began at the belly as instructed.

After shearing just three sheep, Ellen was a lather of sweat. She wondered how her already aching body would stand up to a full day of this. The work was just so physically demanding. To further complicate matters, Ellen also had a two-year-old son to contend with. She had to keep one eye on him as he played with his toys in his playpen, she and Sally taking turns to attend to him when he became bored and started crying. The youngster was none too happy being restricted to the small pen his grandfather had constructed in the shearing shed. The toddler was used to having the free run of the house, as well as the backyard.

On that first, long day, Ellen managed to shear only forty-six sheep. She could not believe that one particular shearer, who looked old enough to be her grandfather, was able to shear 238 sheep during the same period. Nevertheless, she was extremely proud that all but two of her fleeces were removed in one piece. As the days wore on, Ellen became more proficient, and finally, on the last day, was able to shear eighty sheep.

After shearing was complete, and the contractor and his three offsiders had classed and baled the wool, Ellen breathed a sigh of relief. She stood before her wardrobe mirror, dressed only in bra and panties, and could not help but notice how trim and honed her body now looked. She thought she must have lost a full stone in weight due to the arduous work associated with the task.

They certainly earn their money!

Chapter 18

It was March 1944, and still the prisoners had no idea how the war was progressing. The Japanese were the only ones with any outside knowledge and naturally only promoted their own cause. Sergeant Kyoshi spoke of many Japanese victories, pouring scorn on America, Australia and its allies. 'We wait for American and Australian soldier. We have grave waiting,' he said one morning, strutting in front of the assembled prisoners.

That night, Roger and the Australians tried to analyse the situation. 'Does that mean they're coming?' Digger asked.

'He's all piss and wind,' Skeetah chimed in.

'Frankly, I don't think he knows much more than we do,' said Roger. 'I suspect he's just trying to shake us up, although one can never be sure.'

Bluey looked around the group. 'Haven't seen any Jap planes for ages.'

'And there don't seem to be as many of the little yellow bastards around the place,' Scrounger observed.

'That's right,' replied Roger. 'So chins up, chaps.'

By this time, Bluey had doubled the size of the original Japanese garden, and had built another rice paddy. Collecting fertiliser from the privies had become an everyday part of his activities, and his hardened stomach no longer turned at the disgusting odour. Although food production had greatly increased, thanks to Bluey's labours, the amount of food allocated to each prisoner was still severely rationed. They were, in essence, starving – becoming weaker and weaker with each bout of illness.

In mid-1944, the camp was hit with a new strain of malaria. The fever was so debilitating, many inmates were unable to rise from their straw mattresses for assembly. Even the Japanese guards, who usually entered the huts to beat the men who could no longer work, realised they were wasting their time.

It was obvious that the Japanese major and his subordinates were under pressure to complete the airfield, and because so many prisoners had died or were ill, the major reluctantly agreed to temporarily assign Bluey to help with the work. Sergeant Kyoshi smiled crookedly as he spoke to the young Australian at morning assembly. 'Today, you go with other prisoner to work.' His lips curled contemptuously.

'Watch yourself,' Scrounger whispered.

Bluey marched out of the camp with the others, looking longingly towards the horse's enclosure and the vegetable garden. Kyoshi accompanied the six guards. The other prisoners knew this was unusual – he rarely visited the work site, preferring to remain in camp.

After a twenty-minute march through the jungle, the prisoners arrived at the airstrip. It had taken them nearly eighteen months to carve the area out of the jungle. Using only the crudest of tools, they had cut down vegetation and removed every stump by hand, then used shovels and handcarts to gather and spread the fill to level the strip. The prisoners had made so many trips to the quarry that they'd created a deep pathway.

Bluey and Digger were assigned to one of the heavy concrete rollers that compressed the fine gravel into the surface. It took all their will and a Herculean effort to drag the heavy roller backwards and forwards over the long, open area.

After about two hours, the Japanese guards called for a drink break. They had learnt from experience that the workers needed water, otherwise too many of them collapsed and were of no further use for the remainder of the day. Under pressure to meet their completion deadline, the guards had no choice.

As soon as the men were assembled under the canopy of a large tree, Sergeant Kyoshi pointed to Bluey, who had just taken a sip from a canteen. 'You come, now.' His eyes narrowed.

Bluey looked towards Roger, Scrounger and Skeetah, who regarded him with pity. Digger stood up, but the sergeant waved him back, and barked orders at his men who pointed their rifles at the Australians. 'Not you!' he shouted. 'Him!' He pointed the swagger stick at Bluey.

With the blood pounding in his ears, and his heart like a lead weight in his chest, Bluey shuffled towards his nemesis, who pointed with his swagger stick and shoved Bluey along the pathway. Striding along the path, the Japanese man used the stick to poke Bluey in the back. The Australian looked for some avenue of escape through the thick undergrowth, but none appeared.

He knew it would be virtually impossible for him to outrun the strong, fit man behind him.

But I've got to do something!

'I tell you for long time,' Kyoshi taunted. 'Time come, now. You mine at last.'

Bluey's mind raced.

What the hell can I do?

He clenched his teeth, adamant about one thing. He would put up some sort of a fight. A picture of his Irish father came to mind. Dave had once told him, 'It doesn't matter how big they are, son, they can be beaten.'

But this bloke is so strong and healthy.

The pathway led to a small clearing, and the sergeant's command brought him to a halt. 'Stop!' Bluey turned to face his captor. 'I have you now.' Kyoshi placed the swagger stick on the ground beside him.

Despite his life being in grave danger, Bluey could not help but smile as he framed an appropriate response.

'That's what you think, you greasy Jap!' Bluey's eyes flashed fire. He raised his fists and waited, his thin face a picture of grim determination.

Sergeant Kyoshi's expression changed to one of unbridled fury. He removed his shirt, exposing his powerfully built body. 'Now you die slowly,' he growled.

Bluey felt suddenly cold. The fear chilled his spine, but he knew he must keep alert. As the sergeant stepped forward, Bluey could see the big man was light on his feet, like a fighter. Kyoshi crouched as the two opponents circled each other.

'You like small weed,' he scoffed. 'Easy kill.'

'You can try, Tojo,' he replied defiantly, maintaining his fighter's stance.

The use of the Japanese supreme commander's name in such an insulting fashion was too much for Sergeant Kyoshi, who lost control. He charged at Bluey, who quickly sidestepped the onslaught, at the same time delivering hard left and right rips to his opponent's midriff. The blows, however, were ineffectual.

A surprised Kyoshi stopped for a moment to take stock of his smaller adversary. 'I see you fight good. But you see, jujitsu win. You now die.' His face a mask of control, he approached slowly, every step setting off alarm bells in Bluey's mind. When he was close enough, he attempted to grab at Bluey, who dodged his grasp and hit the big man twice in the stomach. He quickly followed with lefts and rights to his face. However, in delivering the blows, he had moved in too close. Kyoshi quickly snaked out a hand, took Bluey's right arm in a vice-like grip and threw him heavily to the ground, kicking him repeatedly.

Gotta . . . get . . . up.

The Japanese sergeant stopped, allowing Bluey to get to his feet. 'You need suffer more.'

The young Australian summoned all of his faculties and remaining strength. He raised his fists and was able to land a few hard blows to the large man's midriff and face, but Kyoshi was unharmed by the attack. As if swatting an annoying mosquito, the Japanese man retaliated with a rain of vicious chops to Bluey's neck, forcing him to the ground. Once down, the brute again laid into him with savage kicks.

This is it . . .

By the time Bluey staggered to his feet to await the next barrage, he barely had the strength to raise his fists. Disease and malnutrition had left him only a shadow of his former self, and with the added punishment inflicted by Kyoshi, he was weak and slow. The sergeant soon had a thick arm wrapped around Bluey's throat, squeezing hard. Bluey struggled violently, fighting for the sweet air that was now denied him. Just as black spots began to dance before his eyes, he heard the hated voice close to his ear. 'Not kill yet. I have you first.'

Kyoshi relaxed his grip just enough for Bluey to take a couple of breaths, before reapplying pressure. Above the sound of his own gasping, and Kyoshi grunting in his ear, Bluey heard a familiar voice from behind him yelling, 'Jap bastard!' Suddenly released, Bluey fell to the ground and looked up. Digger was standing behind Sergeant Kyoshi, his right arm circling the big Jap's throat. To prevent himself from being thrown over the sergeant's shoulders, Digger had wrapped his legs around Kyoshi's thighs. The wide-eyed sergeant panicked, his arms flailing as he tried to remove the grip that was gradually choking the life from his body. He reached back, trying to claw at his attacker's face, but Digger applied even more pressure until the big Jap's eyes bulged repulsively from their sockets. Retrieving Kyoshi's swagger stick, Bluey began striking at the exposed areas of the sergeant's body. Under Digger's weight, Kyoshi began to topple backwards. The two men hit the ground, Kyoshi on top of Digger. Pinned under the weight of the sergeant, Digger's grip slackened for one brief moment and Kyoshi was able to take a breath. When

Digger again attempted to take hold of his opponent's throat, the Japanese man anticipated the move and grabbed hold of Digger's arm, neutralising the attack. But Kyoshi could do nothing to prevent Bluey, who had straddled the two men, from pushing the cane swagger stick hard against his exposed throat. Digger also took a firm grip on both sides of the cane and pulled back with all his strength. Under other circumstances, Kyoshi may have eventually freed himself, but his two weaker opponents were also fighting for their lives – desperation had given them extra strength. He was therefore no match for the Australian pair who applied every ounce of strength to the gruesome task. When Kyoshi's body went limp, Bluey rose to his feet and rolled the big man off his friend. He looked down at his enemy. It sickened him to think that he had killed another human being, but it was kill or be killed.

He helped Digger to his feet and the two men embraced for a few moments. Bluey was choked with emotion. His friend had saved his life. 'I was done for if you hadn't come, Dig.'

'I knew what the bastard was gonna do.' Digger was still breathless. 'You're me mate. I couldn't leave you to him.'

'How'd you get away from the guards?'

'Skeetah and Scrounger started a mock fight with Roger. When the Japs went to break it up, I snuck away.'

'They'll be after us, mate.' Bluey swallowed. 'If they catch us, we're dead. You know that.'

'Yeah, but we probably would've died anyway,' Digger responded dryly. 'What now?'

'We'll head east,' he answered. 'Put as much distance as we

can between us and the camp. We're close to the coast, so that should help.'

'What about him?' Digger pointed to the dead sergeant. Ants had already begun to crawl over his face.

'Leave the bastard. We haven't got time to bury him.'

The two set off through the thick jungle towards the coast. After an hour of bush-bashing, they came upon a narrow track that they followed cautiously. Some time later, they reached a small, almost deserted village, which they managed to skirt without being seen. They heaved a sigh of relief when they first caught a glimpse of the shimmering blue water winking at them through the trees. In the shade of undergrowth edging the beach, the two rested to regain their strength. They had attained their first goal.

'What'll they do when they find him?' Digger was puffing.

'They'll be after our blood,' Bluey replied tightly. 'They'll probably use the locals to track us down.'

'By now they'll know I've gone. They're probably looking for us already.'

'It won't take them long to find Kyoshi's body. They only have to follow the track we took from the airstrip.'

'What are our chances?' Digger's open, good-natured face was tense.

'Not good. But like you said, we probably would've died anyway.'

'Yeah.' Digger nodded sadly.

After a short rest, they were on their way again. It would have been much easier walking along the beach, but because they were just south-east of Padang, Bluey thought it wiser to keep to the jungle. They struggled on until fatigue and approaching darkness forced them to stop beside a small stream. Here, they drank their fill. On the beach, they found coconuts which they quickly retrieved before again taking cover. It took some time, but by using sharp stones and their sappers' knives, they were at last able to reach the milk and flesh. That night they huddled together beside the trunk of a large tree while a tropical storm vented its fury.

In the early light of morning, Bluey awoke with a jolt to the sound of an engine. He shook his companion, placing an index finger to his own lips. 'Shh! Japs,' he whispered.

Bluey and Digger lay prone on the soggy ground, watching as the sleek patrol boat idled by.

'Lookin' for us?' Digger whispered back.

'I reckon so, mate. Seems to be headed in the same direction.'

'Do you think we should go back the other way?' Digger suggested uncertainly.

'There's no point. No. Let's keep going in this direction.'

Only when the vessel was safely in the distance did the two Australians get to their feet.

As they continued their journey in the scrub that lined the beach, they were again faced with large swamps. Exhaustion, and the need to travel fast, forced them to skirt the watery barriers by briefly making their way onto the sandy shoreline. Around midafternoon, they were fighting their way through undergrowth when they heard voices some distance ahead.

Bluey stood still, straining to hear. 'Japs,' he whispered.

'Shit! Where'd they come from?'

'That bloody boat probably dropped them up the coast a bit. We'll have to turn around. Let's go.'

They set off at a full run, the tropical pines tearing at their exposed skin. Fear drove them on, but not for long. After just a few minutes, the weakened pair collapsed, out of breath, their legs refusing to carry them any further, and took brief refuge under the cover of a melaleuca thicket. In the distance, they heard a triumphant shout. Realising the significance, Bluey's hair stood on end.

They've found our tracks!

'Let's go, Dig!'

The two again set off, back in the direction they had just travelled. They came to the first swamp, and were able to make their way across with little difficulty. The second, deeper lagoon, however, proved a much more difficult barrier. Because of his height, Digger was the first to fight his way to the other side. He quickly darted into the cover of thick undergrowth. As ill luck would have it, Bluey became trapped up to his knees in thick slippery mud. The more he struggled, the deeper he sank. On hearing voices approaching, he frantically tried to free himself. The mud sucked and gurgled hungrily around his legs, not willing to let him go. Then Digger was beside him, pulling at his legs and digging at the mud with his bare hands.

'I'm trapped, Dig!' Bluey looked around in despair. 'Get out while you can!'

'No!' Digger grunted as he scraped at the mud. 'I couldn't leave you, Blue. You're me mate.'

Just as Digger freed one leg, they heard a sharp command in Japanese. Turning slowly, they saw six rifles trained on them.

A local villager nodded triumphantly at a Japanese NCO who waved back in recognition of the man's good work.

Once Bluey and Digger had been pulled from the quagmire, the NCO radioed the patrol boat and the soldiers set upon the Australians with rifle butts. Bluey crumpled to the ground beside Digger.

The patrol boat had the escapees back in Padang in little under an hour. They were quickly transported back to camp in the rear of a truck and chained to the flagpole outside the main building. From the huts at the rear of the compound, Bluey and Digger could just make out a number of prisoners pointing in their direction. Chained to the flagpole for the remainder of the day and the entire night, the exhausted Australians had no protection from the tropical storm that hit late afternoon. Afterwards, sitting in the muddy slush at the base of the pole, Digger turned to his companion with a haunted expression. 'I'm real scared, Blue.'

Despite the rain, Bluey's mouth was dry. 'Me too, cobber.'

'Whaddaya think they'll do?'

'Probably kill us.'

'Bastards.'

They sat there like drowned rats through the long, uncomfortable night, trying to snatch a few snippets of sleep to give them the strength they would need to face the following day.

Early in the morning, an official Japanese vehicle entered the main gate, pulling to a halt in front of them. Bluey recognised the two officers who alighted; the colonel and lieutenant from Padang. Both ignored the two Australians. Half an hour later, Bluey and Digger were unchained and dragged up the stairs into a windowless room. A three-man Japanese disciplinary tribunal, headed by the colonel, awaited them. Major Harada occupied the chair on his right, the lieutenant the seat on his left.

The commandant was the first to speak. 'Prisoner now have trial.' Neither of the Australians responded. 'Prisoner murder Japanese soldier!' The colonel's voice was loud with indignation.

'It was self-defence,' Bluey spoke out.

'Prisoner not talk!' the colonel screamed.

Bluey felt the pain of a rifle butt on his back, but stood his ground. 'We're going to die anyway, so it doesn't matter.'

The senior officer began again. 'Prisoner murder Japanese soldier.'

'No,' Bluey responded defiantly. 'He tried to rape and murder me.'

The veins in the senior officer's neck bulged with fury. He seemed incredulous that such an accusation could be made against one of the men under his control. 'Honourable Japanese soldier not do such thing.'

'He's done it before. He was a murdering sadist.'

The Australians were once again set upon with rifle butts and fell to the floor doubled-over in agony. A brusque command brought the beating to a halt. Bluey and Digger lurched unsteadily to their feet, swaying. Forcing his eyes towards the table, Bluey saw the camp commandant whisper something to his senior officer. The colonel nodded then addressed the two prisoners in a much calmer voice. 'You try to escape like good soldier.' He paused, searching for the right words in his limited English. 'Japanese soldier respect, so give honourable death.'

Bluey and Digger looked at each other blankly.

The commandant explained. 'You beheaded.'

Bluey felt urine trickle down his leg. The room swam. He could barely breathe. He'd never experienced such terror. Digger had become crazed. It took four guards to subdue him. The doomed men were dragged to the centre of the compound where all the inmates had been assembled for the ceremony. Catching sight of his fellow prisoners waiting in the jungle heat, Bluey tried to fight his captors, but his efforts were futile. Roger wept quietly. Scrounger and Skeetah, their faces deathly pale, eyes wide in shock, shook their heads in disbelief, unable to comprehend the barbarity of what was about to take place.

The guards bound the men's wrists. The Japanese lieutenant approached and withdrew a long samurai sword from the scabbard at his side. The young officer looked into Digger's eyes, his face displaying the respect a formal execution ceremony required.

The big Australian struggled as the Japanese guards pushed him to his knees.

'Help me, Blue. Please!' he pleaded, his face a mask of terror.

Bluey fought against the arms holding him. The lieutenant lifted the sword and Digger screamed, 'No!'

Bluey watched, transfixed, as the blade rose above his friend's head. Surely this was just a nightmare.

Oh, God. Please help me wake up.

The lethal blade glinted as it reached its full height, then flashed on its way down. Bluey tried to scream as Digger's head rolled onto the ground, but no sound came. Digger's unseeing eyes seemed to look up at him accusingly. The headless body gave a spasmodic tremor, as if in protest, then lay still. The bloodied lieutenant turned to Bluey who was manhandled into a kneeling position. The blade was again lifted.

'Goodbye, Ellen,' he sobbed.

Bluey closed his eyes. Everything slowed. He felt a rush of air just in front of his hairline. Dazed, he opened his eyes. The major was addressing the prisoners. 'It serve Japanese interest for prisoner to work. But he be punished first.'

On a signal from the major, two guards hauled Bluey to his feet and dragged him towards an open doorway in the soldiers' barracks. The whole assembly of prisoners was ordered to follow. Bluey's wrists were roped to a heavy hook above head height on either side of the door jamb. A soldier ripped the shirt from his back. The major stepped forward, nodding in the direction of the lieutenant, who was handed a yard-long strip of rattan. 'Begin,' the commandant ordered.

The cane was lifted high and laid heavily across Bluey's exposed back, the pain forcing the air from his lungs. It was as if the rattan had been heated over a fire. Bluey gritted his teeth and stifled a sob. After the sixth blow, Bluey cried out in agony, and continued to scream each time the rattan came down on his bruised flesh. He passed out on the thirty-first strike, but the lieutenant did not stop until fifty. By this time, Bluey's back was stripped of its skin. Blood had begun flowing from the wounds, soaking his baggy shorts right to the hemline. His unconscious body was allowed to hang while the major addressed the prisoners. 'You try to escape. You see punishment,' he warned loudly.

Still unconscious, Bluey was dragged towards a disused water tank that had been placed in the centre of the compound. About six feet by four feet, the tank had been purposely placed for all the prisoners to see. Two soldiers lifted then pushed Bluey through an opening in the top, letting him fall to the bottom. As an afterthought, a water bottle was thrown in after him. The opening was closed and locked. The same two guards used nails and a hammer to puncture the rusty tank, thus allowing a small amount of fresh air to penetrate the metal structure.

'Use for all prisoner punishment,' the major loudly informed the inmates as the guards began pushing them towards their work duties.

Chapter 19

When Bluey finally came to, some two hours or so later, he tried to sit up in the darkness, but was forced onto his stomach by an excruciating pain. It felt like the whole of his back was on fire. Tears welled up in his eyes as he remembered that his best friend, Digger, was now dead.

Shit, where the bloody hell am I?

Feeling the edges of the tank, he discovered that he was virtually entombed, and that even the slightest movement delivered agonising pain. After groping around the floor of the tank, he was grateful to discover the water canteen and took a swig. He could tell it was still light outside from the tiny holes in the side of the tank, but he had no idea how long he had been incarcerated. Tears again trickled down his cheeks when he thought about his friend.

If he hadn't come back to help me, he might've got away.

Night fell and he was in total blackness. He tried to surrender to the sleep his battered body and mind so craved, but the pain made this impossible. Eventually, overwhelming fatigue finally forced him into a fitful sleep from which he awoke with a howl of anguish. 'Digger!' His voice thundered in the small enclosure. He'd dreamed of Digger's head on the ground, his eyes looking accusingly at Bluey and his mouth open and crying, 'Help me, Blue. Please!'

As Bluey lay on the metal floor of the tank shaking and sobbing, the tropical heavens opened. In no time the bottom of the rusty tank's interior was covered with slush. Bluey was frightened to close his eyes again, but exhaustion won. This time his sleep was reasonably sound, but he was awoken by Japanese voices nearby.

Although it was still predominantly black inside the tank, small slivers of light shone through the air-holes. Sucking in a breath against the pain, Bluey glued his right eye to one of the holes. He watched intently as the prisoners' working party filed slowly past. He saw Scrounger, Skeetah and then Roger, who bravely whispered words of encouragement: 'Keep your chin up, old chap. Don't give in.' Then they were gone.

As the sun rose, the humidity in the tank soared until Bluey could barely draw a breath. The salty perspiration entering the open wounds on his back made him groan in agony. He continued to sip from the water bottle. To obtain some relief from the constant pain, he lay flat on his stomach for most of the time. When this position became too uncomfortable, he rose to his knees, peering through the air-holes at the activity in the compound. At one stage, Little Mudguts strolled past the tank. He turned and shook his head sadly.

By midday, the heat and humidity were unbearable. Bluey

had finished the last drops of water from the canteen and began to slip in and out of consciousness. Night had fallen when he heard approaching footsteps. The small opening was unlocked. 'Give water container,' a voice commanded. It was the Japanese major.

Bluey handed up the water canteen. Another was thrown in and the opening again sealed.

One bottle of water for one day.

He had no idea how long he was to be entombed. If his incarceration was to be for an extended period, he knew he would not survive. To make matters worse, the only food he had eaten in two days was a few mouthfuls of coconut meat. He wondered if the Japanese soldiers also intended to use starvation as a further form of punishment.

That night he was visited by the same nightmare, Digger's decapitated head looking at him with accusing eyes that seemed to penetrate his soul. Bluey woke in a lather of sweat, trembling and sobbing, afraid to go back to sleep.

At midnight, he heard the sounds of quiet footsteps and the opening being unlocked. 'Sshh,' was all Bluey heard before a yam and a banana were lowered to him. The opening was again quickly locked. He had no idea who provided the treasured food. If it had been one of the prisoners, surely they would have spoken to him?

But they wouldn't have had access to the key to open the lock.

The mystery was solved the next day as Little Mudguts strolled by. He looked towards the tank and pointed to himself. As the small man headed towards the main gate, Bluey watched in wonderment.

They're not all bastards.

Bluey ate the hard, raw yam immediately. He was ravenous, but he saved the banana for evening. He would have to be sensible and conserve food and water if he was to survive this latest horror.

The time dragged on and predictably the interior of the metal tank developed into a furnace. Being careful to apportion small sips only, the precious water lasted him until well into the afternoon. Another container was dropped in at dusk. The terrible dream on his third night of torture was different. Digger's grotesque head informed him that he might have escaped if he had not come back to help him. Bluey awoke yelling and sobbing, as tropical rain made a deafening noise on the surface of the metal tank. Nauseated with guilt he was determined to stay awake, but his eyelids would not stay open. They drooped and finally shut. He woke at dawn, to find he was shaking uncontrollably.

Malaria again?

The symptoms, however, weren't the same as the dreaded malaria – it was the pain that was different. The surface of his injured back was burning with a new intensity. His teeth chattered and his body shivered – he almost felt cold in the steamy confines of the small tank. He no longer cared whether he drank from the water container or not. He drifted in and out of consciousness, delirious from the fever that consumed him. Hallucinating, he saw Digger's head on the floor of the tank accusing him of betrayal. There was no escape. How long he remained in the tank, he had no idea, but when he finally regained his senses, he was lying on his stomach on a cot in an unfamiliar room. The commandant and Little Mudguts were standing beside the narrow bed.

'Prisoner have infection from wound on back. Soldier here,' he pointed to the smaller man, 'he bathe wound. Much better after three day. You take sulphur and drink water. He bathe more. You work next day in garden and see to horse, you understand?'

Bluey opened his mouth to talk, but could only nod. The major left the room. Little Mudguts smiled reassuringly, pointing to Bluey's back as he reached for the hot, salty water. Bluey could have cried out in pain when the hot saline liquid was splashed onto his wounds. Instead, he gritted his teeth and made no sound. Little Mudguts completed the task, and carefully patted Bluey dry before leaving. He returned a few minutes later with a small bowl of rice and fish. Bluey had no idea how long it had been since he had eaten. He sat up and used his fingers to shovel the food into his mouth. After he placed the empty bowl on the small bedside table, the Japanese man gave him two large white tablets and a pitcher of cool water. Using his hands, he indicated to Bluey that he must drink all of the water. Little Mudguts then left Bluey to his own devices. He peered out the window to discover he was in a single room at the far end of the Japanese soldiers' quarters.

In the grey mist of dawn, Little Mudguts ushered him into the garden, pointing to the horse and to the plants. As the little fellow turned to go, Bluey mouthed the words, 'thank you', and bowed to the man, who grinned self-consciously before leaving him to his work. Alone once more, Bluey went to the horse who snuffled a welcome.

'G'day, fella,' he whispered affectionately. 'I missed ya.' He rubbed the horse's neck before going to the shed for the bay's morning feed. While the animal was eating, Bluey inspected the garden which had already deteriorated in the week of his absence. Suddenly he saw everything clearly – his ability to raise crops had saved his life. The soldiers needed someone who could provide a consistent supply of food. His knowledge of horses was most likely another advantage, but only a small one.

Maybe the major knew the truth about Kyoshi?

By the time the major strode up to the makeshift stable in his riding apparel, he found the animal groomed and saddled. Bluey bowed.

'Horse look good,' he said appreciatively. He pointed to the garden and frowned. 'You work now.'

Although he was still in a great deal of pain, Bluey set about chipping the weeds that had overtaken the garden. At times during the morning, agony forced him to stop and rest for fear he would faint. He was still extremely woozy from the infection. Occasionally, Little Mudguts returned to watch Bluey's progress. He seemed to be keeping a close eye on him.

That night, when Bluey returned to the hut, Roger Adams was standing out the back, talking to the other two Australians. His mouth fell open in amazement when he saw Bluey. 'Good to have you back, old boy!' he said emotionally. 'We didn't know what had happened. We even thought you might have . . .' Roger couldn't finish.

'I was just lucky.' Bluey was exhausted and in no mood to talk.

'It's none of my business, mate, but what the bloody hell happened?' Scrounger asked.

Bluey looked at the concern in his friends' gaunt faces, and knew he should tell them, but he couldn't bring himself to do it. He looked down at his feet.

Roger could see that Bluey was distressed. 'That's okay, old chap. Plenty of time to talk later. You rest up.'

Skeetah and Scrounger exchanged glances, but left Bluey alone.

With the despised Kyoshi now out of the picture, the tense atmosphere within the camp lessened considerably. None of the guards seemed to hold a grudge against Bluey, which led the prisoners to suspect that they were well aware of their sergeant's depraved behaviour.

Maybe they suffered under him?

Each night, Bluey lay awake, too terrified to go to sleep in case the nightmare came to haunt him. And each night, exhaustion would eventually overcome him and he would sleep poorly until he woke screaming when Digger's head cried out for help.

While life in the prison camp offered no privacy, Bluey's fellow comrades seemed unaware of his nightly torment. Most of them were simply too exhausted to be woken by his yells. There was always someone delirious with malaria or some other disease, jabbering and yelling out during the night.

As time passed, Bluey became increasingly withdrawn. 'He's losing it,' the Englishman muttered to Scrounger and Skeetah after he'd again failed to engage Bluey in conversation.

'Yeah,' Skeetah agreed. 'I dunno how to help him.'

If the men had not been so tired and malnourished themselves, they would have noticed something else – Bluey's eyes. They no longer looked at people, but rather through them. He possessed an almost eerie remoteness, as if he had retreated deep within himself. No one ever mentioned Digger when Bluey was around.

Almost everything Bluey did from that time on became a mere mechanical exercise. He would carry out his duties by day then endure the nightmare most nights – rarely obtaining an uninterrupted night's sleep. The poor sleep and constant stress undermined his ability to fight off disease and he suffered even more frequent bouts of malaria, while dysentery became an everyday part of his life.

Early in 1945, the prisoners began to notice subtle changes in the attitude of their captors. They no longer strutted about confidently, and often huddled in small groups, whispering to each other. There was an air of agitation about them. Another thing puzzled the prisoners. The airstrip, which they had laboured over for over two years, was virtually unused. Most of the air traffic over the island came from Allied planes. Prisoners would stand mesmerised as American aircraft flew overhead towards the town of Padang where the noise of exploding bombs could be clearly heard from the camp. The most able-bodied prisoners were marched to the coastal town to help clear debris from the streets. Bluey's role at the camp remained unchanged. He looked after the horse and maintained the Japanese garden and rice paddies.

On one cloudy morning, just as they were in the process of being mustered outside for the morning count, they heard rifle and machine-gun fire a short distance from the camp. The guards looked nervously towards the gate, but made no attempt to move the prisoners, who were later directed back to their quarters. Even Bluey was confined to the hut.

Around mid-morning, Roger approached him as he lay on the straw mattress. 'What do you think's up, Bluey?'

'Don't know.' He shrugged, staring blankly at the Englishman. He returned his gaze to the thatched ceiling of the dilapidated hut.

Close to midday, the inmates rushed from their huts when they heard an earth-shattering crash from the compound. What they saw would remain with them for the rest of their lives. The front gate of the camp had been flattened by a massive tank, and a platoon of American marines were marching in. The Japanese soldiers laid down their weapons and raised their hands, the marines herding them into a corner of the compound. In total shock, the prisoners could not quite believe what they were seeing. Then the realisation hit home. They were finally free. Most were jubilant, hugging each other and shaking hands, trying to absorb the wonderful event they had dreamed of for years. The Americans handed out chocolates and cigarettes.

'You bloody beauty!' An emaciated Scrounger hugged his small companion who winced with pain.

'Careful, ya big galoot! Ya hurting me.' Skeetah pushed him away.

'Big sook.' Scrounger giggled, and bit on a chocolate bar one of the Yanks had given him.

Skeetah drew deeply on his cigarette, allowing the smoke to tickle his nostrils. 'That's beautiful.'

Bluey knew he should be elated to be going home, but all he felt was a kind of numb confusion. How could he be happy when his best friend would not be going home? He was also anxious that Ellen might have found someone else.

Two and a half years is a bloody long time . . .

Like Bluey, other men just sat quietly, reflecting on their comrades who had not survived the terrible ordeal.

A few of the Americans looked dumbfounded at the skeletal appearance of the malnourished men confronting them.

'Look what these yellow bastards have done to these guys,' a sergeant said gruffly. 'We ought to give them some back.'

A junior NCO at his side agreed. Needing little incentive, a group of marines began to beat the Japanese guards cowering in the corner of the compound.

'Not him!' Bluey yelled as a young marine corporal began to strike at Little Mudguts. Bluey flew across the compound as fast as his thin legs could carry him. He pushed the American aside before reaching down to help the bleeding Japanese man to his feet, placing a protective arm around his shoulder.

'What the —?' said the surprised sergeant.

'He is a good man.' Bluey choked on the words.

The marine sergeant stood his ground. 'Good man or not, pal, he still has to be taken prisoner.'

'Just don't hurt him,' he pleaded. 'He saved my life.'

'Okay, pal. We won't hurt him.'

Now I've seen everything.

Roger Adams, who had witnessed the incident, acknowledged that this was the most animated he had seen the young Australian for months. And indeed, the event signalled a change in Bluey. Helping the Japanese soldier had unlocked something. He wasn't quite his old self, but he was at least more engaged with the world around him.

Later that afternoon, Bluey and the other former prisoners were transported by truck to the new American camp in Padang. The men were provided with proper bathing facilities, before being directed to the mess tent and a hot meal. The Americans also issued two sets of army clothing to every member of the group. Roger approached Bluey as he sat at a table eating a plateful of beef stew. 'I'm leaving in the morning, old boy. A British destroyer is calling for me on its way to Singapore . . .' He hesitated, searching for a way to say goodbye.

'Thanks for everything, Roger.' Bluey could hardly meet his eyes. 'You know what I mean.'

'The same goes for me, old chap. You take care of yourself.'

'Goodbye, Roger.' As the two men shook hands, it struck Bluey that this amazing Englishman had been like a rock to everyone. He had been the stabilising influence that had kept up morale. Now he was going home and Bluey would never see him again. Emotion welling up inside him, Bluey wrapped his arms around Roger in a bear hug.

Roger returned the hug. 'Bye, Bluey.'

The following morning, Bluey was admitted to a field hospital for treatment. Years of malaria, dysentery and malnutrition had all but destroyed his health and he required a special diet to rebuild his strength. As he lay in the hospital bed, Bluey thought of Ellen and his parents, but joyful reflections were chased by nagging doubts.

Will she have someone else by now?

That night, Bluey woke every patient in the temporary hospital ward with his nightmare.

'Bad dream last night?' an American doctor asked the next day.

Bluey looked up with a start. 'You heard?'

'Staff reported it.' The doctor took the clipboard from the base of his bed and flipped the page. 'Do you have these dreams often?'

Bluey felt tired and irritable. 'Sometimes.'

'Is it the same dream?' The American extracted a pen from his shirt pocket and began making notes on the chart.

'Sometimes,' he lied again.

'I'm not a psychiatrist —' the doctor began.

'Well stop asking bloody questions, then!'

The doctor could see the former prisoner-of-war was becoming agitated, so he backed off. He made a further note on the chart. 'I'll recommend to Australian medical authorities that they schedule you for some sessions with a psychiatrist.'

'I bloody well told you,' Bluey said heatedly, 'I don't need to talk about it.'

'You don't have a choice, soldier.' The American's eyes narrowed.

Moving away from the bed, the American officer had to suppress a smile as Bluey's comment drifted after him. 'Bloody Yanks. Think they know every bloody thing.'

The next morning Bluey looked up from his bed to see Scrounger and Skeetah. 'I forgot what you two buggers look like without your beards,' Bluey said, grinning.

'Yeah,' Scrounger stroked his smooth cheek, 'Clark Gable, look out.'

'More like Boris bloody Karloff.' Skeetah chuckled.

'You in here for long, Blue?' Scrounger enquired.

'Dunno, mate. For a little while I think.'

'We're off this arvo,' Skeetah explained. 'A Yank plane is flying us to Port Moresby. An Aussie ship will take us from there.'

'Shit.' Bluey found it hard to swallow.

'When I get up to Goondiwindi, I'll come out and visit you,' said Scrounger. He could see that his friend was taking the separation hard.

'You bloody better.'

'I'll come an' see you too.' Skeetah's tone was unusually soft. 'We'll go for a ride together. See what sort of horseman you are.'

'You little bugger. It'll be great to see you any time.'

'Scrounger an' me wanted to thank you, Blue, you know, for all you done for us in the camp.' Skeetah offered his hand, which Bluey took in a strong grip.

'What about this big galah?' Bluey waved a hand at Scrounger. 'He kept us alive with his wild tucker.'

Scrounger looked embarrassed as he shook hands with Bluey. 'It was nothin'.'

'Good luck to you both,' said Bluey. 'You've been bonza cobbers. The best a man could have.'

After they left, Bluey felt a profound emptiness. Here he was, in a ward full of sick and injured people, yet he felt all alone. He thought about his departing friends.

It was being mates that got us through.

Waiting at the edge of the same airstrip the prisoners had cut out of the jungle with their bare hands, Bluey thought it ironic that he would be using this runway to leave Sumatra. He watched as the RAAF DC 3 circled the small strip before landing. Looking across the open area, he could not believe the number of American aircraft now parked at the end of the runway.

At least the bloody Japs never used it.

On arrival in Port Moresby, Bluey was transferred to the hospital ship. Four days later, he was standing on the deck waiting impatiently for the first sighting of his homeland. One of the crew called out, 'There it is!'

The sight of the Australian coastline sent a surge of patriotism through Bluey. Even though he had not fired a single shot, he had enlisted to protect his country and its people from foreign invaders. He couldn't help feeling proud.

An hour or so later, the hospital ship slowly entered the mouth of the Brisbane River. At Hamilton wharf a fleet of ambulances waited to transport Bluey and the other patients to the Repatriation Hospital at Greenslopes. There he was reissued with a full kit of Australian army clothing as well as personal items. Ribbons and medals were also presented to the ex-prisoner-of-war. Physical examinations then began all over again. Despite Bluey's treatment at the American field hospital, Australian medical staff were unwilling to take any risks, and put him on another high-protein diet.

On his fourth day at Greenslopes, Bluey was wheeled to the psychiatrist's waiting room. He was not looking forward to the visit. He just wanted to get home to Ellen and his family. He'd sent them a telegram as soon as he'd docked, telling them that he'd be home soon.

Dr Richard Stevens turned out to be balding man with steel-rimmed spectacles who looked much older than his thirty-five years. He smiled warmly at the former prisoner-of-war and made small talk, asking questions about Bluey's family, his upbringing, the trip home and so on.

Bluey answered the questions with bad grace, snapping that he wanted to get out of hospital and go home. He'd been told that his father had phoned to pass on their love, and it made the yearning to get home even stronger.

'I'm sure you'll be discharged as soon as you're in good health. You're a strong fellow, and I'm in no doubt that you'll soon be fighting fit.'

The astute psychiatrist deliberately omitted all questions relating to the Japanese prisoner-of-war camp and his treatment there. Bluey felt a sense of relief as he was wheeled back to the ward.

Well that wasn't too bad.

His second visit to Dr Stevens, however, took a different turn.

'On the journey home on the hospital ship, medical staff said you woke everyone in the ward with loud yells following a bad dream,' the doctor said without preamble, closely watching Bluey's face. 'And the same thing has happened since you've been a patient here at Greenslopes.' He examined Bluey's medical chart. 'And there's also a note from the American doctor at Padang reporting the same event. What's troubling you?'

Bluey looked at the doctor coldly. The doctor had caught him completely off guard, which had only served to enrage him. 'I told you before, all I want to do is go home.'

The doctor returned to his notes. Clearly, he'd made a mistake with his surprise tactics, but he would not let the matter drop. 'You know, Sapper O'Donnell, you can block an unpleasant experience from your conscious mind, but your subconscious does not always go along with that. That's why we often have nightmares.'

Bluey's expression was thunderous. 'Unpleasant? Fuckin' unpleasant?' He exploded. 'What a way to describe it!' He looked at the psychiatrist bitterly. 'What the fuck would you know, mate?' He rose to his feet and stormed out of the office, ignoring the orderly waiting for him with a wheelchair. He walked back to the ward, agitated, his thoughts in turmoil. The view from the window beside his bed, of wooded hillsides and the city skyline that usually gave him a sense of calm, could not quiet his racing heart.

Chapter 20

The news that the war was over in Europe was greeted with long celebrations in the main street of Goondiwindi. Despite rationing, the local publicans were somehow able to supply enough liquid refreshments to help the whole town celebrate. For those families who had sons and sweethearts in the Pacific theatre, however, the war was still a constant worry. The news that the atomic bomb had been dropped on Japan left people with bated breath, wondering what would be the aftermath of this action. They received their answer a few days later on 14 August, 1945. World War II was finally over.

The end of the war created a new anxiety and uncertainty for the family at Kilkenny. From the day they were informed that Bluey was a Japanese prisoner-of-war, and in all the months that had passed, they had not heard one word from their loved one, nothing since the letter he wrote while waiting to board the ship. All subsequent enquiries through the Australian Red Cross had proved fruitless. The organisation could not track down any further information on Sapper O'Donnell's condition as a prisoner-of-war. Was he alive? Was he sick or injured? These thoughts inundated their thinking, gnawing at their insides. With no further news, they'd just had to wait patiently to see what eventuated. Three weeks slowly passed, and there was still no word. They were in a fever of suspense. A few more days without word, and they had almost given up hope. Then, just when they were at their lowest ebb, Father Donovan had arrived once more on their doorstep clutching another wire. Dave ripped it open. 'He's alive!' he announced happily. 'He's on his way home on a hospital ship.'

The trio fell into each other's arms and gave thanks through tears of joy. 'Hospital ship?' Sally enquired.

'He's probably malnourished and has perhaps been suffering from malaria and dysentery,' the priest suggested. 'That's typical, I believe.'

'We just thank God he's coming home.' Dave lowered his head.

'Amen.' They all joined in.

A week later, they received a telegram from Brisbane.

In Greenslopes Repat Hospital. Home soon. Love Bluey.

They crowded around the telephone as Dave made the long-distance call to the hospital. They knew they would not be able to speak to Bluey, but they would try to find out about his condition and ask for him to be told that they had called. The hospital was not very forthcoming with their information, only to say he was in a satisfactory condition, and yes, they would tell him his family had called and pass on their love. It was a comfort to them just to have spoken to someone who had contact with him.

After the phone call, they sat around excitedly discussing the possibility of visiting him at Greenslopes. 'With petrol rationing, I don't see how we can make it to Brisbane,' said Dave. 'We're only allowed a hundred and twenty miles a month.'

Sally chipped in. 'What about the train? It leaves in two days' time.'

'But what if we passed him on his way home?' Ellen warned.

'We'll just have to wait to hear from him again,' said Dave.

On the day of his discharge, Bluey was issued with a ticket home. When he learned that the train didn't leave until the following afternoon he was bitterly disappointed.

What the hell do I do now?

And then a thought came to him. This was the perfect opportunity to carry out a task that was weighing heavily on his mind. He caught the mid-morning train to Coolangatta on Queensland's south coast and then a taxi to the address Digger had told him so many times. The cab pulled to a stop in front of a neat low-set cottage perched on a hill overlooking the beach and the Tweed River. He gazed out over the panorama. The blue of the sky was mirrored in the sea.

No wonder you loved it here, big fella.

Bluey stood nervously at the front door. He knew he could never live with himself unless he'd visited Digger's family. In response to his knock, the door to the house was opened by a pretty girl wearing loose-fitting dark grey slacks and a white blouse. She was about Bluey's height, with dark-brown hair worn short, and she had a trim figure. She looked uncertainly at the thin soldier standing in the doorway.

'Sue?' he asked. She nodded, and he said quietly, 'I'm Bluey.'

That was as far as he was able to proceed. She knew of him through the letters Digger had written to her when he and Bluey were training together. She threw herself into his arms, weeping bitterly. As he sought to console her, he felt the tears streaming from his own eyes. Once they had composed themselves, she invited him in.

'The family's heard?' he asked anxiously.

'Yes. The army confirmed it a couple of weeks ago. But we've suspected it for some time.' Her lip quivered again. 'Wait here, Bluey. I'll get Mum and Dad.'

Digger's parents hugged him and made every attempt to make Bluey feel welcome. The brave show did nothing to camouflage the deep sadness pervading every nook and cranny of the Belford home. Digger's mother was a petite woman with short mousy coloured hair, while his father was a giant of a man who had become a little stooped in middle age. They insisted he stay for lunch.

Inevitably, Mr Belford asked the question Bluey had been dreading. 'How did he die?'

Bluey took a deep breath and looked from one face to the next. 'It was from a severe bout of malaria,' he lied.

'Did he suffer very much?' Mrs Belford lifted a small white lace handkerchief to her eyes.

'No. He was unconscious when he went.'

'I'm glad,' she smiled weakly.

Bluey looked up at the kitchen clock and rose to his feet. 'Well, thank you for lunch. It was lovely to meet you. Now I'd better be off or I'll miss my train.'

At the front door, each member of the Belford family hugged him again. 'We appreciate you coming all this way to see us, Bluey.' The big man looked down at him warmly. 'Peter was very lucky to have a mate like you.'

'No, Mr Belford, it's the other way around.' Bluey replied. 'I was lucky to have a cobber like Digger.'

On the return journey to Brisbane, Bluey felt drained. In visiting Digger's family he'd risked facing his own guilt. Telling them that Digger had died of malaria not only spared them terrible grief, but helped him avoid the demons lurking deep in his mind.

One week after receiving the telegram, Ellen, Dave and Sally were sitting at the dining table eating dinner. A storm was brewing, and every now and then, lightning and thunder caused the electric light globes to flicker. After another deafening clap of thunder, the knocking at the front door seemed soft by comparison. The three sat motionless.

'That's the door,' said Sally. They looked at each other. Ellen's heart was pounding as it had with the sound of every car and every door knock in the past two weeks. Nobody said a word. As she opened the door, a lightning flash lit up the homestead's verandah, and Ellen gasped at the figure standing there. The soldier was emaciated, his face drawn and cheeks sunken, the slouch hat seemed far too large for the head on which it was placed.

A bulging kit bag sat on the verandah beside him. Bluey O'Donnell removed the hat and smiled. 'Hello, Ellen.'

'Bluey!' she screamed, and then the three of them were on him, laughing, kissing and hugging. Eventually they broke apart, though Ellen kept her arm in Bluey's as they walked to the table.

'I never thought you'd get here, sweetheart.' Ellen tried to hide her shock at his gaunt appearance.

If it weren't for the curly ginger hair, you'd hardly recognise him.

'Got the train, then a cab from town,' he said with the old familiar grin.

Sally took him by the hand, lost for words. 'Um . . . we're just having tea, love. Pork chops and vegies followed by peach tart and cream.' It seemed such an inane thing to say after all the time he'd been away, but it would do for now.

'Sounds great, Mum,' he said warmly.

Arm in arm with Ellen and his mother, Bluey limped through the open living room to the dining table. Dave followed closely behind. Bluey slowly lowered himself into a chair at the table, while his mother piled a plate with meat and vegetables.

'Shouldn't you still be in hospital, son?' Small furrows creased Sally's brow.

'Bloody hospitals!' he exclaimed. 'I've had a gutful of them.'

'But are you well enough?' Ellen asked. Her heart was still thudding with the excitement of seeing him again, but she could not help feeling distressed at his condition.

'The doctor said it would take a while,' he admitted quietly. 'But I'll be okay.'

'What about the army?' Dave asked. 'Do you have to go back?'

'I'm discharged, Dad. I'm finished with the army for good. But I have to go to Brisbane in a month's time for a medical check-up. They'll pay my way.' As he reached for the salt and pepper, he heard a child begin to cry. 'What the —?' He looked around, puzzled.

Sally smiled. 'This'll come as a bit of a shock, son, but there's been an addition to the family.'

'Not after all these years, Mum, surely?' Bluey looked sceptical.

'No, not me, silly!' She laughed loudly. 'You and Ellen.'

Bluey turned to Ellen, his shocked expression almost comical. Her deep green eyes sparkled like emeralds as the tears formed. 'That's our son, David Liam O'Donnell. He's two years old.'

'What?' Bluey gave a short sharp cry and looked at Ellen in wonderment. 'Bloody hell, I can't believe it. Can I see him?'

Dave took hold of his bewildered son's thin arm, and slowly guided him to the nursery. The two women followed behind arm in arm. Both had dreamed about Bluey meeting his son for the first time, but they'd never discussed it. And now it was happening. When they entered, the crying immediately ceased as the toddler examined the stranger in his room. Bluey looked at the little boy's sweet face, his cheeks still rosy from his nap, his plump little hands holding onto the top rail of the cot.

'My son . . .' Bluey smiled at the toddler and moved towards the cot. 'Can I pick him up?'

Little David looked up at his father and smiled at him as if he had known him all his life.

'He's your boy, darling.' Ellen was crying openly now – tears of happiness.

Bluey lifted the small child, who immediately began to pull at the ribbons adorning his chest.

He stroked the toddler's hair. 'A chip off the old block, isn't he?'

'In more ways than one,' Dave winked.

'Right,' Sally said assertively, 'let's eat or everything will get cold.' She wiped the tears away with her apron. 'Bring David out, son. It won't hurt him to stay up for once.' She chucked her grandson under his chin. 'It's not every day your father comes home after such a long time, is it?'

Everyone was soon re-seated at the table, where Bluey ate the best meal he could remember.

'More, son?' Sally enquired when he had finished.

'I'd love to, Mum, but I can't eat too much at once yet. Stomach's shrunk up a bit, so the doctor says.' He gave a sardonic laugh.

After the meal, Sally and Ellen cleaned up while Bluey nursed his son and sat talking with his father. Finally, the toddler was put to bed.

'Daddy!' the little fellow said happily, pointing to his father. Ellen and Sally had been telling him for days that his daddy was coming home.

'Yes. Daddy! He's home now,' Ellen replied, tucking him in.

'Goodnight,' Bluey said softly, kissing the soft skin on his son's forehead.

Ellen sat on the sofa next to Bluey, taking his hand in hers. He squeezed it. While they sipped their tea, Dave gave his son a brief update on the property. At no time during the conversation was the war or the prisoner-of-war camp discussed. It was like an unspoken agreement between them that he would have to raise the subject himself. Bluey surprised them with his next comment. He placed his arm around Ellen's shoulder, pulling her close. 'We'd better set the date.'

'What?'

'We'd better set the date for our wedding.' He smiled gently and watched her lovely face. 'You know, to make everything official.'

'There's no hurry, darling.' She pressed her cheek briefly against his chest. 'When you're well enough.'

'I'm pretty good now compared to what I was.'

Sally interrupted the conversation. 'And now that you're home, you'll recover in no time, you'll see.'

Bluey changed the subject. 'I see you got a new dog, Dad.'

'Yes, son. Skipper. He's only young, but he's coming along nicely.'

'Get him off Murphy?'

'Yeah, paid five quid for him. Pick of the litter.' Dave rose from his chair. 'Righteo, I've got to get up early in the morning, so I'm off to bed. But before I do, I just want to say welcome home. I'm very proud of you,' he said with a little cough to cover his wavering voice.

'Thanks, Dad.'

Sally took her husband's arm as the two left the room.

Alone with Bluey, her soon-to-be husband, Ellen realised that he was not the same person who had left her crying at the station so long ago. He had left a boy, and come back a man. She felt a bit tongue-tied as she asked uncertainly, 'Do you want to talk, Bluey, or do you want to go to bed?'

'I'm tired, El.' He sighed. 'I think I'd like to lie down.'

When the couple began to undress in the privacy of their bedroom, Ellen was shocked. Ribs and shoulder blades protruded through his yellowish skin. There was not one ounce of spare flesh on his once well-muscled body. When she saw the scars on his back she gasped and tears welled up in her eyes.

Anticipating her reaction, Bluey turned to face her. 'Don't fuss, darlin'. It'll be all right.'

'Oh, Bluey. I had no idea.' She held him tightly and closed her eyes. She never wanted to let him go. His lacerated skin was a stark reminder of how close she had come to losing him.

The two held each other for a long time. Bluey was the first to break away. He sat down on the bed and seemed embarrassed as he began to search for the right words. 'You know, I never stopped thinking about you, El. It was your image that kept me going for all that time in that bloody camp. For a long time, I just yearned to make love to you. For ages, I thought of virtually nothing else.' He looked away. 'Now that I'm finally with you, I have to tell you that I can't. They tell me, for the moment, it's a physical impossibility. I'm sorry.'

The dejected look on his face caused tears to again well up in her eyes. Ellen sat beside him on the bed and placed her arms around him, drawing him close. 'Don't be sorry. There'll be plenty of time for that. I'm just grateful to have you home again,' she assured him. 'Now, let's go to bed.'

Ellen waited until she heard the slow, steady breathing that indicated he was asleep before she allowed herself to drift off. She had no idea of the time when a loud cry of anguish brought her instantly awake. The scream was followed by Bluey's frightened call. 'Digger? Digger! No!'

She gently shook him, and he sat bolt upright, eyes wide. His pyjamas were wet through. 'Bluey. Are you all right?'

His face was a picture of despair, his body shuddering and shaking as he stammered. 'D-did I w-wake you?'

'Yes,' she replied anxiously, 'but it's okay.' She stroked his hair.

When Bluey was again settled, she lay awake for a long time, thinking. It was already apparent that Bluey's experiences as a Japanese prisoner-of-war were far too horrific for her to even begin to understand, and yet his twenty-first birthday was still a few months away. Settling back into a normal home life was not going to be as easy as Ellen had first hoped.

News of Pam's pregnancy filled Ellen with excitement, but her mother's diagnosis with rheumatoid arthritis was a blow. Sally told her it was an extremely painful and debilitating disease. Ellen felt guilty that she would not be close enough to offer practical support to her mother.

I'll have to write more often.

As the days passed, Bluey's terrifying nightmares continued. In the very early days, the horror came almost nightly. After a month, the sleep-depriving ordeals had diminished to around one a week, but were still unpredictable. To exacerbate the situation, Bluey also suffered from recurrent bouts of post-malaria syndrome, a condition that would leave him sweating and shaking. In the morning, his pyjamas and the bedclothes would be soaked.

With a nourishing diet, washed down by numerous glasses of fresh farm milk, Bluey's physical condition slowly improved. When he sat down at the table, he would shake his head at the large amount of food on his plate and smile. 'Bloody hell, how will I get through all that?'

'You'll eat every crumb,' was his mother's terse reply. And he did.

Bluey was not looking forward to his first visit to Greenslopes Repatriation Hospital, especially as his check-up included a consultation with Dr Stevens. But Ellen and Sally wouldn't hear of him missing the appointment.

'How are you?' Dr Stevens asked Bluey on arrival.

'I'm fine.' Bluey didn't care whether the doctor could detect his insincerity.

'That's good news, Bluey. You don't mind if I call you Bluey, do you?' he asked pleasantly.

'No,' Bluey answered quietly.

'But you're still having the dreams, aren't you?' This was more a statement than a question.

Bluey looked away, and pressed his lips together defiantly. 'Not as often. That must mean something.'

'Yes, it does.' The doctor sighed. This was going to be harder than he'd imagined. 'Being back in a stable family environment helps enormously. Have you talked to your wife about the camp?'

At the mention of Ellen, Bluey felt suddenly angry. 'I don't want to talk about it. Why in the blazes can't you leave it alone?' he snapped. 'I just want to forget it. Don't you bloody well understand?'

'Of course I do,' Dr Stevens replied calmly. 'But my experience tells me that it's not that easy —'

'I'm doing okay, I tell you!' Bluey raised his voice.

For the remainder of the visit, the doctor restricted his questions to family matters, which Bluey was only too happy to discuss. The doctor even suggested that he return to some light duties on the farm.

It will keep his mind occupied . . .

When the family asked about his visit to the doctor, Bluey was happy to tell them he'd been given the all clear to return to light work around the property. He suggested that he should take over responsibility for the milking, as well as the odd jobs around the house. Sally did not agree. 'But you've only been home for five weeks, son. Don't you think you need to wait a bit longer?'

'No, Mum,' he said firmly. 'I'm sick of sitting around watching everyone else work their bums off. Don't be fussing over it, please.'

'But it pleasures me to fuss over you, son,' she replied warmly.

'I'll be fine. Don't worry.'

Bluey was keen to help with the fencing, and also had an intense desire to take one of the horses for a gallop, but Dave put his foot down. 'You need to build up your strength before riding, or trying any heavy work.

While Bluey's physical health slowly improved, and the frequency of his nightmares gradually lessened, nothing changed where the intimate side of Bluey's and Ellen's relationship was concerned. When Ellen undressed, he would sit on the bed admiring her beautiful body, the same body he desired so much in his mind, but was continually frustrated with his inability to make love to her.

She's so lovely. What's wrong with me?

But he made no move towards her and Ellen did not say a word. As frustrated as she felt, she knew it would take time. Besides, she was thrilled with the relationship he was developing with his infant son. Bluey was so smitten that he could barely wait for the youngster to wake up from his afternoon nap. Father and son could then be seen walking hand in hand around the house or the yard. Bluey loved to sit the little chap on his lap and point out the different types of birds – galahs, cockatoos and eagles – that flew over the property. Bluey not only fed little David his meals, he sat with him for ages each day, teaching him new words, reciting nursery rhymes and telling stories. When Skipper wasn't working the flock with the other dogs, he wouldn't let little David out of his sight. He'd become the house dog, and took his responsibility to guard it seriously.

It didn't take long before Bluey assumed responsibility for ploughing the wheat fields in preparation for planting. He yearned for the strength to help his hardworking father with the heavy duties. Restricted as he was, he was just happy to be out in the paddocks again. Like his father, he simply loved Kilkenny.

Chapter 21

Bluey detested his monthly trips to the repat hospital, but knew how concerned his family would be if he refused to go.

'I'm just tired of the whole damn thing,' he told them. 'I'm fine, now. You can all see that, can't you?'

Ellen had to admit that Bluey was much stronger, now. The fresh air, healthy diet and care and attention from loved ones seemed to have done wonders. But Sally waved aside his protestations.

'The doctors know what they're doing, son. If you didn't need to go, they wouldn't insist.'

By the time his sixth session was due, Bluey decided it would be his last. Ellen drove him into town to catch the train. As he and Ellen quietly sipped their tea in Goondiwindi's railway station refreshment rooms, they didn't notice Len Humphries drinking at the bar with two of his staff. He sauntered over to their table to offer an outstretched hand to Bluey. 'Haven't seen you since you got back, O'Donnell. Welcome home.'

Bluey took the other man's hand. 'Thanks, Humphries. It's good to be back.'

'Looks like you could do with a feed, mate.'

Ellen intervened, annoyed. 'We're looking after him.'

'Didn't treat you too well in the POW camp by the looks of it.' Though uninvited, Humphries flopped down in a chair.

Ellen looked at the man's drink-inflamed cheeks, shocked at his insensitive comment. It was a subject that was never talked about at home.

Bluey rose to his feet and fixed his childhood foe with a steady stare. Humphries leaned back in his seat and smiled guilelessly back at him. Bluey regarded the other man's well-padded frame with open contempt. 'You don't look to have suffered too much hardship.'

'Don't get het up, O'Donnell,' Humphries muttered. 'It was just an innocent remark. Didn't mean anything by it.'

Ellen could see that Bluey was on the verge of losing his temper. 'It was an extremely insensitive comment, Len,' she interrupted. 'I think you'd better go, now.'

'Yeah, piss off!' Bluey snapped.

Humphries left the table with bad grace. Bluey watched him with a baleful expression.

'You all right, Bluey?' she asked quietly.

He could see she was upset for him. He didn't want to make things worse, so he took a deep breath and tried to relax. 'I still think he's a rotten, fat turd.' They both burst into laughter.

On this visit to Greenslopes, the psychiatrist adopted a different strategy with his feisty red-headed patient. He asked no further questions about the prisoner-of-war camp or the nightmares.

Instead, after initial greetings, he took a different tack. 'Are you working on the farm?'

'Property,' Bluey corrected. 'Yeah, doc, I'm doing more and more as time goes on.'

'You're looking much better,' Dr Stevens said sincerely. 'Put on a lot of weight, I see.'

'Still a fair way to go.' Bluey looked askance, expecting the usual questions.

'What about your love life?' the doctor raised his eyebrows.

Bluey felt embarrassed. 'What about it?' His voice was tight.

'Has your libido returned?'

'My what?'

'Can you get and maintain an erection?'

Bluey shifted uncomfortably in his chair. 'Sort of.'

Stevens scratched his chin. 'By this time, Bluey, we'd expect soldiers who've been through what you've been through to be experiencing an erection when they wake in the morning.'

'Yeah, I do,' Bluey admitted uncertainly. 'And at other times too, sort of.'

'What do you mean?'

'It's hard to explain. It's not like it was before.'

'This is good news, Bluey. You'll soon be back to lovemaking. It's only mind over matter, so the experts say.'

'You sure?' Bluey looked doubtful. 'How come I don't feel that way when I'm with Ellen?'

'You love her, don't you?'

'Yeah, too right.'

'And you find her sexually appealing?'

'You betcha.' He was feeling more positive just thinking about her.

'If that's how you feel, I can't see any physical reason to prevent you from making love to her.'

'But I haven't had the right feelings. You know, here.' Bluey pointed to his heart.

'Bluey, I know this might sound strange, but the problem is not how you feel about Ellen, but how you feel about yourself.'

Bluey looked puzzled.

'Initially, the problem was purely physical, but then your feelings of inadequacy grew to the point where you completely lost confidence in yourself.' He clasped his hands together under his chin, tapping each finger against the other. 'From now on, this is what I want you to do. At every opportunity, I want you to think about all the private moments you've shared with your wife in the past. Watch her as she undresses and think about how it felt to make love to her. I'll give you some medication which may or may not help with your feelings of impotence, and I'll also prescribe something to help you sleep.'

Bluey was dumbfounded. This was great news! He was on the verge of telling the doctor he wasn't actually married to Ellen when Stevens deftly changed the subject. 'I assume you are still having the dream?'

'Yes.' Caught off guard, Bluey answered without thinking. He wanted to roar his disapproval at being tricked in such a way, but was still full of hope about repairing his physical relationship with Ellen. 'Look, doc, I don't want to talk about it, okay? What's done is done. I just want to get on with my life.'

After organising the medication, Dr Stevens terminated the session. He was pleased with his patient's progress, but chastised himself for pushing him too far.

After staying overnight in the Red Cross rooms opposite the hospital, Bluey took the train back to Goondiwindi the next day. He thought about the doctor's suggestions.

I can make love to El. I can.

Ellen and young David were waiting as the train pulled into the platform. He scooped his little son into a warm hug and then embraced Ellen. She looked beautiful – her skirt fitted snugly at her small waist, and hugged her rounded hips, and he could not help but admire the swell of her breasts against the buttons of her blouse. He began to imagine undressing her then decided to hold that thought until they were alone.

On the drive back to Kilkenny, she asked, 'How did it go?'

'All right, I suppose. I had to see this psychiatrist bloke again. He's given me some tablets to take. Says I'll sleep better.'

'That's good news, darling.'

As they chatted about the property and little David, she noticed that Bluey seemed different. He seemed much more self-assured. At home, Sally also noticed the change and took Ellen aside. 'I think the trip did him good, this time, love. He seems more like his old self, don't you think?'

'I think so too, Sal.'

When they were at last alone in the bedroom, Bluey was aroused, but could not bring himself to initiate any lovemaking. As he watched her pull on the short cotton nightie, she turned to him with a tentative smile. 'You all right, darling?'

'Yeah.' He looked into her eyes. 'I was just thinking what a good sort you are.'

'Oh, Bluey. What a lovely thing to say.'

She moved towards him and held his face against the softness of her breast. Her skin smelled sweetly of soap. That night, Bluey had a deep and satisfying sleep. The next morning was Sunday, and with renewed energy, he suggested they go for a ride to the river, or maybe even to the cave. He was filled with confidence.

Today's the day.

They set off after breakfast, choosing the same route they'd taken when Ellen first visited Kilkenny. As they rode through the fields, thick layers of sticky black soil clung to the horses' hooves. The river was milky brown from the recent downpour. On their arrival at the cave, its interior was warm, dry and welcoming. Bluey spread the blanket on the ground, while Ellen removed the thermos flask and scones from a small bag.

'Want a cuppa?' she asked.

'Yeah.' He sat down. 'And I'll have a scone, too.'

While the two sat sipping tea, Bluey examined the walls of the cave. He hadn't been there since before he went away. 'Peaceful here, isn't it?'

'I love it,' she said quietly.

'Remember when I first brought you here, El?' He chuckled.

'You were always looking for opportunities, you naughty boy,' she pretended to chide him and then giggled.

Bluey placed his mug of tea on the ground and removed Ellen's cup from her hand. He turned her gently towards him, kissing her with a passion of old. Surprised and delighted, she returned the kiss. It seemed like an eternity since she'd experienced such feelings. He gently lowered her to the blanket where the kiss continued. With trembling fingers, he unbuttoned her blouse, revealing her breasts, which could hardly be constrained by her lacy, dark blue brassiere. With the bra removed, Bluey kissed her breasts and tenderly caressed them, gently rubbing her nipples between his thumb and finger, causing them to firm and stand erect. She moaned with pleasure. Finally, he broke away. 'Do you remember when I brought you to the cave the first time, and you said it would spoil everything if we did it here?' His voice was husky with desire. 'What about now?'

'I think it would be perfect.' She placed her arms around his neck and drew him closer.

Back at the homestead, Sally noticed the change in the couple. They laughed constantly over lunch, looking into each other's eyes. Their joy was infectious and little David, sitting in his high chair, giggled whenever they laughed.

As time passed, Ellen thought Bluey may have even overcome the nightmare that had plagued him since returning home. It had been more than a month since his last bad episode. She had tried to talk to him about it at the time, but he always became instantly defensive, refusing to discuss it. She did not press the subject, as she was happier and more contented than she could ever remember. While he still had the odd upsetting nightmare, and the after-effects of malaria laid him low from time to time, she felt that at long last, her Bluey was back.

Eight weeks, almost to the day, after the resumption of their lovemaking, Ellen was at the breakfast table when she had to rush for the bathroom, holding her hand to her mouth. Bluey pushed back his chair, ready to follow her, but Sally quickly jumped up.

'You finish your breakfast,' she ordered. 'I'll go.'

Sally knocked at the door. 'Are you feeling sick, Ellen?'

'Come in, Sal.'

Sally entered, and took note of Ellen's pallor. 'You don't look well at all, love.'

'I've been feeling a little sick.'

'How long?' Sally queried, daring to hope.

'For the last three mornings.'

'Oh, love!' she exclaimed happily.

Ellen opened her arms and the two women embraced.

'You'd better go to the doctor and find out for sure.'

'It might be too soon yet. I'll wait a bit longer. Don't say anything to the boys till I find out for sure.'

The two returned to the kitchen.

'Is something wrong with you, El?' Bluey looked up, concerned.

'Just a little stomach upset.' Ellen kissed him lightly on the head.

Two weeks later, the two O'Donnell women drove the ute to Goondiwindi, leaving the men to carry out maintenance duties on the shearing shed. The shearing contractor was due the following week and everything needed to be tip-top.

Three days later, the doctor's office called. Sally could tell from Ellen's smile that she was indeed pregnant. As she replaced the telephone receiver, she turned to Sally and nodded in the affirmative.

'Oh, sweetheart, that's wonderful.' Sally beamed.

'I can't believe it.' She looked slightly bemused. 'I thought it would be ages yet. Mum will be thrilled, especially after Pam's Eric has just been born.'

Sally laughed out loud. 'You know the old saying, love, you play with fire, you get burned.'

'Oh, Sal! You're awful.' They both giggled.

'Have you said anything to Bluey?' Sally asked.

'No. Have you mentioned the possibility to Dave?' Ellen raised an eyebrow.

'Nope.'

'Right then,' she folded her arms, 'won't they be surprised?'

After putting young David to bed, Ellen sat down at the dinner table. Her eyes met those of Sally who raised her eyebrows. A mischievous smile played at the corners of Ellen's mouth. 'We haven't said anything more about the wedding.'

'It's a busy time,' Bluey replied guiltily. 'We'll do it in a couple of months. There's no hurry, is there, El?'

'Actually, in a couple of months I might not fit into a wedding dress.'

Bluey looked at her quizzically, then her meaning hit home. 'Bloody hell!' He stood up. 'You're expecting?'

'Yes.'

He pulled her to her feet and kissed her so tenderly she thought she might melt. She buried her face in his shoulder.

'You little beauty.' It was Dave's turn. 'We're blessed! Congratulations you two. This calls for a celebration.' He pointed to the storage cabinet. 'Bluey, get out the Irish whiskey and we'll toast the expected baby and its mother.'

Bluey was on a cloud for the rest of the day. He'd never known such feelings of peace and contentment.

Ellen phoned her mother and sister with the news, and they agreed to make the long drive to attend the wedding. Pam's husband Barry would take a few days of his annual leave.

Ellen spent a long time mulling over what she would wear to the biggest event of her life. Because they had been living together – something frowned upon in conservative Goondiwindi – and already had a child, Ellen knew she couldn't wear white. This would have really given the gossips some ammunition, as many in the town still tut-tutted every time she walked past. In the postwar environment, rationing was still an everyday part of life, and non-essential items were scarce. It was going to be hard to find the right kind of dress. Sally and Ellen visited the drapery where Pam had once worked to explain Ellen's predicament, and the owners were sympathetic. They had known Sally and Dave for years and had grown close to Pam. They produced a lovely length of cream brocade, some matching lace and a pattern. Over the next two weeks, Sally used her old treadle sewing machine to make a beautiful gown.

The dress taken care of, the next important matter was Bluey's conversion. At this point in time, non-Catholics were expected to convert if they were to marry in the Catholic Church. Even though his mother was a little miffed, Bluey didn't mind. He was just happy that Ellen was to become his wife. Having to meet with the priest and be confirmed into the faith was a small price to pay.

When Ellen and Bluey first approached the new parish priest, they were worried that he might judge them for having children out of wedlock. But Father Fitzgerald shrugged his shoulders. 'As long as you love each other and take your vows before God seriously, that's all that matters.'

The day before the wedding, Ellen's family arrived. They'd been on the road for eight and a half hours in Barry's Willys sedan, only stopping for petrol along the way. When Ellen saw them, she squealed with excitement and ran to the car, little David toddling by her side, to exchange greetings and hug them all.

'Mum, I'm so happy to see you!' she said as David walked into his grandmother's outstretched arms.

'It's a pity it's so far out here, pet.' The older woman's eyes were shining as she took in her grandson's chubby cheeks and ginger curls. He looked especially cute in his cotton shirt and tiny woollen vest. 'It's been so long, little man. I've missed you so.' Joan continued to hug him.

Ellen took baby Eric from her sister's arms and held him. 'He even looks like his grandad.' She kissed the baby's forehead. 'Sorry, Barry,' she said with a smile. 'It's so wonderful to finally see him.'

The group were soon joined by Dave, Sally and Bluey, who renewed their acquaintance before helping with the belongings. 'There's plenty of room in the shearers' quarters, folks,' Dave explained. 'Sal and Ellen have cleaned it up nicely for your stay.'

'But you must be dying for a cuppa. Come on up to the house, first,' said Sally.

After dinner, the families talked well into the night, bringing each other up to date. Ellen didn't comment, but she was worried about her mother. Joan's hands were swollen and disfigured from the arthritis, and she had difficulty walking. Ellen knew that her mother would not want to discuss her health – she didn't like a fuss. She was soon distracted from her concerns about her mother when Pam informed Ellen that she was pregnant again. With Joan and two infants to look after, Ellen knew she would have her hands full, especially now that Barry worked as a salesman for a tobacco firm, a position that took him away from home on country trips.

'That's wonderful news, Sis. I just wish that I lived closer so that I could be more of a help.'

'I'll be just fine,' Pam replied. 'You'll have your own hands full with two little ones. Now there's something important I want to show you.' Pam went to her luggage, returning with a small cardboard box which she handed to Ellen. 'Mum and I found this for you in Brisbane.'

Ellen removed the lid and gazed at a small cream-coloured hat adorned with flowers and a veil just large enough to cover her face. 'Oh! It's beautiful,' she gasped. 'You shouldn't have. It must have been so expensive.'

'It's your wedding, pet.' Joan felt an upwelling of contentment. 'You deserve it.'

A tearful Ellen hugged them both. She felt so lucky, surrounded by such generous, loving people.

If only Dad were here, too.

The following morning the house was abuzz with wedding preparations. As Ellen stood in front of the mirror in the bedroom, Sally, Joan and Pam fussed over her, until she was finally ready.

Sally had washed and set her hair and it shone like silk. 'You look absolutely beautiful,' said Joan, beaming.

Finally, Ellen walked down the aisle of St Mary's Catholic Church with her Uncle Mick at her side, her face glowing with happiness. She was too nervous to do much more than glance at the faces of her many friends and relatives who had chosen to be with her on this important day.

'Haven't been inside a church for so long it's a wonder the ceiling don't cave in,' Dave muttered to his wife as they sat in the front pew.

'I don't know why you don't start going to Mass again,' Sally whispered back.

'Don't like going by meself.'

'I'd go with you.'

'Would you?' He turned to her, surprised.

'Of course, love. It's just that you've never asked.'

When Ellen reached Bluey's side, he turned to her, and all his nervousness dissolved. She was utterly radiant in her new dress, her face alive with love and anticipation.

After the ceremony, relatives and friends congregated in the church grounds before moving on to the Goondiwindi School of Arts hall for the small reception party. To celebrate the occasion, Dave had arranged for a ten-gallon keg of beer, some soft drinks and wine, and had hired a local caterer to provide mixed sandwiches, cold meats and salads and sponge cakes. Aunty Pat had made the beautifully decorated cake as her wedding gift to the young couple. After speeches, followed by a traditional bridal waltz, the band began playing dance music. Everyone got up to dance when they played 'In the Mood'. Afterwards, Uncle Mick placed his arms around Ellen, taking her in a bear hug. 'Eric would be proud of you, Ellen,' he said emotionally. 'Kevin, too.'

'I believe that now,' she replied, wiping away a tear.

Chapter 22

The 1946 shearing season came and went, Ellen relieved that this time she didn't have to manhandle any of the greasy, squirming sheep. Now that the war was over and manpower restrictions were relaxed, the recruitment of shearers returned to the practices of the past. Bluey could hardly believe his ears when he heard about the womenfolk's prowess with the shearing clippers, but was nonetheless happy that his wife no longer had to carry out such a heavy task.

It had been a dry season, but Kilkenny was still able to produce a bumper wheat crop and Dave was finally able to make the last payment to the State Agricultural Bank. In the months that followed, Ellen blossomed in her pregnancy. Restricted to household duties, she helped with the paperwork associated with the running of the property.

Meanwhile Bluey became stronger and stronger. The constant physical work and the security he felt in a loving family helped to ward off his troubling recollections. Yet Ellen sometimes caught him staring off into space with a troubled expression. And if she asked what was wrong, he would just laugh it off, telling her that he was tired. Although infrequent now, the harrowing nightmare still lurked, and every now and then he would wake himself with his own yelling. When she questioned him about the nightmare, his face would close down, and he would shake his head, telling her that it was no big deal. Ellen, fraught with worry, hated being shut out, but thought it wise not to share her concerns with Sally or Dave.

No use worrying them too.

Ellen's waters broke on a sunny Thursday morning as she cleaned the bath. Leaving a trail behind her, she made her way to the verandah where she rang the bell to alert her husband. Sally was the first to come running.

'Is it time, love?' she asked breathlessly.

'Yes.'

'Righteo. You gather your things while I go and get the boys. They're in the bottom paddock.'

'Please hurry, Sal,' she said urgently. 'It's not like the last time. The contractions seem to be very close.'

As Sally rode off, Ellen held a protective hand on her swollen stomach, and made for their bedroom. Halfway down the narrow hallway she was overcome by a severe contraction that forced her to the floor. When the contraction subsided and she was finally able to get up, she was hit with a bout of dizziness and nausea. She made it to the bedroom, where another contraction enveloped her just as she lay down on the bed. She was filled with panic when she heard her toddler wake from his afternoon nap. As she struggled to the nursery, another wave of nausea and dizziness almost brought her to a halt. Barely able to hold on, she managed to guide him to the potty. Then another contraction hit, and she collapsed on the single bed.

Please hurry.

Little David pulled his own trousers up and walked over to his mother, stroking her cheek. 'Mummy sick?' he enquired.

'It's okay, sweetie. The baby's coming.'

Little David clapped his hands and started cooing, 'Baby. Baby.'

Just then, she heard running footsteps on the floor of the homestead. Bluey, Sally and Dave burst into the nursery, and she opened her eyes.

'Take David outside, love.' Sally instructed her husband when she saw the urgency in Ellen's face. Dave gathered up his grandson and left the room, while Bluey and his mother attempted to assist her from the bed.

'Come on, sweetheart,' Bluey encouraged her. 'We've got to get you to the hospital.'

Ellen looked at him, her face filled with pain. 'No,' she said weakly. 'It's too late for that. The baby's coming.'

Bluey swallowed nervously. 'Oh, no!'

'Help me get her into the main bedroom, now son,' Sally ordered, 'then get some towels, clean sheets and my medical kit. It looks like we're going to have a home birth.'

'Oh, Mum —' Bluey could not hide his panic.

'Plenty of babies have been born at home,' Sally reassured him. 'Don't worry. Just do as I ask.'

Bluey returned with the things his mother had asked for and was immediately ushered from the bedroom. 'But I want to be with her,' he pleaded.

'This is no place for men.' Sally pointed to the door. 'Now out with you.'

Not long after, the bearing down began. 'I see the head!' Sally encouraged Ellen. 'Bear down.' As Ellen strained, she heard Sally's cry of triumph. 'The head's clear! Just a couple more, love, and it'll be over.'

One minute later, Cathleen Joan O'Donnell was born.

'It's a girl!' Sally cried excitedly. After a time, she cut and tied the umbilical cord, then wrapped the baby in a soft towel before placing the infant in her mother's arms. When Ellen looked down at her newest offspring, her face, which had so recently been contorted with pain, was now a picture of tenderness. Sally had witnessed the same look when David was born.

'She looks a healthy one, Ellen.'

'Yes, she does.' Ellen eyed her mother-in-law with admiration. 'Thanks to you, Sal.'

'Don't be silly,' Sally scoffed self-consciously. 'Now, let's get her father and grandfather in here to have a look. Then we'll get you both to the hospital.'

Ellen stayed in hospital for a week, during which time the new mother was visited daily by Bluey and his parents. Doctors informed her that the baby was in perfect condition. Ellen was disappointed that her own mother could not be there. Pam had telephoned to say that Joan was very ill. The disease appeared to be progressing more quickly than expected.

When the O'Donnell clan was reunited at Kilkenny, Ellen quickly settled into the routine of a mother with a newborn. But this time it was different; Little David was there to keep her company during the feeding times, and when she decided to wean Cathleen off the breast at night, Bluey got up to feed the baby her bottle. Ellen protested that he needed his sleep, but he turned to her and smiled. 'I missed out on everything the last time, El. So I'll make up for it with Cathleen. Okay?'

Bluey was totally smitten by his new auburn-haired daughter, as was the baby's grandfather. In fact, everyone was so busy and so taken by the new family member that they did not seem to notice that Bluey had stopped his visits to the repat hospital. When hospital staff had called the first month, Bluey had been there to answer the phone, and politely thanked them and explained that he would no longer require their assistance. A letter had arrived since, but Bluey had ignored it.

I don't have *to go. Anyway, with the new baby there's no time.*

The months flew by and soon it was time for Cathleen's baptism. Ellen was disappointed that her mother and sister could not attend, but knew that Joan was pretty much wheelchair-bound, and that the birth of Pam's second child made it hard for her to travel.

Ellen missed her family, and decided to take the children with her to visit them for a week. It had been too long since Joan had seen them, and she wanted to meet Pam's newborn.

Bluey loaded Ellen's suitcases into the train carriage and kissed her and the children goodbye at the station. It had been so long since she'd travelled in an old puffing billy that she'd forgotten how dirty they were. To make matters worse, David was not on his best behaviour. He'd stuck his head out the window and a speck of soot had entered his eye. He was screaming bloody murder, which had set the baby off. It took some time to restore the peace. By the time the train pulled into Roma Street Station, Brisbane, dusk was settling over the city, but her journey was not over yet. She had to transfer to another platform to catch a local train to Coopers Plains and then a taxi to Pam's.

Stepping from the vehicle, she saw Pam descending the front stairs of the high-set Queenslander, her mother waving from the lit verandah. In all the excitement, Ellen soon forgot her tiredness. Joan hugged her grandson and took baby Cathleen from Ellen's arms, gazing down at her with grandmotherly tenderness.

Pam's newborn daughter, Jane, turned out to be a treasure, sleeping most of the time. One-year-old Eric was already taking his first steps. Sharing the care of the little ones, Ellen, Pam and her mother had a wonderful time reminiscing over many cups of tea. It was perhaps fortunate that Barry was on one of his extended country trips. The week flew past, and soon it was time to say goodbye.

A few months later, the O'Donnell family all gathered around the table to help Cathleen blow out the candles on her first birthday cake. Each year seemed to fold into the next as the farming cycle continued, and to Bluey's relief, the nightmare occurred less and less frequently. For the first time in years, he was relaxed, and at last experiencing some degree of contentment. Of course, there were the usual trials and tribulations. Cathleen contracted chicken pox and measles in her second year, one on top of the other, which kept Ellen virtually housebound for two months. It was also the year David started school. The family agreed that he should attend the public school, just like his parents. He settled into the routine like a trouper, no tears, not even on his first day.

By 1950, the situation could not have been much better for the O'Donnells. The overseas price for wheat and wool was at an all-time high, especially high-grade merino fleece, and Kilkenny grew the finest. In fact, during the wool sales of 1951, a world record was set for the price of premium Australian merino fibre. In such a favourable environment, and for the first time ever, Sally and Dave felt comfortably off, so comfortable that they decided to take a long-overdue holiday.

'That's a great idea.' Bluey was excited for his parents. 'Where are you going?'

'We thought we'd go to Burleigh Heads on the south coast, or anywhere on the beach,' Sally said. 'I can't remember the last time I saw white sand and surf.'

Ellen asked enthusiastically, 'When are you planning to leave?'

'In a week's time,' Dave answered. He looked up from his meal. 'You think you can look after things while I'm gone, Blue?'

'Don't give it a second thought, Dad. I'll be fine.'

'Course you will,' Sally chipped in. 'And anyway, a break away from us will do you pair good as well.' She was silent for a few moments, before asking the same question she asked every year. 'Will you be going to the Anzac Day ceremony in town?'

A shadow passed over his features. 'I don't reckon, Mum.'

'Very well, son. Maybe next year.' She placed an arm around his waist.

Sally was like a schoolgirl as they packed their new beige Dodge sedan. She was wearing the cool, colourful sun frock she'd bought especially for the occasion. Dave looked out of place in his shorts, beach shirt and sandals and let everyone know about it. He said he'd rather have worn his jeans and riding boots. Ellen looked on with amusement, pleased that her hardworking parents-in-law were at last taking a break from the constant grind of running the property.

'I wish we could come,' said David plaintively.

'Maybe next time, love,' Sally replied, giving him a parting kiss.

With Cathleen and David at their side, Bluey and Ellen waved as Dave and Sally drove through Kilkenny's front gate.

That night, after the children were in bed, Ellen heard a loud knock on the front door.

'I'll get it,' Bluey called.

In the background, she could hear a low mumble of voices. Then she froze at the sound of a loud thump on the floor. She ran from the kitchen to find her husband collapsed on the front verandah, two police officers trying to comfort him. White-faced, she asked the dreaded question. 'What's happened?'

The sergeant looked uncomfortable. 'We're very sorry to report that a beige Dodge sedan was involved in an accident as it descended Cunningham's Gap. When we arrived at the scene, both occupants, a male and a female, were deceased. Documents in the car indicate that the two were David and Sally O'Donnell. Once again, we're very sorry.'

The word deceased echoed in her head. Her legs buckled and her vision blurred. She felt totally helpless, similar to the way she felt when she'd heard that Bluey's ship had sunk. Sally and Dave were her dearest friends and she had loved them as surely as if they had been her own parents. They were the ones who had supported and loved her through a long and difficult period in her life. And now they were gone. She began to cry openly, her chest heaving with agonised sobs.

She did not notice when the two policemen drove off, although she must have thanked them, she thought.

Bluey was sitting on the verandah steps, staring into the darkness. When Ellen sat beside him, he barely registered her presence. She put her arms around him, wanting to comfort him. 'Oh, darling —' He sat stiffly and did not respond to her touch. Ellen looked at her husband through her own red and swollen eyes and realised that he was dry-eyed.

At that moment, Cathleen came out onto the verandah. She'd been woken by a bad dream. Ellen rose from the steps to take her back to bed, but the little girl saw her parents' faces and knew something terrible had happened.

'Why are you sad, Mummy?'

Ellen knew she would have to tell the children eventually, so she explained as simply as she could to four-year-old Cathleen.

'Does that mean we'll never see Grandma and Grandpa ever again?'

'I'm afraid not, darling.'

Cathleen began to cry. 'But couldn't we drive to heaven to visit them?'

'Oh, sweetie, no. It's a very special place that you can't get to by car.'

Cathleen looked past her mother to her father sitting hunched on the steps. 'I want Daddy to tuck me in,' she said quietly, and walked over to Bluey. She picked up his hand and tugged it gently, 'Come on, Daddy.' Something in the softness of his daughter's touch must have reached Bluey, because he got up slowly and took her back to her room. On his return, he spoke haltingly.

'The police want me to drive to Warwick to identify them.'

'When?' Ellen was relieved that Bluey had finally spoken, but was anxious about him leaving. David didn't know yet, and she wanted him to be there when she told him.

'First thing in the morning.'

'Is there anything you want me to do while you're gone?'

'No, there's not much on.' Bluey couldn't look at Ellen's tear-stained face. 'I'd better turn in.'

They slept poorly that night. The nightmare, the bane of his life, returned with a new intensity, showing him no mercy. Just as he managed to fall into a fitful sleep, he was visited once more by his demons. He awoke trembling. Ellen hardly closed her eyes all night.

Bluey left at seven a.m., before the children were up. It was a long drive to Warwick in the old utility, but Ellen estimated the round trip would take about five hours at the most. She'd kissed her husband tenderly, but he had been distant and uncommunicative. She told herself it must be the shock, and that people cope with grief in different ways.

It was a sad morning. The loss of his grandparents hit eight-year-old David hard, and he went out for a long walk with Skipper. Little Cathleen had blurted out the news to him at breakfast.

'Is that true, Mummy?' David looked at his mother.

'Yes, darling.' Ellen's eyes filled with tears.

'They might come back from heaven,' suggested Cathleen, hopefully.

'No they can't, silly,' chided David. 'When you go to heaven you have to stay there,' he said sadly.

To distract herself from the hollow grief inside, Ellen focused on the many household tasks she had saved for a rainy day. Around midmorning, she could not put it off any longer, and phoned her mother and sister to tell them the bad news. Pam was very upset, especially when she had to excuse herself and her mother from attending the funeral. Joan was in a great deal of pain. She'd developed stomach ulcers from her arthritis medication and was unable to take it any more. Knowing Pam was under immense pressure caring for her children as well as their mother, Ellen told them not to worry. She would pass on their love and sympathy to Bluey.

Lunchtime came and went, but still there was no sign of her husband. As the afternoon slowly passed, worrying thoughts began to enter her mind.

What if he's had an accident? Oh, God, surely not . . .

At five p.m. she put on pork sausages and vegetables for the children's dinner. She would cook more when Bluey arrived home.

Whenever that is.

At seven o'clock she felt a sudden surge of uneasiness, but pushed it aside to bathe the children.

'Where's Daddy?' Cathleen asked plaintively for the umpteenth time as Ellen tucked her in.

'He'll be home soon.'

'But he *always* kisses us goodnight, Mummy,' said David sadly.

Ellen felt another wave of grief and struggled against fresh tears.

'Well, he can kiss you twice tomorrow, then, can't he? Sweet dreams.'

By nine p.m. Ellen began to panic and phoned the Goondiwindi police station to enquire if any accidents had been reported. When a courteous constable informed her that there had been no crashes, she felt a bit better and went to bed. But sleep evaded her.

Where is he?

Chapter 23

Sergeant Simpson had greeted Bluey at the front desk of Warwick's police station that morning. 'I'll take you in the unmarked car, Mr O'Donnell. The morgue's in the basement of the general hospital.' The sergeant, in his mid-forties, wore an ill-fitting uniform that accentuated his pot belly. His awkwardness was strangely comforting to Bluey.

Exhausted from shock and lack of sleep, Bluey would have given everything he owned to be in Warwick for another reason. Why couldn't he just be on a sightseeing trip around the provincial town? Why did this have to happen? The unmarked police car entered the hospital gates and pulled to a halt in the special visitors' car park. The thought of the harrowing job ahead made him go weak at the knees. He took a deep breath.

I will not pass out again.

Bluey followed the sergeant down one flight of stairs to the cold and clinical atmosphere of the basement. It smelled strongly of disinfectant. An orderly in a white coat met Bluey and the sergeant and escorted them to a small sterile room at the far end of a long passageway. In the centre of the room were two covered trolleys, each with a tag tied to a metal leg with string. Bluey knew what the tags said. He also knew what was under the clean, white sheets. He felt suddenly dizzy. Closing his eyes, he tried to think of something else. Ellen's face, his children playing, the river – anything to blot out the reality he was facing. But all he could see was Digger, kneeling on the ground before his Japanese executioner. Bluey wished the cement floor would open up and swallow him.

'Ready, Mr O'Donnell?' Sergeant Simpson asked gently.

Bluey opened his eyes and saw the forms of his dead parents on the trolleys. The jagged pain hit home, pulling him back to the present. He nodded, and the attendant removed the sheet on the first trolley. Dave O'Donnell had died from internal injuries, and his face was unmarked. He looked quite peaceful, as though he was just asleep. Bluey's tough, hardworking Irish father had loved him unconditionally. They'd worked, fished and shot rabbits together and now he was dead – his dear, dear, father. Bluey inhaled sharply when the attendant lifted the second sheet. His beautiful mother – the woman who'd doted on him from the moment he was born – had the whole right side of her face caved in. Bluey fainted into the arms of the burley sergeant.

After Bluey had regained his composure, Sergeant Simpson drove him back to the station to complete some paperwork. Bluey managed to keep himself together as he thanked the policeman. Alone in the utility, Bluey could not hold back his grief. As he bumped along the Cunningham Highway, he thought about his wonderful parents. The way they'd always been there for him, the way they'd welcomed Ellen into their lives, their wisdom and generosity and sense of humour. Surely it couldn't be true that he'd never see them again? Childhood memories streamed through his mind, and the tears flowed until he had to pull over, his body heaving with choking sobs.

Back in Goondiwindi, Bluey forced himself to visit the local undertaker to make arrangements for the funeral. He knew that taking care of his parents in death was the right and proper thing to do. And as their only child, it was a task that fell to him. The undertaker offered sincere and genuine condolences. He had known and respected Dave and Sally O'Donnell. By the time Bluey left the funeral home, he was trembling.

Maybe I just need something to eat?

It was just on two p.m. when he entered the Royal Hotel to order a ham sandwich and a beer. As he lifted the glass to his lips, his hand began to shake and beer spilled onto the front of his good suit trousers. Dabbing at the spill, his attention was drawn to a group of men entering the hotel. They were committee members from Goondiwindi's Chamber of Commerce who had called in for a drink following a meeting. They all approached Bluey to offer their condolences – bad news travelled fast in a small town. Len Humphries was among the group, and when the others made their way to the bar, he stayed behind to chat.

'I'm really sorry to hear about your mum and dad, O'Donnell.'

'Thanks.'

'You look like hell. Let me buy you another drink.'

Before Bluey could reply, Humphries had turned away towards the bar. He returned to the table a few moments later with two whiskies.

He raised his glass. 'Here's to your parents.'

Bluey lifted his drink, stared at the floating ice cubes for a few seconds then downed it in one swallow. The whiskey burned his throat, but the liquid fire had one saving grace; it steadied the trembling.

'This your watering hole?' Bluey asked as he rose to return the hospitality by buying the next round.

'Yeah. Some of the other pubs are bloody dumps. Even let Abos in.' He screwed his face up in distaste. 'We usually come here.'

After downing four drinks, Humphries returned to his colleagues, leaving Bluey to drink by himself. As the alcohol began to take effect, he felt better, much better. Several whiskies later, he could barely remember his name, let alone why he was in the hotel. Finally, the publican instructed hotel staff not to serve him anymore. Slurring and staggering, Bluey told him what he could do with his hotel, then stumbled out to his utility.

Ellen heard the crash just after eleven p.m. She leaped out of bed and ran outside, flicking on the light in time to see Bluey fall out of the truck, which had struck the shed. For the first time in his life he was drunk out of his mind. He picked himself up and lurched towards the verandah. 'Shorry, love,' he slurred. 'It was just too horrible.'

Ellen said nothing as she took in his dishevelled appearance and the despair in his bloodshot eyes. With practised care, she lifted his arm and placed it around her shoulder, helping him to the bedroom. She'd often helped her mother guide her inebriated father to his room. Almost as soon as she lowered Bluey's head to the pillow, he lapsed into a drunken slumber. She removed his shoes before covering him with a blanket.

Ellen readied herself for bed, but the sleep she yearned for would not come. Lying awake, listening to her husband's light snoring, she wondered how this tragedy would affect him. He seemed so much stronger, his old self, but was it a brave front? In the early hours of the morning, she finally fell asleep.

Bluey was up and about before Ellen or the children had even stirred. He remembered Ellen helping him to bed, but that was all. Slipping out of bed a few minutes past five, he could see no sign of the morning sun. He tried to be as quiet as he could, although he knew Ellen was probably half awake.

He milked the cow and fed the poultry and pigs before retrieving the battered utility from beside the wrecked wall of the shed. When he saw the damage, he was filled with remorse and guilt.

Ellen watched out of the corner of her eye as he returned to the kitchen for his breakfast. She felt angry with him for putting her through such an anxious day, but her mood softened as she watched him lift Cathleen up and throw her in the air as he always did. The youngster giggled with delight. Then he did the same to David. 'You're getting too heavy, mate,' he laughed.

'I fixed up the funeral arrangements when I was in town yesterday,' he offered. 'It's the day after tomorrow. There'll be a notice in today's and tomorrow's paper.'

Ellen turned from the stove. She could see he was trying hard. 'Was it bad yesterday?'

'Yeah.'

She was quiet for a moment. 'Were they knocked about?'

'I've seen a bloody sight worse,' he stared helplessly at her then looked away.

'I'm sorry, darling, I shouldn't have asked,' she murmured. When she went on to ask practical questions about the funeral, he started to feel hot and shaky. His heart was drumming and his hands were suddenly wet with sweat.

Maybe it's just a hangover.

She saw the anxiety on his face, and quickly moved to his side to cradle his head against her breast. David watched, puzzled, as his mother stroked his father's hair. When his father had turned away, the boy thought for a moment that he was crying, but told himself that this couldn't be true, because his dad would never cry.

The O'Donnell funeral was not a big affair as funerals go, with only neighbours and a few friends and relatives attending the service. Uncle Mick and Rodney shut the butcher shop so they could attend.

Bluey wore his best suit that Ellen had cleaned and pressed, while Ellen chose the outfit she'd purchased for David's baptism, including the black leather bag and kid gloves Dave and Sally had so generously given to her for the occasion. In accordance with their wishes, there was just a quiet grave-side service presided over by a Church of England minister and a Catholic priest. They were buried in the same grave, the service over almost as soon as it had begun. Ellen sobbed openly, but Bluey had again shut down.

I've got to stay strong for Ellen and the kids.

On the drive back to Kilkenny, his knuckles were white as he gripped the steering wheel of the utility. He turned to Ellen who was nursing Cathleen while David sat between them. He wanted to explain his feelings, but the words would not come. Finally, all he could say was, 'I feel like I'm comin' apart, El.'

'I know, darling,' she said gently. 'Time will help us get over it.'

'But this, on top of everything else . . .' His words trailed off.

'What do you mean, "everything else"?' She looked across at him. 'Is there something worrying you? Please tell me,' she pleaded.

Bluey kept his eyes fixed on the road. He hadn't meant to use those words – a slip of the tongue.

Not now. Not with the kids in the car.

'No, forget it,' he answered dismissively.

'Bluey, I know something's wrong. It has been for a long time,' she said, daring to broach the subject again. 'You're still having nightmares, aren't you?' She took a deep breath. 'Why can't you talk to me about it?'

'I bloody well can't, that's all!'

The children were shocked at their father's outburst and clung to their mother. The rest of the trip was made in silence.

Chapter 24

After the death of his parents, Bluey assumed full responsibility for the running of Kilkenny. For a while he coped admirably, thanks to the expert guidance and training he'd received from his father. But then Ellen began to notice subtle changes. He would often sit for long periods without speaking, and his memory became patchy, as if a heavy fog had settled over the retentive part of his brain. The tragic death of his parents was the exception. His memory of this continually reared out of his mind like an iceberg from a freezing ocean. At times he found it hard to get out of bed, but with a supreme effort of will, he would force himself out to complete his daily tasks. As the days passed into months, he became more and more withdrawn from Ellen and the children.

Most evenings, after work, he sat in front of the radio, but was oblivious to the program being broadcast. He knew Ellen was unhappy and worried sick about him, but he didn't care.

Ellen hardly knew how to approach him anymore. He wasn't even interested in making love. She prayed that the grief and despair would not finally push him over the edge. On one Saturday night, she thought it may have.

The night before David's ninth birthday, Bluey left early to pick up a load from the produce store, but had not returned by tea time. A knot of fear had formed in her stomach as she phoned the police and the hospital. Yet, even as she put down the telephone receiver, little doubts had crept into her mind. Her fears were confirmed when Bluey arrived home roaring drunk a few hours later. As she put him to bed, she had a sick feeling that this would not be the last time she would do this.

He seemed to be his usual self as the family celebrated David's birthday. He even played cricket with the lad in the backyard. David was keen to try out the new bat he'd received as a present. He was also keen to keep his father to his promise that he would take him rabbiting once he'd turned nine. He'd been shown how to handle the .22 rifle, and under the supervision of his father could hit a jam tin from twenty yards. Shooting a moving target would obviously be much harder.

The following morning, Bluey and his son were out in the paddocks at daybreak. Once his eyes had become accustomed to the semi-darkness, David began to look for rabbits. Bluey was first to spot one. 'Look, over there,' he whispered, pointing, 'there's a big one by that saltbush.'

Without hesitation, David raised the rifle and fired. The rabbit scampered away, unscathed. 'I missed,' he said dejectedly.

'You jerked the trigger, mate. Remember, you squeeze it slowly.'

It took ten minutes to spot another one, which David hit

plum centre. 'You got him!' Bluey clapped him on the back. 'Well done.'

David glowed in the warmth of his father's approval. 'Let's try again, Dad,' he cried eagerly.

They returned to the homestead with three rabbits. 'This is the worst part, mate,' Bluey grunted before demonstrating how to skin and gut their kill. David was proud of his achievement and wallowed in his parents' praise. Ellen was thrilled that Bluey had spent time with David, and promised to cook a delicious stew with the largest rabbit.

David's birthday proved to be a momentary respite for Bluey, who soon returned to the pit of despair. Despite working himself to exhaustion, almost every night the nightmare returned to haunt him.

After weeks of disturbed sleep, Bluey was desperate to obtain some sort of relief from the accursed spectre that was tearing his life apart. The next time he travelled to town to pick up a load from the produce store, he called in at the hotel.

I'll just have one drink. That's all I need. A bit of a pick-me-up.

He didn't intend to stay long, but of course, returned to the homestead blind drunk.

The next morning he again played the part of the remorseful husband, apologising for his behaviour and promising that he did not mean to hurt anyone. As time ticked by, this scenario was repeated. Without any notice, he would drop what he was doing and drive to town, only to arrive home hours later completely inebriated. He was always sorry the day after, but somehow, he couldn't stop.

When I drink, there's no nightmare.

Ellen prayed that his need for alcohol would pass, that time would heal the wounds of war and grief and that he would no longer crave oblivion.

During the early stages of his drinking, Bluey still gave a considerable amount of time to his children, whom he idolised. And when he came home late, the children were spared the spectre of a dribbling, staggering father. However, the love he felt for David and Cathleen could not outweigh the need he had for alcohol, and he continued to head into town at every given opportunity, especially on weekends. At those times, David pined for his father's company. They'd often played cricket and gone rabbiting together on Sundays. Now, his father was either working or at the pub.

David remembered the last time they'd gone fishing. He'd made the mistake of asking his father about the war. Other boys at school spoke openly of their father's achievements in the conflict, and he longed to do the same. The lad was not prepared for his father's reaction. His face like thunder, Bluey had spoken harshly, 'Don't *ever* ask me about it.' David was now nine years old, and while he was an intelligent child, he could not understand the reason for his father's angry response. He blinked back tears and tried to concentrate on fishing. He still loved his father, but a new feeling had crept into their relationship – fear.

Fortunately for Bluey, the family's financial circumstances had grown quite comfortable, and money was not a problem. He'd even hired two full-time rouseabouts, who were staying in the shearers' quarters. Ellen cooked their meals, which they collected from the kitchen. With extra help on hand, Bluey was able to slip away to town unnoticed, and be sure that the necessary jobs on the property were completed.

As Bluey's drinking worsened, Ellen didn't know what to do or where to obtain help. She couldn't bring herself to discuss the matter with Uncle Mick or Aunty Pat. It was too personal. And she did not want to burden her mother and sister.

Ellen tried everything to prevent her husband from heading to the hotel. She pleaded with him, attempting to appeal to his better nature. She tried using the children as a means of preventing him going to town, telling him what an adverse effect his drinking was having on them. She even went so far as to hide the keys to the ute. But it was all to no avail.

Things came to a head one night when Bluey arrived home late with a bottle of whiskey.

Ellen looked at him with disgust. 'I'll not have you drinking in my home and in front of the children,' she said angrily.

'It's not your bloody home!' he spat, his eyes narrowing as he swayed in front of her. 'It's mine.'

'You bastard!'

'You bitch!'

Ellen could see that there was no point arguing with him in his present state. Instead, she grabbed the bottle from his hands and darted out into the backyard. Bluey charged after her.

'No!' he yelled, stricken by the thought that his precious whiskey was in danger.

She ran to the rear of the yard, smashing the unopened bottle of Johnnie Walker against an old gum tree beside the back fence, and letting it drop in the grass.

Bluey looked at the broken bottle and his eyes narrowed. 'Bloody bitch!'

He lunged at a terrified Ellen, taking her arm in a vice-like grip, and pulled her towards him. Bluey drew back his fist to hit her, and she cried out in pain and fear. When he caught sight of her face, he let go, crumbling to the ground.

'I nearly hit you, El,' he cried, and began to weep. 'How could I do such a thing?' Sobered by the shock of his own actions, he paused to look at her. 'Oh, God, El. That's it. I'm never having another drink,' he sobbed. 'I'm so sorry.'

Ellen looked at the wreck of a man her husband had become. She could not hate him when he so clearly hated himself.

'It was just the drink, Bluey,' she answered quietly. 'I know in your right mind you would never harm me.'

'I'll stop,' he said, his voice choked with emotion. 'I'll stop.' And for almost three weeks, he kept his word. But the nightmares returned, and again he reached for the bottle to drive them away.

This time, the drinking was even more excessive. Every second day he would take off for town. Even when he was at home, she suspected he had alcohol hidden somewhere on the property. She even searched the barn and agricultural shed, but never found any. To make matters worse, she could no longer hide his addiction from the children. The once attentive, devoted dad rarely spoke to them anymore, let alone played with them. While she could tolerate the lack of closeness in her own relationship with Bluey, she could not bear to see the hurt and disappointment in her children's faces. Ellen had often seen Cathleen trying to start up a conversation with her father, only to have him walk away in mid-sentence as though he did not know she was there. David wondered what he had done wrong to lose his father's attention. After having such a close relationship, he felt as if his father was shunning him.

Please, Dad.

During one particularly long session at the Royal Hotel, Len Humphries entered the bar and approached a hard-faced blonde sitting at a table near the door to the lounge. Bluey had often seen her in the pub, but had never spoken to her. Moments later, he saw the pair approaching him.

'Do you two know each other?' Humphries looked from one to the other.

Bluey struggled to focus on the female who stood swaying before him. The slightly overweight woman had bleached blonde hair and looked to be about thirty-five years of age, though it was difficult to tell. Bluey thought she might have been pretty at one time, but her skin was now mottled and her complexion a blotchy, boozy red.

'O'Donnell, this is Ruby Marks. Ruby, this is Bluey O'Donnell.'

'G'day, Blue,' she slurred. 'Wanna drink?'

'Orright, Ruby.' He reached for his cash. 'What'll you have?' he asked, downing the remainder of his whiskey in one swallow.

She beckoned the barman. 'Full rum and Coke.'

Taking his leave, Humphries winked at Ruby, and that was how Ruby Marks became Bluey's drinking companion. The unlikely pair would meet on almost every occasion he travelled into town.

Bluey felt comfortable around Ruby. She didn't ask questions or look down her nose at him as he felt Ellen did when he drank. She only talked about herself, and asked him nothing about his own life, which suited him. Most of the time, all she wanted to do was get 'blotto'. If she wasn't at the Royal when he came to town, it didn't bother him. If she was there, they drank together, Bluey paying for most of the rounds. While a physical relationship was never on his agenda, there was a time when Ruby sought more. On one hot Saturday afternoon, while the pair sat drinking at a table in the hotel's lounge, she leaned over. 'You wanna do it one day, Blue?'

'Do what?' He looked at her, his eyelids drooping.

'Whaddyareckon? Fuck,' she shot back.

'Nah,' he mumbled, staring at the empty glass that stood on the table in front of him.

'It must be boring havin' it off with the same woman all the time.'

Bluey ignored her.

'A change is as good as a holiday, I always say.' She tossed her head and batted her eyelids coquettishly.

'Forget it, Rube. Another drink?'

She swallowed down the remaining liquid in her glass. 'Yeah. The usual.'

Chapter 25

When Ellen heard about Ruby, it was the straw that broke the camel's back. Brenda Murphy had been in two minds whether to tell her. Brenda's brother-in-law, Sean, was an old mate of Bluey's. He had seen him in one of the town's pubs in company with Ruby Marks, the town's shady lady. After blurting out the information, Brenda watched the expression of shock on her friend's face. She almost wished she hadn't told her.

But she had to know.

Ellen had almost staggered backwards as if she'd been slapped in the face. She couldn't for the life of her conjure up a set of circumstances that could explain his behaviour. To Ellen, a monogamous marriage was something to be treasured, something special. The news left her reeling. In one brief moment, her life had come crashing down around her.

'I'm sorry to be the one to tell you, Ellen. But I thought you had to know.'

Ellen tried to focus on what her friend was saying. 'Oh. Th–that's all right.'

'Do you want me to put the kettle on?'

'To tell you the truth, Brenda, I think I need some time alone to think.'

'I understand. Give me a call if you want to talk.' She hugged Ellen and kissed her on the cheek. 'I'll see you next Wednesday.'

Ellen sat heavily at the kitchen table, her head in her hands.

Ruby Marks had a bad reputation from way back. It had been whispered about town that when Ruby was only seventeen, she'd had a love affair with a married man – a company representative who visited the town regularly. He was never seen again after he learned that Ruby had a 'bun in the oven'. Ruby left not long after, and if gossips could be believed, went to work in a Salvation Army home for unmarried mothers in Brisbane, where she gave birth to a baby that was immediately put up for adoption. Ruby returned to Goondiwindi in due course, and found herself shunned by most of the locals. She did not have much family support, either, as her mother had died when she was only eleven and her father, when he wasn't working for the railways, was to be found drinking in one of Goondiwindi's hotels. Ruby liked to have a good time, and it was often said that she was 'easy'. Ellen had once felt sorry for Ruby, but now felt only resentful and bitter.

That night when Bluey returned, Ellen was waiting. 'I spoke to Brenda Murphy today.' The feeling of dread was so strong she did not think she could bear it.

'So what.'

'She told me about your girlfriend Ruby. Sean saw you together at a pub.'

'She's not my girlfriend!' he exploded. 'And Brenda should mind her own bloody business!'

'You rotten mongrel!' she snapped. 'I'm home alone, out of my mind with worry, and you're on with that, with that *slut.*' Ellen slammed a pot down on the kitchen bench.

'That's not true,' Bluey growled.

'Don't lie!' she shouted. 'You've been seen together. You can't hide in Goondiwindi, Bluey.'

'She's just a drinkin' mate.' The idea that Ruby was his girlfriend was too ridiculous for words. It was all he could do not to burst out laughing.

Ellen saw his amused expression and could not reign in her fury. 'What do you take me for, a fool?'

'I don't take you for anything.'

Her eyes blazed. 'You can say that again. And your hanging around with the town bike just happens to coincide with the fact that we don't have sex any more?'

'No, that's not true!'

'This is it, Bluey.' Her tone was level, icy. 'You give up the grog and your girlfriend, or I'm leaving.'

'For the last time,' his voice rose, 'she's not my bloody girlfriend!'

She glared at him. 'Give up the drink, Bluey, or I'll leave and take the children with me.'

'I'll save you the trouble!' he answered fiercely.

How dare she issue ultimatums!

He stormed into their bedroom and threw a few personal belongings into an old battered suitcase. As he passed the children's room, he looked in on their peaceful, sleeping forms.

Ellen followed him onto the verandah. She couldn't quite believe that this was happening. 'This is it then?' Her voice wavered. 'What about Kilkenny?'

'Do what you like with it,' he snarled.

Watching the lights of the ute become smaller and smaller in the darkness, Ellen felt her stomach twist as if she'd been kicked. She tried to swallow over the sudden lump in her throat.

What have I done?

Numb with shock, she walked back into the lounge room and sat down on the couch. She knew there was no point going to bed that night – she would never sleep.

Is this the end of our marriage? What if he never comes back?

She tried to think of some sort of plan that would enable her to keep Kilkenny going until he returned. At least their current finances were sound, and there was enough money to keep on the hired hands.

But for how long?

Ben Frazier and John McKindley had a reputation in the Goondiwindi area as dependable farm workers who could turn their hands to just about any task. In the past they had earned a good living as shearers. Both were aged somewhere in their fifties and were rough diamonds. Ben had never married, and John had been a widower for many years.

Over their evening meal in the shearers' quarters the next day, Mac looked up from his food. He had removed his hat, revealing his hairless scalp. 'What do you think, mate? The ute's missing. Do you think he's shot through?'

'Dunno,' Ben grunted, loading vegetables onto his fork. 'Silly bastard. Grog's got hold of him. How could he leave her? I mean, apart from being a terrific-looking sort, she's just so nice.'

'How long do you think she can manage by herself?

'Don't know, mate. We'll help as best we can.'

'Yeah, we will.'

A week passed, and Ellen had still heard nothing. In answer to constant questioning from David and Cathleen, she informed them that their father had gone away for a short break. David looked a little uncertain on being told this. His father had never been away for this long before. Cathleen said simply, 'I hope he comes home soon.'

After three weeks without news of her errant husband, Ellen thought it time to make official enquiries. The children were constantly plaguing her with questions about his return. She contacted the police sergeant in charge at Goondiwindi station.

'Have you heard anything about Bluey, Jim?' she asked, a little embarrassed.

'Nothing at all, Ellen,' he answered.

In her quest for information, she called in to her Uncle Mick's butcher shop. 'I'm sorry, Ellen. All I heard was that he left town with some bloody sheila.' He pretended to tidy the butcher's paper on the counter, unable to face the hurt in her eyes. 'The silly bastard.'

Ellen paled.

He's taken that slut with him. How could he!

'Well, damn him,' she said out loud, and stormed out of the shop before her uncle could comfort her.

With a sinking heart, she phoned her mother and sister to explain the circumstances leading to Bluey's departure. Joan was devastated for her daughter. 'Oh, pet! I wish I was well enough to come up and help look after the house for you,' she said forlornly. In all the years Joan had endured her own husband's drinking, she'd never once seriously considered leaving him. She was overwhelmed by the responsibility that her young daughter now faced.

'Don't worry, Mum. I'll be fine.' Ellen wished she believed this.

Chapter 26

No matter how much time passed, David and Cathleen could not understand why their father had left. The boy was now ten, but like his younger sister, blamed himself for his father's leaving.

Maybe he just didn't love us any more.

In their confusion and grief, the children began to misbehave, something they never did. At every opportunity, David would disappear down into the paddocks, too far to hear Ellen's calls for him to come home. Their behaviour increased the pressure on Ellen, who was barely coping. She constantly had to coerce David into carrying out his chores, and the more she chided him, the more sullen he became. Fights between the children seemed to start with little provocation. Cathleen was in tears at the drop of a hat and even began to wet the bed. When David found out, he taunted his sister, which prompted Ellen to severely reprimand him. Their clash led to David withdrawing even further. Ellen had to tread carefully with her daughter lest she make the bed-wetting problem worse.

To Ellen, if there was one plus to the separation, it was the relief she felt at being on her own. She no longer had to wait anxiously for Bluey to arrive home rolling drunk and then endure the subsequent arguments that left her emotionally drained and unable to sleep. Even though she was under immense pressure to keep the property going, the house seemed quiet and peaceful, a sanctuary that she would never take for granted.

The next six months brought about significant change in Ellen's financial situation. While 1953 had been a bumper season, 1954 proved to be the opposite, a complete and utter disaster. A severe drought had settled on the district, and not only was the farm's grain harvest halved, but the new planting was also suspended indefinitely. To exacerbate the situation, the worldwide price for wool had plummeted with the end of the Korean War, and Kilkenny's wool clip was also greatly reduced as a result of the extended drought. Although Ellen just managed to pay the shearing contractor, she found she could no longer afford to pay Ben and Mac. When Ellen gave the pair the bad news, Ben nodded knowingly, his lips narrowing into a determined line. Mac silently stood with his hands in the pockets of his work trousers. Skipper sat by the two men.

'Wondered how long you could keep us on, Missus,' Ben drawled. 'You know, with the poor harvest and all.' He paused. 'Look, we'll keep goin' unpaid for a couple of more weeks if you can feed us. See what happens. If there's no rain by then, we'll leave.'

She was touched by their generosity. 'I can't let you work for nothing.'

'You'd pay us when things get better, wouldn't you, Missus?'

She felt a lump in her throat. 'Of course, but —'

'No buts,' interrupted Mac. Ellen looked at him, surprised. He was usually the quiet one. 'We've talked it over,' he said.

'Thank you.' She choked down an involuntary sob. 'You've no idea what this means to me.'

She was so overcome by the generosity of the two men that tears began to flow as she walked back to the house. Ellen brushed them away with the hem of her apron and reflected on the good hearts of these men. They owed her nothing, yet they were prepared to keep working without wages. She pushed open the back door, and walked into a slanging match between her two children, who were arguing over the last lolly in a packet.

'Stop it!' Ellen raised her voice above theirs.

'But it's mine!' Cathleen cried loudly.

'It's not!' David yelled, his face set.

'It is!' her daughter screamed.

That something so trivial had turned into a heated argument between them was all too much for Ellen, who ran to the bedroom and locked the door. She threw herself on the bed and sobbed into the pillow.

The shock of seeing their mother so upset brought the children's argument to an immediate halt. Guiltily, they made their way to their mother's door. They could hear her weeping.

Swallowing down the gorge in his own throat, David knocked lightly. 'Mum,' he called, 'please don't cry.' He heard his own voice shake. When there was no response, he went on. 'We're sorry for fighting and Cathleen's crying. Won't you please come out? Please?'

After a few moments, the intense weeping faded to a few sniffs. The door opened and her children threw themselves into her outstretched arms. She hugged them and stroked their hair. 'Now that Daddy's gone we have to stick together and help each other. No more fighting because Mummy can't cope with it. Do you understand?' She looked from one small face to the other.

'We'll help, Mum, don't you worry.' Her son wrapped his arms around her protectively.

'Yes, we will,' Cathleen said, wiping away her tears with her sleeve.

Two weeks later, Ellen waved goodbye to Ben and Mac as they rode their packed motorbikes past the homestead verandah. They had wished her the best of luck, and she had thanked them, kissing each man on the cheek and handing them a parcel of sandwiches.

Back in the kitchen, Ellen sat down with a cup of tea.

What will I do?

There was no crop in the ground, the soil was still as dry as powder, and it was the middle of a particularly hot summer. A number of prime sheep in the outer paddock had died due to lack of feed. Prowling dingoes were also on the increase, as were kangaroos, which filled the sheep paddocks at dusk. If the balance of the merino flock was to survive, Ellen knew she would have to drive the remaining sheep into the large river paddock where a limited amount of grass still grew beside the dwindling Macintyre River. Skipper and the other two kelpies, Minto and Bennie, would help.

At least there's some water there.

Taking one paddock at a time, over the next three days she

moved the majority of the flock to the river paddock. She hoped that, without the sheep, the grass in the other paddocks might recover a bit. Under a blazing sun, the task had sapped almost every ounce of her strength.

She stood in the barn unsaddling her bay mare, Sweetie. She was utterly spent, and still she had to prepare dinner and do so many other jobs at the farmhouse. At times like this, the pressure was so great that she felt like running away from the property and taking her children. She would think about the beach at Wynnum, and imagine herself running along the grassy foreshore, the children laughing and wet from swimming.

I can't carry on like this.

At such times, she did what she always did when things got her down, she re-read the letters from her mother and Pam which she kept in a box by her bed.

Ellen still visited Aunty Pat every time she went to town, and still called in at Uncle Mick's butcher shop, but could not afford to buy meat from him anymore. They were surviving on mutton, salted pork and any rabbits that David was able to shoot. The water tank beside the house had run dry, and they were carting water for cooking and personal use from the windmill trough out in the paddock.

Uncle Mick felt bad that he couldn't spare the time to help out his favourite niece on the property. 'I still want you to take this rump steak and some bones for the dogs, Ellen,' he said on one of her visits, holding out a parcel wrapped in newspaper.

'No. I can't do that, Uncle,' she said, overwhelmed by his generous offer.

'You'll take this parcel, do you hear?' He shoved it in her hands and hugged her. 'You look after yourself out there.'

'Yes, Uncle,' her reply was choked. 'And thank you.'

When Ellen visited the grocer, Cliff Smith, to request an extension of her credit limit, he was most obliging.

'You're not on your own, Ellen. A lot of property owners are in the same position with this damn drought.'

'Thank you, Mr Smith. This means a great deal to me.'

'I've always extended credit during the hard times and I've always been repaid when things improve. You can depend on country people,' he said proudly.

Ellen changed the subject. She was starting to feel emotional again in the face of yet another kind gesture, and did not want to cause a scene. 'How is Margaret?'

'She's doing fine. Thank you for asking. She's teaching at Greenslopes State School in Brisbane. She's leaving soon to have a baby.' He beamed.

'Please pass on my congratulations.'

Bill Greensill, the owner of the produce store, was equally obliging when Ellen approached him for extra credit. His son, who'd been killed during the war, had played cricket with Bluey, and Bill knew the O'Donnell family well.

The proprietor of the fuel depot, however, steadfastly refused to extend further credit to the O'Donnell property. 'I don't think it would be wise while Bluey's not there,' the man said tightly. Ellen slammed the door on her way out. Not being able to access fuel would be a major problem. Without it, she couldn't run the tractor or the Dodge sedan. How would she travel to and from town? With every passing second, she felt her confidence diminishing.

Back at Kilkenny, she paced around the kitchen, trying to think of a solution. The burden was becoming too much. Wiping her eyes with a handkerchief, Ellen came to a decision. She would load the car with everything of value she could find in the house and take it to town to sell. The only other alternative was to sell all the wethers to the abattoir, but that would be a last resort. She must try to hold on.

Ellen went into the spare room and began looking through Sally and Dave's things. Her eyes brimmed as she found their treasured possessions – they were so few, and so modest: Dave's gold watch, a couple of gold nuggets left to him by his Irish uncle, and Sally's jewellery case. She baulked at the thought of selling them, but knew that she could not let sentiment interfere with the needs of Kilkenny and her family.

I don't think they'd mind, God bless them.

Yet the more she thought about selling them, the more nervous she became. By the time she'd gathered everything together, her self-confidence had almost completely deserted her and she was in a state of panic. She felt like a thief in the night as she made her way out of the front door to the beige sedan parked beside the house. It was already past midday, and the children would be back from school in less than three hours.

Ellen shut the car door and walked towards the pawn shop, hoping no one would see her. Unfortunately, Len Humphries saw her through the front window of his business – Humphries Agricultural Machinery, nicknamed 'HAM' by the locals – which was one door down and across the road.

This is my chance.

He strode purposefully to the entrance and outside onto the footpath. Dodging a couple of cars, he crossed the street, loudly calling out her name.

He was the last person she wanted to meet, and her face turned pink with embarrassment. 'Len,' she said and stopped.

'How are you?' he asked sweetly, baring his tobacco-stained teeth.

'I'm fine,' she replied, staring at her feet. 'You?'

'I'm good.' Humphries saw the small bag she was carrying. 'Selling something?'

'A few things.' She wished the ground would open up and swallow her.

'Need some dough?' He hadn't meant to blurt it out.

'That's my business, isn't it?' she said, feeling suddenly irritated by his presumption.

'Sorry, Ellen. I'm just concerned about you, that's all.'

Ellen looked at him, surprised by his genuine tone. 'I'm sorry too, Len,' she said. 'Things aren't going too well at the moment.'

'Look, instead of going in there,' he indicated the pawn shop, 'why don't I buy you a spot of lunch?'

Ellen was on the verge of saying no, but then changed her mind.

The hell with it.

'Okay. Why not?' She smiled.

Humphries took her arm as he guided her across the wide street then down the footpath to the cafe. As they took their seats in a booth, he signalled to one of the girls behind the counter.

'Want something to drink?' he asked politely.

'Just something cold, thank you.'

He ordered two pineapple crushes and a plate of mixed sandwiches which were served a few minutes later. She gratefully sipped the drink while he opened the conversation. 'Heard from Bluey?' he asked.

Ellen shook her head.

'The silly galoot. How could he leave you, of all people?'

'Bluey has some problems —'

'You can say that again,' he interrupted. 'You know Ruby?'

Ellen felt her colour rising, but forced herself to stay calm. 'Just from school and her reputation.'

'Rough as bags.' He screwed up his face in disgust. 'He must be mad.'

'I really don't want to talk about it at the moment, Len,' she answered tightly.

'Okay,' he agreed, changing the subject. 'So things aren't going too well out at Kilkenny?'

Ellen was on the verge of telling him to mind his own business again, but changed her mind. It was a relief to be able to discuss her problems with someone. She took a moment to answer. 'Everything was fine until the drought.'

'Yes, even our business has been affected. Fortunately, our company has agencies in areas which are still prospering, so overall there's no problem for us. We're lucky.' He grinned and removed a packet of cigarettes from his pocket.

'I'm pleased for you.'

Humphries looked at Ellen, trying to measure her feelings towards him. She seemed distracted, but not annoyed – vulnerable even. He lit up and sucked the smoke deep into his lungs. 'Look, Ellen, I don't want to interfere, but I have to ask. How are you situated financially?'

Once again, the sincerity in his manner disarmed her. He seemed to have changed quite a lot since the war – everyone had.

'To tell you the truth, things are bad. I've still got credit at the grocery and produce stores, but I can't get any credit for fuel.'

'I see.' He looked thoughtful for a moment, and then his face lit up. 'Why don't you get your fuel on our firm's account?'

'Oh,' she looked shocked. 'I couldn't possibly do that.'

'Why not? We're old friends?'

'I couldn't accept charity.'

'It wouldn't be charity,' he assured her. 'You could pay me back when things pick up.'

Ellen could not believe her ears. This would solve her most pressing problem. She had to accept. 'Very well, Len, and thank you,' she said gratefully.

'That's okay . . .'

Ellen could see he wanted to say something more. 'Was there something else?'

He gazed into her green eyes and smiled shyly. 'Ellen, I don't quite know how to say this. You know how I feel about you, don't you?'

Ellen looked askance.

So that's it.

Humphries saw the change in her demeanour. 'No. Don't think that, please. What I was going to say was, since you know how I feel, you know why I'm doing it. But this is also a business gesture, no strings attached.'

Hell, woman. Don't you realise I love you and want to help you?

'Good.' She gave a sigh of relief.

Len coughed as he summoned his courage. 'I know it's too soon, but I hope there'll be a time in the future when you may consider me —'

'Len, please don't say that.'

'Sorry.' He rose to his feet. 'I'll be off now. Good luck, and don't forget to fill up at the fuel depot before you go home. I'll give Jack a ring when I get back to the office.' He paused again. 'One more thing. If you ever need anything, I'll be there for you.'

'Thanks, Len.' She smiled at him for the first time.

Striding out of the cafe, Humphries had a spring in his step.

She's so beautiful when she smiles.

There were no problems at the fuel depot, the owner all apologies as he used a hand-pump to lift petrol from the underground tank to the wide glass cylinder atop the bowser. On the way home, Ellen looked down at the bag of items she had intended to pawn.

Something for the future.

That night as she sat down for dinner with the children, Ellen looked across at her son who was picking at his braised rabbit and vegetables. He was so tall now, she thought, and was developing a wiry build just like his father's. 'What's the matter?' she enquired.

'Nothing, Mum,' he replied, head down.

'Come on, sweetie, tell me.'

'Is Dad ever coming back?' The pain and misery in his voice were plain to hear.

'I don't know.' The question had caught her off guard.

'Is it something we did?'

'No. Of course not.' She was quick to reassure him.

'I miss him, Mummy.' It was Cathleen's turn. The young girl reminded Ellen of a mixture of Bluey and Sally. Her shoulder-length, auburn hair was beginning to curl at the ends.

'Did you send him away?' David asked tentatively.

Ellen sighed. She knew she could not hide the truth from her son. 'Sort of, I suppose.'

'But why?'

It made her heart ache to see the anguish in his face. 'You're eleven now, David, so maybe you'll understand.' Her mouth was suddenly dry at the prospect of trying to explain adult behaviour to a child. 'I could not have your father drinking like he was.'

'But he never drank before. He could have stopped.'

She looked into her son's lightly freckled face framed by his thick, ginger curls and all she could see was Bluey at that same age. 'He tried to stop . . .' Ellen's eyes misted over. 'I'm sure he wants to stop. He'll come back when he can live without it.'

'But when will that be?' David asked.

'I honestly don't know, son,' she said sadly. 'But I know one thing, you'll have to be the man of the house for a while longer. If we're going to keep Kilkenny going, we'll all have to do a lot more. I'll keep things going during the week, but you'll have to do more at the weekends. I'm sorry.'

'That's all right, Mum.' David got up from the table to hug her.

'I'll help too, Mummy.' Cathleen stood beside her mother.

'Of course you will, darling.' Ellen placed her arm around the girl's waist.

'I can do the chooks and the pigs, can't I? I'm seven now.'

The eagerness in the young voice and the shine in her eyes made Ellen's heart swell with love for her darling child. Impulsively, she drew Cathleen to her and gave her a big hug. Heaven knows, her children had not had it easy, especially David. She knew there had been taunts from other children at school. David had been wearing a few cuts and bruises, evidence of having been in a fight. She would have to have a talk with him if it happened again.

Chapter 27

Bluey had driven away from Ellen and Kilkenny with no idea of what he planned to do. He'd needed to get away, and now that he had, he felt an emptiness inside. He told himself that Ellen's incessant nagging had forced him into leaving, and for this, he blamed her. He gripped the steering wheel hard and shook his head. Her accusations about Ruby had been laughable.

She knows I never look at other women in that way.

His thoughts turned to his children and he felt the guilt like a pain in his chest.

How can I leave them?

Then he remembered Ellen saying that his drinking was hurting them.

Maybe they're better off without me.

He saw his separation from Ellen and his children as something temporary. He would just take a break, a short holiday to sort himself out. Then he'd return and they'd start out fresh. Right now, he needed a drink, and somewhere to think.

Later, as he sat drinking with Ruby in the lounge of the hotel, an idea came to him.

'I'm going to Sydney, Rube.'

Bluey couldn't explain the feeling that came over him when he made the decision. All he knew was that he had a powerful urge to run – to get away from Goondiwindi.

'I'll come with ya,' she offered.

'Orright. If you want to,' he slurred. He didn't care one way or the other.

The improbable pair retrieved her meagre possessions from the flat she rented in the centre of town and set off for Sydney. It took four days for Bluey and Ruby to travel there, not that either of them remembered much of the journey. It was a miracle that they even survived, since at every opportunity during their trip along the New England Highway they stopped for liquid refreshments, sleeping off the after-effects in the ute.

On reaching Sydney, they registered at a run-down, inner-city pub where the accommodation rate was cheap and the grog on tap. After a week, they sought more long-term lodgings and moved to the Salvation Army's People's Palace. Counter staff were less than impressed with their new residents who arrived back drunk every night. After a month and numerous warnings to curtail their unseemly behaviour, the pair was asked to leave. Over the next few weeks, they moved from one flophouse to another.

Eventually, Bluey's money dwindled to the stage where they were forced to sleep outdoors in Hyde Park or any other reserve they could find. The money he received from selling the utility kept them in booze for another five months.

Bluey lost track of Ruby when the money finally ran out. She'd found someone else – someone who sought more in a relationship than just a drinking partner. After the separation, he spent his days in The Rocks and Circular Quay. When there were no police around, he would place his hat on the ground in hopes that passers-by would throw a coin in his direction. He also registered for the dole at the city's Commonwealth Employment Service.

Every morning, when he was sober, he would be overcome with grief over leaving his children. Now they were not around, he missed them – their voices and laughter. If he'd been honest with himself, he would have admitted that he also missed Ellen. He'd lain for a long time thinking about his home and his family. On occasions, he even made the decision to return home, but after a few drinks, any thoughts of returning disappeared into an alcoholic haze.

Although food took second place to drink, when he did seek nourishment, he took his meals at the homeless shelters run by the Salvation Army or St Vincent de Paul charities. While a meal was always available, the beds were taken quickly, and sometimes he missed out. Sleeping outdoors during Sydney's cold winter was an extremely uncomfortable experience, even with newspapers under his clothing. Ernie Longford had taught Bluey how to do this. Ernie was sixty-three, but looked twenty years older, not only because of his filthy clothing and lack of teeth, but also from the deep lines that crisscrossed his gaunt face, and the wrinkled bags under his dull blue eyes.

Bluey had found Ernie in a back alley with a much younger hobo who was trying to rob him of his pension money. When

Bluey intervened, the other man took off. Ernie was extremely grateful, and took Bluey under his wing. They spent the next few hours sharing his flagon of dry sherry.

In Sydney's drop-out society, it was difficult to get close to anyone, but Bluey and Ernie started knocking about together, and they looked out for each other. Having been on the streets for years, Ernie knew every nook and cranny of the place, especially where a dry bed could be had for the night. He introduced Bluey to a number of his contacts, particularly two kitchen-hands, one of whom worked at a leading restaurant. They were always good for a tucker hand-out, or sometimes five shillings, ten bob if they were lucky. Sometimes Bluey and Ernie tried begging at the back doors of other cafes, but were soon sent on their way.

Most weekdays Bluey went to the city Commonwealth Employment Service where casual jobs were handed out. Most of the positions were only for a day or two, but the pay loading for casual work was an incentive – it provided more drinking money.

One employer, a crockery importer, was particularly impressed with Bluey's work as a casual storeman and offered him a full-time position. Bluey accepted, and was determined to give a good account of himself. He was tired of a hand-to-mouth existence, and saw regular work as a way to redeem himself.

If I can just hold down a job for a while, I can save some money.

Bluey knew he couldn't go back to Ellen penniless, and hoped that working hard might help him stay off the grog. Things went well for the first week. He managed to turn up at work on time, and to stay away from the pub until after work. In his second week, he felt he deserved a bit of a reward and popped in to a nearby hotel during his lunch hour. He returned to the warehouse late, and slightly under the weather. He was sacked when he dropped a box of valuable china and the boss smelled alcohol on him.

'You've been to the pub!' Col Stevens accused as he examined the mess.

'Yeah. So what?' Bluey didn't like the manager's tone.

'I warned you, drinking is not permitted during working hours. Get your things and get out!'

'Stick it up your arse,' Bluey raised two fingers, and stormed from the premises. He wouldn't feel the shame and remorse of failing, yet again, to hold down a job until late the next day. Then he would dull that pain the only way he knew how – drinking – and so the cycle continued.

Chapter 28

Time began to lose all meaning for Ellen, the days and nights blurring into one another. It was soon winter, and every day she was out in the paddocks early, rugged up in her moleskin trousers, long-sleeved blouse, sweater, thick topcoat and brown leather gloves. Cloudy days promised rain, but none came, and the land around her slowly dried to dust.

She became more lonely and depressed. Forgetting the reality of their lives together over their last two years together, she recalled only the good times with Bluey. She remembered how good he was with the children, and how she had loved him with every fibre of her being. At times she found herself weeping for no reason. Her dear old school friend Brenda called by every week or so to see her. They shared a cup of tea and her friend brought her up to date with all the local gossip. Without her company, Ellen didn't know how she would have coped.

Ellen still visited her aunt, but felt too embarrassed to call into her uncle's butcher shop in case he thought she was only there for a hand-out.

One evening, as she prepared dinner, Ellen heard a car screech to a halt in front of the homestead. She strode to the front door and swung it open. Her cousin, Rodney, had almost reached the verandah and was carrying a parcel in his arms. 'G'day, Ellen. I was on deliveries out this way and Dad said I should pop in with this.'

'Hello, Rod.' She took the parcel and hesitated. 'I don't know what to say.'

'Dad says to tell you he knows why you haven't been coming into the shop. He says he misses you and wants you to still come. I do too, Ellen.' He could see she was on the brink of tears and was feeling a little uncomfortable at the prospect. 'The meat is only a temporary thing, you know, till you're on your feet again.'

'Thank you, Rod, and thank Uncle Mick too. Have you got time for a cuppa?' Ellen would have appreciated the adult company.

'No, sorry, Ellen. Gotta get home to Beryl and the baby.'

'Give them our love, won't you?' she called after him as he sprinted back to the van.

As time passed, the drought worsened. Ellen was convinced that if not for the river paddock, all the stock would have been lost. To tide the family over financially, she was resigned to selling a number of wethers to the local abattoir. The money she received was enough to pay her bills at the produce and grocery stores and left her with enough working capital to carry on.

Ellen didn't have a moment to spare during the days and weeks that followed. Long before the children left the house to catch the truck to school, she was out in the paddocks, carrying out all the pressing jobs Kilkenny demanded of her. Mending fences, tick control and worming became an everyday part of her life. Bluey had handled these with little effort, but for Ellen, they were extremely taxing.

On top of the demands of managing the property, she also had a house to run and two children to bring up. Under so much pressure, her nerves were fraying, and she was lonely, so damn lonely. Sometimes when she entered the barn she would look longingly at his saddle, her thoughts drifting back to their many rides along the river and the closeness they once shared. Or she'd look at her wedding ring, turning it fondly as she remembered the joy she felt the day they were married. At other times she would be filled with hatred, despising him for his drinking and for leaving her with such an immense responsibility. Her worries were so overwhelming that only abject tiredness allowed her to sleep. Every single day she had to struggle up from the mire of despair into which she had sunk to get her work done. Yet she never gave any hint of the pressure she was under in her weekly letters to her mother and sister.

They have enough problems of their own. And Pam's pregnant again, God bless her.

When the supply of money was almost depleted, it was again shearing season. Although the O'Donnell wool clip was well down against previous years, it would be just enough to keep the family going, though for how long she didn't know.

A week or so after the shearers had left, Ellen heard a vehicle pull up out the front of the homestead, and walked out to the verandah wiping her hands on a tea towel. Len Humphries was manoeuvring a large cardboard box from the rear door. 'Thought you could use some supplies. It's just some fruit and veg, and a few groceries.' He admired Ellen as she walked down the steps towards him. He'd never seen moleskin trousers look so good on anyone.

'You shouldn't have done that, Len,' she smiled, flattered by his attention. 'Come on in. What do I owe you?'

'Nothing,' he replied dismissively. 'It's just a few things I picked up.'

'You didn't have to do that. I will get the cheque for the wool clip soon.'

'That's good.'

'Yes.' She opened the door to let him pass. 'But I still can't afford to pay you for the fuel yet.'

'It can wait,' he said, sitting down at the kitchen table. 'Anyway, I didn't come out here to talk about that. I've got a free day, so I thought I'd come out and give you a hand.' He couldn't stop his eyes from straying to her breasts.

'That's very kind of you,' she answered warmly, unaware of his devouring gaze as she put away the groceries. 'David's taken the dog down to the river paddock to cull some ewes for tick control. Do you want to saddle a horse and give him a hand?'

'I'm not very good at that sort of thing. I'd prefer to help around the yard. Is there anything that needs doing?'

'Wood always needs chopping, I suppose, and the door to the shed is almost off its hinges.' She raised her eyebrows. 'Do you think you could do something about that?'

'Course I can,' he replied enthusiastically. 'I brought my tool kit out just in case.'

Humphries proceeded to chop a week's supply of wood for the stove. He then attacked the more arduous task of re-hanging one of the large doors to the agricultural shed. As he worked under a cloudless sky, the sun bore down on him, and he soon removed his sweat-stained checked shirt, revealing his large, soft frame. He took a handkerchief from the pocket of his work trousers and surveyed the desolation around him; the parched paddocks with hardly a blade of grass and the homestead that needed painting. A sudden gust of wind created a broad willy-willy, lifting a giant cloud of bark litter, leaves and dust skywards as it went.

What a bloody dump.

At midday he returned to the homestead. Standing just inside the back entrance to the living room, he stood in the shadows unnoticed, watching Ellen as she prepared lunch. Admiring the way her moleskin work pants hugged her long, shapely legs, he quickly became aroused and was just thinking of approaching her when he was interrupted by a young voice. 'Who's he?' Cathleen stood out of his view, pointing her finger in his direction.

'That's Mr Humphries.' Ellen turned to face him. 'He's come out to Kilkenny to help us.'

'Hello,' Cathleen gave him her best smile, and he smiled back.

The three had been sitting at the table for a few moments when they heard the back door slam. David entered the kitchen, his eyes wide with shock and indignation. 'What's he doing here?' he asked rudely, looking at his mother.

'David!' Ellen rebuked him, embarrassed. 'This is Mr Humphries, and he's come out here to help.'

'I know who he is,' the youth replied curtly as he sat down to lunch.

Humphries was seething, but didn't dare show it.

Cheeky little shit.

Suppressing the urge to vent his feelings, Humphries gave the youngster one of his most charming smiles. 'Your mum tells me you're the man of the house now and doing a man's work, too.'

David stared rudely. 'Dad'll be back soon. You'll see.'

'I wouldn't bet on it, son,' he said, doing his best to remain polite. He wasn't used to taking cheek from anyone, let alone a child. 'You don't want to get your hopes up.'

David scowled. 'Don't call me son,' he said coldly.

'David! That'll be enough.' His mother's voice courted no argument. David knew she was furious with him, but he didn't care. There was something about the man that made the hackles rise on his neck.

Humphries pushed back his chair from the table and stood up. 'I'll be off now, Ellen. But I'll come out again next weekend. Make a list of jobs for me to do.' He was struggling to control the dark rage that was threatening to erupt.

'Thanks Len.' She saw him to the door, and looked back at David, who was sullenly picking at the cold chicken and salad on his plate.

'I'm sorry about my son's behaviour,' she said quietly.

'That's okay, Ellen,' he patted her arm.

Gripping the steering wheel of his Land Rover, Humphries felt decidedly out of sorts.

What wouldn't I give to kick that little bastard's arse. When she's mine, I'll soon sort him out.

Later that same evening, David tiptoed to his sister's bedroom. 'Cathleen,' he called quietly.

She sat up in bed. 'Yes?'

'I want you to do something for me.'

'What?' she said, suspicious.

'When that Humphries man comes out here and I'm out in the paddocks, I don't want you to leave Mum alone with him. Okay? It's important.'

'What do you mean?'

'I just want you to stay with Mum, whatever she's doing, so they're not alone.'

'But why, David?'

'I don't trust him.'

She was silent for a few seconds. 'All right, I'll try.'

'Good girl.' He ruffled her hair affectionately. It wasn't much of a safeguard, but it was the best he could do.

Chapter 29

Living on the streets of Sydney, Bluey felt like a zombie in some sort of twilight zone, floating from one haze to the next. On the few mornings he awoke sober enough to think rationally, his thoughts always returned to his family and he felt the pain of separation anew. In the thirteen months that had passed since leaving Kilkenny, there had been one positive – he had not had the nightmare for a long time. Bluey hated the city and longed for the open spaces of home. The city, however, had other redeeming features. Grog was easy to get, no one knew him and no one asked him questions.

Things came to a head one drizzly night as he and Ernie shared a bottle of wine under a tree. Ernie suddenly grabbed his chest, collapsed sideways and lay still. Bluey tried his best to wake him, but Ernie remained unconscious. Bluey accosted a passer-by, who reluctantly agreed to call an ambulance from a nearby telephone booth. Ernie was pronounced dead on arrival at the hospital. The loss sent Bluey on a drinking binge. He blacked out for three days.

Early on the third day, as he lay in a drunken stupor on a bench in Hyde Park, two patrolling policemen came upon him. A senior constable took hold of his shoulder. 'Hey! Wake up!' the officer said gruffly. 'You can't sleep it off here.'

Bluey had no idea who was shaking him. He just wanted to return to oblivion. 'Fuck off,' he mumbled.

For the first time in his life, Bluey O'Donnell was arrested and subsequently charged with drunkenness and vagrancy in a public place. Completely sober, he experienced the shame of being brought before a magistrate, who sentenced him to one month's imprisonment. He tried not to think how upset his mother and father would have been.

They'd be so ashamed.

To those in the know, Long Bay Prison was a hell-hole where minor offenders were incarcerated with thieves, rapists and murderers. As well as the stigma of being in jail, Bluey had to endure the physical and mental torture associated with drying out, as well as suffering the taunts and abuse of the other inmates. The Bluey of old would have had little difficulty defending himself against the thugs and bullies who controlled the prisoners. In his current physical condition, he was no match for those who stood over the weaker or older inmates. The worst part was the recurrence of the terrible nightmare. His own yells forced him awake in a lather of sweat. He then tossed and turned on the lumpy mattress on his bunk in the cell, the other prisoners hurling profanities at him.

Without the anaesthetising effect of alcohol, Bluey began thinking straight for the first time in years. He began to analyse his life and where he was headed. The thought that he might end up like Ernie filled him with panic.

I've got to see my children again.

And although it pained him to admit it, he missed Ellen. During his incarceration at Long Bay, he made himself a promise.

I'll go back home.

Although he didn't have much money, and he had no idea how Ellen had managed in his absence, he hitchhiked back to Brisbane. Chatting to the salesman who had picked him up in Tamworth, Bluey felt strong and determined, but by the time he arrived in Brisbane, his willpower had deserted him. Negative thoughts ran wild, and his head began to spin with doubt and worry. How could he face Ellen? What would she think of him? Would she even take him back? More importantly, could he even stay off the grog? He knew Ellen would never tolerate his drinking around the children, and for that, he didn't blame her.

Walking towards Roma Street Station he caught a whiff of beer and tobacco as he passed a pub.

I'll just stop in for a quick one.

Many hours later, Bluey stumbled out onto the dark street, back where he started. After a rough night sleeping in a doorway, he was overwhelmed with shame and self-loathing.

How can I go back to her like this?

Without any money, he was forced to register for the dole at the city Commonwealth Employment Service. He stayed nights at the St Vincent de Paul centre or the Salvation Army, where a meal was always available, but he had to get in quick to score a bed. If these places were overcrowded, he would revert to his small hideout under the Storey Bridge.

One night as Bluey was returning to his hideout under the bridge, three bodgies confronted him in an inner-city laneway. The youths were imposing in their black leather jackets and trendy stove-pipe trousers, their hair slicked back in quiffs. One of them suffered from acute acne, which scarred his cheeks and chin. At first, the three young men just stared at the dishevelled man with two buttons missing from the front of his shirt. They then began to tease him, calling him a drunk and criticising his worn-out clothes. In retaliation, Bluey called the pimple-faced youth 'puss-head' and the youngster struck him. Bluey replied with a great right hook. Enraged by this show of defiance, the three youths set upon him, using him as a punching bag. Bluey was far too weak to defend himself and in his present state was no match for the thugs, who continued with the assault until he fell, unconscious, to the concrete.

Chapter 30

Len Humphries visited Kilkenny once a fortnight to complete odd jobs around the homestead. Ellen was grateful for the company, and the extra help, and felt herself warming to the big man, despite her initial reservations.

After all, she was still a young, vibrant woman with a full life ahead of her and it seemed futile to pine for old times with a husband who had deserted her and his children. Len didn't have Bluey's boyish good looks, but he was pleasant enough looking, she thought. What was more important, he was dependable, and treated her like a queen. He always had something for her when he visited. If it wasn't a bag of groceries, it was a box of chocolates. He had even surprised her with a lovely bunch of flowers on his last visit.

Ellen had been feeling particularly depressed, and the flowers had lifted her spirits and brought the sparkle back to her eyes.

'Oh, Len, they're lovely.' She took them from him and breathed in their perfume, keeping her head down to hide her moist eyes. 'Come inside and we'll have a cuppa before work.'

He followed Ellen into the kitchen. Cathleen was sitting at the table, seemingly immersed in her homework. Humphries smiled at her. 'Hello, Cathleen.' Unlike her brother, she did not feel the same animosity to this man. He was always being so helpful around the place, and whenever he visited, their mother seemed so much happier.

'Hello, Mr Humphries.'

'Call me, Uncle Len.'

'Okay,' Cathleen said shyly.

Len was happy with the headway he was making with the young girl. Maybe a gift or two for her wouldn't go astray, he thought. He would need all the help he could get to win over her mother. It surprised him, but he genuinely liked the little girl.

She's a sweet little thing. Nothing like her brat of a brother.

Ellen was pleased with the positive connection that was building between Cathleen and Len. She knew he was making an effort, and appreciated it.

He sat down at the dining table and addressed Ellen. 'The ladies at the CWA got the flowers for me. You know,' he said, casting a sideways glance at her, 'we do quite a bit to help them by way of cash and goods.'

She opened a cupboard above the sink and removed a vase which she began filling with water. 'That's very generous of you.' She tried to hide the surprise in her voice as she started arranging the flowers. 'I'm sure a company as successful as your father's does a lot of good work.'

With her words of praise ringing in his ears, Len thought he would try to press home his advantage. 'Yes, we do. Not many people know it, but we donate to church charities and the Salvos, and we're on their committee and the hospital board as well.' He strained to remember the lofty words he had heard in a speech his father had given at a charity function. 'Our objective is to help all people in need, no matter who they are,' he repeated.

Ellen smiled. This was a side of Len she had never seen, and it came as a pleasant surprise. 'I never knew.' She spooned tea into a pot and thought how mistaken people were about him. Was this the same man Bluey had often derided?

'I know my father was behind a lot of this work but I've also got plans of my own.'

'Really?' Ellen passed him a cup.

'I want to raise money for a swimming pool – you know, for the kids – and dedicate it to the memory of fallen diggers.'

'Oh, Len!' Ellen felt like hugging him. 'I think that's a wonderful idea!'

'Me, too!' Cathleen couldn't resist piping up.

Len beamed. He was on a roll now. 'I've got quite a few ideas like this one.'

Especially for you, sweet Ellen.

What Ellen didn't know, was that Len wasn't being entirely honest. He'd left her with the impression that he was involved with this community work, but the truth was, it was all his father's work, and he had no intention of following in his footsteps.

Humphries didn't involve himself in any work associated with the property itself, leaving that to eleven-year-old David. He stayed for only a few hours at a time, but by the third month had became frustrated that he'd never been able to discuss his feelings with Ellen. Cathleen had carried out her brother's instructions to the letter, and never left her mother's side when Humphries visited. If the truth were known, Cathleen enjoyed being near her mother on his visits. Ellen smiled a lot and was teasing and playful. And to Cathleen, Humphries always seemed polite and kind. What she didn't know, was that David had had an unpleasant encounter with Humphries in Goondiwindi that had confirmed his fears.

David was running an errand for the school principal and was on his way to the newsagent to buy a box of HB pencils when he'd rounded a corner and almost bumped into Humphries. David grimaced.

'Well, well, well,' Humphries said nastily. 'I've been hoping we might have a little man-to-man talk.'

'I've got nothing to say to you,' David responded sullenly, trying to step around him.

Humphries placed a heavy hand on his shoulder. 'You stay put and listen carefully until I've finished.'

'I won't.' David struggled, but could not get free. Humphries squeezed the lad's shoulder hard.

'Now, listen good, you little troublemaker. I'm keen on your mother and I'm going to be the new man in her life, so you'd better get used to it and show me some respect when I come calling.'

Jerking out of his grasp, David hissed, 'I'll never show you anything but hate!'

Humphries smiled crookedly. 'It doesn't matter what you feel, does it, boy? Your dad's gone for good, and I've won over your sister already. It's just a matter of time.'

David fought the tears and ran all the way back to school.

He'll never take Dad's place.

Chapter 31

Bluey opened his eyes, but a thick fog blurred his vision. He blinked and gently shook his head to try to clear away the murkiness, but the agony resulting from even the slightest movement forced him to lie still. On top of the pain, he felt extremely confused. Slowly, he began to focus. A white image floated into view.

An angel. This must be the end of the line.

The angel floated to his bedside. 'Himself is awake, is he?' The Irish brogue was unmistakable.

The fog eventually cleared, and Bluey realised he was in a hospital, and that the angel at his bedside was a nursing nun. A white habit covered her body from head to toe, leaving only her face and hands visible. Beds filled with male patients lined both sides of the large public ward. On the wall at each end of the open room, a large crucifix looked down upon the poor suffering unfortunates who were lying there.

'Shit! What the bloody hell am I doing here?' Bluey tried to raise his voice, but he was too weak.

'That'll be enough of that sort of talk here, me bucko.' The nun's kindly face hardened slightly. 'You rest a bit more and I'll arrange for a cup of tea and some food. Now, lie back.'

To isolate him from the other patients, the nun pulled a curtain around his bed, and he soon drifted back to sleep. Out of the blue, however, the terrible dream returned to haunt him. He yelled and his eyes flew open in horror as they always did.

The nun was at his bedside in an instant. 'You're all right. You're all right,' she whispered soothingly. His exhaustion was such that it didn't take long for blessed blackness to again envelope him.

The next time Bluey opened his eyes, the curtain around his bed had been drawn back and the lights switched on. Gazing through the panes of glass at the far end of the open ward, he saw it was dark outside. In the distance, he could see the lights of the city centre. Although his head was spinning, he still had a good idea of where he was. Recognising the outline of buildings on the horizon, he came to a quick conclusion.

I must be in the Mater Hospital, over near the Gabba.

Several minutes later, another nursing nun came to his bedside. She was much older than the Irish one who had visited earlier. She had a pale lined face, which lit up when she noticed he was again awake.

He looked up at the kindly face and enquired, 'How long have I been here, Sister?' He was still feeling bewildered.

'Five days, I'm sorry to say.'

'What's the date?' he asked, frowning.

'It's the twenty-first day of January, 1955,' she answered quietly.

'What day is it?'

'Thursday.' The nun paused. 'You had no identification on you when they brought you in. All I can tell you is that an ambulance delivered you to casualty, bleeding and unconscious. You've suffered concussion and you have three broken ribs. Now, I'm going to give you some soup to keep you going. When you've finished that, you can sleep some more. Here. Let me help you sit up.'

The nun took hold of his shoulders, pulling him forward as she tucked pillows behind his back for support. The pain from his broken ribs caused him to cry out in agony. 'Hell! Be careful!'

'Don't blaspheme here if you don't mind,' she said, shaking her head in disapproval. She lifted a steaming bowl from the tray and began feeding him warm vegetable soup. When the food reached his stomach, however, he began to shake and the nurse had to stop for a few moments. He felt so empty inside, as if he hadn't eaten for a long, long time. After he'd finished, and the nurse had left, he lay back to rest and the shaking started all over again. This time it lasted much longer.

He tried to think back to the events leading up to his being hospitalised. He remembered being curled in a foetal position, and pointy-toed shoes kicking into him, but then nothing more. Yet his memory was absolutely clear on one thing – how he had come to be in Brisbane. An image of her floated across his mind.

Ellen.

The following morning, an orderly helped him into a wheelchair and wheeled him to a communal bathroom to be shaved and showered. When Bluey looked in the large mirror above the row of sinks, he was horrified by his reflection. His lips and nose were crisscrossed with cuts, and dark bruising surrounded his swollen eyes. On removing his blue-striped hospital pyjamas, he noticed his torso was covered in dark bruises and welts, especially around his rib cage. But it was his emaciated body that shocked him the most. He stared at his reflection in utter disbelief, and wondered how he had let himself get to this state.

God, I need a drink.

Later the same morning, the house doctor visited Bluey on his rounds.

'So how are you feeling?'

'A bit better today, Doc.'

The doctor was aged somewhere in his mid-thirties and was nearly bald, the few remaining strands of hair combed neatly across his scalp. His pronounced, dark moustache gave him a sort of Groucho Marx look.

'You took a pretty bad beating. You had concussion, and your ribs are on the mend. But you're not out of the woods yet, Mr O'Donnell,' he said, looking over the top of his glasses at Bluey. He had a habit of blinking his eyelids a couple of times before closing them tight in a squint.

'What do you mean?'

'I think I'd better start from the beginning. When you were admitted, we took some routine blood and urine samples.' He picked up his patient file and opened it. 'What we discovered, Mr O'Donnell, is that you are suffering from some kidney and liver damage due to excessive consumption of alcohol. If this continues, I must warn you, the condition will be life-threatening.'

'Shit!' Bluey began to shiver again, his mouth suddenly dry. 'Where do I go to from here, Doc?' The severity of his condition was beginning to sink in.

'We'll need to transfer you to a rehabilitation clinic to dry out. The shivering you're experiencing – the d.t.'s – is caused by withdrawal symptoms. You haven't had a drink in nearly a week and your body is craving it.'

'Let's see if I've got this right. I can't drink at all? Not even a beer?'

'Exactly,' the doctor answered emphatically. 'Not unless you wish to die a relatively young man.'

'And if I don't drink?' Bluey asked, watching the doctor squint again.

'You're still young. Stay sober, and there's nothing to stop you from regaining your health.' He checked his file. 'It's just as well you've never been a smoker.'

That night as he lay in the hospital bed, Bluey's mind began to clear. His thoughts returned to his childhood on the property with his parents; carefree days spent in a loving environment. A picture of Ellen and his two children interrupted his thoughts and he felt awash with guilt. His kids – he missed them so much. As always, memories of the POW camp came, and he gritted his teeth to force them from his mind. In the end, weariness overcame him and he fell into a deep sleep, waking when the first light of dawn filtered into the ward.

As he lay in his bed thinking, the tremors that wracked his body were not created by the withdrawal symptoms alone. Indeed, the shivering increased markedly when he thought about the total mess he'd made of his life. What had become of his beautiful children? And what had become of Ellen? Guilt returned, suffocating him. He resisted the urge to close his eyes again.

On the day Bluey arrived at the rehab clinic, torrential summer rain dampened his first impressions. Set on top of a hill overlooking New Farm Park and the Brisbane River, the clinic provided a quiet, peaceful environment for the recovering inmates.

Bluey presented himself at the reception centre, where he was issued with shoes, a hat, socks, two sets of clean clothing, sheets, towels and shaving equipment, all donated to the clinic by various Christian charities. He was allocated a private room on the first floor, though like the other inmates, he had to use communal bathroom and toilet facilities at the far end of a long central hall. His room had a single bed, wardrobe and a porcelain sink, with soap, toothpaste and a new toothbrush neatly arranged beside the cold-water tap. Cheap green-checked linoleum covered the floor, and two French doors led onto a balcony.

On his first afternoon at the clinic, Bluey had an immediate appointment with a visiting clinical psychologist. Jim Thallon was a short, barrel-chested man with a pleasant face. His grey hair was thick and tightly waved as if it had been set with butterfly clips. 'Please take a seat,' the psychologist said in a well-modulated voice, then examined a folder in front of him. 'So is Bluey your correct Christian name?' he asked courteously.

'It'll do,' Bluey grunted.

'Is there a reason you can't tell me your correct name?'

'Because that name's never been used, mate.' Bluey felt annoyed. *Bloody wanker.*

'Fair enough.'

Jim Thallon quickly deduced that his fiery-headed patient was not going to be a pushover, so he adopted a different approach, cautiously persuading the supposed reformed drinker to complete a number of aptitude tests. After analysing the results, Thallon explained the physical and mental degradation associated with alcoholism, and gave his patient a number of strategies to assist him in overcoming his addiction. Then, just at the end of the session, Thallon mentioned Bluey's nightmares.

'Your medical file states you awoke screaming after having a bad dream.'

'So what?' Bluey was instantly on the defensive.

'Do you wish to discuss the dream?' Thallon asked.

'No!' Bluey felt unusually irritable, even aggressive. He hated being there, being asked about things that he felt were deeply private. He didn't like baring his soul to anyone.

Thallon persisted. 'Is the dream associated with your alcoholism?'

'How the hell would I know?'

Thallon decided not to pursue the matter for the time being.

The rehabilitation clinic prided itself on its orderliness. Each morning, inmates were encouraged to rise by six a.m., at which time Bluey made his way out onto the balcony. Looking down into the park below, he would watch the homeless men shuffle away from their benches, rotundas or makeshift shelters.

Oh, God. That could be me . . .

The dishevelled men were a constant reminder of the fate that awaited him should he renew his love affair with the bottle.

By seven a.m., all patients in the men's wing had to be showered, shaved and fully dressed. A cooked breakfast was then served in the communal dining room. Meals were the only time male and female inmates were permitted to intermingle. A lunch, usually mixed sandwiches, was taken at twelve-thirty on the verandah. Dinner was served at six p.m., again in the communal dining room. Apart from doctor's appointments and interviews with the psychologist, the inmates' time was their own. In the men's activities room, many of the males played cards or monopoly while others read or listened to the radio, especially Bob Dyer's quiz show. Bluey kept pretty much to himself, and spent a lot of time in the library, trying to get up to date on what had been happening in the world.

After a week of treatment, his shaking had decreased significantly. To improve matters, the dark bruising on his torso had almost disappeared. His appetite had also returned, and he began to put on weight, though he was still many pounds lighter than he had been before he'd begun drinking. But Bluey was still woken every few nights by the nightmare.

After two more weeks of rehabilitation therapy, the constant longing for alcohol still plagued him, so he sought another interview with the psychologist.

'The craving's still there, Doc.'

'I'm not surprised, Mr O'Donnell. It will remain with you for some time yet.' There was a long pause. 'In fact, you may always have a longing for alcohol. It's extremely difficult to determine. Every case is different.'

'Bloody hell!' He looked at the psych in dismay. 'You mean I'll just have to live with it?'

'I'm afraid so.'

'Shit! Isn't there anything I can do?'

'Not really, though a more supportive environment would help. Haven't you any family you can turn to?'

'I left my wife and kids over a year ago. I shot through with another woman.'

The psychologist nodded, but made no comment.

'No, it wasn't like that,' Bluey added, seeing the look on Thallon's face. 'Not sex and the like. She was an alcho, like me.'

'Where is this woman now?'

'Wouldn't have a clue.' Bluey shrugged.

'Would your wife take you back?'

Bluey paused. He knew he needed to face this question head on, but it was hard. 'Knowing Ellen, I doubt if she'd take me back. You see, I did some pretty rotten things to her.'

'But you must have had feelings for each other once.'

For the first time in months, Bluey broke into a smile. 'Yeah, you can say that again, Doc. We grew up in the same district and went to school together. By the time we were sixteen, we couldn't keep our hands off each other. Then there was the stinkin' bloody war. I went overseas when I was only eighteen.'

'But that wouldn't have been permitted.'

'I lied about my bloody age.'

'I see.'

'Stop saying you see, when you don't!' Thinking about the war had raised Bluey's ire.

Thallon ignored the aggressive tone. 'Does your involvement in the war have anything to do with the nightmares you experience two or three times a week? Night staff have heard your cries.'

Bluey sat in silence, his face set hard. Jim Thallon suspected it wouldn't be long before Bluey was swept into a rage. 'Well, do you dream about something that happened in the war?'

'I don't want to talk about it!'

'But you'll have to some day.'

Bluey took a deep breath. 'Yes,' he spat, 'the dream has something to do with the war! Satisfied?'

'I'm sorry, Mr O'Donnell. Please continue.'

'No, I don't think I can,' he said gruffly.

'Very well. What about going home and giving it a go?'

'I don't know if I could handle it.'

Thallon looked at him intently. 'Tell me honestly. Do you miss your children?'

'Yeah.' Bluey gazed out the window. 'They're beautiful kids. My son, David, he'd be eleven now. He's a crack shot with the rifle. And my little girl, Cathleen – smart as a whip.'

'And your wife?'

Bluey was taken aback by this question. 'I don't know. I suppose I still love her. It's not something I let myself think about.'

Thallon looked directly into Bluey's eyes. 'Go home, Mr O'Donnell. Go home.'

A week later, Bluey stood beside the Cunningham Highway, near Ipswich, hoping to hitch a ride back to his home town. He was dressed in khaki trousers, a neatly pressed red-checked, short-sleeved shirt and a hat. It was half an hour before an FJ Holden pulled to a halt beside him. The elderly man was looking for company on his drive back to Warwick. The man talked about everything, from his business to his grandchildren, and Bluey answered in monosyllables. Gazing absently out the front window, he watched the dry scrubland flash past, parched under a relenting sun. He had never seen the Downs in such poor condition.

Bloody drought.

At three o'clock that same afternoon, a semitrailer dropped Bluey outside the Goondiwindi post office. Nothing much seemed to have changed in his old home town, although the place seemed noisier somehow; maybe because there was a lot more traffic on the streets. He walked past the drapery shop where Ellen's sister, Pam, had once worked, and the newsagent. He passed the milk bar where he'd sat with Ellen, nursing milkshakes, and the picture theatre where they'd touched each other tenderly in the dark. A wave of nostalgia surged through him as memories of his courtship came flooding back. How naïve they had been! What he wouldn't give to be starting again from those times. He squared his shoulders, and sighed.

You can't go back.

PART TWO

1955–

Chapter 32

Bluey's room in the cramped shearers' quarters was just about large enough for a small sink and a narrow bed. An outside earth closet was provided for the workers. Lying on the bunk, Bluey thought about how Ellen had received him.

I don't blame her, I suppose.

Still, it had hurt him deeply to see the look of utter revulsion on her face when she spoke to him. He had never seen such hate in her eyes before (well, at least not when he was sober). She had always been the one to forgive and forget, hardly ever harbouring a grudge. However, he accepted that during his absence, she would have been under enormous pressure, running a house, looking after two children and maintaining a property, all at the same time and all alone. To make matters worse, fortunes on Kilkenny had changed considerably since his departure.

How could I have done this to her?

He felt suddenly exhausted, and stretched out on his bunk. He didn't want to think any more about the mess he'd made of his life. It was too depressing, and he knew he had to stay positive to be of any help around the place. He closed his eyes and was soon asleep.

David stood for a long while, looking into the face of his sleeping father. When his mother had told him his dad was back, he couldn't believe it. It was as though all his secret dreams and prayers had been answered at once. He had missed him so much. On his way down to the shearers' quarters he had wanted to run as fast as his legs would carry him, and he had started to, but then slowed.

What if Dad doesn't really love us any more?

His heart was thudding against his chest.

But he must love us because he's back.

'Dad,' he called softly, not wanting to wake him with a fright. 'Dad,' he repeated a little louder, excitement starting to bubble around the word.

Bluey didn't know how long he had been asleep when the happy call awakened him. He opened his eyes to see the shining face of his son looking down at him. 'David!' There was an instant lump in his throat. He swung out of the bed and wrapped his arms around the boy, whose eyes filled with tears.

They held each other for a long moment. Eventually Bluey stood back.

'I missed you mate,' he said, his voice quavering. He tried to cover his emotion with a quip. 'Bloody hell, you're taller than me now!'

'Why'd you go away, Dad?'

Bluey knew it was time for some honesty – his son deserved

an explanation. 'I was mixed up, after the war, and the grog got me.'

'Are you okay now?' The adult tone took Bluey by surprise.

'Yeah,' he replied. 'Don't worry about me, I'll be fine.'

'What about me?' a voice asked softly from the doorway.

Bluey turned towards his daughter.

'Cathleen.' He looked at her in wonder. She'd changed so much. She was taller, now – her thick, honey-blonde hair swept into a ponytail.

'Daddy.'

He held out his arms. 'Come an' give your old man a hug.' The youngster needed no further encouragement, and practically threw herself at him.

'I'm so happy now, Daddy.'

'Me, too, sweetheart.' He held her close.

David patted him on the arm. 'Mum said tea's ready and to wash up before you come.'

Bluey walked into the kitchen, unsure how Ellen would receive him. Her rage a few hours earlier was understandable, but he'd been unprepared for how wounded he felt. She'd since showered and changed into the sleeveless floral summer dress he'd always admired on her. She still looked beautiful.

I must have been mad.

Seeing her estranged husband with the children, Ellen's own feelings were mixed. On the one hand, she was furious that he'd abandoned them, but on the other felt moved to see them with their father. The smile on their faces was enough to convince her she had done the right thing in letting him stay.

'Cathleen, pull the chair out for your father. He can sit at the head of the table.'

'Yes, Mummy.'

During the meal, David plied his father with questions about his absence, and what he'd been doing. Sensing Ellen's disapproval, Bluey was deliberately vague, or only told stories about his various stints of employment. He often changed the subject, encouraging his children to talk about their experiences at home and at school over the previous year. But David wouldn't give up, and eventually Ellen put an end to the questioning. 'We don't want to hear about it,' she said sharply, before turning to her daughter. 'Cathleen, you can help me with the dishes while David does his homework.' She looked to the head of the table. 'Bluey, you can find sheets, pillow slips and blankets in the usual place. Most of your clothes are still where you left them. In the morning, David will do the milking because we have to be in the paddocks early. We've had trouble with dingoes lately. I've made up some baits.'

At one-fifteen a.m. Ellen was woken by a blood-curdling yell from the shearers' quarters. She knew that sound could travel far on a still night, but she was still shocked to be able to hear Bluey from the homestead. She imagined him sitting up in his bunk, trembling and sweating, and began to think about how he had managed all those months in Sydney.

She longed to return to the dreamless sleep that had been so rudely interrupted, but her mind was now too active. At around three a.m. she drifted off at last, only to be awoken what seemed like seconds later by the shrill noise of the bedside alarm clock. It was five a.m.

As Ellen stepped into the shearers' quarters, she came face to face with her husband, who was wide awake and dressed.

'You had that dream?'

'Yes.'

'You'll have to do something about it. You know that, don't you?'

'Yeah, I suppose so. But there's too much to worry about on Kilkenny right now. It'll have to wait.'

It was not until Bluey rode into the sheep paddocks with Ellen that he appreciated the full extent of the devastation inflicted by the drought.

There's hardly a blade of grass left.

'Most of the time I've kept the flock in the river paddock. At least there's still a small amount of grass growing along the bank, and there's some saltbush as well. I've cut off the branches and the sheep have been eating that. If we could only get a bit of rain, the outer paddocks would pick up enough to take most of the flock again. That would give the river paddock a chance to recover.'

'You've done a great job,' he said admiringly. He wanted to place a comforting hand on her shoulder, but thought it might anger her.

As if sensing his hesitation, she too resisted making a sharp retort. *What can be gained by saying such things?*

As they rode deeper into the river paddock, they came across the carcasses of two sheep with their throats ripped out. Otherwise they were not marked in any way. Surprisingly, no part of the carcasses had been eaten by the dingoes.

'Bloody things kill for the sake of it!' she said angrily.

'How many have we lost?'

'With the drought and the dingoes,' she said, 'I reckon we've lost just over twenty per cent.'

'Shit!' he exclaimed. 'That's a lot of money down the drain.'

'Yes.'

They spent the morning dropping baits and crutching severely fly-blown sheep. The fly menace was even worse in such dry, hot conditions. At midday, they rode to the river bank for a brief lunch break. Bluey dismounted and hooked his reins into the branch of a small red gum at the edge of the river and poured himself a drink from his waterbag. Two crows cawed and a flock of galahs rose as a pink and grey cloud from the gums above. 'Bloody hell, look at the river!' It was only a trickle.

Ellen tied her horse beside his and sat down at the top of the river bank. 'I made some sandwiches.' She reached into a saddle bag.

Bluey took a packet from her and opened it. He forced a small smile. 'Cold rabbit. Smells good.'

'Leftovers.' She shrugged. 'I didn't bring any tea. You'll just have to wash it down with water.'

As she bit into the last of her sandwich, he looked intently into her face, noticing for the first time the little creases that had appeared around her emerald eyes. They did not detract from her beauty in any way. Despite the fact that she wore working jodhpurs and a checked shirt and her face was dirt-smudged, he doubted she'd ever looked more attractive than she did at that moment.

She caught him looking at her and he coughed to cover his

embarrassment. 'I remember this spot well. It was where David was conceived.' He smiled properly this time.

'It seems like a long time ago,' she said quietly.

He exhaled deeply. 'We had it made then.'

'Yes, we did.' It was her turn to clear her throat. 'Okay, time to get back to work.'

By the time they returned to the homestead at dusk, he wondered whether he even had the strength to dismount. He felt completely and utterly spent. The long period of alcoholism, his sleeping rough, and his poor health had all combined to weaken him more than he thought possible, and he hadn't done this demanding type of work for more than a year. The evening meal over, he quickly kissed the children good night before retiring to his spartan accommodation. That night, total exhaustion ensured his sleep was a dreamless one.

The following work day turned out to be another he would like to forget. With virtually every muscle in his body aching in protest, he repaired fences and made preparations for the flock's dipping, programmed for the following week. That night, he was again asleep as soon as his head touched the pillow.

Chapter 33

The first Saturday after Bluey's return, Len Humphries visited Kilkenny as usual. The big man couldn't believe his eyes when he saw his old nemesis sitting at the breakfast table. Just as he'd begun to believe that a life with Ellen seemed possible, Bluey had reappeared. Humphries' eyes narrowed. Bitter disappointment turned to anger.

'You're back,' he snapped.

'Yeah,' David couldn't contain himself, answering for his father.

'That's right,' Bluey replied evenly.

Humphries' top lip curled contemptuously. 'I don't know how you've got the hide to come back after what you did.' He was determined to put up a fight for her.

'That's none of your business, Humphries.' Bluey stood up.

'That's enough, you pair.' Ellen looked from one to the other. She was grateful Cathleen had stayed in town overnight, with the family of a friend.

Humphries was too angry to let go. 'Is it now?' he growled.

'Well let me tell you, O'Donnell, I've spent most of my weekends coming out here to help. And my company has been paying the fuel costs for this property.'

Bluey looked askance. 'Is that right, Ellen?'

'Yes.' Her tone was defiant. 'Len was there for us when we needed him.'

'I didn't need him,' David interrupted.

Humphries lost his temper. 'You keep out of it, you little prick!' he exploded.

Ellen looked at Humphries as if seeing him for the first time. 'How dare you speak to my son like that.'

'I'm sorry, Ellen. I didn't mean it.'

'I'm just as sure you did,' she answered quietly.

'Get out, Humphries.' There was no mistaking the threat in Bluey's voice.

Knowing he had lost Ellen, the big man's darker side came to the fore. If he couldn't have her, then they both had to be punished for his loss. He placed his hands on his hips and eyeballed his old adversary. 'And what are you going to do about it if I don't, O'Donnell?'

'Just what I always have.' Bluey gritted his teeth.

Humphries' expression changed from contempt to mirth, and he laughed out loud. 'Look at you, you drunk. You can hardly lift your fists.'

'Get out.' Bluey took a step towards the larger man.

'Please go.' Ellen wiped her brow nervously. 'You're not wanted here.'

They followed Humphries as he walked out the front door,

across the verandah and into the driveway. As he reached his vehicle, he suddenly swung back towards them. Only a yard separated him from Bluey. 'Right, you lot.' He slammed a fist into the palm of the other hand. 'I want your account paid in full. You have until the end of the week.'

'Get stuffed, Hum—' was all Bluey managed to say before the large fist connected with his face. He didn't see it coming. As Bluey lay in a daze on the dusty ground, Humphries began kicking him.

'Stop!' Ellen screamed. She tried to step between them, but Humphries roughly pushed her aside.

Bluey scrambled to his feet, but barely had the strength to raise his fists, let alone block the relentless pounding to his face and body. Each time he fell to the dirt, he became a target for Humphries' boots. Blood began to flow from his nose and mouth. Just as the big man was about to kick Bluey again, two bullets lifted the dust near his feet.

'Leave him alone,' said an icy voice.

Humphries turned to confront the speaker. David was standing on the verandah, pointing a .22 rifle at the big man's stomach. Humphries' eyes bulged at the sight of the weapon. 'Gimme that, you little shit.' He took two steps towards the verandah, but was stopped in his tracks as a third bullet ripped through the fabric of his shirt tail, which was flapping loosely at his hip.

'I'll put the next one in your guts.' Bluey heard his son's voice through the mist that was slowly evaporating around him. 'Now, piss off!'

'David!' Ellen looked at him in shock.

'Sorry, Mum.'

'I'll get you, you little bastard!'

Ellen glared at the panting, red-faced man in disgust. 'Get going, Humphries,' she said coldly, 'or I'll take the gun from him and shoot you myself.'

Humphries stared at her, anger clawing at his heart. He'd lost Ellen, his plans for a happy life with her disintegrating before his eyes, and the bitterness rose up within him like a tidal wave.

'If payment for the fuel is not made by the end of the week, I'll see to it that you're ruined. Do you hear me? You'll lose everything.' He got into his Land Rover and drove off in a cloud of dust.

Ellen and David helped Bluey to his feet, sitting him on the top step of the verandah.

'Are you okay, Dad?'

'Yeah.' Bluey looked at the boy through swollen eyes. 'That was a bloody good shot.'

'I've been practising,' David said proudly. 'I'll go and saddle the horses now, Dad, if you're okay.'

'Sure.'

As David headed to the stables Ellen took a white handkerchief from a pocket of her work trousers and began wiping blood from Bluey's lips and nose.

'Don't do that,' Bluey protested weakly. 'You'll mark your hanky.'

Ellen looked at him in surprise. 'That's what you said at the pictures that day.'

'Did I?' He pretended not to remember.

'Yes,' she replied wistfully.

He noticed the softness in her voice and decided to broach a difficult subject. 'I meant what I said, you know. There was nothing between me and Ruby Marks. We just drank together.'

'But you left with her. I know it and so does the whole town. How do you think that makes me feel?'

'I'm sorry, El. But I want you to know there's never been anyone else but you. Ever.'

She wanted to believe him, but something was stopping her. The hardship she'd suffered over the past year stood like a barrier between them. She changed the subject. 'Come into the house and I'll bathe those cuts.'

Bluey couldn't help feeling a little satisfied as she fussed over him. After she had bathed the cuts in a saline solution and stemmed the flow of blood, she said worriedly, 'You'd better stay home and rest.'

'Like bloody hell.'

'But you might have broken bones.'

'I know what a fracture feels like.'

'Are you sure?' Ellen applied some sticking plaster to a large cut above his eye.

'Compared to Japanese punishment, that was a cakewalk.'

'Oh.' She raised her eyebrows. This was the first reference he'd ever made to his war experiences, and it filled her with hope that perhaps he was close to talking about what happened in the POW camp. But she was also worried about pushing him too far, and decided not to pursue the subject.

He's mentioned it himself. He'll talk about it again when he's ready.

Bluey and Ellen were grateful that the unfortunate incident with Humphries had occurred on a weekend, as David was available to help them with the work. Bluey's chest almost burst with pride as he watched his young son handle the work with the expertise of an experienced property hand. At lunchtime they shared sandwiches and billy tea by the river. Bluey's father's face drifted into his mind.

Dad would have been so proud of him.

Out in the paddocks, Bluey noticed bachelor buttons and paper daisies growing beside the river. In spite of the drought, they were back in profusion. After scooping up an armful, he lifted his head to gaze across the waterway and found himself staring into the eyes of a dingo watching him from the other side. It was unusual to sight them during daylight hours. It stood deathly still, its yellow eyes unmoving, until he dropped the blossoms to draw the .22 rifle from a long, narrow leather pouch behind the saddle. Instinctively, the animal scooted off into the scrub. 'Bastard!'

On his return to the homestead, Bluey left the flowers on the sink and then made his way to his quarters.

The native blooms were the first thing Ellen saw when she entered the kitchen. She picked them up and inhaled their delicate fragrance. He'd never picked flowers for her before, and the tenderness of the gesture melted a little more of the ice in her heart – but only a little.

It's going to take more than a few flowers.

Ellen got the call from Humphries' solicitor just as Bluey walked through the back door.

'It's Benjamin Edwards, Ellen.' The man sounded apologetic. 'Len Humphries has insisted that I phone to chase up the money you owe him.'

'We had no formal agreement, Ben,' she replied. 'But I fully intend to pay what we owe. He'll just have to wait till we sell the wool clip.'

'He isn't prepared to wait,' the solicitor replied.

'He has no choice.'

'Then he'll take you to court.'

'Yes,' she said evenly, 'but that'll take time, and by then we'll have sold the wool clip. Don't worry, he'll get his money.'

The solicitor was obviously uncomfortable about having to make this phone call. He knew both families well, and was aware of Humphries' reputation as a bully. But he had to do his job.

'He'll probably want me to start legal proceedings immediately.'

'Look, Ben, you know most property owners pay their major bills when they receive the cheque for their wool clip. Everyone knows this. Humphries must have other property owners who settle their accounts after shearing?'

'I can't comment on that, Ellen.'

'If Humphries singled us out for legal action, he'd certainly get a large number of property owners offside. They'd never forgive him for not being prepared to wait a few months for Kilkenny to settle its account. Dave and Sally were held in high esteem around here. Humphries' reputation would be shot to pieces. Has he considered that?'

'I don't think so. I'll put it to him. Hopefully, he'll see the logic of your argument.' The solicitor rang off.

'Bastard didn't waste any time,' said Bluey.

'No. It's a shame though.' She frowned. 'We need the money from the wool clip for the tractor repairs, among other things.'

'Don't worry,' Bluey assured her. 'I have a few cards left to play.'

Ellen was curious, but the children's noisy arrival stopped her from any further questioning.

The following Monday morning, Bluey drove into town to meet the manager of the Commercial Banking Company of Sydney, the bank the O'Donnell family had always used. He figured that he might have had a better chance with the State Agricultural Bank, but being a government-sponsored organisation, it took far too long to process applications. Kilkenny couldn't wait.

The bank was a dark brick, two-storey building with arched double doors that created a grand entrance on the corner of two intersecting streets. The manager's office was located on the top floor.

Facing his client, a knowing look appeared on the face of the experienced banker. He knew exactly why this property owner had come to see him. Many others had come before.

'Sit down, Bluey,' the manager pointed to a straight-backed chair in front of his old oak desk.

'Thanks, Glen.' Bluey removed his hat.

The portly man sat back in his leather chair and donned his rimless spectacles. He sucked on his cigarette, the smoke curling around his nostrils. 'What can I do for you?'

'I'll come right to the point,' Bluey began. 'We need a loan to carry on. The drought's killing us.'

The manager removed a thick file from a desk drawer, took out a typed sheet of paper, and placed it on the blotter. As he shifted the cigarette in his mouth, some ash fell onto his lap. 'You're not alone there,' he said, brushing away the ash. 'And as you are probably aware, Ellen has been here before, but as she wasn't the owner, there was nothing I could do to help.' He frowned. 'Not that the bank would loan money to a woman anyway, you understand?' Bluey could just imagine what her response would have been to that statement. 'With this drought,' the manager continued, 'the bank is somewhat overextended, particularly around here. I'm not sure if head office would approve another loan in this area.'

Bluey leaned forward. 'Look, Glen, as you know, our property's debt-free. The O'Donnells have banked here since my father first moved to the district and we've never sought a loan from you in the past. You know we are good for the dough and you'll have Kilkenny as collateral.'

The manager handed the sheet of paper to Bluey. 'I will submit your loan application and strongly recommend it be approved.'

Bluey exhaled with relief.

'How much were you looking to borrow?' He took up his pen.

Once Bluey had finalised matters at the bank, he headed to the fuel depot to arrange extended credit with the same man who had previously refused Ellen. His next task was to obtain a utility. Ellen had used the boot of the car in his absence, but had often had to make several trips – to Bluey this was an inefficient use of time and fuel. He drove the Dodge sedan to a local motor dealer who swapped it for a reliable, '38 model Chevrolet flat top. He gave Bluey an additional seventy-five pounds because his sedan was a much newer model, and was in good condition.

Ellen was extremely pleased when Bluey told her of his morning dealings.

He's trying so hard.

That night, as Bluey removed his boots, he heard a light knock at the door. It was Cathleen. 'I wanted to come down and keep you company for a while, Daddy,' she said, smiling.

Bluey was caught off-guard. 'Does your mother know you're here?'

'Yes.' She walked in and sat on the other chair.

Bluey felt awkward. He had always been much closer to David. Cathleen had been so young when he left.

'How is school going?' He was sure this must have sounded like a dumb question, but if Cathleen thought it was, she didn't seem to care. She went on to tell him about her class and the subjects she liked best. 'Tell me about your friends,' he said. He was beginning to relax, and his young daughter had no trouble chatting away about her life. He sat back, grinning, as Cathleen took over the conversation.

They talked for over an hour before she rose. 'I'd better go. Mummy said I had to be back by nine.' She wrapped her arms around his neck and kissed him on the cheek.

He felt his heart melt. 'Sleep tight, sweet dreams and God bless.' He followed her to the door and watched her skip back to the homestead.

What a sweet child.

Two nights later, she visited him again. This time she carried a deck of cards. 'Will you teach me how to play please, Daddy?'

'Of course I will.' He drew up two chairs next to his small table. It soon became part of their regular special time together. Once or twice a week after doing the dishes, she'd visit her father in the shearers' quarters and they'd play the card games Sally had taught him as a child: coon-can, switch, snatch and poker for matches. Bluey looked forward to Cathleen's visits, and was glad to be making up for lost time.

Chapter 34

As the weeks passed, Bluey settled back into the routine of property life. The hard, physical work and wholesome food soon built up his strength, and at nights he was either too tired or too busy with his children to let his craving for the bottle overtake him.

The doctor said it would kill me, and the kids need a father.

A few days a week Ellen assisted Bluey, and David helped on weekends. Whenever time allowed, father and son began to go shooting and fishing again.

Sitting by the river on one Sunday morning, David reeled in a small yellow belly.

'Not much around today, Dad,' he said, expertly twisting the fish from the hook.

'Hang on to that one, mate. We'll set the big line and try for a Murray cod. I've never caught one of those big bludgers. They're too cunning.' Bluey reached into a sugar bag for the necessary tackle. 'We'll set it up near that submerged log over there near that deep hole.' He pointed. 'Your grandfather once told me they like to lurk about in places like that.'

Once the line was set, they settled back to wait. David eyed his father uncertainly. 'Remember how I asked you about the war that time, Dad?'

The comment caught Bluey by surprise. 'Yeah.'

'And you told me never to ask you about it?' David waited.

'It's not something I want to think about, son. I've tried to put it behind me.' He looked into David's innocent eyes, his young face a mixture of anticipation and apprehension, and sighed.

Where to begin . . .

'I was in a Japanese prisoner-of-war camp. Things happened there that I want to forget. That's about it, mate.'

David opened his mouth to reply, but the ratchet on the set line began to zing. Something big had hit it. 'You land him, son.' Bluey jumped to his feet.

David took hold and tried to reel in some line, but whatever was on the other end was too strong. 'It's too big, Dad!'

'Let some more line out!' Bluey cried with exhilaration. 'We'll play him!'

Over the next twenty minutes, they moved upstream and downstream with the fish as it tried to extricate itself from the hook embedded in its mouth. With each minute, it began to tire, and slowly but surely David began to reel it in. Finally, the large Murray cod was in the shallows. Bluey grabbed it behind the gills and lifted it clear. 'Has to be thirty-five pounds if it's an ounce!' He grabbed his son's shoulder, shaking him with excitement. 'That'll feed us for a week.'

David stood looking down on the fish which was now

thrashing about on the grassy bank. 'I don't want to keep him, Dad. I want to put him back.'

'What?' Bluey was stunned.

'He's old and he's brave. I think he should live.'

Bluey was flabbergasted, but was also proud of his son's compassion.

'Very well, mate. You caught him, so it's your decision.'

Autumn came and went, followed by a bitterly cold winter with frosts that killed off any remaining green grass. To ensure the flock had food, Bluey cut branches off the saltbush and obtained a load of hay and grain from the produce store, using the animal feed sparingly.

The depleted merino flock was shorn two months later, and Bluey forwarded Humphries a cheque for the full amount owing. The five shearers who came to the O'Donnell property were somewhat amused that they'd had to share their drab accommodation with Kilkenny's owner. The good-natured men teased Bluey mercilessly about not being allowed to sleep in the house.

With the money from the bank loan, Bluey employed a mechanic to repair the old tractor. It would be needed to prepare the wheat fields when the rains finally came. The fencing around the paddocks was in a state of disrepair, so some of the precious money had to be apportioned to that, too.

Weeks passed, but still the drought continued. On two occasions, passing showers tantalised the hopes of the O'Donnell family. Other farmers in the district received some good falls, but not Kilkenny. It didn't seem fair that some properties could now plant a crop while others were left devastated. The O'Donnell's optimism faded, with cloudless blue skies greeting them every morning. The remainder of the merino flock was just hanging on, with Bluey and Ellen alternating them between the river paddock and the smaller enclosures away from the dwindling stream.

By now, Bluey's health had improved greatly. His complexion took on a fresh, healthy look, while his body hardened with the constant manual work. Taking his meals with the family, he always made sure he was clean shaven and presentable. His improved appearance did not go unnoticed by Ellen, who had always been attracted to his boyish good looks. Watching him eat his evening meal one night, she couldn't stop herself from thinking.

Why does he have to look so good?

It had been years since they'd made love, so long that she'd almost forgotten what it was like to be aroused. Ellen appreciated that Bluey went out of his way to help her. He was particularly attentive when she came down with a bad dose of influenza, cooking her meals and fussing over her while still attending to the needs of Kilkenny. This was all new for him, and while his good behaviour couldn't fully remove the bitterness from her heart, she was forced to admit that he was making a concerted effort.

Then, just when he thought everything was going along fine, without warning the nightmare of his past returned. He wondered if it might have been that his body had adjusted to the hard work, and that he was no longer utterly spent at the end of each day. Indeed, he did not always fall asleep when his head hit the pillow, and he could no longer rely on the dreamless sleep of exhaustion.

To help overcome the problem, instead of sitting in his room, he went to the agricultural shed, where his father's heavy punching bag still hung from a beam. Under the admiring gaze of his two children, he worked out until he could no longer raise his fists, in the hope of reaching a state of fatigue that would, with luck, suppress the nightmare. It gave him an opportunity to pass on to David the same boxing instruction his own father had passed to him.

'I can't believe how quick you are now, Dad.' David marvelled.

'You should've seen your grandad.' Bluey smiled. 'He was like lightning.'

David looked thoughtful. 'I can remember him you know. He used to ruffle my hair a lot, and he was always singing.'

'Yeah, son. He was a great man.'

Bluey still continued to sleep in the shearers' accommodation, but was tired of using the temporary shower facilities there. Enclosed by a hessian screen for limited privacy, this primitive affair consisted of a canvas bucket, with a shower head screwed into the base, suspended by a rope over a beam. One afternoon, after a full day in the paddocks, he walked into the house to take his shower.

'Ellen, you there?' he called out loudly.

When he heard no response, he walked towards the bathroom and strode right in. The vision before him caused his eyes to pop and his mouth to drop open in amazement. Ellen stood dripping wet, without a stitch of clothing. The body that left him weak at the knees was there before him in all its wondrous glory. She looked back at him in surprise, but said nothing. Then he was gone. As she heard his loud footsteps quickly retreating, she had to suppress a giggle.

Did you see the look on his face?

Her wall of resentment was beginning to crumble.

Bluey returned to the shearers' quarters and sat for a long time on his bunk. All he could think about was that image of Ellen, naked in the bathroom. The desirable body and lovely face were still the same.

She's so beautiful. What an idiot I was.

Bluey felt himself begin to harden.

Bloody hell.

He knew he loved her and wanted her back, but seeing her naked brought out the intense physical attraction he still felt for her. He'd not allowed himself to think about her in this way until now – the risk of rejection had seemed too great. But she hadn't shouted at him when he burst in on her. Maybe he'd imagined it, but she looked as if she was about to break into a smile. He sat there daydreaming, thinking about the future and what could have been if there had not been a war. He tried to marshal his thoughts into some sort of order. He knew she was the only woman he could ever love, and that he wanted her as his wife in every possible way. He was gripped with a fierce determination to win her back.

Later, when he made his way into the kitchen for dinner, Ellen did not turn from the stove. 'Bathroom's free now, Bluey.'

'I'm sorry, El. I didn't know you were there.'

She swung around, and her eyes met his and held. 'That's all right. You've seen it all before.'

He sat in his seat, and out of the corner of her eye, Ellen saw him smile. She then realised that she, too, was looking like the cat that got the cream. Handing him his plate, she looked at his full head of ginger hair. A few flecks of grey now highlighted his temples, but the curls were still there in abundance. For a brief moment, she wanted to reach out and run her fingers through them, just like she did when they were young.

That wouldn't be right.

Throughout the meal, whenever she looked up, he was gazing at her. For the first time since his return, there was much less tension between them. The children also noticed the relaxed atmosphere.

'I can't come to the shed tonight, Daddy. I have too much homework. Can you help me with my history project?' Cathleen asked sweetly.

'Of course, love.' It was a simple request, but he felt an upwelling of contentment. It seemed Cathleen longed for his company and he suddenly felt a wave of guilt for ever leaving her. 'Then David and I are going out to the shed for a workout, right, mate?'

David beamed.

Almost as if to challenge his rehabilitation, the nightmare would not go away. Every week or so, Bluey's cry of anguish would sometimes wake David as well. The boy knew his father had problems that stemmed from his time as a prisoner-of-war, and had seen the scars on his back. He felt he was old enough now to speak up. While working out on the large punching bag one evening, he turned to Bluey. 'I hear you, Dad,' he began tentatively.

'What do you mean?' Bluey replied, puzzled.

'When you scream out at night.' The youngster paused. 'I know you don't want to talk about it, but I hate to hear you like that.'

Bluey shrugged self-consciously. 'I'm sorry, mate. I can't help it.'

'Mum says you used to see a doctor about it.'

'Yeah, I did.'

'Why don't you go back and see him again?' David asked boldly. 'You're not getting any better, are you?'

Bluey sighed deeply then grinned, trying to make light of the situation. 'You're a wise little bugger, aren't you?'

'Dad, I'm worried about you and I know Cathleen is too. You've got to do something about it.'

The compassion and anxiety in his son's eyes tore at Bluey's conscience. His children were growing older, and his problems could no longer be hidden from them. That night he lay awake thinking, and came to a decision he never thought he would make.

Ellen was preparing breakfast when he broke the news. 'I'm going back to see Dr Stevens, El.'

Ellen froze. This was the best news she'd had in years.

Bluey continued. 'The kids are worried. I don't want this to affect them. I don't want it to affect you any more, either.'

Ellen turned to him. 'I think that's a good idea.' She didn't want to be too enthusiastic or too patronising in case she put him off, but was secretly thrilled that at last he was serious about trying to resolve his problems.

On the drive to Brisbane Bluey tried hard to remember his last visit with the psychiatrist, but too much had happened since. When he'd phoned to make the appointment, there had been no difficulty. The receptionist at the repatriation hospital had returned his call immediately, saying that Dr Stevens would be pleased to see him the following week.

Dressed in light grey slacks and a cream, short-sleeved open-necked shirt, Bluey entered the psychiatrist's office. The balding man looked up from his desk and smiled warmly. 'It's been a long time, Bluey.' He rose and held out his hand.

Bluey took it in a firm grip. 'Yeah, it has, Doc. Been living the good life I see?'

'Yes.' The doctor chuckled, patting his paunch. He sat down and crossed his hands over his stomach. 'So how have you been?'

Bluey gave the psychiatrist an honest account of his life since his last visit, telling him about his parents' deaths, his alcoholism and his life on the streets. Once he began talking, he felt a great weight lift off his shoulders. He couldn't stop until he was finished.

Dr Stevens took a deep breath. 'It seems you've either drunk yourself into a stupor or worked yourself into the ground in the hope that the nightmare would go away, but it hasn't, has it?'

'No, Doc, it hasn't. And now it's affecting my kids.'

'Can I take it that this time you really want to do something about it?'

'Yeah.' He paused. 'The war was a long time ago. I don't feel as bad about things as I did before.'

'Bluey,' the doctor began in a reassuring tone, 'you were just a kid when you were taken prisoner. You must have seen some terrible things.'

Whether it was the memory of his son's pained expression, the doctor's gentle tone or his own mellowing, Bluey didn't know, but for the first time he felt ready to talk about the war. And talk he did. He told the doctor everything – about his friendship with Digger, the sinking of the ship, Digger saving his life in the water, the prisoner-of-war camp, the punishments, the disease, and the sadistic Japanese sergeant they subsequently killed to save their own lives. He started to weep when he admitted that Digger might have escaped had he not come back for him.

'I remember Digger's words, Doc, as if it was yesterday.' His voice choked with pain. 'He said, "I couldn't leave you, Blue. You're me mate."'

Bluey began to sweat as he described the punishment that was meted out to them. Finally, Bluey attempted to explain the profound sense of guilt he felt at being left alive after Digger's execution. For the first time, he revealed to another living soul what took place in the nightmare.

When Bluey had finished, the doctor sat quietly for several moments, slowly shaking his head. 'And I thought I'd heard it all.' He swallowed down the lump in his throat.

'What can I do?'

The doctor leaned forward in his seat. 'Bluey, you felt you owed Digger your life because he saved you when the ship was sunk. Right?'

'Yeah,' Bluey replied uncertainly.

'And when Digger came back for you when you were stuck in the mud you think he might have been able to escape?'

'That's right.'

'And he was killed and you are still alive.' The doctor raised his eyebrows.

'Yes.' Bluey looked down at his hands, which were gripping his knees.

'Bluey, you are suffering from a guilt complex that manifests in your subconscious, that's why you have the nightmare.' Drawing in a deep breath, he continued. 'Look, let's get things clear; you've done nothing wrong here. You were virtually a child. The Japanese only let you live because they needed you. You had no control over the situation. Do you really think Digger would blame you?'

Bluey was quiet for a long moment, but he knew the answer instinctively. 'No. Digger was one of the kindest blokes I've ever met.'

'Then don't blame yourself.'

'I understand what you're saying, Doc, and it makes sense, but I'm not sure it will help.'

'Trust me, Bluey. Talking about it will help enormously, but we're going to do more than that, I can assure you. Do you know anything about hypnotism?'

'I remember seeing an ad for a hypnotist show in the *Courier-Mail* once. A Yank I think he was. He put people under and got them to do silly things.'

'Yes, you're right. Hypnotism has been used as a form of entertainment. Volunteers are chosen from the audience and put into a trance and made to believe they are drunk, or that they are an animal.' He grinned. 'It's been around a long time. It's recently been endorsed by the medical profession as a treatment in cases such as yours. I think it would really help in your situation.'

'Okay, Doc. Sounds good to me.'

'I'm going to put you under and attempt to reassure your subconscious.' He left his chair and stood before Bluey, holding a small pendant. 'Sit where you are and make yourself completely comfortable. Now I want you to concentrate your full attention on this pendant. As I swing it backwards and forwards, keep your eyes glued to it. Don't think of anything else except the movement of the pendant.'

Bluey watched the small circle of silver and felt his mind drifting . . .

When he awoke, he felt relaxed and peaceful. 'I feel great, Doc.'

The psych looked at him with a serious expression. 'You're not out of the woods yet, Bluey. I'm afraid there's no quick fix. You'll need a number of sessions, and the nightmare may still return from time to time. Guilt is a strange bedfellow and takes a lot of persuasion to shift.' He stroked his chin. 'You must tell your wife about Digger and the prisoner-of-war camp so she can fully appreciate what you went through. You must also give your children a brief outline so that they can understand why you left them. But avoid the details – they're far too young to cope. Make an appointment with the receptionist. We'll have another hypnosis session next month.' He smiled as he stood to see Bluey to the door.

'Thanks, Doc.'

Bluey stayed overnight in a Red Cross room at the hospital, and was up early, anxious to start the trip home. It was midafternoon by the time he drove the old ute through the gates of the property, feeling tired, but peaceful.

'How'd it go?' Ellen anxiously scanned her husband's face, and was relieved to find no sign of tension there.

'Really good,' he assured her. 'I'll talk to you about it later.'

At that moment, Cathleen and David bounded out of the house to greet their father. David couldn't have felt happier. His father was home for good, and he wasn't drinking. What was more, he'd gone to the doctor to get help for his nightmares. Even though David was only thirteen years old, he knew this was important.

'Do you reckon we'll be able to go shooting later, Dad?' David asked. 'There's heaps of roos around.'

'Maybe tomorrow evening, son. We've got a lot of work to catch up on. I've got to load grain on the ute to drop off in the paddocks in the morning.' He smiled at David. 'And you've got your jobs, mate – feeding the pigs and the dogs.'

'I'll do it now, Dad.'

'And Cathleen, you can feed the chooks and collect the eggs as usual.'

'Yes, Daddy.'

Later that night, after the children were in bed, Bluey led Ellen to the sofa. For the second time ever, he revealed to another person everything that had befallen him after he left Australia for overseas service. When he told her about Digger's execution and his own punishment she began to weep. As he continued to speak, he felt hot tears on his own cheeks. He could not look at her when he explained the horror of his nightmare. He told her of Dr Steven's diagnosis and his treatment by hypnosis. He withheld nothing from her, repeating the doctor's warning that he was a far cry from being cured.

'It's going to take a lot more counselling and hypnosis, but even then the dream might return from time to time. The doc says a major hurdle has been overcome because at least I can talk about it now, especially to you.'

She sat mute, tears rolling down her cheeks. Then, finally, drew him tenderly to her breast. 'Oh, Bluey. I had no idea. You poor darling. How could I have been so self-centred?'

'You didn't know, El.'

She called me darling!

A feeling of contentment suffused him, seemingly spreading to every pore in his body.

'What are we to do?'

He sat up and placed an arm around her shoulder, tilting her chin with his free hand to look into her glistening green eyes. 'I love you, El. I always have and always will. There's never been anyone else.'

His words sent a surge of longing through her being. 'And I love you, Bluey.' She held him tightly and closed her eyes. She never wanted to let him go.

He kissed her, and she thought she would melt. It had been so long. He rose and pulled her to her feet, lifting her into his arms. He carried her to the bedroom.

Digger appeared in his dream again that night. But this time, he was the friend of old, looking as he did when Bluey first met him. The big man bestowed on Bluey the most beatific smile. 'Stop blaming yourself, Blue. Have a good life.'

Bluey awoke with a start and lay back thinking about the new dream. While acknowledging it was most likely a result of the hypnosis, he could not help but smile.

That's probably just what Digger would've said.

He went back to sleep with Ellen's arm draped over his chest.

David's face lit up when his parents emerged from the bedroom the following morning.

'You look happy today, son.'

'Yes, Mum. I am.'

That evening, David and Cathleen were just about to begin clearing the table when Ellen spoke. 'Your father needs to talk to you, so I want you to listen closely to everything he has to say.'

The children looked at each other and remained seated. It had to be something important if their mother was speaking so formally.

Bluey pushed back his chair and looked from one young face to the other. He had discussed what he was going to say with Ellen. 'You both know I went to the doctor yesterday.'

'Yes, Dad,' David replied. Cathleen nodded.

'I will be going back to see him a few more times. He says I need to tell you a little about the war and why I was away last year.' When there was no answer, he continued. 'I was very young when I went to the war, only a few years older than you, David. The truth is I never really got there. Our ship was sunk and we were captured by the Japs. It was a terrible time and it left me with a recurring nightmare about a good friend who died over there. I'm not making excuses for my drinking, I'm trying to explain what happened. God knows if I had that time over again . . .' He trailed off.

'You don't have to go on if you don't want to, Daddy,' Cathleen said gently.

'I'm okay.' He took a deep breath and continued. 'I suppose it was because I was so young. It was difficult to cope. I found out that when I drank, the nightmare didn't come. My drinking caused problems between Mum and me.' His eyes met Ellen's. 'It wasn't her fault. She was just trying to protect you. Anyway, that's why I left, even though I loved you both so much.'

Cathleen went to her father, wrapping her arms around him. David's mind was racing, remembering his father's blood-curdling screams in the night and his heavy drinking. 'Thanks for telling us, Dad.'

Bluey put his arm around his daughter's waist and ruffled his son's hair. 'That's okay, mate. Things are going to be good from now on. You wait and see.'

Chapter 34

When rain finally came to Kilkenny, it seemed the downpour would never end. After five days of constant rain, the Macintyre River was running a banker, and the road to town was cut off by rising floodwaters. The children couldn't attend school. Eventually the river paddock became inundated. To prevent stock losses, Bluey, Ellen, David and the dogs gradually moved the flock to higher ground in the bottom paddock. The homestead had been built on a small rise, so was fairly safe, but the barn and the agricultural shed were vulnerable to the floodwaters. Both would be inundated if the river got much higher. On returning to the barn, they unsaddled the soaked horses.

'Get the brushes will you, David?' Bluey asked.

As David walked to a darkened corner of the shed, Skipper started after the lad, growling and barking. A large eastern brown snake had made its way into the dry barn to escape the rain. The dog was too late to prevent the venomous reptile from striking at the boy as he walked past a stack of lucerne hay. At first, Ellen looked mystified then her expression changed to one of horror as she watched her son clutch his leg, and the dog take on the angry snake. With his powerful jaws, the dog latched onto the slithering creature's neck and bit down hard. It was soon over. The snake lay dead.

Ellen and Bluey ran to David. 'Did it get you?' his father asked, dreading the reply

'Yes. Here.' David pointed to the lower half of his leg.

'Oh, no. What'll we do?' Ellen had never felt such gut-wrenching fear. She felt the pulse pounding in her throat.

'We have to get him to the hospital, and fast.'

'The road's cut off.' Her eyes were saucers of panic.

'Don't worry. I'll get him there.' Bluey's face became a picture of grim determination. 'But before we go, we have to tie up the leg. Go get the first-aid kit will you. And hurry, love.' As Ellen ran out of the barn, he turned back to his son. 'David, don't move a muscle.'

'I'm scared, Dad.' His voice quivered.

'Don't be.' He placed a comforting hand on his shoulder. 'You've got to try to stay relaxed. I know that's hard.'

Bluey heard a whimper coming from behind them and swung around to see the dog staggering.

Bloody thing got him too.

Out of breath, Ellen was soon by his side with the first-aid bag. Bluey removed the snake-bite kit and a small sharp knife. 'This'll hurt, mate.' He examined his son's face, now wet with perspiration. Quickly nicking the flesh around the punctured area, he allowed the blood to flow. He then leaned over his son's calf muscle, and sucked at the wound for several seconds, spitting the blood and poison onto the dirt floor of the barn. Bluey then used his leather belt as a tourniquet on David's thigh.

'It's so tight, Dad. It hurts.'

'It has to be tight, mate.' Watching her son grimace with pain as his father went about the gruesome task, Ellen couldn't stop shaking. David clutched his head as the poison began to take effect. Perspiration oozed from every pore of his body and his shivering increased.

'The ute won't make it to town, but a horse will.' Bluey said, thinking aloud. 'Ellen, phone the hospital and tell them to have an ambulance waiting on the other side of Ellis Creek.'

'How'll you get across?' she asked anxiously.

'I'll swim the horse. Tell the ambulance I'll meet them there. Tell them it was an eastern brown snake and to bring the right antivenene.'

He re-saddled old Ned, reining him tightly then assisted his son into the saddle. Ellen held David as Bluey swung up behind him. As a final gesture he turned to a petrified Ellen. 'Don't worry, El. I'll get him there,' he said, knowing his words were of little comfort. 'You and Cathleen wait by the phone. I'll call you when I get to the hospital.' Before she could reply, he was gone from the shelter of the barn.

Passing through the front gate of the property, he took hold of both reins in one hand, holding David in the saddle with the other. He knew the job before him was not going to be easy. Ellis Creek was a fifteen-minute ride away. He then had to swim the horse across the swirling current to the other side where, hopefully, the ambulance would be waiting. Ned, the ten-year-old gelding on which the two were seated, was dependable and sure-footed, but would need extra courage to enter a flooded river.

Riding at full gallop, the heavy rain seemed to pierce their faces like shards of glass. As Bluey approached the flooded creek, the rain began to ease off slightly, but the sight before him made his heart sink. Ellis Creek, usually a trickle about ten feet wide, was a raging torrent at least fifty yards across. On reaching the edge of the muddy waters, he saw the ambulance pulling to a halt on the opposite side.

Bluey knew that if they were to reach the other side anywhere near the ambulance they would have to enter the swirling waters some distance upstream. After riding for a half mile or so, he stopped and urged the horse towards the river. Wrapping both arms around his son, he looked into the face resting against his shoulder. 'Hang on, mate,' he pleaded. 'Please, hang on.' Bluey heeled the bay towards the current, but sensing danger, the animal propped. Bluey dug his heels in harder, yelling, 'Come on, Ned! Get up!'

The frightened animal refused to budge. Bluey took a deep breath. He knew the horse needed to feel secure if it was to enter the swift-flowing water – it must not sense the desperation and panic consuming its rider. With a free hand, Bluey patted the side of Ned's neck. This time he spoke softy and calmly. 'Come on, mate. You can do it.'

Bluey again lightly dug the bay with his heels, and the nervous animal slowly began to step into the swirling waters. Horse and riders were immediately swept downstream. With words of encouragement from Bluey, Ned struck out for the other side. It took all Bluey's strength and expertise as a horseman to stop them slipping off. 'Come on, Ned. Swim, boy!' he urged the animal. 'Swim, you old bugger!' Above the noise of the water he could hear the animal snorting with determination, using its powerful legs to strike out for the other side.

They were halfway across when Bluey saw the ambulance. Seconds later, they were swept past the vehicle. The ambulance officers followed them by running along the bank and calling out, 'Hang on, mate! Hang on!'

Hearing their calls of encouragement gave Bluey renewed strength, and a few moments later, horse and riders at last reached shallower waters. Bluey quickly heeled Ned towards the grassy bank where they were met by the two officers. Bluey was the first to speak. 'I'll ride back to the ambulance. You fellas run behind.'

On reaching the vehicle, the two men took David from his arms, placing him on a narrow stretcher inside.

'It was a brown, right?' the older one asked.

'Yeah, an eastern brown.' Bluey swallowed.

The other officer reached for a black medical bag. 'We'll give him a shot of antivenene right now.'

'I'll unsaddle old Ned and let him go.' Bluey turned to the horse whose flanks were still heaving from its ordeal. 'I'll track him down later.'

The ambulance sped towards town with its siren blaring. Bluey sat by David's side, his eyes never leaving the face of his son.

At the hospital, David was rushed into the emergency ward and Bluey was ushered outside by a nursing sister who directed him to a telephone. Ellen answered almost as soon as the phone rang. 'Bluey!' she cried. 'How is he?' Her mouth felt suddenly dry.

'The doctors are with him now.'

'I don't know what I'd do if anything happened —' Ellen's voice cracked.

'He's strong, El. He'll be fine. I'd better get back.'

'Ring me as soon as you know anything.'

'Of course.'

Back in the hospital's waiting room, Bluey was oblivious to the looks people gave him. Muddied and wet through, he cared only about the condition of his beloved son. He sat near a large window, and could see the river below. Only the giant red gums stood defiant against the swollen waterway, the smaller trees were almost completely submerged – their tips swirling like kelp. Bluey kept glancing at the electric clock on the wall above the doorway. He thought it must have stopped, the hands moved so slowly. He took a magazine from the small table at his elbow, but could not focus his mind on anything but David. He was just about to make enquiries when the doctor appeared at the doorway. 'I'm pleased to report that David will make a full recovery.'

'Thank God.' Bluey dropped his head into his hands.

'What you did made a difference, you know.' The doctor laid a hand on Bluey's shoulder. 'Good work.'

Bluey rang Ellen immediately to pass on the good news. She couldn't answer him through her sobs of relief.

Cathleen took over the phone. 'Daddy, Mummy's crying and laughing at the same time. Is David going to be all right?'

'Yes, sweetheart,' he said soothingly.

Ellen came back on the line, and Bluey told her that he didn't know when he would be able to return to Kilkenny.

'I'm stuck here till the creek goes down. Will you be all right?'

'Don't worry about us!' replied Ellen, clearly euphoric.

Bluey was allowed to visit his son for a short while. David slowly opened his eyes and smiled as he heard his father enter the darkened room. 'How do you feel, mate?' Bluey asked quietly.

'I'm still a bit wonky, Dad. But I feel much better.'

'I should've warned you that snakes would come into the sheds with the rain.'

'Don't blame yourself. I'm old enough to look where I'm walking. And I see them nearly every day. They usually shoot off quick.'

'The bloody thing must have felt trapped.'

'What about Skipper?'

'Sorry, mate. Snake got him.'

Tears rolled down his son's cheek. 'He saved me from being bitten again.'

'Yeah, he was a top dog.' Bluey stroked David's hair. 'Don't be upset, mate, he was getting on. Murphy's bitch has just had another litter. You can pick one out.'

'Okay, Dad.' His eyes began to droop.

'You try and get some rest now. I'll stay with you until you nod off.'

Leaving David's hospital room, Bluey was surprised to see Mick Sommers waiting for him in the passageway. 'How's he feeling, Blue?' The two men shook hands.

'He'll make a full recovery. He's asleep now.'

'Thanks be to God,' Mick said and blessed himself. 'Ellen phoned and gave us the news. Pat and me want you to stay with us till the river drops and David's fit to go home.'

'That's very kind of you, Mick. I appreciate it.'

'You can come home with me now, if you like.'

'Nah. I'll wait and see when David wakes up. I'll walk over later. It's not that far.' A thought struck him. 'My saddle and bridle are at the reception desk. Can I leave them at your place?'

'I'll take them home with me now.' Mick clapped him on the shoulder. 'I'll tell Pat to set another place at the table for tea.'

'Thanks, Mick.'

After two more days of treatment, and a stream of visitors including his aunt, uncle and cousins, not to mention school mates, David was discharged. To his peers, David was a sort of a hero because he had survived a killer brown snake bite.

Bluey contacted Ellen to come and pick them up. The creek had dropped enough for the road to be reopened. She entered the hospital foyer where Bluey and David waited, and ran to her son, throwing her arms around the embarrassed boy. 'Not in front of everyone, Mum.' He wriggled self-consciously.

'Come on. Let's get you home.' She smiled warmly. 'Your sister's all by herself.' In spite of David's protestations, he nevertheless took comfort in the loving arm that was draped over his shoulder as they left the hospital.

As Ellen prepared David's favourite dinner – braised steak – she thought about how fragile her relationship with Bluey was. It had only been a short time since their reconciliation, and they were both working hard at repairing their life together. The deep wounds of the past were healing, but if anything had happened to David . . . She shuddered to think how another tragedy would have affected them. Their resurrected life together would have come crashing down. But David had recovered, and his father's contribution to that recovery only strengthened the love and admiration she felt for him. She shrugged away the melancholy mood and said a small prayer of thanks.

The flood damage to Kilkenny was significant, especially to the river paddock fencing. Water had also found its way into the barn and the agricultural shed, spoiling some of the feed stored there. It took the family a full week to clean up. Surprisingly, the merino flock was in reasonably good condition and at last there would be fresh green grass. But the fencing would need to be repaired and the feed replaced, and they had no money for that. In fact, they were broke.

Bluey made a loan application to the Agricultural Bank, but his request was denied. The produce store, however, was prepared to extend them credit until things improved. Bluey was grateful because he would soon require seed and more fertiliser to raise a crop.

That night, as Bluey and Ellen sat alone in the living room, he broached the subject. 'El, we're out of dough,' he said bluntly. 'Shearing season's a long way off . . .'

'Well, we'll just have to hang in there and see what turns up. What would Dave have done?'

'Just that.' He lifted his chin stubbornly. 'He'd never let Kilkenny go. Not while he had life in him.'

'What about a summer crop?'

'Good idea. I might put in one of those new ones. What about sunflower?'

'Why not?'

In preparation for the expected planting, Bluey spent the next three days in the old tractor ploughing the grain field, using up the remaining fertiliser. He visited the produce store for the promised sunflower seed and soil enrichment, and was stunned when Bill Greensill refused. 'Sorry, Blue, I've sold the business to Len Humphries. I'm only looking after it till a new manager's appointed.'

'And I want payment for all you owe here, O'Donnell,' a loud voice demanded.

Bluey swung around to face Humphries, who was leaning against the front door, idly smoking a cigarette. The puffed up, satisfied look on his face made Bluey see red. 'You!'

'Yes, you little shit. I own this place now, and I want you to pay up.' He fell silent, as if letting the victory of the moment settle over him.

'Get stuffed.'

'You can say and do what you like, O'Donnell,' the larger man replied smugly. 'All I have to do is take you to court. With what you owe the bank and this business, you'll be declared bankrupt. Then I can pick up your precious Kilkenny when it's sold from under you.' He gave a raucous laugh.

'You bastard! I'll die before I let that happen.' Bluey strode towards Humphries.

'Be careful,' he warned. 'Don't forget the last time we tangled.'

Bluey's eyes narrowed. 'I haven't forgotten.' The wound of defeat remained open and was still festering

As Bluey passed by the big man, he was unable to resist a parting shot. 'You know, Humphries, you haven't changed a bit from when you were a kid. You're still a rotten, fat turd.'

Bluey turned away, and just managed to duck the large fist that sailed towards his head. Humphries lost his balance, falling sideways against a pane of glass in the front window of the store. As the glass shattered, the big man regained his composure, turning again towards Bluey. He wiped away blood dripping from a small cut to his elbow. 'Right, you little bastard,' he said darkly, 'it's time you learned another lesson.'

Humphries threw off his hat and raised his fists. Bluey did likewise. The two men circled each other, the scene drawing a small crowd of shoppers. Drinkers began to pour out of a nearby hotel. One local shook his head in wonder. 'This has been going on for bloody years.'

A confident Humphries directed most of his blows to Bluey's face, and while one glancing blow did stun him for a brief moment, the smaller man was still able to rip hard lefts and rights into the other man's midriff. As the confrontation progressed, however, Humphries became less and less sure of himself. He had been living the good life and was no match for his fit and sure-footed rival. Because he was in no condition for a protracted fight, Humphries increased the intensity of his blows in an effort to finish off his opponent. But the harder he tried to hit, the slower he became, and Bluey was easily able to block or dodge the misdirected fists.

At one point, Bluey stepped aside to avoid a heavy punch and lost his footing. He slipped backwards over the gutter to the bitumen street, lying for a moment, stunned. Humphries leapt on him, kicking at him, and driving the wind from his lungs. Just at this moment, a rough-looking character emerged from the Victoria Hotel and yelled out, 'Kicking's for sheilas, Humphries.'

This outburst momentarily distracted the big man, giving Bluey time to struggle to his feet. He began taunting his enemy. 'Yeah, you're a fat sheila, Humphries.'

The crowd roared with laughter, enraging Humphries, who again lunged towards his opponent. Stepping to one side, Bluey rained blows into his midriff, before delivering stinging punches to his face. Blood poured from Humphries' nose and lips. From that moment on, he was a defeated man. Barely able to lift his fists, he fell to the bitumen road.

Bluey reached down, grabbing the beaten man's shirt front. 'Don't ever come to my property again, Humphries, or you'll get more of the bloody same.'

Striding towards the old ute parked outside the produce store, he heard a slurred voice from behind him. 'You still have to pay, O'Donnell. Not even a fist fight changes that.' Bluey spun around, to see Humphries sitting on the road, grinning through the blood filling his mouth.

Sick bastard.

'What happened to you?' said Ellen, shocked, when Bluey came through the back door.

'Len Humphries has bought the produce store and wants payment for what we owe. He told me he'd get Kilkenny if we don't pay.'

'Are you okay, darling?'

'A lot better than him.'

'Tell me all about it, Dad,' David asked excitedly.

'No, son,' Bluey answered firmly. 'Fighting's a poor way of settling things. But sometimes you have to defend yourself.'

'I bet you gave him a hiding.' The admiration in David's voice was plain.

'I don't want to discuss it. Understand?'

'Yes, Dad.'

'How can we possibly pay him?' asked Ellen.

'I've got no idea, El. But my father and mother worked their fingers to the bone to build Kilkenny, and I'll die before he gets it.'

'That's my Bluey.' She wrapped her arms around him and he winced.

'Mongrel kicked me in the ribs while I was down.'

'Big coward,' she muttered. 'Come and I'll tape your chest.'

A week later, a letter arrived from Humphries' solicitor. As good as his word, it demanded payment be made in full for outstanding debts, and threatened court action if such debts were not paid immediately.

'I can't let him get this place!' Bluey slammed the letter onto the table.

'Legally, he's probably got us. But I'm not going without a fight.'

'Good girl.' They hugged each other hard, united in their resolve to save their heritage.

Bluey's solicitor advised there was no legal avenue left open to them. The following week was a sleepless one for both of them, as they lay awake desperately trying to think of ways and means of saving their property. It always culminated in a dead end.

Chapter 35

Ellen met Brenda Murphy at the front door, and the first thing she noticed was the local newspaper tucked under her friend's arm. She couldn't tell whether the flush in Brenda's cheeks was from the exertion of her pushbike ride, or from excitement.

'Have you seen the paper?' said Brenda, too aflutter to offer a greeting.

'No, I haven't. Come inside and I'll put the kettle on.'

In the kitchen, Brenda spread the newspaper on the table. 'Take a look.' She pointed to an article on page three.

Ellen leaned over and examined the piece. It was an invitation to all local property owners to attend a public meeting to gauge interest in growing cotton.

'Cotton? Here?'

'Mike's going. As you know, we haven't been doing all that well lately. He says it won't do any harm to listen to what they have to say.'

'Can you leave the paper? I'll talk to Bluey about it.'

The two women continued their usual catch-up over a cup of tea and scones. After Brenda's departure, Ellen's mind kept returning to the newspaper article. She read it over and over, taking in every word as she waited for him to come in from the paddocks.

After reading the story, he turned to her. 'What do you think?'

'Why not?'

Around forty property owners attended the meeting, many of them landowners with small holdings. Listening to the speakers as they outlined the benefits of growing cotton, Bluey became more and more engrossed. Cotton was a crop that needed a large area to be viable, and he had seven thousand acres – more than enough. On hearing this information, a few of the smaller property holders quietly left the meeting.

Bluey was starting to feel excited. This was an opportunity to end his financial problems. He could sell the merinos and farm cotton. Then he thought about how disappointed his father would have been to see his beloved Kilkenny change beyond recognition, and he felt guilty.

But times change! Circumstances change! And he'd want me to save Kilkenny first.

At the end of the meeting, the senior officer from the Queensland Department of Primary Industries, Mr Ambrose Palmerson, said his officers would remain to discuss issues with individual farmers.

'What do you think, Bluey?' asked Michael Murphy who'd been sitting beside him.

'I don't know. It sounds good, but I'm going to find out a

bit more first.' Bluey made straight for Palmerson. 'G'day, Mr Palmerson. I'm Bluey O'Donnell.' The two shook hands.

'How can I help you, Mr O'Donnell?'

'Well, first of all, the name's Bluey.'

'Ambrose.' He grinned.

'I've got to admit that I've never really thought about cotton as a crop before.'

'Yes, it's never been grown on a commercial basis in Queensland. The government is keen on its cultivation here. How big is your property?' Palmerson enquired with interest.

'Seven thousand acres.' Bluey told him it was a wheat and sheep property and that he had experienced some financial difficulties. He spoke of his wife and two children who were dependent on him. It was no time to be embarrassed.

'What about available water?'

'It's right on the Macintyre.'

'That's perfect. The river gives you a major advantage. You could be the forerunner of this venture. We will give you all the assistance we can. We want this project to be successful.'

For several moments, Bluey stood there, turning the information over in his head. His mind was racing. This could be the end of his financial problems. But then doubts crept in.

'Hell, Ambrose. I don't know the first thing about growing cotton. What makes you so sure I could handle it?'

Palmerson smiled encouragingly. 'As I said before, my department will provide every assistance.'

'To tell you the truth, I don't think I've got much of a choice.'

'You've made the right decision, Bluey. And there's also

tremendous Japanese interest in the crop for their developing clothing industry.'

'Japs?' Bluey frowned.

'Yes.' Palmerson noticed the change in Bluey's demeanour. 'The war's been over for a long time,' he said gently.

'I was in a Japanese prison camp,' Bluey replied bitterly.

'Oh.'

'Don't worry,' he cleared his throat. 'I can let bygones be bygones.'

'You sure?' The senior officer raised his eyebrows.

'Yeah.'

'There's a Japanese executive visiting the area with me right now.' He looked Bluey in the eye. 'Would it be all right to bring him out to your property?'

'I suppose so.'

'Just say so if it isn't,' Palmerson said evenly. 'We can still go ahead without him. It's just that I'd like him to meet some of the locals.'

Bluey knew he had to come to terms with his animosity. 'Bring him out for tea tomorrow night. It'll be fine.'

'What do you think, El?' Bluey asked that night after he'd explained the cotton proposal.

'It may be the answer we were looking for.' She grabbed hold of his hand and squeezed it hard. 'Are you sure about the dinner tomorrow? There's still time to ring Palmerson and cancel.' Ellen sensed his disquiet.

'Yes. I'll bite my tongue. We need this.'

The next day he could think of nothing else but his impending visitor. He felt odd – as if he was somehow letting his country down. He knew this was ridiculous, but his anxiety only increased as the day dragged on. David and Cathleen were fed early, both retiring to their respective rooms and their homework. At six-thirty p.m. Bluey heard the car pull up. Acid gnawed at the wall of his stomach.

A bloody Jap in my home!

Then, quite suddenly, Bluey was reminded of Little Mudguts. He hadn't thought about him for a long time. He thought about how kind he'd been – how he'd helped him out when he didn't have to, indeed when it was risky for him to do so.

He was a good bloke. They can't all be bad.

Ellen looked at her husband's worried expression and knew this was going to be an ordeal for him. She reached for his hand.

'We'll open the door together,' she said.

Bluey pulled back the heavy farmhouse door to the smiling face of Ambrose Palmerson. By his side stood a slightly built man in his fifties, his arms full of gift-wrapped parcels. The man was immaculately dressed in a grey suit, white shirt and black tie. Bluey stood transfixed. It was the first time he'd come face to face with a Japanese person since the war. Bluey's mouth opened and closed, but no sound emerged.

Palmerson broke the silence. 'Bluey, I'd like you to meet Mr Hayashi Akio. He is the manager of Nippon Cotton Industries. Mr Hayashi, this is the man I spoke to you about.'

'I pleased to meet you.' The Japanese man smiled warmly and bowed awkwardly, trying not to drop his parcels.

'G'day,' said Bluey, and introduced Ellen to both men.

'How do you do?' Ellen responded.

'It Japanese tradition to give gifts. I hope you like.' He handed Ellen a small, neatly wrapped box. 'And this for you, Mr O'Donnell.' He bowed once more.

'Just call me Bluey. Please come in.'

Once they were settled, Ellen went to the kitchen to check on the meal she had prepared. Hayashi Akio handed Bluey the remaining gifts. 'Mr Palmerson tell me you have two children. Boy would like cricket bat, yes? And little girl like doll? My three granddaughter love them.'

'Thank you.' Bluey was unprepared for the man's generous gesture.

'I suppose we'd better get down to business.' Palmerson opened his briefcase. Bluey was surprised that at no time during the talks, or the subsequent meal, did his hatred for the Japanese come to mind. This man was nothing like the guards that had made his life a misery for all that time.

He's more like Little Mudguts.

Palmerson informed Bluey that a cotton gin would be established locally to service the needs of growers in the district. Farmers would also know the approximate value of the crop at the time of planting.

'That's a change from having to take pot-luck,' said Bluey.

'Yes, with cotton, at least you know pretty much what you're going to get. Once you've sold your flock and are ready to proceed, I'll arrange for one of my officers to visit the property to help you with the setting up process.'

Hayashi Akio sat quietly, trying to follow the conversation taking place between the two Australian men.

Later that night as they prepared for bed, Ellen unwrapped her gift. She drew in a sharp breath – it was expensive perfume. She spayed her wrist and sniffed. 'It's beautiful.' She turned to Bluey. 'What did you get?'

Bluey removed the coloured paper to find a boxed gold fountain pen. 'Bloody hell! It must have cost him a fortune!'

'He seemed quite nice,' she offered quietly.

'Yeah,' he admitted. 'He wasn't too bad at all.'

Bluey called a stock agent to Kilkenny the next day. Tom Fielder had known the O'Donnells for years, and arrived in his battered truck at lunchtime. Tufts of straw-coloured hair escaped from beneath Tom's well-worn akubra hat. Bluey gave him a guided tour around the paddocks so he could inspect the flock.

After the usual small talk, and discussion about cotton and its impact on the area, Tom got down to business. 'You said you have around sixteen hundred prime merinos?' he asked, drawing a notebook and pen from a pocket of his jacket.

'Yes, two per cent rams and of the remainder, roughly sixty per cent ewes and forty per cent wethers. They produce fine grade wool, the best.'

After doing a few rough calculations, he turned to Bluey. 'The lot should fetch around twelve and a half thousand pounds.'

'Bloody hell!'

'You don't think that's enough?' Tom Fielder looked at Bluey, surprised.

'It's enough, Tom.' Bluey assured him. 'I'm just a little bit overwhelmed that's all.'

'The flock's worth every cent and they'll sell well at auction. When it comes to business matters, I'm pretty conservative.'

'When will you pick them up?'

'I'll get in touch with a Warwick trucking firm that I've used in the past. I reckon they'll be able to get here by the weekend. Can you arrange to have the flock penned by that time?'

'My bloody oath!'

The rest of that week was a busy time for the O'Donnells. Every minute was spent bringing in the valuable flock. It was a particularly time-consuming task with only two dogs – Skipper was sorely missed. Since the sheep were to be sold and most likely transported to another district, Bluey thought it best if they were dipped, so David took time off school to help. During the week, Bluey had his doubts that they would make the deadline. Then, finally, the double-decker trucks arrived as planned on Saturday morning, and all was ready. Watching the sheep being loaded, he felt a wave of sadness. The flock had been the core of his and his father's working lives.

'Sorry to see them go?' Ellen asked. Standing by the pens, she placed an arm around his waist.

'They'd have to be the stupidest animals God ever put breath into. But yeah,' he grudgingly admitted, 'I'll miss 'em.'

When the last truck pulled out, an eerie silence seemed to settle on the property.

A week later, Bluey drove to town to repay his loan to the Commercial Banking Company of Sydney. He had received five hundred pounds more for the flock than expected and he was in a good mood. Next stop was the produce store, where he found Bill Greensill and Len Humphries deep in conversation. Humphries' face contorted with rage. 'Get out, O'Donnell.'

'I only came to give you this.' Bluey extracted the bank cheque from his shirt pocket and let it drop to the floor. 'Paid in full.'

'Wha—' Humphries was flummoxed.

The look on Humphries' face made Bluey laugh out loud as he walked out of the store.

In preparation for planting the new crop, Bluey had to make a few alterations to Kilkenny. First and foremost, the fencing to the various paddocks had to be removed so that much larger fields could be established. He purchased up-to-date irrigation equipment, as well as a heavy-duty pump, which he bolted to the concrete floor of a small shed he'd built by the river. He hired a bulldozer to construct a dam and filled it by pumping water from the river. He also bought a larger tractor with a much wider cut to plough the extensive area needed to produce a viable yield of cotton. Bluey identified the most fertile tracts of land for the new crop. In the process, he made a conscious decision not to clear the scrub surrounding the cave.

When the primary industries officer visited Kilkenny, he explained that the ploughed land had to slope slightly, and that furrows had to be dug between each row. If there was no rain, water would be released from the dam into a deep trench at the higher end of the field and allowed to flow into each furrow. He provided in-depth instruction on the cotton plant's growing cycle, as well as advice on fertilisers and insecticides. By the time the officer left Kilkenny, Bluey felt confident he would cope.

Standing at the sink preparing pork chops and vegetables for her family, Ellen felt a wonderful glow of peace and contentment. Life had definitely taken a turn for the better. Her relationship with Bluey had blossomed. It was as if they were courting again, or on the honeymoon they never had. She could actually see the love in his eyes every time he looked at her. They had two wonderful children and at last their financial woes seems surmountable. An impish smile hovered on her lips as her thoughts turned to another, more personal matter. It was wonderful, she could hardly believe it – not after all this time . . .

At the dinner table that night, Ellen turned to her husband. 'We will be all right now won't we, darling?'

Bluey gazed at the face of the woman he loved so much. She'd washed her hair and drawn it back into a ponytail. 'Course we will, El. We've got enough to keep us going and the crop's virtually sold even before I plant it. We'll never be millionaires, but we'll survive.'

'That's all I need,' she said, and reached across to stroke her husband's hand. The children exchanged happy glances.

At breakfast a few mornings later, Ellen suddenly jumped up and ran to the bathroom. Bluey followed. 'You all right, El?' he asked anxiously, lightly tapping at the bathroom door.

'Come in.' She wiped her mouth. 'I'm okay now.'

'What's wrong?' He noted her pale complexion.

'Oh, I'm just a bit off colour,' she replied vaguely, splashing water onto her face.

'Well, you'd better stay in the house today.'

'There's something else . . .' She looked at him with a tiny flicker of a smile and it hit him straight away.

'You're pregnant!'

'I think so,' she smiled.

'Beauty!' He let out a triumphant whoop and wrapped his arms around her, hugging her fiercely.

Their father's excited cry brought the children running. 'What's happened?' David asked, looking from one beaming parent to the other.

'Are you okay, Mum?' said Cathleen.

'Yes, darling. I was just telling your father that we might be having another baby.'

David seemed momentarily uncomfortable – the news had caught him off guard – but when he saw the happiness in his mother's face, he responded with a huge smile and big hug. 'I hope it's a boy.'

'Oh, but I want it to be a girl!' Cathleen cried.

'As long as the baby's healthy, I don't mind either way,' Bluey said.

Sally Pamela O'Donnell was born seven months later – naturally, she was a redhead – and was nursed and adored by her doting parents and siblings.

On 25 April, 1958, Bluey attended his first Anzac Day service. With encouragement from David, he had applied for and received his medals, four in all: the 1939–1945 Star, the Pacific Star, the King George VI Medal and the Australian Service Medal. He wore them proudly on the left breast of his suit coat as he marched with other veterans down Goondiwindi's main street. Uncle Mick had been granted permission to walk beside him with Kevin's medals pinned to the right breast of his coat. Both sides of the road were packed with locals who clapped and cheered.

With Sally in her arms, and flanked by David and Cathleen, Ellen waited for her husband to pass. The children were bursting with pride. Bluey knew where they would be waiting, and as he walked by, he turned his head and winked at them. After the march, there was the laying of wreaths, and speeches at the memorial, followed by the Last Post. Listening to the haunting sounds of the bugle, Bluey's thoughts turned to Digger and his family.

God bless you, Dig.

Bluey's war was won.

Acknowledgements

Having been raised in the suburbs, I know little about sheep or wool. I'd therefore like to first of all thank Reuben Brumpton, a renowned expert in the industry, for all the information he imparted to me. Secondly, I must mention the ladies at Goondiwindi's Information Centre. They were so helpful during my visit to the provincial centre to carry out research. I'm very grateful, girls. I would now like to thank three marvellous young women from Penguin Australia – Jo Rosenberg, for first recognising the book's potential; publisher Ali Watts, for her faith in the work, as well as her encouragement and support, and lastly, Miriam Cannell, for her editorial work and advice. Ali, Miriam and Jo have helped me in every possible way and I can't express my gratitude enough. They're simply wonderful. To my darling wife. Lyn, I couldn't have done it without you, sweetheart. My daughter, Rhonda, and my son, Scott, are always there in the background, giving me confidence and feedback. Love yas.